"When Lana Ferguson said she was going to write a book about the Loch Ness Monster, I had no idea what I was in for. I should have known it would include a funny, relatable heroine, copious amounts of spice, and the sexiest hero that ever graced a kilt. You WANT to read this!"

—Ruby Dixon, *New York Times* bestselling author of *By the Horns*

"*Under Loch and Key* is Lana at the top of her game. Unique, atmospheric, playful, and so hot you'll be looking for the nearest loch to cool off in, her books are everything I'm happy to reach for time and time again."

—Tarah DeWitt, *USA Today* bestselling author of *Savor It*

"Ferguson puts her own ingeniously clever and wonderfully whimsical spin on the Loch Ness Monster legend and the Scottish romance with a delightful rom-com that delivers plenty of cheeky banter and heartfelt musings on the importance of family, as well as love scenes hot enough to warm up the coldest Scottish loch."

—*Booklist*

"Lana Ferguson is the only author so far who can convince me to read ANY genre of romance I normally wouldn't pick up, just to devour the book in a single day and absolutely love it."

—The Gloss

Praise for

The Game Changer

"It is no secret that I have and will always devour anything Lana Ferguson writes. *The Game Changer* is her first dab at sports romance, and boy, I was immediately obsessed. This book has Ferguson's addictive brand of delicious spice and storytelling, plus one of the tropes I'll never get tired of reading: brother's best friend. Besides, we get to follow a giant ginger on skates around the ice and a baker who calls him Cupcake. It doesn't get better than this."

—Elena Armas, *New York Times* bestselling author of *The Fiancé Dilemma*

"*The Game Changer* is a fun tale to read that revolves around the world[s] of hockey and baking. Ian and Delilah are two likable characters trying to do the right thing even as those around them try to tell them what to do. Readers will enjoy their banter and watching them fall in love. Don't miss this enjoyable tale."

—Romance Reviews Today

"A real banger. . . . *The Game Changer* has sensuality, banter, wit, and romance in spades, and I promise you will not be able to put it down once you start reading it."

—Romance by the Book

Praise for
The Fake Mate

"An overall delightful experience. . . . Funny, sweet, and very hot, *The Fake Mate* is the ideal venture into mystic romance."
—Shondaland

"A steamy, worthwhile romance with plenty of banter, tapping into the popular grumpy-meets-sunshine trope." —*Kirkus Reviews*

"Charming. Funny. Primal. Ferguson's paranormal romance manages to be sweet and spicy at the same time, with two likable leads who can't ignore their wolfish urges. . . . Readers will tear through this omegaverse novel." —*Booklist*

Praise for
The Nanny

"Ferguson makes the will-they-won't-they sing with complex emotional shading and a strong sense of inevitability to her protagonists' connection. . . . Rosie Danan fans should snap this up."
—*Publishers Weekly* (starred review)

"This steamy romantic comedy puts a modern spin on traditional tropes, bringing the falling-for-the-nanny and secret-past storylines into the twenty-first century." —*Library Journal*

"Everything about *The Nanny* is enjoyable: the plot, the pacing, the compelling characters, and especially Ferguson's wise and funny voice. It's also extremely refreshing to see sex-positive characters who approach intimacy with maturity. . . . If you're a fan of dirty talk and slow-burning chemistry, you'll love *The Nanny*."

—*BookPage* (starred review)

BERKLEY TITLES BY LANA FERGUSON

The Nanny
The Fake Mate
The Game Changer
Under Loch and Key
Overruled
The Mating Game

The Mating Game

LANA FERGUSON

BERKLEY ROMANCE
NEW YORK

BERKLEY ROMANCE
Published by Berkley
An imprint of Penguin Random House LLC
1745 Broadway, New York, NY 10019
penguinrandomhouse.com

Copyright © 2025 by Lana Ferguson
Excerpt from *The Final Score* copyright © 2025 by Lana Ferguson
Penguin Random House values and supports copyright.
Copyright fuels creativity, encourages diverse voices, promotes free speech, and creates a vibrant culture. Thank you for buying an authorized edition of this book and for complying with copyright laws by not reproducing, scanning, or distributing any part of it in any form without permission. You are supporting writers and allowing Penguin Random House to continue to publish books for every reader. Please note that no part of this book may be used or reproduced in any manner for the purpose of training artificial intelligence technologies or systems.

BERKLEY and the BERKLEY & B colophon are registered trademarks of Penguin Random House LLC.

Book design by Alison Cnockaert
Interior art: Wolves, moon and paw © happy.designer / Shutterstock

Library of Congress Cataloging-in-Publication Data

Names: Ferguson, Lana, author.
Title: The mating game / Lana Ferguson.
Description: First edition. | New York : Berkley Romance, 2025.
Identifiers: LCCN 2025013619 (print) | LCCN 2025013620 (ebook) |
ISBN 9780593953693 trade paperback | ISBN 9780593953709 ebook
Subjects: LCGFT: Fiction | Fantasy fiction | Romance fiction | Werewolf fiction | Novels
Classification: LCC PS3606.E72555 M38 2025 (print) | LCC PS3606.E72555 (ebook) |
DDC 813/.6--dc23/eng/20250428
LC record available at https://lccn.loc.gov/2025013619
LC ebook record available at https://lccn.loc.gov/2025013620

First Edition: December 2025

Printed in the United States of America
1st Printing

The authorized representative in the EU for product safety and compliance is
Penguin Random House Ireland, Morrison Chambers, 32 Nassau Street,
Dublin D02 YH68, Ireland, https://eu-contact.penguin.ie.

To Keri,
for always being willing to listen to me talk about knotting.

The Mating Game

1

Tess

"WELL, THE GOOD news is... you're not dying."

I gape at the pretty, smiling ER physician—Dr. Carter, she said her name was—who is regarding me carefully, having looked up at me from her clipboard, which I assume has the results of all the blood tests we did earlier.

"Do you know what's wrong with me?" I wring my hands together. "Is it some sort of weird twenty-four-hour bug?"

This seems unlikely to me, given the severity of the symptoms I've been experiencing the last several hours, but I suppose it's still a possibility.

Dr. Carter glances down at her clipboard again, flipping a page and reading something there. "I wanted to ask a few follow-up questions if that's okay?"

"Sure," I answer tightly, wishing she would just give me some clue as to what's wrong with me. "That's fine."

"Your parents... You listed them both as betas?"

I nod. "That's right."

"And your siblings?"

"Also betas. We all are."

She presses her lips together briefly. "Do you have any family history of crossbreeding with shifters?"

"Excuse me?"

"Sorry." She gives me another polite smile. "It's relevant."

I think hard, trying to mentally tick through my family tree for as far back as I can recall. "I think . . ." I frown, trying to remember. "I think my great-grandmother was a shifter, actually. I never met her though. She died before I was born."

"Hmm."

I watch as she scans through her notes again, every passing second making my anxiety climb higher. Twenty-four hours ago, I was perfectly healthy and packing for my trip to Denver, excited about a new job. Travel is nothing new to me; my contracting business, Rustic Renovations, takes me all over the country, but this is the first time I've had to get off a plane and take an Uber straight to the nearest emergency room.

It started with cramps—terrible, *terrible* cramps—followed by a fever, cold sweats, and lots of nausea, and by the time the plane landed, it was clear all the other people on my flight were worried I was carrying some sort of plague, given my awful appearance. Even now I can feel my chestnut bangs clinging to my forehead with sweat, and it's only the IV in my arm feeding me occasional doses of high-powered nausea meds that's keeping me from hurling all over the speckled white tile of the little room I'm in.

"Well," Dr. Carter starts carefully. "Your blood tests yielded an abnormal spike in your hormone levels. Your progesterone, estrogen, and cortisol levels are all three times the amounts they should be. Your endocrine system is having a hard time processing the influx. That's what's causing all the unfortunate symptoms you're experiencing."

"I don't understand. Why would my hormones be out of whack all of a sudden? Is it like menopause? I'm only twenty-eight!"

"Nothing like that. It's . . . Well." She sighs, pulling the clipboard to her stomach and holding it against her white coat as she offers me a sympathetic look. "This might come as a shock, Ms. Covington, but . . ."

I lean in, my ass scooting to the edge of the hospital bed, which has me instinctively reach behind to make sure my panties aren't flashing anyone from the gap in the back of my paper gown. "What? What is it?"

"What you're experiencing isn't entirely out of the ordinary. In fact, it's something most shifters experience at the end of puberty."

I blink. "But . . . I'm a beta. Betas can't shift."

"Yes, well. It's not *entirely* unheard-of for a recessive gene to present itself later in life."

"That's . . ." I run my fingers through my hair, no doubt making my bangs stick straight up, but I can't focus on that right now. "That's impossible."

"Not impossible, I'm afraid," Dr. Carter says gently. "Just unlikely."

I try to process what she's saying, but it sounds faraway, like she's speaking to someone else. There's no way I could suddenly be—

I force a swallow. "So, what? Am I going to suddenly sprout ears and a tail?"

"No, no," Dr. Carter assures me with a laugh as she reaches to tuck one honeyed tendril of her hair behind her ear. "Nothing so sudden as that. You will, however, feel the urge to shift in the near future. I have all sorts of pamphlets I can give you that are chockfull of information about what your body is going through. Although, I've never seen a case with such a late presentation as yours . . . so I can't guarantee your experiences will be exactly the same."

"I just . . . don't see how this could happen."

"It's basically a little hiccup in your genes," she says with a shrug. "It will be an adjustment, but I can promise you your life won't be turned upside down entirely."

Easy for her to say.

"Any other surprises I have to look forward to?" I know I sound petulant, but I think it's allowed after the day I've had. "Am I going to start craving more red meat and sniffing strangers?"

Her smile is a little tighter, and I realize I'm being slightly offensive.

"Sorry," I amend quietly. "This is just a lot."

"I get it," she says. "It's funny, my mate eats his steaks practically rare. I'm always teasing him about it. I can tell you *I've* never had any special feelings about red meat, and as for sniffing strangers . . . you *will* start to experience a sharpened sense of smell. Every shifter has a particular scent, and unless they elect to use suppressants—which is usually only the case in certain professions or environments—you are going to pick up on those. It might cause headaches at first, but with time you will become more acclimated to the sensation."

"Great," I mumble dejectedly. "Just great."

"If I'm being candid," Dr. Carter goes on, "I have other suspicions about your lab results."

I stifle a groan. What else could possibly be going on with my body? "What?"

"It's only . . ." She holds out her chart, indicating a sloping graph that makes no sense to me. "Your particular levels of these hormones are indicative of a secondary designation."

"A secondary designation?"

"It's rare—incredibly rare, even—but then again, so is your situation as a whole. So it wouldn't be all that surprising at this point."

"I'm not following."

"I think you might be an omega, Ms. Covington."

I'm blinking dumbly again. "What?"

"Like I said, it's very rare, and in this day and age . . . it really isn't all that different from being a shifter."

"I know what an omega is," I say absently. "I have a friend who—" I swallow thickly. "How can you be so sure?"

"Well," she laughs. "I *am* one, for starters."

Fuck. Foot in mouth. Again. "Sorry. I'm sorry. I am not usually this much of an asshole."

"It's fine. Really. I can't imagine what it must be like to face this so suddenly."

"If you're an omega as well, can you tell me what I can expect? If that's the case?"

I could always ask my friend Ada, but I haven't even figured out how I'm going to tell her, or anyone else for that matter.

"Like I said, it really isn't all that different in most cases. If you start googling, you're likely to go down some undesirable Reddit rabbit holes that are mostly nonsense, but you can just ignore those. All it means is that your heats might be a little more frequent. Possibly more intense as well."

"My *heats*?"

Oh God. That absolutely hadn't crossed my mind yet.

"Yes," Dr. Carter explains calmly. "Usually, a shifter going through puberty will experience less intense heats—we call them 'juvenile heats,' to be exact—meaning they won't last the full ovulation cycle and won't have the same level of, ah, need."

"Need?"

"Need to, um . . . copulate."

"Oh fuck," I groan.

Dr. Carter gives me a small smile. "Precisely."

I might laugh if my entire world weren't tilting on its axis.

"So . . . what do I do in the meantime?"

She considers this for a moment. "I'm going to prescribe you some hormone regulators, but the dose will be very mild. Just enough to alleviate some of your symptoms. We don't want to interrupt your body's cycle of change, after all. I can also get you something for the nausea and cramps. Other than that . . . I would strongly suggest that you spend the next few weeks or so at home if at all possible. I can't predict exactly what other symptoms you might experience while your body adjusts to the new hormone levels, and being around other shifters might make things more uncomfortable. Shifting isn't permitted inside city limits, but I can get you a doctor's note explaining your condition in case there are any unplanned incidents. Otherwise, there are several nice heat clinics on the edge of the city, where you would be able to shift comfortably. Normally, you would need to schedule weeks in advance, but again, I can get you a doctor's note explaining your special circumstances."

My mind whirls. Unplanned shifting? Heat clinics?

"I can't hole up for weeks," I argue. "I'm here for a job."

"Any chance you could work remotely?"

"I'm a contractor. I do renovation for cabins and lodges and such."

"Ah. That's a pickle."

"It is," I remark dryly.

"Well, I obviously can't force you either way," Dr. Carter says. "I can only suggest. But I would keep a close eye on your body. You don't want to overexert yourself."

"But the meds should help, right?"

"A little," she says. "As I said, we don't want to medicate you so much that your body can't process the change it's going through. This is a natural thing. For the most part, we just have to let it run its course."

Perfect, I think. *Just perfect.*

"Okay," I say with a nod. "Okay. This is fine. I guess . . . if you could get me those prescriptions you mentioned, I can deal with the rest."

"If you have any more trouble, don't hesitate to come back in, okay?"

"Sure," I answer, knowing that's unlikely. The jobsite is almost two hours away. I won't have time to pack up and head out every time I get a cramp. "Of course."

"Right. I'll get you those prescriptions before I release you." She starts to turn toward the door but pauses, giving me one last concerned look. "Oh. One more thing. It's very unlikely, but I should mention that you should steer clear of alphas."

"Alphas?"

"Another secondary designation," she tells me. "Their pheromones, like yours and mine, are stronger than your average shifter's. Being around one might wreak havoc on your system—could even possibly trigger a juvenile heat if you're compatible enough." She shrugs. "It's probably a nonissue. They are also incredibly rare." A small, strange smile touches her lips. "But then again . . . you never know."

I watch her go, still stuck on *pheromones*. Nothing about any of this feels like real life.

I check my phone when she leaves and see that my brothers have responded to the group text, asking if I landed okay. It takes all I have not to laugh at that. I am definitely not ready to have this discussion with my family. I don't even know what I'm going to say to my brothers when they drive in to join me on the job at the end of the week.

The job.

I groan. I'm still expected to show up at the small ski lodge this evening—a little place just up the mountain, near the town of Pleasant Hill. The woman I've been speaking to, Jeannie, seems nice enough, and I can only hope she won't notice if I have to escape to the bathroom to deal with an influx of cramps or sweating or God knows what else during the next few weeks while I oversee the renovation.

I laugh dryly.

At least things can't get any worse.

"MADE IT TO Nowheresville yet?"

In hindsight, I probably should have let Ada's call go to voicemail. It's only been a couple of hours since the nice doctor at the ER informed me my entire life was changing, but since my best friend is like a shark smelling blood in the water when it comes to sussing out my moods, I doubt I can keep any of this from her for long.

"Almost," I tell her, slowing for a stop sign. "It's really off the beaten path."

"Never a good sign. That's how you get axe-murdered."

I roll my eyes. "I'm not going to get axe-murdered."

"That's what every person who gets axe-murdered thinks. No

one wakes up thinking, 'Oh, today I'm going to get axe-murdered,' but then, before you know it, you're human firewood."

"I am officially putting you in time-out from those true crime podcasts."

"You'll change your tune when I keep you from becoming human firewood."

"How about we stop using the term 'human firewood' when I'm this close to a secluded ski lodge that I'll be staying at by myself until my brothers fly in?"

Ada snorts on the other end of the line. "Thomas and Chase are in more danger than you are. They're pretty, but they don't have the same hardware upstairs as you. Kyle might stand a chance."

"Hey, now," I laugh. "That's not very nice."

"I'm kidding," she says. "You know I love those big lugs. But still, there's a reason you're the brains of the operation and they're the muscle."

"And cameraman," I correct, thinking of Kyle.

"And cameraman," she agrees.

"How cold is it there?"

"Somewhere between frozen toes and cracked lips."

I can practically hear her shudder. "No thanks."

"Definitely a far cry from Newport."

"I'll think of you while I'm on the beach later," she says with sympathy.

"That makes everything better."

"Obviously. How are you feeling? Did you end up going to get checked out?"

I bite my lip, considering. Ada would understand. I've never asked for the ins and outs of what she is, but that doesn't mean I haven't picked up bits and pieces over the years. I'm . . . not ready to tell anyone yet. Not when I haven't figured out my own feelings about it. I'm already half panicking enough as it is without her hysterics added to the mix.

"I feel better," I tell her. It's not a *complete* lie. I *do* feel better after taking the meds Dr. Carter gave me. "Not dying, at least."

"Just make sure you get checked out if you start feeling shitty again. It sounded like you were really suffering when I talked to you last."

"Maybe I ate something bad," I offer, knowing that's not the case. It *could* be a possibility though, in an easier turn of events.

"Have you heard anything back from HGTV?"

"Not yet," I sigh. "They said it could be a couple of weeks."

"Yeah, well, they'd be stupid not to green-light the show. You haven't had a TikTok fall under a million views in months."

"My brothers are optimistic, but . . ."

"You're the worrywart."

"That's me," I laugh. "It just comes down to the fine print. I don't want to jump into anything that's going to make our job not fun anymore, you know? I don't want to totally be beholden to *their* whims."

"I get that," she says. "What does your dad think?"

My hands tighten on the steering wheel, my jaw clenching. With everything happening today, my problems back home are the last thing I want to discuss.

"I don't know," I tell her honestly. "I haven't told him about it yet."

"You haven't told him?"

"No, and I told my brothers not to tell him either."

"But why?"

"Because..." I frown, thinking of the awful year he's had. That we've *all* had. "I don't want to get my parents' hopes up if it doesn't come through. I'll tell them when I have good news."

"Babe, that's a lot of pressure to put on yourself."

"I know," I sigh. "But what choice do I have?"

I can practically see the sympathy in her eyes even from so far away, my chest constricting when I think about everything riding on this deal. Of the *good* it could do when it comes to dad's medical issues.

"This is all contingent on whether or not HGTV passes," I grumble.

"Shut up," she tuts. "If they do, then they're walnuts."

"Walnuts?"

"Felt appropriate," she replies. "If they *do* pass on it, they suck, and I will boycott their channel."

"You and I both know the day you give up *Property Brothers* is the day you're six feet under."

"They're hot twins with hammers. I won't be judged for this. Just a sec." I hear her shuffling on the other end for a moment before her voice returns. "Can I call you back? That's Perry's school on the other line."

"Absolutely. I'll talk to you later, okay?"

"Sure. Call you later."

She disconnects the call, and I'm suddenly even more glad I decided not to tell her yet about everything happening with me. It's not that I don't trust Ada enough to tell her what's going on, it's just that I know how much she worries—it's the mom in her—and if I tell her about everything that's happening, there's a good chance she'll be packing up herself and her son, Perry, and hopping on the first flight out. She has enough going on with the whole single mother thing; she definitely doesn't need any of my drama stressing her out even more. I'll give myself a few days to wrap my head around it first.

It isn't long after I hang up with Ada that I see the end of the driveway. A faded wooden sign that reads THE BEAR ESSENTIALS WILDERNESS LODGE leans at a not-so-straight angle to signal that I'm at the right place. I can just make out the lodge nestled in the pristine white of the surrounding snow as I drive up, the log siding stark amid the wintery scenery. A deck wraps around the front to lead down to a set of stairs, and on either side of the heavy wooden door is a series of wide windows that go all the way up to the roof. The sky behind it is now painted in a rich array of pinks and purples as the sun begins to sink below the horizon, giving the entire thing more of that postcard feel—save for the wear and tear.

It's still . . . pretty, mostly. But it's definitely seen some hard years. There are broken rails on the stairs that I notice as I get closer, a few missing shingles on the roof—even the sign above the door is faded and chipped, as if long overdue for a touch-up. I'm already making a mental note of all the people in Denver I'm going to have to call to contract some work out to.

It's less picturesque than the one (literally *one*) photo I saw on the very basic website, and I'm gathering now that it was most likely dated. I doubt they've updated the lodge since it was built.

"Kind of a funny name for a lodge," I mutter to myself as I shift my rental car into park.

I sit in the car for a minute so I can shoot a text to my brothers, following that up with one to my dad to let him know I arrived at the jobsite. I stare down at my phone as I watch the little dots pop up with his impending response, a small smile touching my mouth when he replies, You be careful out there, kiddo.

It feels weird keeping all that's happened today from him, considering I tell him everything, but with what he's going through . . . I don't want to add to his stress. In fact, it's imperative that I don't, what with the state of his heart.

I step out of the car, letting the door shut behind me, to get a better look at the place. There's an old Bronco parked just outside, the forest-green paint still shiny despite the vehicle being at least thirty years old by my best guess, and it somehow looks like it's in better shape than the lodge itself. I eye the broken railing that seems to have cracks and rotting wood as far as the eye can see; I *really* have my work cut out with this one.

I'm staring at the railing so intensely that I almost miss it when the front door opens and someone steps outside, but I catch a large, dark shape out of the corner of my eye, stark against the light flakes of the gently falling snow—and it's hard to focus on much else when the person finally comes into view. He's heading right for me, and I can feel my mouth part as I take in the hulking size of the man walking down the rickety stairs.

Tall is an understatement; this man looks more than a foot taller than I am, and I'm five foot four. But more than that, he is *wide*. Shoulders that seem to go on for miles in the thick red plaid of his coat, a broad chest that stretches the black-knit thermal beneath—it's like he stepped right out of *Lumberjack Weekly*, with his trimmed beard and gray beanie with dark curls poking out of it that are just a shade or two darker than his eyes. I most likely spend a second too long studying the soft-looking mouth that peeks out from his scruff, but honestly, given that this stranger might be one of the most attractive people I have ever seen—and I have seen a *lot* of people—I think it's probably excusable. He comes to a stop right in front of me, and my gaze goes up and up and *up*, to the point that I'm forced to crane my neck as I gape at this giant of a man.

"You Esther?"

I blink, the abruptness of his question catching me off guard. "Tess."

"Jeannie said an Esther was coming."

"Yeah," I answer. "I go by Tess."

He shrugs. "Fair enough."

"Sorry." I stick out one gloved hand. "I'm the contractor Jeannie hired for the renovations. Do you work here?"

His eyes flick to my outstretched hand, but he doesn't take it. "Looks that way."

Jeez. Talk about frosty.

He's still frowning at my hand, so I draw it back slowly, my eyes lingering on the way his mouth turns down at the corners. The expression only makes him look more rugged, and I think to myself that he really does give off a lumberjack vibe, albeit a very terse one. I'm pretty sure there's a Harlequin romance on my shelf at home that he was the cover model for at some point in his life. All that's missing is an axe, really.

I can't help but laugh at that, recalling Ada's and my conversation about being murdered out here. The guy arches a brow at the giggle that escapes me.

"Something funny?"

I wave my hand in front of my face. "Not unless you think murder is funny."

"Excuse me?"

"Not, like, *actual* murder," I correct, sort of. "I mean, well, okay, I guess *kind of* actual murder. My friend made this joke when I was on my way that I was going to get murdered out here, and I was thinking you totally give me lumberjack vibes, and that got me thinking about axes, which got me thinking about the murder again, and—"

I notice he's staring at me as if I've lost my mind.

"This is probably one of those things that should have stayed in my head."

He continues to frown at me for exactly four more seconds, then: "I'm not gonna argue with you there."

"Right. Um." I clear my throat. "Is Jeannie around? I would love to introduce myself in person after all the emails we've exchanged."

"Jeannie's down the mountain. Had something come up at her place."

"Oh. When will she be back?"

"Tomorrow, I figure."

"Oh."

I don't really know what else to say to that. This is all going very different from how I pictured, but I guess that's par for the course, considering how this entire trip has been.

The bear of a man nods toward my car. "You got luggage?"

"Hmm? Oh. Yes. Sorry. I can—"

He sort of grunts in response but says nothing. It surprises me when he steps toward the car to open the back door and grab my bag—so much so that I reach out to try to stop him, which earns me a puzzled look.

"You don't have to," I tell him, a little distracted by how dark his eyes look up close. "I can get my things."

There's a scent tickling my nose—one that reminds me of rain and sunshine—and I think to myself that it seems terribly out of place here in the snow. Maybe it's his cologne? It's really . . . nice, actually.

He looks from me to the bag and back again—finally shrugging before he releases it to turn and stomp up the steps onto the main deck. He taps his boots against the last stair, and I'm left to my own devices. I remember myself after only a few seconds, grabbing my bag and hurrying after him. He leaves the front door open when he slips inside, disappearing into the warm glow of the lights beyond.

"Sorry," I offer again as I step in after him. "I didn't catch your name."

"Didn't give it," he tosses over his shoulder as he shrugs out of his flannel coat.

"Totally something a murderer would say," I tease with a cluck of my tongue.

He turns to look at me strangely even as I try for what I hope is a friendly smile. "Hunter," he concedes. "Hunter Barrett."

Hunter.

I almost laugh at the utter appropriateness of his name. He definitely looks like a Hunter.

I close the door behind me and let my eyes sweep the room. There's a giant elk head mounted behind the front desk—its horns decked in dusty old Santa hats despite it being October. An old brass chandelier that has seen better days hangs above us in the wide entryway; thick cobwebs dangling between the fixtures make me grimace as I stare up into them. The walls are a rich stained wood that feels warm even covered in dust, and I think to myself that with a little TLC, they could shine up nicely.

All that's missing is a bearskin rug.

Honestly, I'm not convinced I won't find one with further exploration.

I notice Hunter rounding the front counter, which is built of treated cedar, reaching up to pull off the beanie he's wearing. The hair beneath is a thick heap of dark curls that frame his face and make him seem wilder somehow—not to mention the way I'm filled with a sudden curiosity as to what it might feel like if I pushed my fingers through them. He climbs up to take a seat on a wooden stool, settling there as he braces his hands on the counter in front of an open ledger.

"So, you do work here, right?"

"Sort of goes with owning the place, yeah," he tells me with a slight smirk.

I blink dumbly. "You're the owner?"

"Last time I checked."

My mouth parts in surprise, and it takes me all of three seconds to realize that I made murder jokes to my new would-be employer of sorts, most likely giving him the impression that I'm completely unhinged.

Perfect.

2

Hunter

WHEN JEANNIE TOLD me she was hiring someone to renovate the lodge, I was wholly against it for a myriad of reasons. I still am, truthfully. I've fought my headstrong aunt every step of the way, from the conception of this half-baked plan right up to her informing me that someone was well on their way, but I have to admit, of all the people I might have pictured showing up at the lodge with a mind to "fix up the place," this tiny scrap of a woman is the furthest thing from anyone my imagination toyed with.

Her soft chestnut hair falls in her eyes, her bangs just long enough that she seems to make a habit of blowing them away from her face. Her big brown eyes give her a permanent quizzical expression that would almost be cute if I weren't determined to dislike her. Plus, she really is positively tiny. How in the fuck does she expect to overhaul this entire place? I don't think they even make stepladders that would allow her to reach some of the higher bits.

Her owlish eyes are even wider as she comes to terms with the fact that it is actually *me* who she'll be working for rather than Jeannie, more or less, and her admittedly plush pink mouth makes a perfect O shape as she blinks her long lashes repeatedly.

"But I . . ." Her lips purse in a pout. "But I've been talking to Jeannie all this time."

And I can't help it; the irritation that she's here in the first place is still bubbling just beneath the surface, and her puzzled look and scrunched nose, which are one step away from being downright adorable, aren't enough to eradicate it.

"Probably because I didn't want to hire you."

Her mouth drops open. "Excuse me?"

"Nothing to excuse," I answer flippantly.

"You didn't want to hire me?"

"Wasn't as convinced as Jeannie that we need all these renovations." I shrug, eyeing the way her arms cross over her chest, her shoulders hunching up around her ears, making her look like a cat that's three seconds from hissing. "You been doing this for very long? Kind of tiny for a contractor."

That gets the rise out of her that I'm looking for. "*Excuse* me?"

"Didn't mean anything by it," I say, using that same disinterested monotone. "Just an observation."

I watch her bristle, her fists clenching at her sides as she takes what I assume is meant to be a menacing step toward me moments before she thrusts a finger in my direction. "I've been doing this for *ten years* now," she sputters. "My dad did it for eighteen years before that." She gestures wildly around the room. "I could rip this dingy little place down board by board and put it back together twice as nice if I wanted to."

I feel a pang of irritation at her assessment, a memory creeping forward of another time someone called it as much. "Dingy, huh?"

"Shit." Her expression turns sheepish as she reaches to unwind the scarf from around her neck, suddenly looking flushed. "I shouldn't have said that." She narrows her eyes, pointing a finger at me again. "But you shouldn't go around making snap observations. If you don't want me here doing this job, just say the word, and I'll turn right around and go back to the airport."

I still don't really want her here—that hasn't changed—but honestly, now I'm almost intrigued to see what she has planned. I eye her cheeks, which are tinted pink with an ire that seems bigger than her stature, and I'm strangely curious about this woman who looks like she would have no qualms with, at the very least, *attempting* to kick my ass despite being half my size.

"By all means," I tell her drolly. "But then again, you're already here. I'm sure you'll do a bang-up job, Miss Fixit."

I'm rewarded with another gaping expression, her lips mouthing the moniker back at me in a daze. "Oh, sure," she huffs, throwing up her hands. "Since I'm already here."

"Exactly." I lift my arms above my head in a stretch, and my black Henley strains across my chest. "Well . . . there's no one staying here right now, so you can pretty much take whatever room you want. The suites are upstairs. They're all available except the one to the left of the landing. That's mine. There's an attached bath in every room. Living area is just through there." I nod my head toward the wide entry across the room. "Got a pool table if you play. Jeannie cooks breakfast, lunch, and dinner—gotta be down by eight in the morning if you want to catch breakfast though. Lunch is at twelve, give or take a few, and dinner is at six. Got it?"

She nods at me with visible confusion, and I round the counter, sticking out my hand. She glances at it with a brief frown, flicking her gaze back up to my face warily before sliding her palm against mine.

"Okay," she says. "I think I've got it."

"Good." This close to her, I smell a blast of something heavy and sweet, and my nostrils flare of their own accord as I try to breathe in more of it, but it's gone as quickly as it came. *The fuck was that?* "Well . . ." I say, clearing my throat and wrenching my hand from hers. "Welcome to the Bear Essentials Wilderness Lodge."

I move to leave her there, because I suddenly feel strange, but I barely make it to the stairs before she's calling out, "I just . . . pick my own room?"

"Seems the only way you'll get the one you want," I toss over my shoulder. And because I can't help myself, I turn to give her a smirk. "Probably don't want me to know where you're staying anyway," I say seriously. And when she gives me a puzzled look: "Since I might be an axe-wielding murderer."

She flushes again, and I feel a tinge of satisfaction at her discomfort.

"Don't you want to show me around and tell me some of your plans for the place?" she calls.

"Not really," I answer, already starting up the stairs. "Jeannie is the one insisting on this little redecorating project."

She makes an indignant sound. "I'm not a *decorator*."

"Of course not, Miss Fixit." I raise my hand above my head to offer her a little wave. "Breakfast is at eight," I remind her. "Have a good night."

She makes that same disgruntled squawk, and I hear her shoes slapping against the floor as if she's following me. Even from several paces away, I'm hit with that strange scent, one that makes my steps heavier for the briefest of moments before it dissipates. I frown at my feet, turning again and narrowing my eyes at her as she skids to a halt. Jeannie definitely would have told me if—But it's hitting me again, causing goose bumps to break out across my skin, and without even realizing I'm doing it, I'm stomping back down the stairs to loom over her.

She shrinks only for a moment before rising to her full height to stare me down. It might be amusing if my heart weren't beating so fast.

"Are you an omega?"

She visibly blanches. "W-what?"

A pit forms in my stomach, because there's no way Jeannie would have subjected me to this. Not after everything.

But I know this woman has no idea about my past, so I try my best to keep my tone from sounding as irritated as I feel.

"I'm only asking because," I try again, going for less aggressive but fearing that I might be failing, "I'm not on suppressants."

"Why would you even ask that in the first place?"

"Because . . ." I lean toward her, dragging in an inhale as if compelled. "You smell like an omega."

Her mouth falls open. "That's—that's a really rude question, isn't it?"

She asks it as if she isn't entirely sure of the answer.

"Maybe," I say truthfully, "but if you're going to be staying here, it would probably be a good idea to take precautions. I wouldn't want you to have an incident."

"An *incident*?"

She acts like I'm being outrageous. Surely she can scent me? She has to know how bad an idea it is for us to cohabitate in this enclosed space for however long without any kind of barrier.

"I . . . Yes," I say, genuinely confused by her confusion, but what's more, I can't fathom having to endure sharing my space with another omega. Not after what happened. I can hear the aggravation in my tone now. "Something like this would have been nice to know ahead of time. It's honestly a bit rude not to disclose this sort of thing knowing you'd be sharing a space."

She snorts. Actually *snorts*. "Wow. Day one, and already I'm dealing with this crap."

"What?"

"I'm fine," she says through gritted teeth. "I can do this job regardless of what I am, and I'm not going to let you sit there and discriminate just because I'm—because I'm a—"

"An omega?"

Her cheeks go bright pink. "Yes. That. You have another thing coming if you're going to insinuate I can't do my job because of some hormonal bullshit."

Huh.

I have to admit her answer takes me by surprise; I've never met an omega who seemed almost offended by their own designation, but then again, I've only met one other (two if you count my cousin Noah's mate), and *she* certainly wasn't embarrassed by what she was. On the contrary, she reveled in it. Which is exactly why the idea of being forced to live under the same roof as another omega for so long makes my insides twist.

I suppose I could grab some suppressants from the pharmacy in town if she insists on being stubborn—maybe she has some sort of condition that makes her incapable of taking them?—but then again, this is *my* place. Why should I?

Because she smells fucking mouthwatering.

There's something in an omega's scent that calls to someone like me; it's a tiny zing of unbridled want that creeps up my spine with even the smallest of inhales, one that I know all too well. It's bone-deep in our DNA to feel these things in each other's presence, and even if I'm currently the only one apparently feeling them, that doesn't mean it's not still a terrible idea to have her here.

I take a step back from her, sort of at a loss. She still looks offended.

Worked up, even. And while I have no desire for her to be here, doing what she's planning on doing, I wasn't intending to be outright *rude*—regardless of how uneasy she makes me.

"Oh . . . kay," I say slowly. "Well . . . all right then. Just thought I'd mention it, considering."

"Considering," she scoffs.

I wonder if Mackenzie was this hostile to Noah when they met.

Miss Fixit is still glaring at me as I slowly turn back toward the stairs, and I hold my breath while I take them two at a time, needing to put distance between me and the tiny, sweet-smelling contractor who might actually want to murder me.

I don't slow down until my bedroom door is closed and locked behind me. I'd had a lot of expectations about meeting the contractor after Jeannie finally wore me down to hire one, but nearly being barreled over by her big brown eyes wasn't even remotely within the realm of possibilities I'd dreamed up. I'd prepared myself to be cold to her, even downright unwelcoming if I had to be—anything to put up some sort of final protest against this entire debacle that Jeannie insists is necessary. And I tried. I really did.

But Little Miss Fixit wasn't having any of it.

There's a ghost of a smile on my mouth as I remember the way she tore into me; she's such a tiny thing, and yet, when she let me know what's what, she reared up like a brown bear protecting her cubs on the mountainside. And I shouldn't find that cute. I also shouldn't have found myself at a loss for words even for a moment while studying her soft waves the color of tree bark and her full mouth the same blushed shade of the hellebores that grow up the mountain.

And her *scent*.

I can still practically taste the richness of it—like baked apples and cinnamon with a touch of something headier, something that could make me dizzy if I let myself have too much of it.

Tess. I test her name in my head, liking the sound of it. Soft, like her. Except she isn't. Not really. I can tell that Tess is nowhere near as soft as she looks. I can discern that after only a few minutes with her. Which means it's going to be a hell of a lot harder than I anticipated to treat her like I originally planned. To make sure she's all too aware of how I'm against the changes she'll bring. I close my eyes, letting my head thunk against my bedroom door as I try to push out of my mind the way she pursed her mouth. No, I can keep my distance, I think. I can make sure she knows exactly how I feel about her being here, sweet scent or no. Because I can't let someone like her rush into my life and turn it upside down. Not again.

The last time nearly broke me.

3

Tess

"HAVE YOU BEEN sleeping?" Ada asks. "You're too young for eye bags."

I pause from unpacking to glance over at the mirror above the dresser and press my fingertips to the obvious dark circles that have started to form under my eyes. I frown at the overall shittiness of my appearance—my bangs look stringy, and my complexion seems somehow *paler* than usual. It's like I didn't sleep at all last night. Which, fair.

"I look that bad, huh?"

"You look stunning." My lips purse at her tone as she adds, "For an extra on *The Walking Dead*."

"Hysterical," I mutter.

"You didn't answer my question."

"Just a rough night," I say, shoving another pair of jeans into a dresser drawer. "Didn't get much sleep."

Hardly any, thanks to my infuriating new employer. Even now I feel myself tensing at the memory of the bizarre exchange I had with Hunter last night—from the coarse initial greeting to the infuriating remarks over my new designation I'd barely had more than a few hours to come to terms with.

If you're going to be staying here, it would probably be a good idea to take precautions. I wouldn't want you to have an incident.

I snort. What an asshole. An *incident*. What, does he think, I'm going to start howling at him and begging for his dick or something? Fucking shifter men. Which I assume he must be, given that the pleasant scent of sunshine and rain lingered long after he shut himself in his bedroom, something I'm now gathering was most likely *not* cologne.

And not to mention his obvious disdain at my being here in the first place. I spent most of the night fuming over his snide *Little Miss Fixit* comments—having half a mind to spend the rest of the evening boarding that asshole up in his own bedroom just to show him I'm perfectly comfortable around a hammer.

He's lucky my brothers are bringing all the tools.

I want to know how he could even tell what I was in the first place. It's not like there's some sort of sign stamped on my forehead now, is there? Will *every* shifter I meet know that I'm some sort of medical anomaly right away? That seems . . . inconvenient. Hopefully there's more information in the pamphlets Dr. Carter gave me.

"Did you pack appropriate pajamas?" Ada asks. "Are your toes in danger of frostbite?"

I roll my eyes. "I brought plenty of wool socks. I *have* seen snow before, you know."

I catch Ada's shiver even on my tiny phone screen. "I could never."

"You'll have to leave Southern California sometime," I laugh.

"Right. I could join you in Axe-Murderer Land and lose my toes. No thanks."

"What happened with Perry's school yesterday?"

I peek over to catch her teeth worrying at her lip. "He's acting out in class again."

"What does that mean?"

"He refused to participate."

"He's six," I scoff.

"I know that," she says. "I just worry about him socially. He doesn't seem interested in making friends at all. I thought moving him to private school this year would help get him some more one-on-one attention, but he keeps saying he hates the place."

"He'll adjust," I assure her. "I wouldn't worry about it too much. He's still so little."

"I hope you're right." She sighs, then waves a hand in front of her face. "Now tell me why you're not sleeping."

"It's not a big deal . . ."

I'm just apparently something entirely different than I thought I was for my entire life. Oh, and my new employer not only doesn't want me here but might think I'm going to rampantly hump his leg at some point.

Ada narrows her bright green eyes, leaning in a little so that her auburn hair falls into her face. "Tess."

"Fine," I sigh. "Just . . . still feeling a little under the weather."

An understatement, really. I tossed and turned the entire night—the meds the doctor gave me hardly even touched the cramps, the night sweats, and the strange itching sensation all over my skin. Between that and my irritation with Hunter, I'm positively exhausted.

"I thought you said it was clearing up?"

"I know." I spin to plop down on the edge of the bed, frowning at my phone, which I propped up on the dresser so I can look at my friend properly. "And it . . . is. Technically. Sort of."

"Oh my God," she groans. "Tell me you aren't dying."

"I'm not *dying*," I huff. "I'm just . . . not entirely well."

"If you want to make sense anytime soon, that would be great."

"Look, it's not a big deal, okay? The doctor said it's not unheard-of and that when I'm fully adjusted, everything will be as normal as—"

"*Tess.*"

"I'm not a beta."

Her head cocks, her freckled nose scrunching. "Come again?"

"Or, I mean, I might be right now, but I won't be soon? I don't know. It's all very confusing."

"Still not making sense."

"She called it a . . . late presentation."

"So, what . . . you're . . ." Her eyes widen. "Are you a shifter?"

"Among other things, apparently," I grumble.

"Oh my God. Have you shifted? Jesus Christ. What's that even like for the first time as an adult? I did it when I was thirteen, and I swear, *Twilight* didn't get it *entirely* wrong. I mean—"

"I haven't," I tell her, cutting her off. "Not yet. But I guess I will. Soon."

"Wow." She shakes her head, looking as stunned as I still feel. "That's insane, Tess. How are you holding up?"

"I'm . . . okay. I don't think it's entirely sunk in yet. Since my body is apparently still . . . changing."

"Okay. Yeah. Good. I just . . . Fuck. Do you have any questions I can answer? I know I'm not a doctor, but it's probably going to be easier to ask *me* about your biannual horny parade than it would be to ask a stranger."

"Ah." I shift on the bed, feeling uncomfortable. "About that. She thinks I might be having those . . . more frequently than others."

"Why? I mean, I have them four or five times a year, but that usually only happens with . . ."

She blinks at me, understanding dawning on her features, and I nod back at her, the realization hanging between us.

"Holy fuck," she whispers.

"Yep." I end the *p* with an audible pop. "I guess we can join the Omega of the Month Club."

"That's not a thing," she snorts.

"Whatever. I get to be nonsensical right now."

Ada gapes at me, looking dazed. "Wow, Tess. That's . . ." Her brows shoot up. "Do you think it's because you've spent so much time with me? Like . . . maybe we synced up? Like periods?"

I shake my head. "Pretty sure it doesn't work like that."

"I just . . . *Holy shit*. Seriously, are you okay? Have you told your parents?" She grimaces. "Have you told your *brothers*?"

I make a face. "No and no. Just you for now." I wince, realizing that there is actually *one* other person in the immediate vicinity who might know. "I'm having a hard enough time letting it marinate while at the jobsite."

"Oh shit. I didn't even think of that. Is that going to be weird? What about the woman you're working for? Is she a shifter?"

"I . . . haven't met her yet. She wasn't here when I got in last night. I met the owner though—who apparently is *not* Jeannie—and he was . . . a character."

"Shifter?"

"I . . ." I recall the soft scent of warm, sun-heated rain and frown. "I'm not sure." Okay, I have a very strong inkling, but I don't say that. "It's very possible though."

"Is he one of those old bearded guys who's always got on some type of fur?"

"He's not much older than me, actually," I tell her with a scoff. "But he does have a beard. No fur so far, just a lot of plaid."

"Oh?" Her voice takes on a much more interested tone. "Is he hot?"

I chew at the inside of my lip, a flash of Hunter's dark eyes and full mouth cropping up unbidden even as I try to shrug it off. I will *not* be romanticizing the gruff asshole, not even in my head. "I mean, he's not unattractive by any means."

"Oh my God. He's hot, isn't he?"

"I guess," I mumble. "Objectively."

"How *interesting*," she practically purrs.

I roll my eyes. "Well, given that—like you said—I look like a *Walking Dead* extra and I made an axe-murderer joke right after meeting him—your fault, by the way—he's probably going to do his best to avoid me."

I don't mention that at this point, I'm hoping he does, given that our first meeting went as disastrously as possible.

"Shut up. A shower and some good sleep and you'll get back to being the fresh-faced hottie I know and love."

"Actually, I get the sense he doesn't like that I'm here. Apparently this entire job was Jeannie's venture. I don't even know what their connection is yet. Hunter wasn't very . . . forthcoming."

On all sorts of things, I don't say, trying not to think about the way he sniffed me.

Fucking *sniffed* me.

That's going to take some getting used to.

"Hunter," Ada snorts. "How appropriate."

"I thought the same thing."

"Seriously, though. Do you have any questions?"

"I don't know . . . I still don't know what to think of it. I don't *feel* different yet, you know?" I consider everything for a moment. "What was it like when you found out?"

"I mean, I was thirteen, so it was sort of a nonissue. I didn't have my first heat till I was nineteen, so until then, it was just this thing about myself that I knew was going to be a big deal one day."

"Were you scared? Knowing you were different?"

"I don't know. My entire family are shifters, so I knew that was likely in the cards for me, but I'm the first omega in a couple of generations, according to my mom. Have you thought about asking your mom about where this might have come from?"

I wince. "She has enough going on."

"I'm sure she'd want to support you, babe."

"I know that. I do. But she's so tired all the time, being the only one working, and with everything going on with Dad . . ."

"You're not a burden, Tess," Ada stresses. "I know you think that anytime you have problems, you have to keep them to yourself, but people *want* to help you."

Deep down I know she's right, but it's hard to shake off literal years of trying to make myself as little of a problem as possible to the people I love. They have enough to deal with.

"Maybe," I mumble. I check the time on my phone. "I'd better go find my new boss, who might hate me."

"Mm." Her serious expression gives way to mischief. "Well. I'm sure you could make him *come around*."

"You're disgusting."

"One of us should be getting some action."

"You could get plenty if you stopped swiping left all the time."

She rolls her eyes. "The last guy on that app who looked promising said in his bio that his anthem was a G-Eazy song. Didn't exactly spark confidence. I think I'm going to delete it altogether. It's not like I use it for anything more than entertainment purposes."

"One of these days you're going to have to give *someone* a chance."

"I've done just fine without penis so far, thank you very much. Artificial works as well as the real thing." Her expression falls then. "Besides, you know why I don't date."

That gives me pause, and I feel a surge of guilt course through me. I *do* know why she doesn't date—and even if she's never really gone into the full details, given that it happened before we met, I know enough to understand *why* she continues to swipe left.

"Yeah, I know." I check the time. "I guess I should get downstairs and see if Jeannie ever made it in. It would be nice to discuss the project with someone who actually *wants* it to get done."

"Mr. Hunter is probably looking for a place to lay his log."

I push up from the bed, reaching for my phone on the dresser. "Okay, back to work for me. You can go back to mocking people's Tinder bios."

"It's a hard job, but someone has to do it."

"Whatever. Tell Catherine I said hi."

"Tess says hi!" Ada shouts behind her.

I hear a faint *Hi, Tess* from somewhere out of sight, and I wince. "Has your mom been around for this entire conversation?"

"I think she left around the time I suggested you should make him come."

"Good talk. Bye-bye, now."

Ada makes a kissing face right before I hang up the FaceTime call, and I shake my head as I stow my phone in my pocket. I try to situate my bangs into a less nightmarish situation, but given the way I'm still sweating slightly even *with* the frigid temperature, I reason that this is as good as it's going to get. It's not as if I have anyone to impress anyway. I'm going to get a lot sweatier than this when we start getting into the real work.

And I don't care in the slightest what anyone in this lodge thinks of my appearance.

Not at all.

THE LODGE LOOKS different in the morning sun—no less dusty or aged, but there's something about the sunlight gleaming on the soft mounds of powdery white outside that makes the walls seem to shine a little brighter. Honestly, it makes the entire place feel more charming.

The heat isn't quite as strong as I might like, a fact that became entirely apparent about eighteen minutes after I settled into bed last night in my usual bedtime attire of a T-shirt and panties. I was jumping back out of bed in no time at all to pull on pajama pants and the thickest pair of socks I own. Socks that I am currently still wearing inside the fuzzy snow boots I've shoved the ends of my sweatpants into. Socks that I'd wager I won't be taking off for the entirety of my stay.

I'm not looking where I'm going as well as I should when I step off the last stair, nearly tripping over a black mass of . . . *something* that gives a yowl when my foot collides with it. It bounds off in a fluffy blur toward the other room, leaving me blinking at the spot where it just was and wondering what in the hell I nearly stepped on.

One day here, and not only does my host hate me and think I'm some sort of biological ticking time bomb, but I'm already upsetting the local wildlife. Great.

I follow my nose, tracking the smell of cooked meat and, beneath that, something sweet that I very much hope comes with syrup, stalking it like a hungry predator as it leads me down an adjoining hall attached to the room where the front desk resides. It spills out into a long dining room that houses a wide (*surprise!*) wooden dining room table, each leg made of an untreated log and the benches on either side of a similar material. An older woman who looks to be in her sixties with thick graying hair piled on top of her head works at the other end, setting out plates and trays of bacon, eggs, and—most importantly—*pancakes*. She looks up when she notices me entering, giving me a kind smile that makes her eyes crinkle. Almost like we're old friends.

"Oh, hey," she greets me. "You must be Esther."

"Tess," I correct gently. "Everyone calls me Tess."

"Of course," she says, still smiling. "It's good to have you here. Why, you're the first guest we've had since May. No one to look at most of the time but Hunter and Reginald, and they're not great company even on their best days."

I wrinkle my nose. I'd been under the impression that I was the only guest. "Reginald?"

"Sorry." She nods her head down toward the floor, and I notice now that the same massive black *something* from the stairs is skulking in from the opposite door, which I assume leads to the kitchen. "He only *acts* like an asshole," she assures me as the very fluffy, very *large* cat takes a seat near her feet. "He's really kind of sweet once you get to know him."

"His name is Reginald?"

"Yeah," she laughs. "Named him after my late husband. Believe it or not, he sort of favors him a little."

I look into the slightly squashed face of the massive feline, trying to picture it. "Well. It's nice to meet you both."

"Sleep well?"

"Like a baby," I tell her. "Once my teeth stopped chattering."

"Well, shit. I'll put some extra blankets in your room after breakfast. These old ducts aren't what they used to be. I'll talk to Hunter and see if we have enough in the budget to do something about the furnace." She nods her head toward a wide window that overlooks the snow. There are so many *windows* in this place. "Hunter actually mentioned chopping some more wood later for the big fireplace. Haven't started it up in a few months—but it's right toasty to sit around when it gets going." She nods to herself as she gazes out the window, finally giving her head a little shake as if remembering herself. "Sorry, you'd think I'd never met anyone before." She wipes her hands on her apron, then steps closer, extending one for me to shake. "Jeannie. It's good to finally meet you in person."

"You too," I reply warmly. There's a whiff of something sweet coming from her, something not too unlike the pancakes she's just set down—and I have no way of knowing if it's batter on her clothes or one of those scent things the doctor warned me about. I can't decide if it's rude to ask. "I'm really excited to get started."

"I follow you on the TikTok," she says. "You do some good work."

I beam. "I appreciate that. It's really cool doing what I love with my family."

"Right. You have those brothers. They around?"

I shake my head. "They're driving. Bringing all the tools. I wanted to come ahead and get a feel for the place."

"Ah. Of course. Well, I'm thrilled you guys took the job. Took some convincing with that grumpy nephew of mine, but I know you're gonna do wonders here."

"Nephew?" I raise an eyebrow as I shake her hand. "Are you related to Hunter?"

"Aunt," she clarifies. "By marriage. My Reg was Hunter's uncle."

I guess it would be a bad idea to tell her that her nephew is kind of an asshole.

"Oh. Yeah. I met him last night. He seems great."

Jeannie laughs at that. "You don't have to sugarcoat it with me, hon. I'm sure he was a big ol' sourpuss. He isn't as keen on renovating as I am."

"I . . . gathered he has some reservations."

"Just ignore him. He isn't big on change when it comes to this old place."

I'm not sure what else to say about that, seeing as her remark feels like a major understatement, if Hunter's attitude last night was any indication. I give an appreciative look around the room in lieu of responding. "Well, it's really a lovely place you've got here."

"Oh, I know it's not what it used to be, but if you keep an open mind, this place really can be quite . . ." She smiles a little to herself, looking at the snow outside the window again. "Magical, really." She snorts out a laugh. "Listen to me, acting a fool."

"No, no," I tell her. "I get it. If Hunter is agreeable, we should probably all sit down to go over the budget and talk about the different projects I have planned for this place. A lot of the work my brothers and I can do by ourselves, but some of the larger jobs we'll have to get people to drive in from Denver for."

"I'll make sure he gets his panties out of a bunch long enough to do that," she assures me. "He can be reasonable when he wants to be." She nods to herself. "Anyway, I imagine you're hungry."

"Starving," I admit with slight surprise. The nausea is pretty much under control at the moment, and I'm realizing how long it's been since I've eaten properly.

"Well, sit down, sit down. Better dig in before the food gets cold."

I waste no time in obliging, lowering myself onto the carved bench at one side of the table, then grabbing one of the empty plates waiting there. I load up on eggs and two pancakes (my hips won't thank me for it, but honestly, I sort of love my curves), then tear into a crispy strip of bacon with an actual moan as I close my eyes.

"That's fantastic."

Jeannie chuckles to herself as she settles into the only actual chair, which sits at the head of the table near where I'm perched. "Glad you like it. I don't get to cook for many people anymore. Business has been so slow, you see."

"Oh?" I shove a forkful of eggs into my mouth. "Why is that?"

Jeannie sighs. "Used to be full up all winter long," she tells me. "Then a few years back, they built that new highway that bypasses the town . . . took all our travelers right around us and straight on to Denver. Business hasn't been the same since."

"That's too bad."

"We manage." She gives a soft shrug as she reaches for a strip of bacon. "Still get the locals up here around Christmastime every year. Reckon it's only to help us out, but it gets us through the rest of the year. Not to mention the few stragglers we get off the main road hankering for the *scenic* route."

I keep my voice casual as I start to cut into my pancakes, which are now drowning in syrup. "And it's only you and Hunter up here? No other staff?"

"We have a lady who comes in once a week to clean a bit," she answers. "But other than that, it's just us."

I chew thoughtfully as I let my eyes move about the room, noticing similar signs of neglect that could easily be fixed with minimal effort. "You know, I actually don't think it will take much to spruce the place up." I'm looking at the thick curtains that have begun to gather dust and thinking about how easily they could be cleaned. "I already have a few ideas, just from a quick look around, that I can run by you. Also, the website could use a bit of an overhaul. It's sort of hard to navigate." I shrug idly. "I don't know. Might help a little?"

Jeannie chews at her food, nodding her head quietly. "You're probably right. I'd love to help get the place more up to scratch myself, but these old bones don't get around like they used to. I'd throw out my damn back trying to climb some ladder to get all the cobwebs off these ceilings. Hunter does all the major upkeep we need, but like I said, he isn't really keen on the idea of changing anything too much. Sort of set in his ways, that one."

"He does seem a little . . ." I tilt my head side to side, thinking. "Rigid?"

God, maybe that was a poor choice of words.

Now I'm thinking about those shoulders again. I reason that it isn't *my* fault I was confronted with a physique that nearly defies the laws of nature within five minutes of arriving. Honestly, I'm just pondering the idea that he has to order all his shirts in a custom size. The absurdity of that possibility is enough to distract me from the grumpy innkeeper.

Jeannie simply laughs, taking another bite of bacon before she holds the last little bit under the table for the cat. "He wasn't always. The pup has had a rough go of it these last few years." She snorts. "Last decade, really."

"Pup?"

"Old habit," she tells me. "He shifted so early that first time. Practically a puppy. I haven't really been able to shake the nickname."

"So he's a shifter then," I press.

"Sure is," she says. "We both are."

"Ah, I thought I smelled . . ."

"Reginald used to say I smelled just like cake batter," she sighs wistfully. Her nostrils flare then. "You smell pretty lovely yourself."

I feel my cheeks heat. "Yeah, I . . ." And what do I say to that? I can't go and dump all my recent problems on this woman I barely know. Not when I don't know how to feel about them myself. "Thank you."

She leans in then, inhaling deeply. "You actually smell so familiar to me. It's odd."

"Oh, I . . . Your nephew seemed to have a bit of an issue with it, actually."

Her brows raise. "Did he now?"

"I don't think he likes me very much, truth be told."

"Oh, I'm sure that's not true," she argues.

I must be making a face, because Jeannie reaches over to give my forearm a pat. "He's a lot like Reginald," she tells me, nodding her head toward the giant cat, who is happily snacking on his bit of bacon. "He's really kind of sweet once you get to know him."

"Are we talking about me?"

I tense at the sound of Hunter's voice and turn to find him standing in the doorway.

"There you are," Jeannie says. "We were just saying we all needed to have a sit-down about the plans for this place."

He cocks a brow. "Oh, do we?"

"Don't be like that," she scolds. "Tess is here, and she's willing to help, so you need to be respectful."

"I'm plenty respectful," he mutters as he steps farther into the room.

His scent bombards me as he plops down on the other side of

the table, folding his arms over the top and eyeing me warily. This scenting business is still so new, and I haven't quite figured out how to get a handle on it. On the one hand, they both smell really good, but on the other . . . *Jeannie's* scent doesn't make me squirm in my seat.

"I was just telling your aunt that we should probably go over the budget and pin down what we absolutely can and can't do."

"Oh?" Hunter purses his lips. "Like what?"

"Well, for starters, Jeannie said the heat in this place isn't what it used to be. Do we have room for a new furnace?"

Hunter scoffs. "I highly doubt it. We can barely afford the cosmetic stuff Jeannie mentioned."

"We really need a new generator," Jeannie points out.

Hunter makes a face. "And where are we supposed to get the money for that?"

"Okay," I say, placating. "So we focus on cosmetics for now, and hopefully more business will come in to help offset the cost for some of the bigger projects."

"What exactly do you plan to do here?" Hunter asks.

I push my plate aside, crossing my arms. "Well, Jeannie and I discussed new flooring, some renovations in the bathrooms—that will mean new showers and vanities. I want to redo the foyer if we can; the front desk needs to be sanded and restained, and for that matter, the stairs need to be redone as well. The wood is scuffed to hell. From what I can see, the fireplace is still great—we just need to refinish the mantel, maybe, but I like the rustic charm of the original stonework there. Based on your budget, I don't think we have enough to rip out all the wood paneling, but we can most likely refinish it, at the very least. Plus, there is definitely some cosmetic work that needs to be done outside. I'd love to get the roof replaced with sheet metal if we can, but I'll have to go over the numbers to see if I can contract it out."

"That sounds like . . . a lot," Hunter says flatly.

I nod back at him. "There are other projects that might come up after I see the whole place—I'm going to want that tour later, by the way—but we can discuss those then."

Hunter's jaw works subtly, and I can tell he's bothered by this whole conversation. I remember what Jeannie said about him not liking change, and I can imagine that this definitely is a *lot* for him. Still, this is what I was hired for, and I can't let his aversion stop me from doing my job.

Hunter huffs out a breath then, shaking his head and pushing up from the table. "Sounds like you have it all figured out."

"I mean, I don't want to do anything without your approval. You're still the owner."

His mouth turns down in a frown as he looks between me and Jeannie, and for a moment I imagine a flash of vulnerability in his eyes that's gone as quickly as it comes. "Whatever Jeannie wants that we can afford," he says finally. "I'll deal with it."

He stalks out of the room then, and I feel as if he's left more questions than answers.

"Don't mind him," Jeannie sighs. "Like I said, he's really attached to this place. Doesn't like the idea of changing things."

"I don't want to step on any toes," I say.

She shakes her head. "You're not. He knows we need this, he's just having a hard time accepting it. He'll come around. Promise."

"If you're sure . . ."

"I'm positive."

She stands from her chair and wipes her hands on her apron, informing me that she's going to wash dishes and to holler if I need anything, then leaves me to puzzle over the conversation (however one-sided) I just had. It bothers me to know I'm unwanted here, because it's a problem I've never had to deal with before. Still, with HGTV looking for footage of this place to use as a pseudo interview for a chance at my own show, I can't afford to back down. Not as long as Hunter isn't outright chasing me off.

My eyes move to the enormous mass of fur. The cat is currently giving me a bored expression while he licks his lips, and I feel myself frowning as I remember the way Hunter implied I don't look the part when it comes to this job.

I tell myself that maybe Jeannie is right. Maybe Hunter isn't much of a people person. I even convince myself that it's possible we just got off on the wrong foot. I mean, I did sort of imply he might be a murderer—but it was a *joke*. Plus, I guess if he really doesn't want to make any renovations to his place, it's understandable he would be wary of me. I've got nothing for all the omega stuff though. I'm actively choosing not to think about it, or else there won't be any hope of getting along with Hunter. I tell myself I'll find him later, give him my sunniest smile, and we'll be right as rain for the remainder of the job. I reach over tentatively to give Reginald a head scratch, but he quickly slinks out of reach, looking almost offended.

Awesome.

THERE'S A BETTER signal on the deck, and I hold out my phone to check my appearance, making sure my hair isn't windblown before I hit record.

"Hey, guys! I'm here in Pleasant Hill, Colorado, for a new project." I turn the camera toward the lodge to get a panoramic view.

"And as you can see, I've got my work cut out for me. Stay tuned for more updates!"

I'll need to get some shots from the inside later to post to my account, but for now, that should do.

I move down the stairs in search of Hunter after I finally get my video to upload to TikTok and find him chopping wood like Jeannie mentioned. Remembering that I am a sensible twenty-eight-year-old woman who *shouldn't* be rendered temporarily incapable of speech at the sight of an overgrown man all dressed in plaid and chopping wood proves to be another matter entirely.

I don't *mean* to wind up at the deck stairs, one hand on the railing and short a few dozen brain cells (the important ones, ones that help unglue my tongue from the roof of my mouth in moments like these) as I try to process rolled-up sleeves and thick forearms. It also doesn't escape my notice that even from where I'm standing at the top of the stairs, Hunter might still be eye level to me. Needless to say, I'm decidedly less than eloquent when I meet the surly innkeeper for the third time since my arrival in Pleasant Hill.

God, this guy could create an entire TikTok account of just him chopping wood and make a killing.

I find him mid-swing, which means I'm forced to watch the way the plaid button-down hugs his shoulders as they strain with the effort of rolling to wield an axe—leaving me an addled mess with parted lips and wide eyes. Honestly, at this point, I hope I still look like a functioning human woman. His chest heaves against the fabric of his shirt as he looks up at me with a furrowed brow, then reaches with his free hand to wipe away the sweat that clings there.

That's when I remember that I'm still staring at him.

"Hey." My voice comes out all wrong. "I didn't mean to interrupt."

He swings the axe enough so that the blade is wedged into the wide log that he's using to prop up the smaller ones—and that's not supposed to be hot, is it? "Did you need something?"

"Oh, no, not really," I say a little too quickly. "I just wanted to—" I'm momentarily distracted when he tugs at the edge of his shirt to bring it up to his forehead to wipe the sweat there, revealing hard lines and ridges and a trail of dark hair that disappears into his jeans. I refuse to think about how far it goes. "I wanted to apologize if I was rude yesterday," I manage. "It was a long flight and a weird day. I didn't mean to insinuate anything about your place. It's really great."

One dark brow arches with something that almost seems like amusement, but it's so hard to read Hunter Barrett. "Nah, you meant it," he says with a shrug. "But you didn't say anything that wasn't true."

"Still," I say through gritted teeth, ignoring his blasé demeanor. Also, how is he wearing *only* that flannel out here? Is he some sort of yeti? "I really wanted to say I'm sorry."

Another shrug. "It's why you're here, isn't it? Help out with my dingy lodge?"

"Look, I gather that you weren't completely on board with hiring me, but I'd love it if we could sort of work together on this. I want to be sure that any changes I make are ones that you'll be happy with."

"Got your work cut out for you then," he snorts.

Don't scowl. Don't scowl.

"I can handle it," I say with my sunniest smile. "I'm sure we can do some great things here. I don't know if you're on TikTok, but I've handled way bigger renos than this."

He looks at me like I'm speaking French. "Not on . . . TikTok. Sorry."

I almost laugh. That definitely tracks. I'm trying not to let my eyes settle on the tiny bit of dark hair that escapes the unbuttoned collar of his shirt. *So it's top to bottom then, eh?* "I'm sure you're the type that has a private Facebook with just family and friends, huh? Stranger danger and all that?"

He shakes his head. "Nope. Don't have one."

"You don't have Facebook?"

"Nope."

My brow knits. "You don't strike me as the X type."

"Don't know what that is," he says matter-of-factly. "Don't really use the internet, aside from the website for reservations."

Now I'm probably looking at him like *he's* started speaking French. "Everyone uses the internet."

"Except me, I guess," he says dryly.

I find myself staring at him again, but now it's in a way as if he's sprouted another head. He's talking like a seventy-year-old man, but by my best guess, Hunter can't be more than thirty. If that. Who in the hell *doesn't* use the internet in this day and age?

In my disbelief, I can hear my voice coming out an octave higher than it should be.

"Why?"

He shrugs. "Just have better things to do with my time."

I have about a dozen other questions I could ask about my new acquaintance's particular oddity, but even knowing as little as I do about Hunter, I still recognize that he'll probably have little to offer on the subject other than some dodgy monosyllabic answer.

"Okay, Grandpa," I snort, shoving my hands into my pockets. "What do you do with your free time? Whittle?"

His mouth does something I've yet to see it do, turning up at the corners until I'm blasted with straight white teeth that make my stomach flutter a little. I decide then and there that should I ever find myself miraculously given a seat in Congress, my first order of business would be rendering Hunter Barrett's smile *illegal*.

"Something like that," he laughs quietly.

He reaches down to gather up a few logs he's finished splitting, beginning the process of piling them in his long arms, presumably so he can carry them inside.

I shuffle my feet, trying to calm the swooping that lingers inside my belly in the aftermath of a full-blown Hunter smile. "Do you need help with that?"

I'm rewarded with another low chuckle. "I've got it. Better save your strength for all the fixin'."

I ignore his obvious joke at my expense. "Sure. How far away is town, by the way? I was hoping you guys had a pharmacy."

"A pharmacy?"

I avert my eyes, crossing my arms over my chest. Definitely don't want to get into *that* discussion with Hunter. Especially not after his weird comments about my designation, which I barely know anything about myself. The doctor only gave me a small supply of the meds, writing a prescription for more that I could fill. I'm sort of regretting not taking care of it in the city now.

"Just need to pick up a few things," I mumble.

"Your car won't make it down the mountain."

My eyes snap up to meet his. "What?"

"Had a big snow last week. Your tires aren't wrapped. Not even sure how you made it to the lodge without winding up in a ditch."

"I'm perfectly capable of driving in snow," I snipe.

His mouth quirks. "Well, you can capably find yourself on the side of the road in a snowbank if you try to make it down the mountain in that little car."

"What am I supposed to do then?"

"If you need a ride"—he straightens with his arms full of wood, his dark eyes settling on my face—"I'd be happy to give you one. If I'm not busy."

I feel my cheeks heat a little, and I remind myself that this is a perfectly innocent statement, regardless of what my stomach is doing in response. It takes me a moment to answer, because my initial urge is to argue, but there's a slight hint of warm rain creeping into my nostrils now that he's a little closer, and it's making me sort of dizzy. I blink, trying to remember words as a twisting sensation ensues in my stomach.

"That'd be great," I half squeak as he starts to move past me.

He's at the top of the stairs and towering over me in a matter of seconds, the corners of his mouth tilting up as he gives me a glance from the side, one dark curl escaping his might-be-staple beanie and falling into his eyes. "You know, in between all my whittling."

His eyes move over my face as my lips press together in a tight line, and he finally moves to carry the wood inside. It takes me at least three seconds to remember how to form words as I spin on my heel to call after him, pushing down the still-writhing feeling in my stomach that's quickly progressing to something more and more uncomfortable with every second.

"Oh, hey, what's the Wi-Fi password, by the way?"

His answering laugh doesn't bode well.

4

Hunter

I DON'T SEE Tess for a few hours after running into her out back, and I can't say that I'm not grateful for the reprieve. I thought I might have imagined it, how appealing she is—with her wide brown eyes and her pert nose that wrinkles when she's irritated and her soft-looking mouth that seems to be developing a habit of pursing in my vicinity—but it's clear now that she's just as lovely as my brain remembers from last night. It makes my newfound resolve to ignore her as much as possible all the more difficult.

In the short time since meeting her, I've thought a lot about how doing so is in both our best interests; I know better than anyone that continued exposure will only lead to awkward situations, given how enticing I find her scent, and there's nothing I want less than to find myself ruled by my hormones and then make an ass of myself all over again. I've had more than enough of that in my life already, thank you very much.

But my plans to steer clear are thwarted when I find her crouched in a corner of the great room sometime after I put the wood away, holding out her hand to a very bored-looking Reginald, who is eyeing her with utter disinterest as she tries to entice him out from the little table he's hiding under. I watch for a few seconds as she baby-talks and coos and makes *pspsps* noises at him while he looks at her like she's lost it.

"Here, kitty kitty," she coos.

I cross my arms, leaning against a wall as amusement washes over me.

"Come here, you mean-ass furball," she huffs. "Let me love you."

After a beat, I decide to put her out of her misery. "You might as well give it up now," I call to her, noticing the way she jolts slightly before her head whips around to look at me. "That cat hates everyone but Jeannie."

As if to drive home my point, Reg chooses that moment to bound away, flicking his tail as he goes so that it whips Tess in the face.

"Damn it," she mutters. "I'm dying to pet that cat."

"Better men have tried."

I catch a sudden whiff of her scent. It's so potent, it seeps into my nostrils and seems to almost drip down my throat.

Is it somehow stronger than it was yesterday?

I clear my throat, looking anywhere but at her. I can't help but notice the cobwebs collecting in one corner of the ceiling and frown. Not exactly helpful for my stance that we don't need her here making changes.

"So," I start. "What do you think of my dingy little lodge?"

She frowns. "Look . . . I shouldn't have said that. It was really unprofessional." She squares her shoulders, taking a step closer to me and thrusting out her hand. "Can we start over? I'm really sorry that we got off on the wrong foot. It was . . ." Her frown deepens then, her brow furrowing. "It was a weird day yesterday."

I want to tell her that *no*—we can't start over, if only for my own sanity, given that being on friendlier terms with her will most likely only make it harder for me to ignore her delectable scent. Still. It seems that she's here for the next several weeks, and I know that realistically, being at odds with her at every turn because of my own hang-ups isn't exactly feasible.

"Sure," I say as I slowly take her hand, if a tad bit begrudgingly. "I guess we can try that."

Her answering smile feels like a blow to the chest, the brightness of it making everything feel too tight. Her soft hand in mine makes the skin of my palm tingle, and before I realize what I'm doing, I'm jerking my hand away and shoving it in my pocket. I try to pretend that I don't see the flash of disappointment in her eyes.

"You are Miss Fixit, after all," I tell her with a shrug.

She narrows her eyes at me. "Cute."

She rises to her full height—which is still much shorter than me—crossing her arms.

"Get all that whittling done?"

My lips twitch, but I snuff out the smile before it has time to form. "Not quite." I eye the pink sweatpants that hug the generous curve of her hips, my eyes dipping to her ridiculous fuzzy socks before I scold myself for even looking. "What are those?"

"What?" She follows my line of sight, eyeing her feet before cocking a brow back at me. "Socks?"

"Those are *not* socks."

"Of course they are."

"They look like you skinned the Lorax."

She rolls her eyes. "Sorry. You weren't around to consult when I was getting dressed." She lets her gaze sweep around the room. "I was actually about to start exploring a little more . . . Mind giving me a tour of the place?"

Actually, I'd like to get far away from you, because you smell like something I want to take a bite out of.

"I guess I can do that," I say instead like a jackass.

She gives me a little mock bow, extending her arm as if to say, *After you.*

I shake my head, turning to leave the room so she can't see the smirk that touches my mouth.

Tess Covington might be trouble.

I'VE NEVER HAD someone wax poetic about my banisters before, but Tess found out they're original to the property and hand-carved by my great-grandfather, and she hasn't stopped talking about them since.

"I really want to highlight them in the remodel," she's saying. "The mantel too. You said he carved that also?"

I nod mutely, a little dumbstruck by her good mood. It's like once she slid into her element, she became an entirely different person. Or rather, she started actually being *friendly*. Her attitude up until this point has probably been my fault, so I can't really blame her for it.

It's actually kind of . . . sweet. How into this she obviously is. That makes it hard to look away when she starts going on and on about the original flooring she finds under the old carpet and starts gushing about it.

"This is fantastic! We have to rip all the carpet up and refinish this hardwood. I can't believe it's just been sitting here for who knows how long. Did you know this was under here?"

Another probably dumb-looking nod, because I haven't yet figured out how to get a word in edgewise with the way she's chattering on.

I *shouldn't* find it cute.

Or her in general, really.

You'd think I would know better, that my body would have formulated some sort of omega defense system, considering the last one I got close to practically ripped my heart out, and yet here I am, openly admiring this woman who apparently knows her way around a hammer.

It's ridiculous.

"—and if you meant it about driving me into town, I'd actually really appreciate it."

I blink, coming out of my own head and back into the conversation.

"Hmm?"

She looks slightly embarrassed for some reason, turning her head away and reaching to rub at her neck. I wonder if she realizes how much this makes her scent bloom in the air, the soft smell of cinnamon and baked apples tickling my nostrils and making my mouth water.

"It's just that I really need to get to a pharmacy," she tells me. "I've been a little under the weather; I actually saw a doctor before I came here, and she gave me these prescriptions, and I need to—"

"I'll take you," I tell her. My body's tensing with her burgeoning scent, so it comes out as more of a grunt. "It's fine."

She visibly relaxes, her face breaking into a grin. "Great. I'd definitely appreciate it."

"We can go whenever you're ready," I tell her as she turns to study the paneling on the wall. "Just let me know when—"

She takes a step, not looking where she's going, and I watch as, almost in slow motion, her foot catches the corner of the upturned carpet that she tugged loose to reveal the hardwood underneath.

Her eyes widen as she loses her balance, and in a matter of seconds, she goes from tumbling backward to pressing against my chest. One of my hands wraps around her wrist while the other cradles her neck, holding her close so she doesn't fall.

My lashes shutter in a blink as I'm hardly able to recall how we got like this; it's as if I saw her in danger and my body just... reacted. Which is odd. This close, I can feel the warmth of her seeping through my clothes, can feel her soft skin brushing against my rough palms, and for a few seconds, I can't seem to remember how to speak.

When it comes back to me, my voice is rougher than it was when I last spoke. "Are you okay?"

"I..." Her pupils dilate under my scrutiny, and I feel a rush of... something in my gut that would probably thrill me if it weren't so alarming. Pleasurable but terrifying. "I'm fine," she says. "Wasn't watching where I was going."

"Clearly," I mutter.

Her brow furrows like she might return the sarcasm, but then her lips press together, making them look fuller, pinker. As I watch her throat bob in a swallow, I'm struck with the realization that with my hand cradling her neck, my wrist is dangerously close to her scent glands. That with one flick, I could scent her, and she would smell like me.

And why the *fuck* is that so appealing?

It's enough to have me untangling myself from her with more force than necessary, because these are *not* feelings I need or want. Not again. Putting your faith in the wrong omega is enough to make anyone wary of doing it again.

I clear my throat when she's out of my hands and at a safer distance, ignoring the way my palms tingle, almost as if in protest.

I clear my throat. "Good. Try to be more careful."

The thought of her getting hurt also sparks a visceral reaction in me, and even though I know what it is—even though I *know* it's simply biology—it makes my insides twist. With need or disgust at myself . . . I can't be sure.

"If you still need to go to the pharmacy," I say, changing the subject so I can hopefully escape and actually *breathe*, "we can go in twenty. I just need to . . . I have to . . ." I point aimlessly, having no actual excuse to get far away from her but needing to do so all the same. "Just have to check on something first."

She nods slowly, her eyes wide and seeming to see right through me. "Sure. Meet you at your truck?"

"Sounds great," I tell her, already spinning on my heel.

It occurs to me then that I'm actually *trapped* here. For the next several weeks, I will be forced to endure living under the same roof with the exact type of person I swore I never wanted to have anything to do with again.

And even if that's not her fault, it doesn't change the way part of me feels the need to keep my distance. Even if only to protect myself.

You can't be friends with Tess Covington, I repeat over and over as I head toward my bedroom for a moment of peace before I'm trapped in the Bronco with her for half an hour. *It's not a good idea.*

There's a reason alphas and omegas drive each other's hormones so out of whack; we're made to perfectly complement one another. Merely being in close proximity is enough to draw us to each other, to make us *want*. It makes it way too easy to get in over your head without knowing what the other person is really like. Something I know all too well.

I tell myself I'll just let her do her job, interacting with her as little as I can possibly get away with. That way nothing is complicated.

That way no one gets hurt.

I touch my fingers to my nostrils when I'm safely tucked away in my bedroom, allowing myself to breathe in her scent even though I know I shouldn't. I close my eyes and let the sweetness of it fill my nose, releasing a shuddering breath when it makes my mouth water all over again.

I have a feeling it'll be easier said than done.

5

Tess

"SO HOW EXACTLY did you get into this? This thing you do."

I turn my face from the passenger window, catching his expression, which I assume is him trying not to seem overly curious. There's a little scrunch between his eyes and a purse to his lips, almost like he's trying to make sense of his own question.

"This thing I do?"

"Yeah," he semiclarifies. "On the internet."

I consider that. It's not really a question I've ever had to answer, largely because most people who know about my account have been following me for years, even if the explosion in popularity is fairly new. They saw it happen in real time.

"I started working with my dad's business when I was still in school. I always loved what he did—taking a place that needs a lot of love and turning it into something gorgeous. I don't know. There's something simple and beautiful about that."

"You said your dad *did* this for eighteen years when you were yelling at me yesterday."

I roll my eyes. "I didn't *yell*."

"Sure you didn't," he snorts. "But past tense? He doesn't do it anymore?"

"No, he . . ." I frown, trying not to let the familiar melancholy creep in. "He had a stroke," I tell him. "When I was eighteen. He hasn't really been the same since."

"I'm sorry," Hunter offers.

I shake my head. "He can still get around, but his hands don't work the way they used to."

"That must be tough for someone who's spent their whole life using them."

My chest clenches. He has no idea how *tough* it's been, and I doubt he'd care to hear it.

"Yeah," I manage. "It was . . . an adjustment. He still consults sometimes."

"Okay, most of this makes sense. It's the TikTok thing I don't get."

I chuckle under my breath. "You really are way too young to be so old."

"It's a curse," he responds dryly.

"I was doing this job in North Carolina," I tell him. "TikTok was starting to become a whole *thing*, and I just started posting some footage for fun. We never expected to go viral."

"'Viral'?" he echoes.

I outright laugh this time. It's like he's eighty, and what I don't say is he is entirely too *hot* to be this old.

"It sort of blew up," I clarify. "Got a million views practically overnight."

Hunter makes a face like the idea of a million people seeing anything he's done makes him uneasy, and there's something endearing about that.

Or maybe I'm still a little hung up on the way he touched me not half an hour ago.

If I concentrate, I can still feel the phantom press of his fingers against my throat, the skin there prickling with interest as if silently asking for more. I'd never felt such a strong reaction to anyone's touch before, and after the haziness in my brain cleared up, I concluded that it has to be some sort of hormonal garbage, nothing more.

Even if I'm still thinking about it. Just a little.

"So you said your brothers are on their way?"

"Mm-hmm. They should be here tomorrow."

"Great," he deadpans.

I cross my arms. "Why are you so against the renovations? Jeannie told me about how business has been slower. Don't you want to try to do something about that?"

The way his expression tightens . . . I almost feel bad for asking.

"It's . . . complicated."

"I can do complicated," I assure him.

"I suppose . . . it has a lot to do with my parents."

He looks like he'd rather be talking about anything else, but I can't help it. Strangely, I have this overwhelming desire to *know* what it is that makes the grumpy innkeeper tick.

"Your parents?"

He glances at me from the side. "They died. Car accident. Ten years ago now."

"Oh," I answer quietly. I feel like a dick for asking. "I'm sorry."

He shakes his head. "It's fine. It was a long time ago."

The pup has had a rough go of it these last few years. Last decade, really.

Well, shit.

I did *not* need to hear anything that would endear me to the grumpy innkeeper.

"Now I'm feeling even *more* shitty for calling the place dingy."

He surprises me with a barely there grin, the action making the scruff on his face crease with what *might* be a dimple hiding underneath.

"Don't worry," he tells me. "It wasn't really me you insulted, just my dead parents."

I narrow my eyes. "Are you actually kind of a shit?"

"Maybe a little."

I can feel myself grinning too now, and I wonder if maybe Jeannie was right—if Hunter isn't as mean as he seems.

"I forgive you for being so oblivious," he teases.

His phrasing gives me pause, and without even thinking, I laugh bitterly, replying, "Wouldn't be the first time."

He eyes me curiously, and I feel a sudden wave of embarrassment, something that's commonplace when I think about my dad and all the things I've missed this last year. How I could have been so oblivious to how he's been struggling. Hunter is still looking at me from the corner of his eye as if he'd like to say more, but for some reason, the idea of spilling my guts about my family woes makes my stomach twist with distaste.

My eyes flick to the radio, and I suddenly reach to turn up the knob. "I like this song."

Hunter doesn't prod at my blatant diversion, thankfully, but I can feel him watching me from the driver's seat as I keep my eyes trained out the opposite window. He doesn't ask me any more questions while we continue on the winding path that takes us down the mountain toward town, leaving me with nothing but my own thoughts for company.

"**I HAVE TO** pick up a few things," Hunter tells me when we both step out of the Bronco on Main Street. He points in the opposite direction. "The pharmacy is down that way."

"How do I find you again when I'm done?"

Hunter's mouth tilts up in a lazy grin, that hint of a dimple now obvious beneath the scruff on his cheek. I feel a brief flash of curiosity as to what it might feel like under my palm, which I quickly shake away.

"It's not exactly a big place," he assures me. "I'll find you."

"Well, let me give you my number. Just in case."

Hunter's brow furrows as if he thinks this is unnecessary, but after a moment he reaches down into his pocket to fish out his own phone. Something that immediately makes me reel.

"What is *that*?"

Hunter glances down at the phone—if you can even call it one, and the jury is still out as far as I'm concerned—in his hand. "My cell phone?"

"Tell me that's not a flip phone," I press incredulously.

Hunter looks amused now. "Looks that way."

"I didn't even know they still *made* those."

"Wouldn't know," he tells me. "I've had this one forever."

"And by 'forever' I assume you mean since they first started making cell phones, judging by that thing."

"It gets the job done," he assures me. "Your number?"

I rattle it off and watch in wonder as Hunter taps it in on the ancient keypad, flipping it shut with a *thwip* sound after. A *thwip*. That sound brings back all kinds of nostalgia from what feels like a billion years ago. Is Hunter an *actual* modern-day version of the caveman? I'm still staring at him with a blank expression as I try for the dozenth time to puzzle this man out, but he's already shoving his phone back into his pocket and adjusting the gray beanie he seems so fond of.

"Don't take too long," he urges. "Gets colder after dark." He frowns as he says it, eyeing my jacket. "You *did* bring something heavier than that, right?"

I frown down at my choice of attire. "No? It's warmer than it looks though."

"Not for Colorado after dark in the middle of October it isn't." He huffs out a breath, and before I even register what he's doing, he's shrugged off his brown Carhartt coat, leaving him in only his thick flannel as he thrusts it toward me. "Take this."

"I can't take your—"

"I can't have Miss Fixit freezing to death on me," he counters before I can finish. "Too much to do."

I scoff at his smirk, but at that moment, a stiff breeze chooses to gust over us, and I shiver. Damn it.

"Fine," I say, snatching his coat and putting it on. "Thank you."

He pauses, eyeing the way I'm shrugging into his coat like he's now understanding what he's done. A mask of indifference slides over his face, his jaw clenching a bit. "It's just a coat. Don't think much of it."

"If you say so," I huff. "I guess tell me where I can buy a warmer coat as well."

"Check out Cat's place," he tells me. "It's that way"—he dips his chin opposite from where I need to go first—"but it's not far."

I nod dumbly, watching him turn to stalk off, his broad, plaid-clad form obvious against the stark white of our surroundings. I can't help the way I turn my face and press my nose to the dense fabric of his coat, inhaling deeply and getting a lungful of his fresh, enticing smell. One I'm realizing now must not be some sort of cologne but instead is just *him*. His scent hits me like a freight train, seeming to seep into my skin, and going deeper, as if settling on my bones. It's an odd sensation.

My skin prickles and my cheeks flush, and for the briefest and most embarrassing of moments I imagine a pulse between my legs that comes on so suddenly it gives me pause. I quickly jerk my face away from the coat, debating whether or not I should take it off, but honestly, it *is* really warm.

I finally remember I came here to do something, putting away my incredulity of everything that is Hunter Barrett to turn and head toward the pharmacy. As I walk, it dawns on me that I didn't get *his* number.

I FIND THE pharmacy without much difficulty, and thanks to the elderly shopkeeper, Martha, I walk out with my prescription as well as a rather large tub of saltwater taffy that she convinced me I needed after I casually mentioned I'd never tried it. I'm not usually one to argue against candy, so it didn't take much nudging on her part, truthfully.

I carry my items in a brown paper sack with twine handles, exploring the quiet sidewalk of Pleasant Hill as I make my way back to where Hunter parked the Bronco. The people here are all bundled up in winter coats as they pass me by, but still they take the time to offer a wave or a kind smile if their face coverings allow for it. I can't help but notice how different the atmosphere is from California—and not just the weather. People back home barely look up when they're crowding sidewalks, too busy checking their texts or their fantasy football picks or whatever else is so important on their phones.

My own phone buzzes in my pocket, and I fish it out to swipe it open and read the text there.

> **DAD:** Everything looks great, kiddo. Don't work yourself too hard out there.

A smile touches my face, though I still feel a pang in my chest. I sent my dad some pictures I took this morning of the lodge with some of my initial ideas, something I always do when I start a job, but now there's a tinge of sadness to the ritual that comes from wondering how much more time I get to do this with him if I can't land the signing bonus with this HGTV deal.

Shrugging off my potential melancholy, I pass a storefront window that holds several outfits on vintage-looking dressmaker's mannequins. A hand-painted logo across the glass that reads CAT's CLOSET catches my eye and makes me stop on the sidewalk.

I realize this must be the store Hunter mentioned. I pull his coat a little tighter around me as another breeze blows through, and I can't pretend that it isn't partly because it smells so good. It's like being wrapped up in a spa towel, the smell of clean sunshine and rain enveloping me, making me feel strangely calm and more than just a bit warm. Instead, my limbs feel a little laxer, my skin thrumming with heat. Maybe the whole scent thing isn't *so* bad.

I wager it wouldn't hurt to check things out considering he was *so* confident he could find me at any given time within city limits. With that in mind, I pull open the wooden door to the sound of a bell jingling, signaling my entry. There are more mannequins boasting various pieces of winter clothing scattered about the inside, as well as hanging displays on the walls and even some home decor here and there. I pick up the end of a knitted scarf that catches my eye near the entrance and rub the soft material between my fingers as a voice calls out from somewhere in the back.

"Hey, be right there!"

I decide that the scarf is a must-have as I pull it from around the mannequin's neck, and I'm moving on to check out a rack of sweaters when I hear footsteps sounding nearby. A woman who's a tad shorter than me with thick dark hair appears from between the clothes racks, her smile warm and genuine as she notices me browsing.

"Sorry about that," she says. "I was nuking some leftovers in the back."

"Oh, that's fine," I tell her. "I just saw the display outside, and everything looked so cute."

Her nose wrinkles as her head cocks to the side. "You're not from around here."

"What gave it away?"

Her lips quirk. "Because I know everyone from around here." Her brow furrows. "You look familiar though. Have you visited before?"

I shake my head. "No. First time."

"Hmm. I swear I've—Oh my God." She snaps her fingers. "Are you Tess Covington?"

I reel a little, blinking. "Yes?"

"Oh my God! I'm sorry, total stalker moment," she laughs. "I follow you on TikTok."

"Oh!" I laugh nervously. I always feel awkward when people recognize me. "Right."

"I've been following you since the North Carolina remodel," she laughs. "I swear, I have an entire reno wish list, thanks to you. My boyfriend is *so* excited about that." She says this last bit with a hint of sarcasm, smiling good-naturedly. "Jesus, I'm sorry. I'm having a starstruck moment." She sticks out her hand. "My name's Cat. Cat Campbell." She shakes my hand enthusiastically when I give it. "Well, *technically* my name is Catalina—named after my grandma, mind you; she's full Greek—but after *Step Brothers* came out, it was all 'It's the fucking Catalina Wine Mixer!' shouted after me everywhere I went in high school, so you can imagine—" She presses her lips together suddenly, looking sheepish as she releases my hand, which she's realized she's still shaking. "Sorry," she offers. "I'm told I talk too much when I get excited."

I can't help but laugh, deciding on the spot that I like Cat. "It's fine. Totally get the nickname. Did you know my real name is Esther?"

"Shut up. Really?"

"Really. Also named after my grandma. Not Greek though. Just very old and very into her seven cats."

"I think it's a rule that all Esthers have to love cats," she teases.

I shrug with another laugh. "Well, she put all seven of them in her will, so . . ."

Cat laughs with me now, her smile morphing into a confused look. "So what are you even doing here? Pleasant Hill doesn't really seem like your usual."

"I'm renovating the Bear Essentials Lodge up the mountain, actually."

"Oh! Hunter's place?"

I nod. "You know him?"

"Oh yeah. He and my boyfriend graduated together. They're old friends. I was two years below them though—I'm always teasing them that they're old now, since they turn thirty-two next year."

The bell over the front door rings, interrupting her and yielding the broad frame of the man in question as he ducks inside. He brings with him that same sharp scent I'd only *just* started to get used to from his the aroma of it washing over me and making me feel that same embarrassing pulse between my legs. Is that even normal? Am I going to get horny for every shifter man I meet now?

"There you are," he murmurs, his low voice doing nothing for the situation between my legs. "I thought you were going to meet me back at the Bronco?"

I shrug, giving him a smile as I shift uncomfortably. "I thought you said you could find me."

"I did, didn't I?"

"Just testing out your theory," I tease.

He notices Cat standing there, and when I turn back, I find her looking between us curiously. "Oh, Hunter gave me a ride into town."

"Ah." She flashes a grin in his direction. "Hey, stranger. About time you came down from your mountain to dwell with us townies."

Hunter rolls his eyes. "Been busy. That's all." He frowns at the bag I'm carrying. "Seems like you found more than a prescription."

"The nice lady at the store talked me into some saltwater taffy."

Hunter makes a face. "That's bad for your teeth."

"I'm sorry," I snort. "Should I have gotten you some Werther's Original instead, Gramps?"

Cat bursts out laughing, catching my attention. "Wow. I might love you, Tess. I'm glad someone is finally roasting Hunter about his Stone Age ways. Did you know he still carries a flip phone?"

"I *know*," I guffaw. "I thought I had suddenly time traveled to 2007."

"So glad the two of you met," Hunter harrumphs as he frowns

down at us. It's weird that even his frown does something strange to me.

"Mm-hmm. Especially since you were hiding her," Cat accuses him. "I think the fact that you have a *celebrity* staying at the lodge warrants a text."

"Oh," I cut in. "I'm not really a—"

"I doubt she wants you guys pressing your noses to the windows like she's a zoo animal or something."

"I would *not*," Cat huffs. "But this is great, right?" She beams back at me then. "You can get the lodge some amazing exposure, right?"

Hunter frowns back at us both. "I'm sure that she's not worried about—"

"I mean, I do have some friends over at *Travel Quarter* who might—"

"There's no way any of them would be interested in my dingy little lodge," Hunter snorts. I feel guilt creeping up at his use of *my* term, but he looks mostly unperturbed by it. Disinterested, if anything. He shoves his hands into his pockets. "You ready? Jeannie will be cooking dinner before long."

I nod back at him, his tone cutting off any further discussion. "Yeah. Just let me pay for this scarf and look at the coats really quick."

"Okay." He bobs his head in agreement. "I'll go start the truck."

We watch him leave the way he came, and I hear Cat's sigh after the door closes behind him, drawing my attention. "Don't mind him," Cat offers. "He's not nearly as grumpy as he makes himself out to be."

"Right. I'm sure."

"How long are you staying, anyway? You should totally come

out to Fred's with us the next time we go. I mean, if you want. No pressure or anything."

"Fred's?"

"Oh, sorry. It's the only bar in town." She grimaces. "I know. It's a terrible name for a bar, but it's been there for, like, fifty years. The owner refuses to change it. He thinks it's *fun*."

"That sounds awesome, actually," I tell her honestly.

"Yeah?" Her smile widens as she claps her hands together. "Great! It's usually just me and my boyfriend, Jarred, and maybe a few locals, but at least you can meet some new people, hopefully? And there's always dancing, if you dance. Oh, and Paula makes the *best* cheese fries in the state. Well, I'm assuming. I haven't had *every* rendition, obviously, but I—" She sighs. "Shit. I'm doing it again. I'm sorry. You're just, like, probably the most famous person to ever visit," she laughs.

"It's fine," I assure her. "Fred's sounds great. I'd love to come."

"Awesome!" Cat reaches into her back pocket for her phone. "Can I get your number? I can text you when I figure out when we can come after you for Fred's. My boyfriend is out of town right now, but he should be back in a week or so. You'll still be here, right?"

"I will be," I tell her before I give her my phone number. "That sounds great."

She taps out a text, and I feel my phone vibrate in my pocket. "I can't believe I have your phone number! I promise not to make you give me an autograph or anything."

"It's fine," I chuckle. "I promise."

I follow her back to the cash register after she shows me the coats, continuing to happily chat at me from over her shoulder, and I find myself genuinely excited to have made something of a friend here. Well, someone other than Hunter, that is. If I can even call him a friend—and I'm still not sure I can. It isn't lost on me that Cat is the second person to hint that the stony innkeeper is warmer than he appears to be.

I find said innkeeper standing by his truck, stoically looking out at the rapidly sinking sun with a serene expression. His hands are shoved in his pockets, and standing like that, he looks younger somehow. Less burdened, if that's even a thing.

I shrug out of his coat as I approach, and his normal frown colors his lips when I hold it out to him.

"Grabbed a better coat," I tell him. "But thanks for lending me yours."

He's still frowning at the garment like it offends him, looking from it to me as if he doesn't believe I actually got a warmer one. He finally takes it after a beat, and when his fingers accidentally brush against mine, it feels like a current of electricity passes between us, one that I feel zapping deep in my belly. Even when it passes, I still feel the echo of the sensation, like it's reverberating through me.

Huh, that's weird.

"Ready to go?" Hunter's voice is a little rougher as he tucks the coat under his arm.

"After you, Gramps," I tease, trying to ignore the strange sensation currently coursing through me that has me wanting to snatch his coat back and bury myself in its warmth again.

Hunter rolls his eyes, but it doesn't stop him from walking me to my side of the truck, yanking the door open, and holding it until I climb inside. I try to remember the last time anyone opened a door for me but then scoff at my own line of thinking.

He's just being nice.

THE MATING GAME

The thought almost makes me laugh, since *being nice* doesn't seem to be Hunter's forte.

And as he climbs back into the Bronco, I tell myself that the twinging desire to ask for his coat back is just the chill clinging to the cabin of the truck. That the strange tightness of my skin can be attributed to this also.

Because honestly, I have no other idea what it could be.

6

Hunter

I DO MY best to ignore the fact that Tess smells like me on the drive home, but it proves difficult. I wasn't thinking when I offered her my coat; seeing her shiver had forced my hand, and before I even knew what I was doing, my coat was off my body and thrust toward her.

Fucking hormones.

It's strange that she could be so self-sufficient and fiery and still so small and fragile. Everything about her seems to invoke my protective instincts, which in turn makes me more and more irritated with myself. Even knowing all the facts—knowing *why* she affects me like this—doesn't curb the knee-jerk desire to ask her to leave if only to spare myself the slow torture that is being in her presence.

As we're getting out of my Bronco, recovering from a quiet drive during which neither of us seemed too keen on conversation, it's like I can feel her on my skin. Her scent is melded with mine, seeping out from the coat under my arm and into my clothes. It's intoxicating.

It's also really fucking annoying.

"So, your brothers will be here tomorrow?"

Her head jerks up as we walk up the stairs to the front door, her expression distracted. "Hmm?"

"Your brothers," I repeat. "You said they'd be here tomorrow."

"Oh, right. They will be." She nods aimlessly, her brows furrowed. A breeze flutters past, and I can smell her scent in the air, causing me to tense. "Around lunchtime, I think."

"That's . . . good. You can get started then."

Her brow lifts. "Oh, so you're on board now?"

"Don't think I have much of a choice now, do I?"

Even with my dry tone, the corner of her mouth lifts. "Not unless you're up for chasing me away."

Oh, I'd chase you. The thought comes unbidden.

I brush it aside.

"Seems easier to let you get on with it," I say. "I'm looking forward to seeing you rip this place down board by board."

She rolls her eyes as I unlock the front door. "You're never going to let that go, are you?"

"Not anytime soon, no."

I move aside to let her walk past me, and as she does, she stumbles a little. Once again, my reaction is immediate, and my hand cups her elbow to steady her.

"Are you okay?"

Now that I'm looking at her in the light of the foyer, she does seem a little pale. There's a thin sheen of sweat on her temples, and her pupils are dilated, her expression a little dazed.

"I'm . . . okay. I think. Just got a little dizzy there." She laughs softly. "Must not be used to the elevation yet."

I want to press her, to ask if she's sure, but that's my instincts talking. I still haven't stopped touching her, and I jerk my hand away with the realization. I stuff it in my pocket, eyeing her to make sure she really is all right.

"Nothing some water and a good night's sleep won't fix," I tell her.

She nods. "If I don't freeze to death tonight."

"Jeannie had me put more blankets in your room."

"Oh . . . great." She bobs her head. "That will help a lot."

And my mouth is opening before I can stop it, my stupid hands lifting as if they have a mind of their own. I thrust my coat toward her like an idiot, knowing full well that she just bought her own. That she doesn't need it. Doesn't stop me from offering it.

"You can borrow this if you want," I say. "I have another."

I assume she's going to laugh at me, because I would if I were her, so she surprises me when she reaches for it instead. Quickly, like it's a bit of instinct on her part as well. And why do I like that?

You know why.

That alone should have me rescinding the offer, but I can't seem to open my mouth to do it. Instead, I watch as she carefully gathers my coat up in her arms, holding it to her chest. Her smile is small, hardly even enough to be called a smile, but the gratitude in her eyes is apparent.

Dangerous, my brain screams, even as my urges shout, *Protect*.

"Thank you," she says quietly.

She still looks a little under the weather, and as much as I want to do something about that—what, I don't know—I resist the urge, shoving my hands into my pockets instead. My skin feels stretched, and my muscles twitch with restlessness. I can feel the wolf just beneath the surface, like he's bursting to get out.

"Well, good night, Hunter," she offers, still holding my coat.

I nod stiffly. "Night, Tess."

I watch her climb the stairs, not missing the slight shake in her step. Is she sick? Should I offer to help her to her room?

No, you shouldn't, jackass.

Still, I stand there like I'm exactly that, not taking my eyes off her until she's safely tucked away in her room. Even after, I linger for a few moments, at war with myself and not even recognizing what it is that's making me so restless but feeling it anyway.

I scrub a hand down my face, rubbing my beard as I shake my head.

Trouble.

THE CRISP MOUNTAIN air does wonders for my thoughts; the snow is powdery and chilled against my paws, and as it flurries up behind me while I bound through it, I urge myself to keep going faster, to push myself harder.

Running in this form always makes things seem clearer, and now is no different.

Like this, it's easier to be reasonable about the lovely omega I've only known for twenty-four hours. It's easier to recognize that the urges I feel for her are nothing more than our biology, that our proximity and our hormones are more than likely running the show in our interactions—something I think maybe I should discuss with Tess. Maybe she hasn't met an alpha before, I reason. Maybe that's why she doesn't seem to be as aware of the danger here.

Then again, maybe she is. The prescription she picked up might have been a bottle of suppressants, for all I know.

I pause in the moonlight, snuffling out a breath as displeasure courses through me. The idea of not being able to scent her sweet, heavenly aroma anymore doesn't instill good feelings, but I know that's just hormones. It would probably be for the best if those *were* suppressants she picked up. And if not, maybe I should grab some of my own.

It's been almost ten years since a woman has affected me this way, and it's no coincidence. What we are . . . the universe itself is conspiring to bring us together. I fell for that once, and I'm not keen on doing it again.

I take off through the snow, feeling lighter with the clarity that shifting has brought me. Snow clings to the smoky gray of my fur, and I shake my head back and forth to dislodge it, never slowing my pace. I even let out a howl as I break through the trees, the pleasure of the simple act a primal, ancient thing. It reminds me of what I am and why I should be more mindful of it.

I wonder what color Tess's fur is . . .

A growl resonates in my chest, the wolf equivalent of cursing myself. I skid to a stop, flicking my tail in irritation. *I really am a jackass*, I think. Even with clarity, even with reason . . . I can't get her out of my head.

I should talk to her. That would be the smartest course of action. Tess seems reasonable. Intelligent. If I talk to her about what's happening, we can come up with a solution for how best to avoid any sort of . . . incident. Surely she isn't interested in succumbing to some instinctual nonsense with someone she just met either. Most likely, there's nothing about me that would attract her anyway, hormones aside. I'm too moody, too surly at the best of times, and people have never been my strong suit. I'm better off staying out of her way as much as possible while she's here.

Even if the thought of it has another involuntary growl rumbling in my chest.

I take off running into the night, changing course to head back to the lodge with every intention of falling into bed and passing out before I have a calm, sensible discussion with my houseguest tomorrow. Whether it be suppressants for her or for me, we'll make sure that our proximity isn't a problem for either of us.

Another howl escapes me as I pad through the snow, but I ignore it.

BACK IN MY bedroom and freshly showered, I do my best not to mourn the loss of Tess's scent on my clothes. My pajama bottoms and my clean skin smell only of me, and I tell myself this is a good thing. It's one step toward a smooth reno, free of any complications or distractions. Something I'm sure Tess wants too.

I toss the towel I was using to dry my hair into the hamper in the corner, then plop down onto the end of my bed and lean back on my hands. The knowledge that Tess is only a few doors away makes me restless, almost like I shouldn't be here. Like I should be with *her* instead. Which is insane. It makes no sense. Not unless—

A sudden pounding at my door has me jolting upright on my bed, frowning at the wood even as another series of sharp knocks sounds in the space. It hits me then—overwhelming, like a lightning strike—and I'm on my feet before I even know what I'm doing, wrenching the door open and throwing it wide, though I already know what's waiting for me. I can *smell* it.

And suddenly so much makes sense—the restlessness, the urges, all of it. Because there's only one thing that could send my system into overdrive so quickly, one thing that could override all my good sense and turn me into little more than an animal just going on instinct.

And she's currently outside my door, her skin pink and flushed and her *scent* so potent it might as well be a drug. It's so thick I can practically taste it on my tongue, and her eyes are little more than black pupils, her mouth parted as she pants raggedly.

"Hunter."

My name on her too-red mouth, like she's been biting her lips—it makes every muscle in my body draw up tight, and I feel my own resolve crumble into nothing. Feel it burn up and float away.

Because Tess Covington is outside my door, saying my name sweetly and looking at me like she's desperate, like she's needy—like I'm the only one who can give her what she's looking for. On some level, I reckon that could be true. Because the way she smells right now . . .

She is absolutely in heat, and she's looking at me like she needs me.

Fuck.

7

Tess

I FEEL LIKE shit.

I did my best to hide it while Hunter drove me home, but the symptoms that plagued me yesterday in Denver seem to be creeping back with a vengeance, making my head swim and my stomach cramp. I manage to get through a very stilted good-night, clutching his coat under my arm for reasons I can't even fathom.

Strangely, when he'd offered it, I felt like I'd never wanted anything more.

Which is insane, really. Who gets giddy when someone offers them a coat?

Back in my room and freshly showered, I find myself doubled over on the bed, the meds I took doing very little to ease the discomfort. I grit my teeth as I squirm on the mattress, sweat beading at my temples and tremors racking my body.

What the fuck is wrong with me?

I roll onto my back, my hand brushing the stiff material of Hunter's Carhartt and rustling it as I try not to writhe. The action stirs up the potent scent that seems to cling to the fabric, the scent of sunshine and rain going from overly pleasant to oddly mouthwatering as my body instinctively shifts farther toward it.

Oh God.

It's like *heaven*.

I bury my face in the lining, drawing in deep lungfuls of the delicious fragrance that, strangely enough, seems to make the cramps abate, if only a little. I'm questioning the logic of this when my body wakes up in a new way, making my torment suddenly crystal clear, even if it's something I've only heard about secondhand.

Because suddenly I'm drenched between my legs.

And I'm not talking about a little, I'm talking about soaked underwear and a throbbing *need* that seems to hit me out of nowhere, making everything below the waist positively *pulse* with want.

"*How?*" I groan as I bundle up Hunter's coat and shove my nose deeper into it.

The nice doctor in the ER certainly never mentioned *this*.

For the most part, we just have to let it run its course.

Run its course, my ass.

I revel in the utter relief that is Hunter's coat, struck with the sudden urge to seek relief of a different kind. The need to touch myself is overwhelming, and before I realize what I'm doing, my hand is slipping into my sweatpants, my fingertips skimming over my lower abdomen and tucking into my underwear. I hiss when they glide through the moisture between my legs, which is unlike anything I've ever experienced before. It's not like my usual arousal. No, this is something altogether different. More copious, more viscous, and somehow just . . . *slicker*.

But the momentary relief I feel when my fingertips glide over my wet clit is palpable, and my lips part on a silent cry as I circle the swollen bud. Suddenly all I can think about is coming, and with that in mind, I start to work my wrist, teasing and stroking myself as the cramps in my belly turn to a more pleasant simmer.

"*Fuck,*" I groan.

Is this really what Ada has to deal with?

And you too now.

I clutch Hunter's coat to my nostrils as I roll onto my back, the smell of him somehow making my touches more potent, more enjoyable. It's like his scent is giving me a high, making my skin tingle and my pussy clench. Even as I shake with an orgasm that is satisfying but somehow still not enough, I feel myself slipping into some sort of delirium, one that begs me to somehow get more of it.

Or, better yet, get it straight from the source.

A more rational part of my brain screams that this is a terrible idea—I'm even a little terrified by these current events—but that thought is lost to the rhythmic chanting that's taken up somewhere in my hindbrain, one that shouts that there's someone nearby who can make this feeling go away, that he can make it *better*. I don't know where it comes from or what it really means, but before I can question it, I'm on my feet and stomping to my door.

Hunter's coat is abandoned on my bedroom floor, but my needy body isn't even perturbed by this, because it seems to know what I'm after. It seems to recognize that in a few moments, it will have something much better. Or at least I hope so.

I barely register that I'm beating on Hunter's door; I have no idea what time it is or how long has passed since I saw him, but it's fully dark outside now, so I have to assume a little while. He doesn't answer at first, but I can see a shadow under the door, and the sight of it makes me even giddier, the anticipation in my blood actually *singing*.

I pound again, and when the door wrenches open moments later to reveal a wet-haired, shirtless Hunter Barrett looking like sex and sin, with his dark smattering of chest hair and his abs that look like I could wash clothes on them, I think I actually let out a *whimper*.

"Hunter."

He looks at me for a long moment with shock in his features, and I can tell by the widening of his eyes that he *knows*. He knows what's wrong with me. *And maybe*, my fevered brain whispers with delight, *maybe he's going to make it better*.

"Tess?"

Jesus, his *voice*. Was it always this deep?

"Don't feel good," I tell him. "Hurt."

He sucks in a breath when I fall into him and rub my cheek against his chest hair, brushing my fingers over his stomach to tease the hard muscle there. He feels like heaven against me, and I loop my arms around his neck and tug myself up, having the strangest urge to lick his neck.

"How are you—*Jesus*, Tess."

Okay, so I definitely licked his neck. That is a thing I just did.

"You smell so good," I murmur into his throat, running the flat of my palm down the center of his chest, gliding it over one of his nipples as he gasps. "Why do you smell so good?"

"I think you're in heat," he says through gritted teeth. "Fuck, this is exactly what I was talking about."

It seems surreal. I've known I was an omega for an entire *day*. How can I already be in heat?

Maybe if I wasn't so concerned with the possibility of dropping to my knees and wrestling Hunter out of his sweatpants so I can see what his dick looks like, I might have a better answer to that question. As it is, my brain is still hung up on the promise of the aforementioned dick.

His massive hand wraps around my wrist even as I'm going for that particular prize, tightening his grip. This also turns me on for reasons I can't explain. He's just so *big*. Was he always this big?

"We can't," he says. "You don't know what you're doing right now."

"I know exactly what I'm doing," I purr, using a voice I have absolutely never used before. "If you'd let go of me."

"Tess," he says more firmly, but I detect the strain there. "I'm not touching you. Not when you're like this."

"That's okay," I hum. "I can just touch you."

He groans, a noise that from here sounds painful.

Me too, buddy.

"Tess," he rasps, his voice suddenly sounding tortured. "I can't."

And as if my body seems to get the message, realizing it won't be getting what it wants, the cramps return with full force, threatening to cut my knees out from under me with how much it hurts. I cry out as I wobble, and Hunter's arms are there, holding me close so I don't fall. It feels so nice I don't fight the urge to nuzzle into his sternum.

"Hurts," I say again, sounding small and pathetic all of a sudden.

"Shh," he soothes. "I know it does. I'm sorry."

"Can't you just touch me?"

I don't even know how I *know* that he can help me, but I do. I fucking know it. Why won't he help me?

"No, omega," he says forcefully, his tone making me shiver. "I'm not going to touch you."

I can feel tears welling in my eyes, and distantly I know that tomorrow, I'm going to be really embarrassed by that. Now, though, all I care about is the fact that Hunter is seemingly going to abandon me to my predicament.

I look up at him with tears clinging to my lashes, and the pain I find in his features, the intensity there—it makes me wonder if I'm not the only one suffering. His thumb strokes my cheek, and I lean into the touch, begging him without words for more. When I turn my face to lick at the pad, the sound of his sharp intake of breath washes over me.

"Don't cry," he says soothingly, his expression gaining resolve as he brushes the hair from my face.

"Hurts," I say again.

He holds my face in his hands, staring into my eyes with a look of resolve and maybe even regret. At any other time, I would be wary of that look.

"I'll help you," he says softly.

I blink back at him, trying to register what he's said. "You will?"

"I will," he promises. His expression takes on a hard edge. "But I'm not going to touch you."

I frown at this, because I don't see how he can do one without the other, but before I can question it, he's gathering me up in his arms. He kicks the door shut as he pulls me into his embrace like I'm some sort of princess, and I cling to him for dear life as he carries me to his bed, my needy body thrilled by this development.

But then he sits with his back to the headboard, situating me until I'm cradled between his legs with my back touching his front. His arms go around my middle as if anchoring me, and his cheek presses to my throat, his nose following after it as he breathes in.

"I'm going to give you my scent," he tells me. "It will help. Okay?"

I'm nodding vigorously, not even entirely sure what he's referring to but wanting whatever it is that he's willing to give.

I feel the prick of his beard against the delicate tissue of my throat as he pulls me tighter, and only seconds later it gives way to his clean-shaven neck, the skin sliding against mine in a way that, for whatever reason, *lights me the fuck up*.

"*Oh.*"

"That's it," he murmurs. "That's good."

The guttural quality that his voice has taken on makes my pussy throb even harder, and I swear to all that's holy, if he asked me to get down on my knees for him right this second, I wouldn't hesitate.

"I know it hurts," he hums. "I've got you."

I nod, whimpering when he rubs his throat across mine again.

"Jesus. You smell . . ." His nose skirts along the length of my neck, his shuddering breath washing my skin, warming it. "*Ripe.*"

I don't even know if that's good, but he says it like it is, and my entire body quivers with the praise. Just fucking absorbs it like a sponge and then asks for more. My back arches slightly as I squirm, and I can feel him hard and insistent against my ass.

God, I *want* that.

"Hunter," I mewl. "Please."

"Hand in your panties, Tess," he commands, clearing his throat as he tugs his face from my neck. "You'll need to touch yourself."

I shove my hand into my pants so fast I could be in a professional competition to get there first—my modesty apparently a thing of the past—hissing between my teeth when my fingers meet my wet, oversensitized flesh. I let out a shaky breath of relief when my fingers slide into my slick folds, the relief immediate.

"That's it," he praises. "Feels better?"

I nod jerkily. "Uh-huh."

"Mm. Good."

I'm already moving to shrug out of my sweatpants when he stops me, holding me tighter.

"Uh-uh," he says. "That isn't what this is. I'm trying to be the good guy here." I feel the ghost of his lips against my throat, can practically *feel* him murmuring, "So don't tempt me, Tess."

"Please," I whimper, barely even knowing what I'm asking for.

"You're going to make yourself come," he tells me. "That's all that's going to happen here. I don't want you to stop until you soak those little fingers. Can you do that?"

I suck in a breath. "Y-yes," I manage. "I can do that."

"That's a good girl," he breathes, then his grip on me tightens, like he's realizing what he's said.

What is *wrong* with me that those words have me seconds from combusting?

I circle my fingertips around my throbbing clit, hyperaware of the weight of his arms under my breasts, the scratch of his beard on my neck, the press of his hard cock against my lower back.

I want fucking *all* of it.

"Don't stop," he says through gritted teeth. "Keep touching yourself."

I nod as I resume my pace, every swipe of my fingers making my thighs clench and my skin feel just a little tighter. My head lolls back against his shoulder, and from the corner of my eye, I can almost make out the darkness of his hair, his face turned to mine as if watching me. I feel the gentle press of his lips skirting along my jaw, and I work my hand faster, chasing that promise of release, trusting Hunter that it will make everything better.

I grunt in frustration when I can't seem to get there fast enough, and Hunter's answering hum comes from deep inside his chest, his voice sounding raspy and somehow *more* than usual.

"I know it's not quite enough," he says. "You need a knot. Don't you?"

I don't even know what that is, but I feel myself nodding.

Is that what I need? Would that make the ache go away?

I tease myself harder, my body arching into my own touch as Hunter's voice in my ear takes me to new heights.

"You'll just have to make do," he goes on. He breathes in deep. "*Fuck*, Tess. I can smell you. I can smell how fucking wet you are. What are you doing to me?"

I have no idea how to answer that, too lost to the sensations of my impending orgasm and his deliciously deep voice.

"That's it," he groans. "You're close, aren't you? I want you to make yourself come. *Now*, omega."

"*Fuck*."

I shudder and shake as my orgasm hits me, teasing myself relentlessly through it as wave after wave washes over me. I can hear Hunter talking through it, muttered praises of *Good girl* and *Pretty little thing* touching my senses from what seems like far, far away. My entire body feels like one frayed nerve, my system seeming to be in overdrive.

Somewhere, deep in the recesses of my mind, a memory triggers.

Being around one might wreak havoc on your system.

Dr. Carter's warnings come back to me, and suddenly, even in the haze of my dwindling orgasm and the growing fatigue that creeps into my limbs because of it—the possibility of what she said makes itself known.

"Alpha?"

It's the only word I manage as fatigue seeps through me, and even the sharp intake of Hunter's breath and the rumble in his chest sound far away. Right now, I feel boneless and spent, even *happy*. Like all my problems floated away with my orgasm, and in a similar fashion, despite the audacity of what I've just done—I drift off.

It's the best sleep I've ever had in my life.

8

Hunter

ALPHA.

Alpha.

Alpha.

I need to let her go, and I know that. It's just that her fucking scent is swirling around me, keeping a chokehold on my senses. My cock throbs against her back even as I draw in ragged breaths at her throat, and every instinct I have is screaming at me to touch her, to *take* her—both things I can't do.

Untangling myself from her is actual torture; my body protests with every nerve ending, every cell angry at me as I carefully lay her across my bed and slowly back away. I stare at the picture in front of me—her soft brown hair fanning across my sheets as her chest rises and falls slowly, her hand still delicately tucked inside her sweatpants—and it takes everything in me to walk away.

I stomp to the attached bath with difficulty, shutting the door behind me to try to gain a reprieve from her scent, knowing it would be better to leave the room altogether but seemingly unable to put that much distance between us with the way she still smells so . . . vulnerable.

I can smell her in my bathroom even with the door shut, her scent clinging to my clothes and my skin, and I hiss when I palm my aching cock, feeling the base throb as my knot threatens to swell even without the promised warmth of her body fitting snugly around it. I quickly shed my clothes, which are saturated with her, kick them aside and turn on the hot water as if I might somehow be able to wash her away and save myself from the madness that's creeping in from having a sweet-smelling omega in heat only a few feet from me.

The hot water barely helps; even under the spray, my cock continues to pulse with want, my muscles taut and my senses on high alert. I curse under my breath as I stare down at my angry-looking erection, knowing deep down that it won't go away without some sort of relief. Not with Tess's scent still lingering in the air. I close my eyes and count to five, steeling myself for what will surely be an unsatisfying experience. Nothing could ever satisfy me with the heat-drenched scent of a lovely omega in the other room.

Still, I reach down and begin to angrily pump myself, trying not to imagine Tess, because I know it's wrong, but unable to help it. The *sounds* she made are still ringing in my ears—soft cries and sharp gasps—and the weight of her body might as well be imprinted against mine for the way I can still feel her touching me. I stroke my fist up and down my shaft as copious amounts of pre-cum drip from the slit at the head, hissing under my breath as pleasure and pain war with each other.

I hate that she's affecting me this way, hate that I'm helpless against what her scent does to my body. It feels too much like before, when I let myself get wrapped up in someone just like her only to have my heart ripped out and stomped on.

My mouth falls open as I start to fuck my fist, the action rough and raw and nothing like what it might feel like had this happened under different circumstances. If Tess weren't a stranger who had only asked for my help out of desperation. Maybe in that alternate reality I might have her on her stomach right now, maybe I'd be teasing the head of my cock against her slick entrance, pushing inside her ever so gently even as she keens for more. Maybe I'd be feeling the warm, wet stretch of her enveloping my cock, sucking me deeper inside even as she begs for my knot. Maybe I'd—

"*Fuck.*"

Cum jets from my cock and coats my palm, but still I don't stop. I stroke myself with my warm release, my breath sawing out of me roughly as my knot starts to swell, even without being snugly fitted inside an omega in heat. It's brutal and a bit painful, and all I can do is reach lower, wrapping my hand around the useless swell and massaging it with my fist to try to bring some relief.

Alpha, I recall. *She called me alpha.*

Like I was hers.

Like she was *mine*.

I shiver with every touch, my eyes shut tight as flashes of Tess's hand working inside her sweats flit through my thoughts. I think about how pretty she might be between her legs. I think about how her little fingers might look working her swollen clit while I tell her what to do.

Because my omega was so *good* for me.

I grip my throbbing knot tightly, clenching my teeth as I try to get ahold of myself. She's not *mine*. I know that. It's just the hormones talking. I *know* that.

Doesn't make any of it better.

Even minutes later, gripping my knot and willing it to soften as I brace myself under the hot spray of the shower, I'm still thinking about her. About how she sounded, how she felt, how she looked. I can't *stop* thinking about it.

When I finally get out of the shower to change, my knot is still slightly swollen but more manageable, even if it hurts like a bitch, almost like it's angry with me for not putting it where it belongs.

I don't even know her, I argue weakly.

The omega in question remains sprawled across my bed, sleeping peacefully, oblivious to the turmoil she's caused. I watch her from my bathroom doorway, telling myself to leave her there, to sleep somewhere else, to put *distance* between us—but I can't seem to move away.

I know, I can't sleep *with* her. That would make for a whole new onslaught in what will surely already be an awkward conversation.

Leave.

Just leave.

I stand in place for seconds more, simply staring at her.

Then, with a curse, I plod over to the chair in the corner and plop myself down in it. I know without a doubt that I'm going to sleep like shit tonight, but it seems my alpha is refusing to let Tess out of our sight. I watch her until my eyes grow heavy, worried for what the morning will bring.

Worried that if she asks for my help again, I won't be able to refuse her next time.

WHEN I JOLT awake the next morning, the sun streaming in through the blinds, the first thing I notice is that my bed is empty. I sit up straight, my heart immediately starting to pound, and my head whips back and forth as I try to make sense of the fact that my sheets are now sans Tess.

My skin feels itchy with her absence, and despite knowing that my instincts are apparently still running the show, I find myself stalking to my bedroom door and throwing it open with the intention of finding her and making sure she's okay anyway. The door to her bedroom is closed, and figuring that turnabout is fair play, I don't hesitate to raise my fist and beat against the wood. I hear her shuffling around in there immediately, her shadow appearing at the crack under the door.

"Tess," I call, but there's no answer.

I knock again, a little harder this time, but her door remains frustratingly closed.

"We've got to talk about it, Tess," I sigh, still feeling restless because I can't see her.

It seems that despite the fact that we didn't *actually* get physical, my alpha has decided she's ours to take care of until she's . . . better. Something that will prove difficult when another wave hits. I don't know if I can survive another without touching her.

Which is why we need to talk.

"Tess! I'm not leaving, and I live here, so you can either open the door, and we can talk about it, or I can—"

She wrenches the door open, and then she's standing there, her hair a mess and her teeth worrying at her bottom lip. Her cheeks are flushed pink, her pale skin rosy at the apples, and her wide brown eyes even more owlish than usual. The dark circles underneath them certainly aren't helping matters.

"I was hoping if I pretended you weren't real long enough, maybe you'd go away," she mumbles.

"Clearly not," I remark.

She sighs, leaning against the doorframe as she scrubs a hand down her face. "A girl can dream."

"We have to talk about it. We have to decide what you're going to do before another wave—"

And then it hits me.

I can't scent her heat anymore.

I lean in despite her garbled protests, inhaling at her throat deeply. Nothing. She smells normal now. Granted, even her *usual* scent is mouthwatering, but it doesn't have my knot threatening to swell, at least.

I rear back, confused. "How can it already be over?"

"Yeah . . ." She rubs at the back of her neck. "About that . . ." She winces. "Are you sure we can't just pretend nothing happened?"

I grit my teeth, still remembering the hell that was last night, when I was forced to stick close to her despite being tortured by her delicious scent.

"No," I tell her resolutely. "We can't." I feel frustration building inside me. "How could you be so careless?"

Her eyes go wide. "*Excuse* me?"

"You come here on the cusp of your heat—no suppressants—and you just don't say anything? Do you have any idea how dangerous that could have been? What if I'd been a bad guy? What if I'd taken advantage of you?"

And I'm realizing how much that thought angers me. The possibility that there might have been someone with less scruples than me whom she could have found herself with. Someone who would have *used* her.

My alpha *hates* that.

I immediately feel guilty when her eyes go wide with shock, but the very real fear I feel when she's imagining it keeps me from apologizing. Her mouth parts, her eyes going to the floor as she considers the question.

"I didn't know, okay?"

This gives me pause. "What?"

"I didn't know this was going to happen!"

"Like . . ." I struggle to think of reasons as to why that might occur. "Like you're off schedule?"

She snorts, rolling her eyes. "Like there *isn't* a schedule. Or . . . there wasn't. I guess there is now." She throws up her hands. "I don't know!"

"You're going to have to give me more than that."

"Listen," she says with a huff. "Two days ago? I woke up a beta. The same way I've woken up for the last twenty-eight years. The same as my parents and my brothers and everyone else I know in my family. Then suddenly, after Satan's sky ride of a flight and the worst flu symptoms I've ever had, some random ER doctor is telling me that, surprise! I am apparently a shifter. And not just any ol' regular shifter, but an *omega*."

My nose wrinkles. "That doesn't make sense."

"You're telling me," she scoffs.

I eye her incredulously, earning me another roll of *her* eyes.

"It's called 'late presentation,'" she tells me.

"And that's . . . a thing?"

"Apparently."

"Huh." It's definitely nothing I've ever heard of, but then again, she's only the second omega I've spent any real time with. So what do I know? "And that causes you to . . ."

I wave my hand aimlessly, hoping she'll throw me a bone so I don't have to say it.

Her brow cocks. "To throw myself at the first guy I can get my hands on? Apparently."

Her phrasing leaves a sour taste in my mouth, because I'm

thinking of the possible scenario where someone *else* might have been around last night. Again, my alpha hates this very much.

Fucking hormones.

"To be fair," I say, clearing my throat. "It being *us* trapped in the lodge probably isn't making things any better."

Her head tilts to the side. "What do you mean?"

"Because of what I am."

She looks lost. "And . . . you are?"

"An alpha," I answer flatly. "My pheromones are going to make yours go haywire."

"You are?"

"You didn't know?"

Her eyes go wide. "I had no idea. How would I have? I didn't even know what *I* was two days ago."

"But you said . . ."

Alpha.

Alpha.

Alpha.

I take a deep breath. "That's what you called me. Last night."

I watch as her cheeks tinge pink, no doubt remembering everything that happened last night. Not that I can blame her. It's playing on a loop in the back of my mind.

"Oh" is all she says.

"Oh?"

"I mean . . . the doctor mentioned that I should steer clear of . . . people like you. I don't even remember saying that. Maybe I was thinking out loud?"

Silence stretches between us, both of us no doubt trying to decide how to move forward. I can feel irritation brewing inside me, an emotion that makes no sense. Why on earth would I be *annoyed* that she hadn't meant to call me that last night?

"Can we just . . ." She shuffles her weight from one foot to the other. "Can we please just pretend last night didn't happen?"

"Pretend," I echo dumbly.

"Yeah, I mean . . . I still have a job to do."

"And what if this happens again?"

Her mouth forms an O shape, her brows lifting. "Again?"

"It seems like this came out of nowhere, right?"

"Kind of," she admits.

"And it only lasted a few hours? I'm no expert, but that's not normal."

"The doctor said that I might experience some . . . issues. While my body changes."

"There's a chance this will happen again, Tess."

She bites her lower lip. "Maybe it won't."

I want to grab her and shake her. I'm too on edge thinking about this happening when someone else is around. When she's *vulnerable*.

"And what if it does?"

"Then I'll deal with it," she says primly. "Contrary to the way I acted last night, I *can* take care of myself."

I stare back at her, thinking. The words on the tip of my tongue go against everything I've ever sworn to myself, but the thought of her finding herself in a situation where someone might use her makes my stomach twist. I can't let myself get wrapped up in . . . whatever this is. I know where that road leads.

"You need to be on suppressants," I say through gritted teeth.

Her brows knit. "The doctor said we shouldn't hinder my body's natural changes."

"And how is that fair to me?"

She rears back. "Fair to *you*?"

"You think it was *easy*? Turning you down like I did? It causes me physical pain to be around you when you're like that."

"Wow," she snorts. "I'm sorry that my life blowing up is inconveniencing *you*."

I wince, trying to get my aggravation in check as I realize that this whole thing most likely *is* a nightmare for her—the fact that she can't control it. Part of me feels like an asshole now.

I'm opening my mouth to try to smooth things over, maybe even offer to stay with Jeannie while Tess is here, as much of a hassle as that will be for me, but then—

"Oy, Tess! You here?"

I take a step back to catch sight of three random men pushing through the door in the foyer at the base of the stairs, each carrying a bag and looking around with interest. When I turn to Tess, I notice relief in her features, her mouth even twisting up in a smile.

"Be right there!" she calls, leaning past me. Then she gives me her attention once more. "Look. I'm sorry to *inconvenience* you—but I can handle myself. I'm really sorry I put you in that . . . position last night, but it won't happen again. I can do this job, and now that I know what to expect, I can handle whatever *issues* arise on my own going forward."

I can feel the argument trying to escape my mouth, but she's already pushing past me to bound down the stairs. I move to brace myself on the banister as I watch her throw herself at one of the men, feeling a prickling sensation in my skin as I watch them take turns hugging her tight. Just watching them makes my stomach churn for some reason.

Am I . . . jealous?

No. Absolutely not. It's just my fucking instincts and hormonal bullshit. Besides, I reason—to myself or my alpha, I can't be sure—these have to be her *brothers*. Her *beta* brothers, she said. They pose no threat to me.

Not that there would be any reason for them to.

I know I should go introduce myself and play nice or whatever, but right now . . . I can't seem to muster up the desire to do anything more than push off the banister and skulk back to my room. My room, which still smells completely saturated with *her*.

I tell myself that in a day or so, these urges will abate. Everything I'm feeling is just a direct result of what happened. It's a natural response, that's all.

I take a deep breath, letting her sweet scent fill my nostrils, only realizing what I've done when I feel myself start to harden in my sweats.

Natural response, I scoff at myself.

Right.

9

Tess

"TODAY WE'RE GOING to be tearing up this old carpet. I think once it's gone the room is going to look like an entirely new space already!"

Kyle pans around to show the entire floor, and I go through the motions of explaining everything we're about to do as I try not to focus on the fact that I watched Hunter walk through this room to the back deck not half an hour ago.

Which is a problem because . . . I can't look at him.

It's been three days since the Incident, as I'm calling it in my mind, and every time I catch a glimpse of Hunter, be it passing in the hallway or sitting across the dinner table, I can't seem to look him in the eye.

I tell myself that this is a reasonable response to approaching a veritable stranger while being high on sex hormones and begging him to touch you only for him to outright *reject* you, but it doesn't make it any less awkward. I know deep down that Hunter didn't *reject* me—I know that. If anything, I'm grateful for the way he . . . handled things. Had he actually given me what I begged for, I'd probably be halfway across the country right now, wallowing in my mortification.

I can smell how fucking wet you are.

God. Is that a wolf thing? They really should print up some better pamphlets.

I can't remember everything that was said between us that night, but the flashes I *do* remember are . . . a lot. Fuck, I can't even lie down in bed at night without scattered memories of *Good girl* and *Touch yourself* flitting through my thoughts.

It's enough to make my current working conditions . . . strained.

Beyond my mortification is a sense of overall aggravation at having been seen like that—vulnerable, needy—for the first time in a long time. And in the most carnal way, I *needed* someone. I can't pretend I'm not grateful to have lucked out, to have that person be Hunter, who took care of me in a way that minimized my humiliation as much as he could. Come to think of it . . . I haven't thanked him for that. It really seems so ludicrous, *thanking* someone for what happened.

"You gonna just stand there looking at that carpet or do you wanna help tear it up?" Chase asks when we're done filming.

I shoot a scowl at my brother, but Chase only gives me his usual lopsided grin. He's the baby of the family and looks more like me than Thomas, which means it's like looking at a less-stressed version of myself currently smirking at me.

"I was thinking," I tell him.

He chuckles under his breath, handing me a hammer. "Been doing a lot of that the last couple of days."

"Well, I have a lot on my mind."

"Both of you shut up so I can get a good clip of this," Kyle grumbles, steadying his camera.

Kyle is a mix of all of us—my brown hair, Mom's blue eyes, and

Dad's stubborn brow. He's also the only one who knows his way around the camera, so we try not to piss him off.

"Hey," Thomas cuts in, entering the room from the foyer. "Anyone seen the boss? I swear that guy is like a vampire or something."

Thomas looks more like our mom; his blond hair has the same slight waves that hers does, and his blue eyes are to die for and a constant source of my envy. Much prettier than my dirt-brown ones.

I cock my head. "A vampire?"

"Yeah, dude only seems to come out of his room at night. Think I caught a glimpse of him hanging from the rafters while I was checking out the pool table last night."

"He's not a vampire," I say, rolling my eyes. "But he's not very keen on this project."

Not to mention the fact that I begged him to fuck me three days ago.

But of course I don't say that.

"I need the green light on what color stain he wants for the new mantel," Thomas says.

"But we're not supposed to start that until next week," I point out.

Chase is frowning. "What do you mean, he isn't keen on the project?"

"I mean . . ." I trail off, throwing up my hands. "You talked to him. Did he seem very excited?"

"I just thought it was a vampire thing."

"Vampires aren't real," Kyle says matter-of-factly.

Thomas's brow wrinkles. "Wolf people are real, why can't vampires be real?"

I pinch the bridge of my nose. I love my brothers, but sometimes herding them through a job is like taming feral opossums. They're too much like our mom—which is to say that they take *free-spirited* to new heights. Of course it would fall to me to be our dad's carbon copy—too serious, a workaholic, and, if any of the Tinder dates I've had in the last year are to be believed, no fun.

"So, can you get his opinion?" Thomas asks.

I stiffen at the idea of seeking Hunter out. "Can't *you* ask him?"

"No way," Thomas says, cringing. "I'm not talking to the might-be-a-vampire dude."

"He's *not* a vampire," I groan. "Kyle already said they aren't real."

Chase leans in conspiratorially. "But if wolf people are real, then it begs the question, right?"

"Don't call them 'wolf people,'" I chide.

Especially since I'm apparently one of them.

I wince. Definitely still not ready for that discussion. Especially after the whole begging-for-sex fiasco.

"You know Hunter is a shifter, right?"

Thomas's brows raise. "Really?"

"Yes," I tell them. "Jeannie too."

"Wow, that's so cool. I wonder if he'd shift for me," Chase says.

"Please do *not* ask him to do that for you," I groan.

Kyle shoots me a look. "Wait, how do you know this?"

I feel my neck heat. "It came up in conversation when we were talking about accommodations."

"Ah." Chase bobs his head. "Makes sense."

"Anyway." Thomas waves two sample cards at me, fluttering his lashes. "You're the boss, right? Go do boss things."

"*Fine.*"

I snatch the cards from him, grumbling under my breath as I dust off my jeans. The last thing I need is to talk about *wood stain* with the guy I tried to not quite dry hump. I catch a glimpse of myself in an old mirror hanging outside the great room, frowning when I notice the state of my hair. My bangs are sticking straight up again; I tell myself at least once a day to stop running my fingers through them, but it's a futile effort. I do my best to straighten them before catching myself, realizing that it's silly to try to make myself *presentable* for Hunter. Especially after I gave him that whole speech about keeping things professional.

Hunter isn't in the entryway, dining room, or kitchen—although Jeannie is in the latter and informs me that a little while earlier she saw him through the window that looks out onto the back deck. I shrug into my new coat before I step outside; Hunter was definitely right, my old one was not up to the task of Colorado air in October.

I don't see Hunter at first. A quick scan of the grounds beyond the deck shows that the place is entirely empty, and I frown at the undisturbed snow, wondering where he might have gone off to. There's an empty hot tub back here and a few deck chairs, but it's the lump of cloth a few feet away that catches my attention.

I know that plaid.

I step over to the bundle and toe it gently, noting a pair of jeans, a flannel shirt, and some boots.

Are these Hunter's *clothes*? What the hell?

I turn my head this way and that again to try to spot him, but just like before, there's no sign of him. Did he really run off into the woods without his clothes? Why on earth would he do that? Could he be—

A rustling in the tree line catches my eye, and I squint at the blinding layer of white that sparkles under the sun. The bushes shake like something might be moving through them—a rabbit maybe? But no, this seems bigger.

And it seems like it's coming this way.

I take two steps back with the intention of scuttling inside; I'm not equipped to meet the local wildlife, and I've heard too many horror stories about bears to take any chances.

Before I can get even halfway to the door, the bushes part in a flurry, something large and gray hurtling over the snow with purpose. I squint as it gets closer, and it takes a few seconds to make out what exactly is currently barreling toward the deck I'm occupying, but when I do, a gasp escapes me.

Because it's a very large, very *fast* wolf that's bounding in my direction.

My first instinct is to scream, to run maybe, but then I remember where I am and who I'm currently staying with. Surely that isn't . . . It *can't* be—

I'm so busy ruminating that I completely forget to try to escape, and by the time the thought occurs to me, the wolf is trotting up the steps to the deck like he owns the place, casting me a glance that feels too human, too *aware*.

He sits on his haunches and tilts his head as he looks at me, and I can imagine for just a second that there's a sparkle of amusement in his eyes. He gives a short yip before bending to nose the pile of clothes on the deck, then straightens to look at me again pointedly.

My brow furrows. "Hunter?"

He yips again, placing his paw on the pile of clothes to draw attention to it once more.

"I don't know what you're trying to say," I tell him.

A low rumble sounds in the wolf's chest, and he does something with his eyes that looks suspiciously like a roll, and then, before my very eyes, the wolf starts to change, his fur receding and his bones twisting until, in a flash, Hunter stands before me.

And he's utterly naked.

I stare with an open mouth for a total of three seconds before I realize what I'm doing—carefully avoiding anything below the belt—finally spinning on my heel as quickly as possible while my cheeks flush with heat.

"You could have warned me," I squeak.

I hear his low chuckle followed by the rustling of clothes. "I tried."

"You could have tried *harder*."

"Yeah, well. It's cold out here."

I wait until I no longer hear the sound of him dressing, even waiting for him to clear his throat before turning around.

I blink back at him as I try to make sense of what I just saw; I've always known *in theory* what happens when a shifter changes, but since Ada rarely stays in her other form for very long—let alone lets me watch her shift—it's not something I've ever experienced in person.

"Does that . . . hurt?" I ask.

He shakes his head. "No." He purses his lips. "Maybe in the beginning? But you get used to it."

I can feel myself frowning, suddenly filled with fear at the idea of that happening to me, because in the midst of all the chaos this week, I haven't given much thought to *that* element of things. But that's going to happen to me, right? The thought suddenly fills me with panic, because what if it *does* hurt? I mean, how on earth could my body change that way?

"That hasn't . . ." Hunter must notice the sudden wariness on my face, because his expression turns to one of concern. "That hasn't happened to you yet?"

I shake my head vehemently. "No."

"Fuck." He crosses his arms over his wide chest, the flannel of his shirt straining with the effort. "Are you nervous? Have there been any signs?"

Of course I'm nervous, I don't say, not wanting to appear as vulnerable as I feel.

"How would I even know what signs there might be?"

His brow furrows. "I guess that's fair."

Silence passes between us, both of us no doubt realizing this is the first time either has spoken directly to the other since the Incident.

"Were you looking for me?"

My eyes snap up to meet his. "Hmm? Oh. Yes. Sorry." I hold up the two sample cards on either side of my face. "I need an opinion on stain."

"Stain," he echoes.

"For the new mantel. We brought a couple of options but wanted to let you have the final say."

He frowns, stepping closer. When his hand reaches out to let his thumb brush against my cheek, I suck in a breath, holding it in my chest as he swipes at something on my face.

"You had a little dust there," he explains.

I let the breath out through my nostrils, trying to look unaffected. The scent of him seems so much sharper now, making my heart beat faster. Like just being in his presence is enough to make my body wake up.

I clear my throat, shaking the cards that I'm still holding on either side of my face. "So . . . stain?"

He eyes each card, finally reaching to pluck one from my hand. "This one, I think."

"Good choice," I say, my voice a little too high.

He just . . . *smells* so good. It's making me dizzy.

He fiddles with the card as he looks at his shoes, his expression carefully blank.

"So . . . how have you been feeling?"

I blink back at him, taking a second to ascertain his meaning because his scent makes my head feel all floaty. "What?" I snort. "You mean have I tried to maul anyone else for sex lately?"

"No," he says with a frown. "I meant, 'How are you feeling?'"

"Oh." Well, now I feel like a dick. I shuffle my weight from one foot to the other. "Fine, mostly. I've had some weird symptoms, but nothing like . . . that."

He nods. "Good."

"Good?"

"I imagine it's scary," he says. "What you're going through. So it's good you aren't having anything too wild happen."

Not again, I'm sure he's thinking

"For now, at least," I mutter.

I immediately regret it, because his eyes widen a little, no doubt thinking of the *last* time something "wild" happened.

I can smell how fucking wet you are.

I clear my throat again, pushing those thoughts aside. "Anyway, good choice on the stain. I'll tell my brothers."

I'm turning around to escape when his voice stops me.

"Tess."

I turn slightly, looking back at him. "Yeah?"

"I'm sorry."

I pause, tilting my head. "What for?"

"For . . . being so harsh with you the other day," he says. "It's been eating at me. I know it isn't your fault, I do, it's just . . . I've had bad experiences in the past. With omegas. I know that's not your fault either, though I reckon that's why I acted like an ass about it." He rubs at the back of his neck, nudging his beanie he's wearing a little and making it sit slightly off-kilter. "My alpha has been . . . restless. I know we barely know each other, but that doesn't change what we are or that I've been worried about you. I don't want you to think you have to go out of your way to avoid me."

Ah, so he noticed. Great.

"Your . . . alpha?"

"It's hard to explain," he says. "It's like there's this wilder side to me. Almost like my wolf runs the show sometimes."

"Will that happen to me?"

"Probably," he tells me. "After you come into it more, I imagine. Anyway . . . Again. I'm sorry."

"It's okay," I say after a beat. And, weirdly, I mean it. "It's actually a relief to know that I'm not the only one losing it because of some hormonal bullshit."

He chuckles softly, the low sound enough to warm me from even a few feet away. "Wouldn't be the first time."

My eyebrows shoot up. "You've really dealt with this before?"

He looks aggravated, like maybe he said more than he meant to, but nods heavily. "Like I said . . . you're not the first omega I've met."

Wow. The pure shock of something that feels dangerously like jealousy coursing through me is powerful and potent. And ridiculous. Definitely ridiculous.

He heaves a sigh as he goes on. "What we are . . . it's like we're designed to be drawn to each other. The more time we spend together . . . like *that*—the more we'll want it. It's just our nature. It's not . . . *you* that I'm wary of, Tess. It's the situation. I've played this game before and lost. But I want to help you if I can." His brows shoot up as he realizes what he's said. "With questions, I mean. If you have any. If I can answer them."

"Well, I mean . . . that's good, I guess." My lips part as I shake my head. "For *me*, at least," I correct, laughing awkwardly. "I'd definitely love to be able to ask questions if they come up."

"Of course," he says. "Anything you need."

It's a foreign sensation for me, the possibility of needing someone, and I don't know what to make of it. Normally, it might irritate me, the thought of having to rely on someone, but for some reason, with Hunter, it just . . . doesn't. Is that what he was talking about? Is that just what we are?

Anything you need.

All I can do is hope that it doesn't come down to me needing his dick again, because will I really be strong enough to not go to him next time? I don't know if I can survive another embarrassment like that.

"I appreciate it," I tell him. "Really."

He shoves his hands in his pockets, offering me a thin smile. "No problem."

"And . . . I guess I should actually say thank you."

He cocks his head. "Thank you?"

"For . . ." My cheeks heat. "For helping me. For being the good guy. You could have really taken advantage of me that night, but you didn't. And now that I know you've had bad experiences with people like me . . . Well. Thank you."

"Oh . . ." He rubs at his neck, shifting his eyes to his feet. "It was no problem."

And right there on the tip of my tongue are questions about the omega he knew—what she was like, how they met—all sorts of things that aren't my business to ask or even to *think*, but they're waiting there anyway.

I open my mouth, not even sure what's about to come out of it, but thankfully, Chase saves me.

"Yo, Tess!"

I turn to my brother. "Yeah?"

"Can you come look at this? I need your eyes."

"Be right there," I say.

He goes back inside, leaving me alone with Hunter again.

"Well," I say. "I guess I'd better get back to work."

"Lots of fixin' to do," he answers with a wry smile.

I match it with one of my own. "Lots."

I leave him there, feeling better than I did before I found him. Maybe we can put the weirdness behind us. It's only hormones, after all. It's not like it meant something. Provided my body behaves, maybe the rest of my time here will go by smoothly. Maybe Hunter and I can even be friends.

Flashes of his naked chest flit through my thoughts, from the defined muscles to the thick fur there that shouldn't be as appealing as it is.

Friends, I remind my stupid, horny brain. *Just friends.*

10

Hunter

THINGS HAVE BEEN slightly less strained after my talk with Tess on the deck a few days ago. At least... outwardly. I still think about the way she sounded and smelled in my arms at least fourteen times a day, but who's counting?

She and her brothers have gotten quite a lot done in their first week; the carpet in the great room has all been ripped up, and they've even started working on the mantel over the fireplace. I have to admit... the changes are already an improvement, and there's still so much more to be done. My few discussions with Tess prove that she's doing her best to plan her updates without changing the heart of the place, and I can't tell her what that means to me. I probably should, but then again, I can barely speak to her for more than five seconds without remembering her touching herself in my bed. It makes for an awkward working relationship, to be sure.

Which is why I've resorted to calling what I *hope* will be a more expert opinion.

It rings twice before he picks up; ever prompt, my cousin.

"Hello," Noah greets.

"Hey," I answer. "Busy?"

"Most days, yes," he tells me in that dry tone that garners no nonsense. "Did you need something?"

"I needed to ask for . . . some medical advice."

"Are you hurt?"

"No, it's not for me."

A stretch of silence before: "Well, go on then."

I remind myself that Noah is practically an android and that I shouldn't be offended by his brusqueness.

"There's a woman—"

"I'm the last person that you should be asking for advice on women."

I scoff. "Says the happily mated man."

"Yes, but"—his tone goes a fraction softer, as it often does when he speaks of his mate—"that was mostly Mackenzie's doing."

"Are you telling me I should call your mate?"

I smile at the prickliness in his tone when he answers, "No. You can ask me."

"There's a woman here working on the lodge, and—"

"What's wrong with the lodge?"

"Are you going to let me finish a question or are you going to keep rudely interrupting?"

"You introduced a new topic into the conversation," he says. "It's not rude to ask for clarification."

Literally an android.

"The lodge is fine," I explain. "Jeannie—" I frown, not exactly wanting to put it out there that my aunt strong-armed me. "I mean *I* hired a team to do some renovations."

"That's nice," Noah says. He's quiet for a second before: "Even the corner bedroom upstairs?"

"Yes, I'm sorry to say we will be touching your unspoken heat room."

I can practically hear him frowning; I don't want to think about all the reasons that room is *special* to him—it took a week of uncomfortable boners to air out the scent of Mackenzie's impromptu heat last year.

"I suppose if you have to," he says petulantly. "What about this woman?"

"She's heading up the team doing the renovations."

"And?"

"*And* she's experiencing some . . . strange symptoms."

"What sort of symptoms?"

"Like, a-week-ago-she-was-a-beta symptoms."

"Ah."

I rear back. "'Ah'? That's all you have to say?"

"I've heard of this happening," he tells me.

"You have?"

"Mm-hmm. This isn't the first case I've been made aware of. What sort of symptoms is she experiencing?"

"*Heat* symptoms," I tell him through gritted teeth, tensing from just the *thought* of Tess spiraling into another episode. "Ones that go as fast as they come."

"How long do they last?"

"So far, it's only happened one time, but it lasted at least a few hours. I don't know. She was gone when I woke up."

"You *slept* with her? Someone experiencing heat for the first time?"

"*No*," I huff. "I'm not a fucking monster. I just gave her my scent and . . . talked her through it."

"Talked her through it."

"She needed something! She was suffering."

"I suppose it *would* take considerable willpower to resist a shifter in full-blown heat. That was good of you."

"Not just any shifter," I say. "She's a fucking omega."

He's silent again, and I hear the creak of his desk chair as he no doubt leans back into it. "That is a pickle."

"I'd say it's a whole damned jar of them."

"And she's . . . staying there?"

"That was part of the agreement when she took the job. I can't kick her out. It would take her, minimum, thirty minutes to get here in the mornings from town. It's not safe for her to be driving on those roads like that in her tiny little car."

"Oh boy."

"What?"

"You like her."

I blanch. "What? No. I barely know her."

"And yet you're sitting here worried about her well-being to the point that you're calling me for advice."

"I just don't know what to do if she has another episode."

"Did you talk to her about it?"

"I . . . may have been a bit of a dick to her about it afterward."

Noah makes a sound that accurately mirrors my own discomfort. "I guess that's to be expected after Chloe."

I wince at her name. I've done my best to think of her as little as possible in the years since I last saw her, but this week with Tess has definitely made it harder to brush the thought of her aside.

"I don't know what came over me," I admit. "I was just so angry that she could be so careless. Then she told me everything that was going on, and I couldn't help but feel . . ."

"Feel what?"

"Responsible? Somehow? Like I needed to help her."

"Alpha instincts," Noah says with a hum. "They'll only get worse the longer you stay in close proximity to her," he warns. "Trust me."

I run a hand through my hair, mussing it. It's no secret what Mackenzie and Noah went through last year when they started seeing more of each other only to have her accidentally go into an early heat, and while that worked out for *them*, I'm certainly not interested in playing their little mating game.

"Can't you prescribe me some suppressants?"

"I can," he says. "Although, if she's experiencing heat symptoms, even they won't be enough to ensure you won't be affected by it."

"So, what? I just ride it out? Hope that I don't maul her next time?"

"If she doesn't want your . . . help, then I suppose that, yes, that's all you can do."

"Great," I groan. "Good talk."

"I'm a cardiologist," he says, "not a relationship guru."

"There is no relationship," I huff.

"Be that as it may."

I scrub a hand down my face, realizing that this conversation is pointless. Noah is so wrapped up in his own mated bliss, he probably can't even see the true gravity of the situation. It's night and day how different he is after mating with Mackenzie.

Still an android though.

"Well, just . . . send a prescription to the pharmacy in town, would you? I need all the help I can get."

"Does she smell that good?"

I think back to her soft scent of baked apples and cinnamon that makes my mouth water, knowing that I'm in danger of running into it around every corner, no escape to be had. I sigh, resigning myself to my fate.

"You have no idea," I tell him.

His answering chuckle offers no comfort as he answers, "You'd be surprised."

I RUN INTO Tess about an hour after I hang up with Noah, and immediately upon finding her, I can tell that something is . . . off. Her hair is mussed and her expression is pinched, and she sucks on her thumb while holding a hammer and cursing at the offending tool.

"You all right?"

She jolts at the sound of my voice, turning her big brown eyes on me as her lips part in surprise. I'm hit with her scent, exactly as I knew I would be, and I have to take small, shallow breaths just to try not to be overwhelmed by it.

"I'm fine," she says. "Caught my thumb with the hammer."

"Ouch."

"Yeah, it's not my best day."

There are dark circles under her eyes, a paleness in her cheeks that makes the freckles I'm just now noticing look more prominent, and it makes my alpha stir, makes him perk up and take notice. "You look . . . tired."

"Tired," she scoffs. "Is that code for 'like shit'?"

"No, just tired," I chuckle.

"My fucking skin feels too tight. Is that normal? I keep getting these weird cramps in my legs, and I feel so . . . so *restless*. I can't seem to shake it. It kept me up half the night."

Uh-oh.

I try to keep my tone gentle because I imagine that coming into all this as an adult has to be scary. "Um . . . have you still not shifted yet?"

"What?" Her brows shoot up. "Of course not. I don't even know how."

I chew on the inside of my cheek for a moment while she studies the red tip of her thumb, telling myself to keep my mouth shut. It's not like the last time I offered her help went so well. Still, I can already feel it, how I won't be able to walk away from her without saying something. It's a fucking pain in my ass, truth be told.

"I could show you," I tell her. "Or try, at least. I can't say I've ever taught someone how to shift."

"You don't have to," she argues hesitantly. "You've already done so much. I don't want to be a burden."

I frown. "It's not a burden. And it's okay to admit you need the help, Tess. Who else is going to show you?"

To my relief, *she* looks relieved. "Really?"

"If you want."

"Actually, that would be . . . kind of great? I've been reading some of the pamphlets the doctor gave me, and it gives all these descriptions of what it *feels* like—but not how to actually *do* it."

"Probably because most people do it for the first time as teenagers. It's just an instinct, really."

"Well, it sure as hell doesn't feel like an instinct."

"Tell you what," I say. "Meet me out back when you're done here, and we'll go through it together."

There's gratitude in her eyes, and that has my alpha preening, practically puffed up with pride at the idea of coming to her rescue.

Down, boy.

"Are you sure? I don't want to put you out."

"It's fine," I assure her. "Someone has to do it, and I doubt your brothers will be much help."

She winces. "Especially since they don't know."

"You haven't told them?"

"No." She shakes her head. "I haven't figured out how to broach the subject of me turning into a fucking wolf and begging strangers for sex yet."

I can't help it, I snort out a laugh. "Oh, is that all?"

"I know, right? No big deal."

She's smiling at me now, and I can feel my own face mirroring the action. It's funny how when she's out of my sight, all I do is worry about interacting with her, and yet when I'm actually doing so, it's strangely easy. I don't know what to make of that.

"An hour good?" I ask.

She nods. "Sounds great."

"All right," I answer. "I'll see you then."

She gives me another nod and a small smile before going back to what she was doing—and I turn to escape the vicinity of her potent scent so I don't drown in it. It doesn't occur to me for several more minutes that she's going to have to be naked for this little lesson.

Fuck.

I'M TRYING *VERY* hard not to be distracted from what I'm trying to teach her, but it's more than a little difficult, given that my hand is currently curled around her calf. Sure, I'm only teaching her the best way to bend when she's getting ready to shift, and her clothes are still most definitely on, but tell that to my fucking hormones.

It's like my body can't seem to reconcile the innocent gesture. Not with her smelling like she does.

We're in a small clearing just out of view from the lodge; Tess was afraid her brothers might stumble upon us while we were going over things, and apparently she's not ready to tell them anything. Not that I blame her. I don't know that I would have an easy time explaining this either.

"You're going to want to lean into a crouch," I tell her. "That makes it easier when you go from two legs to four."

"This is so fucking weird," she mutters.

"Just wait till you eat your first rabbit."

She audibly gasps. "I will *not* be eating a rabbit."

"You get caught out in the snow one good time? You'll eat a rabbit."

She makes a disgruntled sound, and I chuckle under my breath. She's kind of easy to rile up.

"But how do I . . . you know?" she says. "Is there some sort of magic word to change?"

I bark out a laugh. "No, there's no magic word. Your body is meant to do this, and once it realizes that, it will be as easy as breathing."

"*Breathing* doesn't require me to eat poor innocent rabbits," she grumbles.

"That restlessness you're feeling in your skin? That's because your body wants you to change forms. The wolf is a part of us, you know? You have to let it out sometimes, or else it will get . . . cooped up."

"You talk about it like it's a separate person."

"I suppose in a way . . . it is? There's the human part of my brain, and then there's the wolf. After so long . . . I can recognize who has hold of the reins."

"This is . . . so fucking weird."

"It'll get easier," I tell her. "I promise."

"So how does it work?"

"You have to imagine your wolf like an actual entity," I tell her. "It's a part of you, but it's also its own being."

"Because *that* isn't cryptic."

"Hey, it's not like I've ever had to explain this to someone."

"You're right," she sighs. "I'm sorry. Go on."

"You need to focus on that restlessness you're feeling. Tap into it. You need to imagine it like a string you can pull. Don't fight it, but instead seek it out, yeah?"

"That still seems cryptic as hell."

"You'll just have to try, and we'll go from there, okay?"

"Maybe you should go first," she says. "So I can see it happening."

My jaw works, dreading the next part that still hasn't occurred to her. "Well . . . I'll need to get naked."

"*Naked?*"

"Yeah. This isn't news. You remember when you came across me when I'd shifted the other day? It's just something you have to do. Unless you want to tear through your clothes. I've done it before, and it's a bitch."

Her mouth hangs agape, her eyes narrowing like she's suspicious of me.

I roll my eyes. "I'm not trying to get you naked, but you *will* have to be to do this. Even if you want to try it by yourself."

"Ugh, fine," she concedes. "Take your damn clothes off. Can you at least hide your . . . you know?"

"I'll do my best not to flash you."

She angles her body, no doubt watching from her peripherals while I start to shed my clothes. It's fucking freezing out, but thankfully, I run just a little hotter than a beta. I save my boots for last so I don't accidentally freeze my toes, shoving it all into the nylon bag I brought for us before I stand up straight. I turn to the side with one hand covering my dick, doing my best to maintain some modesty.

"Okay," I tell her. "Ready when you are."

She peeks over at me, and I can tell by the slight widening of her eyes and the more than slight bloom of her scent that she likes what she sees. A part of me wants to preen under her attention, but I shove it down. That's not what we're doing here.

I close my eyes and draw on that feeling inside that's a bit more animal than I am—almost like calling out to an actual wolf and bidding it to come closer. It's like breathing now, the change, but as my limbs shift and my fur sprouts, I can only imagine how shocking it must be for Tess, who has no prior experience.

When I'm down on all fours, I settle on my haunches, staring back at a now wide-eyed Tess, who is looking at me like I'm some sort of alien. She waves at me like she's testing to see if it's *actually* me, and I yip at her while throwing my head back in answer.

"Fucking freaky," she mutters.

I trot over to her side, tugging at her coat sleeve with my teeth to try to pull it from her shoulder. I know that without some sort of nudge, she'll put this off for as long as she can until she spontaneously shifts in the middle of a grocery store or something.

"I get it, I get it," she huffs. "Get naked." She points down at me. "But *you* turn around."

I dutifully do as she says, circling in place and settling again to face the opposite direction. I can hear the rustling of her clothes as she slowly sheds them behind me, and even as a wolf, I shudder at the thought of her without them. It's something I didn't get to see before, and I can't pretend that this isn't a little disappointing. I'm only human, after all.

Well, mostly.

"All I'm doing is freezing to death," I hear her grousing behind me, the chatter of her teeth clicking in the stillness. "How the hell am I supposed to pull at some invisible string?"

I yip again, pawing at the snow and bending the front half of my body as if readying to pounce. Thankfully, she gets my meaning.

"Yeah, yeah, lean into it, I got it."

If I could, I would smile. She might be pricklier than I am sometimes.

I hear her feet shuffling in the snow, her muttered curses and deep breaths, and I don't know if it's her own body's need to do so or just a stroke of luck, but after a few minutes, I hear something plop down into the snow, followed by the soft whimpering of another wolf.

And when I finally turn . . . I find the most stunning creature on four legs I've ever seen.

11

Tess

HOLY TWILIGHT KNOCKOFF, Batman.

I stumble around on four legs—repeat, *four legs*—letting out little sounds that only further my panic because they're not shouts and curses; they're howls and *barks*. I stare down at my feet—or rather, *paws*—flexing my toes in the snow and marveling at how much warmer I feel already. I idly think, *I guess fur will do that for you.*

"How do you feel?"

My eyes snap up to meet those of Hunter's wolf, and I'm stunned all over again, because I'm aware that he just made a sound that wasn't at all human, and yet I understood it perfectly.

"This is so fucking weird."

Jesus Christ. Apparently, not only do I *understand* wolf, I speak it too.

Hunter trots over to me, sniffing at my ear, and I wince away self-consciously.

"What are you doing?"

"Just getting your scent," he tells me. *"It's slightly different in this form."*

If I had a nose still and not a fur-covered snout, I would wrinkle it with distaste. *"Does it smell . . . bad?"*

Hunter makes a low sound in his chest, one that is both human and very much not human all at once. *"It's definitely not bad."*

I try to steady myself—it's much harder to stand on four legs than you might think if you've never done it before—taking in my surroundings with a sort of clarity that makes me realize my *eyes* are better now. I can see the tiny flurries of snow as they're unsettled by the wind. I catch sight of the leaves trembling in the breeze from my peripherals. I can even see the slight flick of Hunter's tail as he studies me quietly.

"Well," I warble. *"How do I look?"*

His eyes are still the same dark brown that's almost black, even like this, but they seem sharper somehow, and I guess given what I just observed, that makes sense too. He snuffles at me, making another a low sound, and I understand his words so well he might as well have spoken them.

"Gorgeous."

I don't think wolves can actually blush, but if they could, my face would be on fire.

God. This is so fucking weird.

"What do we do now?" I ask.

He gestures with his head over his shoulder, drawing my eyes to the clearing beyond. *"Let's get you used to four legs."*

"And how do you propose we do that?"

I swear, if wolves could smile, he would be grinning maniacally.

"By seeing whether or not you can catch me."

And before I can manage a response, he's kicking up snow as he makes a mad dash out of the clearing, leaving me teetering alone like a baby deer. Talk about throwing a girl in the deep end with no floaties.

I take one step, and then another, putting one paw in front of the other until it comes easier, until the shakiness lessens and my steps seem surer.

Okay, I think. *I can do this. I can.*

I see Hunter in the distance, perched on a raised boulder and staring down his nose at me almost as if smirking. I dig my claws into the earth beneath the snow, gearing up to try to run.

As I take off in a sprint, following after the sleek, dark gray of his form that stays paces ahead of me, I can't help but think he's sort of gorgeous too.

I NEVER DO catch him, but I give it my best effort. I reason that he's had fifteen years or so to get the hang of this, and it's perfectly fine that I can't seem to catch up to him after just one day of practice. Even if it does stir my competitive side.

Hunter seems to be enjoying all of it; he makes playful sounds and a noise that's suspiciously like the wolf equivalent of a laugh when I get close, only for him to bound off in the other direction, and by the end of our little game of tag, I'm about ready to bite him. Which I'm aware is a thought that would have struck me as highly strange only a week ago.

"*This is exhausting*," I tell him.

He trots slowly back and forth a few paces away, looking like the picture of energy. He doesn't even seem out of breath, while I'm panting like . . . well, like a dog.

"*You get used to it*," he answers.

I make a sound that's meant to be a snort. *"When? When my fur turns as gray as yours?"*

I ponder that for a moment, wondering if that happens to wolves. I have *so* much more research to do, clearly.

"You did good today," he says. *"Really. Shifting for the first time is never easy, but you're already moving like a natural."* He cocks his head. *"How is your sense of smell?"*

"Well, if the fact that I can tell there's some sort of animal over there is any indication, I'd say it's pretty good."

He flashes me an *actual* wolfish grin—something I've never heard of outside romance novels—yipping in a way that makes me think he's laughing.

"Rabbit," he tells me. *"If you're hungry."*

"I'm not eating a rabbit." If I could, I would scowl. *"How are you so damn fast anyway?"*

"Years of practice. You'll get there." Another sound that seems suspiciously like a laugh. *"Maybe. Eventually."*

I feel my hackles rise. *"Maybe I'm just warming up."*

"Sure you are."

I check the sky where the sun has started to sink, grateful that I told my brothers I wasn't feeling well. I didn't mean to stay out this long, but I know they won't come looking for me since I hinted that it was "female stuff."

Boys.

I know we should probably head back, but my bruised ego is still sore that I didn't even come *close* to catching Hunter. My muscles feel more alive than they ever have, and my body's so light, it's almost like it's poised to take flight. Once you get over the fact that you've changed into an *actual wolf*, it's pretty amazing, actually.

"Maybe we should go one more round," I muse.

He snuffles. *"Are you that desperate to lose again?"*

"Who says I'd lose again?"

"The other three times you tried."

I let out a little growl, surprising myself.

Hunter notices. *"Did you just growl at me?"*

"You're being smug."

"Of course I am," he says *smugly*. *"I'm currently undefeated."*

"One more time," I urge.

His head tilts to look at the sky, noting the same sinking sun I just did. *"It will be dark soon."*

"You scared, Grandpa?"

"Of you?" He takes a step closer, imposing his full height on me, which is easy, since his wolf is so much larger than mine. *"Hardly."*

"Then I suggest you run," I all but purr, unsure where the sound comes from.

The thrill of the chase has my blood pumping harder, and I can feel a frenetic energy in my limbs urging me to move, to *go*, and I'm determined to make full use of it.

Hunter stares down at me for a moment more, then surprises me by leaning in close to press his snout right under my ear. I can feel his breath puffing against my fur as he inhales deeply, and when he pulls away, I can feel my legs get shakier.

"Your scent is off," he says.

"Stop making excuses."

"I'm not making excuses, I'm saying that your scent is—"

I can't ignore the urge to move any longer, taking off at a full sprint as I bound away from him and call out, *"Fine, you can chase me this time then!"*

I revel in the icy wind that rushes past me as I move as fast as I'm able, the powdery white that kicks up all around me feeling *right* somehow. Have I ever felt as free as I do right now?

I can hear Hunter behind me, hear him howl his acceptance of my challenge as I continue to run from him, and I can almost sense the way he follows after me. It's like a disruption in the air, a ripple in the current of my surroundings. Like an old instinct of giving chase, of being *hunted*.

There's nothing like it, really.

It doesn't hit me that I feel strange until I'm weaving between the trees to try to outmaneuver him, but when it does, it spreads like wildfire. I can feel a sort of boiling in my blood, one that makes me hot all over despite the wintery wonderland I'm currently traipsing through. Strangely, it makes me sink deeper into instinct, makes me feel more like a wolf than a person for a handful of moments.

I don't know what to make of it, but I find that I *like* it. I like it very much.

Hunter is so close behind that I can practically hear his heartbeat—no, literally, I can *hear* his heartbeat—but the thought of being captured by him doesn't upset me, oddly enough. No, as the urges and the heat inside me grow, I find that I *want* him to catch me. I want him to take me to the ground and prove that he's stronger, that he's *faster*—I want him to—

I yelp when a heavy mass collides with me, the force of it so strong that a sharp tingling sensation spreads through my body, so forceful it feels as if my skin begins to fizz. I roll instinctively against the force of the blow, snarling as a heavy weight moves with me until it settles beneath me.

It takes longer than it should, I think, for me to realize that something is different—my heart is beating so fast in my chest and in my ears that I don't notice it at first. That I'm looking down at a very human, very *naked* Hunter currently cradled between my equally human thighs.

I pant as I stare down at him, taking note of his enlarged pupils, his heaving chest—realizing that this urgency I'm feeling . . . I don't think it's only me. Not if the way Hunter is looking at me is any indication.

"You caught me," I rasp.

I watch his throat bob with a swallow. "I didn't mean to . . . pummel you like that. You just—you smell so—"

And for reasons unknown to me, my very being seems to hinge on the end of that sentence.

"I smell so . . . ?"

"You smell like you *need* me."

And it doesn't occur to me until the words leave his mouth that I *might*. Because all at once—between the urgency and the overwhelming sensation of being completely free for maybe the first time in my entire life—I realize that the throbbing in my skin is even *worse* between my legs.

I recognize it for what it is—it's the same sensation that had me begging him to touch me only days ago—but with the way my body is keyed up from our afternoon, I'm more in tune with it this time. It feels less like a siege of my body and more like the way I've been feeling all afternoon. Like *letting go*.

And all at once, I forget why I protested Hunter's attempt to help in the first place.

"I'm sorry," I tell him. "I didn't—"

"I know you didn't," he assures me. "I know."

That same heat ratchets even higher, the throbbing in my core damn near painful. I grit my teeth, shifting slightly and gasping when I feel Hunter hard between my legs.

"Sorry," he grits out. "I can't help it."

I swallow thickly, trying to shift away but only managing to rub against him again, causing us both to groan.

"I could..." He shudders beneath me. "I could help you."

My skin feels like it gets tighter around my bones as a cramp tears through me. "You... could? Like last time?"

I feel the ghost of his fingertips skirt along my thigh, so warm despite the chill in the air.

"I don't want to take advantage of you," he says. "But you could... you could use me."

I can't help it; I rock my hips once—just *once*—gasping when I feel something long and hard between my legs. I realize that I'm absolutely drenched, and there is no way Hunter doesn't feel it. Not when I'm two steps away from riding him.

"It feels like I'm taking advantage of *you*," I groan.

He shakes his head. "Just because it's instinct drawing you to me... doesn't mean I don't want it."

Oh. That makes me shiver all over.

"What if we just—" I let out a shuddering breath. "No sex. Just... just touching. Maybe that will... help it not get too complicated."

I watch his eyes darken even further, the pupils swallowing up his irises until there's almost nothing left of them.

"You mean"—his nails bite into the softness of my thighs right as his hips tilt to let the hard length of him grind against my aching core—"like this?"

I throw my head back with a gasp, my eyes fluttering shut as sparks course through me. It's the basest level of satisfaction I've ever felt, like a desperate need that's being met to the fullest. I nod dazedly, chasing after the motion with another rock of my hips.

"Just like that," I rasp. "Again."

Even as the fire tears through my body, threatening to consume me, the feel of Hunter beneath me, the clash of his own heat—*all* of it has me careening into some higher plane where nothing feels real and yet everything feels *too* real.

We find a rhythm—I rock my hips to meet the rolling of his, each slide of his cock along my slick folds sending sparks across my skin and deep in my belly that take me even higher.

And then he opens his mouth and sends me right into the stratosphere.

"Fuck, *look at you*," he grinds out. "You look so pretty riding me." His hands curl around to grip my ass, pulling me down harder against his cock until I'm gasping for breath. "That's it," he croons. "That's a good omega. Use me. Take what you need."

And I do, I fucking *do*. In a display that is more wanton than anything I've done in my entire life, I start to undulate my hips faster and faster, chasing the relief I know he can give me. Like this, I can feel every ridge, every hard inch of him—and every touch only makes me want more. I grind down against him again and again, shutting my eyes tight to focus on the feeling of him, on the raw power he exudes. He's so *big*. Everything about him seems to call to this part of me that I never knew existed, almost as if simply being near him forces that part of me to wake up, to take notice of him.

"*Fuck*," he grunts. "I'm going to come if you keep doing that, Tess."

I nod frantically, because I want it. I want to know that he's as lost to this as I am.

"Please," I manage, my voice no more than a whimper.

"You want my cum?"

I brace myself against his chest, digging my nails into the hard muscle of his pecs until he hisses with it. "*Yes.*"

He grips me tighter, forcing me to roll against him even faster than before, and the delicious friction of his cock sliding along my clit has me shaking, has my entire body strung tight like a bowstring. And it's so close, it's *right there*, and I—

"*Oh.*"

My body seizes up even as I quiver with my orgasm, and if I weren't so far gone, I might be embarrassed by the gush of fluids that escapes me, wetting his pelvis to the point that I can *hear* the sloppy slide of his cock through my folds.

"Look so pretty when you come," he says through gritted teeth. "When you make a mess of me. *Fuck*, I'm gonna—"

I feel a hot splash of fluid as his cock pulses between my legs, and I have an irrational, fleeting thought mourning the fact that he's not inside me. As if my instincts are angry with me for not keeping his cum for myself. I even have the brief, mortifying urge to reach down and stuff it inside me, one that takes the last remaining bit of my restraint to resist.

And when I come down from the high of it all, it hits me that I'm straddling Hunter, naked, both of us planted in the snow, out in the open where anyone might come across us. Endorphins still flood my system, accompanied by the chill creeping into my flushed body, making me shiver.

I stare down at Hunter with wide eyes, feeling a flush of embarrassment creep into my chest. "I—"

And Hunter, sensing my rising panic, seems to know just what to do.

"Shh." He gently rubs my thighs, his glazed eyes half covered by heavy lids. "You're okay. You're safe. Just let me take care of you."

He coaxes me down until I'm curled into his chest, his large hands smoothing over each notch in my spine.

"It's okay," he coos. "I've got you."

"I don't know what's happening to me," I admit, feeling a rush of fear. "What's happening to me, Hunter?"

"You're going to be okay," he urges. "All right? I promise."

"What if this happens again?"

His hand stills near the base of my spine. "If it happens again . . . then you'll let me help you. Okay? It doesn't have to mean anything. It's just biology."

"Biology," I echo.

"It's clear that all these new hormones being introduced into your system are triggering these sort of mini . . . heats. That's the only explanation for you to smell like heat only to lose it after being . . . satisfied."

"Satisfied," I snort.

"I'm not a doctor," he chuckles. "But it's the only thing I can think of."

"I guess it makes sense," I sigh.

There's a beat of silence before: "I don't think my alpha will allow me to let you suffer, Tess," he admits quietly. "You're not the only one affected."

"Is it wrong to say that makes me feel better?"

He chuckles softly once more. "No. I can't imagine how scary this is for you."

"So we're . . . friends? Who help each other?"

"Friends," he agrees. "Who help each other."

I sigh, relaxing into his hold. "Okay. I can live with that."

"Good. Now let's get you back to your clothes before the adrenaline leaves your system and you freeze. Can you change again?"

I nod into his chest, strangely reluctant to let go of him just yet. I know we need to talk about this more, but with his cum drying on my skin and the air growing increasingly more frigid—I don't think I can manage it right now. Maybe when we're back in the warm lodge and more . . . clothed.

I feel his lips at my hair as he murmurs, "Race you back?"

His question eases some of my embarrassment, and my lips curl into a grin.

"I'm going to destroy you."

He laughs again, giving my ass a soft pat. "Sure you are."

12

Hunter

THE PROBLEM WITH calling myself Tess's *friend* is that I don't think that *friends* think of each other the way I've been thinking of her for the last week. We've been perfectly *friendly* when she comes to me with questions or asks for my help in making decisions regarding her current project; her brothers have also been a tad friendlier when interacting with me. Even if one of them keeps asking me if I have fangs.

I have to assume that's a shifter question.

The problem, I think, is that after that day in the snow . . . I can't stop looking at her. My eyes gravitate toward her whenever she's in the same room; they search for her when she isn't. And even if it's biology, if it's just instinct, it feels impossible to stop. I'm doing it right now—watching her chatter into the camera that her brother Kyle holds as she gushes over the original wood floors she's unearthed by ripping up the seventies-style carpet that was covering it. She's so much more animated in front of the camera, so light and not nearly as serious as she normally seems, and I . . . like this side of her. It makes me want to get to know *that* side of Tess.

"If you keep staring at that girl, you're going to burn a hole in the side of her head."

I jolt in my seat at the front desk, whipping my eyes away from the opening to the great room, where Tess is working, to find Jeannie looking down at me with an amused expression.

I feel my cheeks heat. "I don't know what you're talking about."

Her lips purse; she's holding Reginald in her arms, the massive fur ball giving me a look much like his mother's that screams, *Bullshit*.

"You wanna tell me why I can smell you on her?"

I tense. I've been so concerned with making sure Tess's brothers didn't suspect anything that I didn't give any thought to my very much *shifter* aunt, whose sense of smell would no doubt be the biggest threat to our little secret. I try to make myself look busy by typing something nonsensical on the ancient Gateway computer—I'm not even sure how it still works—and shrug.

"Maybe we bumped into each other."

"'Bumped into each other,'" she echoes blandly.

I shrug again. "Maybe."

"One hell of a bump," Jeannie chuckles.

I glare up at her from my seat. "Say what you want to say."

"I'm not saying anything," she urges. "Just worry about you is all."

"Well, I'm fine."

"I just remember how you were after Chloe—"

"It's not like that," I cut her off forcefully. "She's . . . going through some things."

Jeannie cocks her head. "What sorts of things?"

I glance back at Tess, who is still recording. It's not really my place to spread her business, but then again, I know that Jeannie won't say anything, and honestly, I could use advice from someone who *isn't* my android cousin.

"She didn't know she was an omega until two weeks ago."

Jeannie rears back. "What? How is that possible?"

"We talked about it." *After I talked her through an orgasm.* "Apparently, it's called 'late presentation.' Her entire life, she thought she was a beta. Then the day she shows up in Colorado, she finds out that she's *actually* an omega."

"Wow." Jeannie glances in the other room, scratching Reginald's head idly. "Poor girl." Her eyes widen suddenly. "Wait, does that mean she's never shifted before?"

"She hadn't," I tell her. "Not until a week ago. I . . . taught her how. I've gone out with her a couple evenings this week to help her practice."

Unfortunately, with no more happy endings.

Wait. Unfortunately? That's not right. It's a *good* thing she hasn't shown any more symptoms.

"That must have been terrifying," Jeannie notes.

I think back to Tess's alarm after first shifting, nodding idly. "Yes, I imagine so. She seems to be doing better now though."

"And you're just . . . helping her? Out of the goodness of your heart?"

My brow furrows. "Is that so hard to believe?"

"Well . . ." Jeannie chuckles to herself. "You aren't exactly known for doing anything out of 'the goodness of your heart,' so . . ."

I roll my eyes. "You make me sound like an asshole."

"I prefer the term 'stern,'" she says.

"Whatever. There's no one else around to show her."

Her brow cocks. "You could have asked me."

That gives me pause. Mostly because it's the simplest solution, but it didn't even *occur* to me until this very moment. Even now, considering it, something inside me withers at the thought. As if my instincts have decided it's *my* responsibility to help Tess.

Jeannie, sensing my internal struggles, just laughs.

"Goodness of your heart." She hums. "Right."

"Don't you have something you should be doing?" I grumble.

She pats my shoulder. "Yes, bothering my favorite nephew."

"I'm your only nephew," I mutter.

Which is true, since she's my only aunt on my dad's side.

"Still."

Movement catches my eye, and my heart rate picks up slightly when I notice Tess heading toward us from the other room. Then I have a mini internal inquisition about why my heart rate would be picking up at all from such a thing. I conclusively reason that it's definitely because I know what she looks like naked.

Which is to say . . . good. Very good.

Jesus, it's been too fucking long since I've been with someone. I'm practically acting like a virgin when it comes to Tess.

"Hey," she says. "Thomas and Chase have finished sanding down the floor in there. Want to come look at the stain samples we brought? I'm leaning toward a cedar-esque shade; I think it will go really well with all the rustic elements we're keeping original without overpowering the shiplap we're putting up on the walls. But I want to make sure you agree before we move forward with staining."

I've noticed she talks with her hands a lot when she's excited about something, which is usually only when it has to do with the project. Even now her slim fingers are waving around her face and her animated expression lights up while she's describing something as simple as wood stain.

I glance over at Jeannie, who clearly caught me staring at Tess while she talked, ignoring her smirk as I answer, "Sure, I can do that."

"Great," she answers with a grin, one that makes her cheeks dimple and her eyes crinkle at the corners. They're a few shades lighter than mine, with green flecks near the iris, which somehow makes her eyes seem even larger than they are, and her moods easy to read just by the shape of them.

"You should come see too, Jeannie," she says.

Jeannie shakes her head. "No, no, I need to get started on lunch. I'm sure Hunter has everything covered."

She winks at me as if sharing a joke, and I roll my eyes again. Of course she would have fun with this entire situation. Heaven forbid she ever finds out about Tess's mini heat situation; I'll never hear the end of that one. Jeannie will have us mated off in her head by sunset.

I hop down from the stool at the counter, circling it and following after Tess as she explains the shots Kyle needs to get while they're staining the floors. I have to admit, I know absolutely nothing about the TikTok side of the things she's doing, but she sounds so confident when she talks about it, so sure of herself, that it's a little hard not to sit up and pay attention. It's a far cry from the uncertainty she exudes regarding her sudden change of designation.

Her brothers are in the opposite corner of the room, by the fireplace; the new stone they've brought in admittedly makes the old thing look warmer and more inviting even being only half-done.

The largest brother, Chase, nods at me when our eyes meet. "Hey, man, tell my sister her cedar is too light, yeah?"

"Don't listen to him," Tess grumbles. "He doesn't know what he's talking about."

"I know you don't pair cedar floors with this sandstone fireplace," he chuffs.

She rolls her eyes. "You do when the walls are going to be as dark as they are. You need the contrast."

Chase gives me a look that seems to say that his sister is off her rocker, and my alpha prickles at his ribbing her, so much so that I have to shove it down. *This is her brother*, I remind myself. They're just teasing each other. It's fine.

"So this is the cedar I was talking about," she says, pointing at a swatch of stained wood. "And then there's this one, which leans more cherry. I personally think this one overpowers the space, but Chase likes it, which means we've been arguing about it all morning—"

"Because it's better!" he calls from the other side of the room.

"—*which* means that you get to be my tiebreaker."

I look between the two wood samples, honestly not seeing much of a difference other than one being darker. I can tell by the look in Tess's eyes that she's dead set on the one she's holding out just a little closer to me, as if this will influence my decision, her eyes big and hopeful in a way that's actually . . . adorable.

Adorable?

I brush the thought away. Truthfully, if it were up to *me*, I would go with the one Chase seems to be championing. I also can't see the lighter color working in the space, but then again, there's still so much to do that it's hard to visualize. I can tell that Tess is completely sure in her assertion that it will work, and the pleading look on her face calls to the baser part of me.

That means I'm opening my mouth before I'm even fully aware what's about to come out of it.

"I like this one too," I tell her, pointing at the cedar swatch. "I think you're right about the contrast."

I have no idea if that's true, but with the way her face lights up, I decide it's the right answer anyhow.

You know you're just trying to appease her because of your instincts, my brain whispers, right as I emphatically tell it to shut the hell up.

"Great," she says cheerily. "I think so too."

"You're going to give her a big head," Chase calls.

She waves him off. "It's not Hunter's fault he has better taste than you."

I notice there's sweat on her brow, and whether or not that's due to her work or . . . something else, I can't be sure. Again, my mouth opens before I figure out what's leaving it.

"How are you feeling, by the way?" I ask, lowering my voice.

Her cheeks tinge pink, and her eyes dart over to her brothers, who have begun to talk among themselves while Kyle films some close-ups of Thomas and Chase working on the fireplace.

"Okay," she admits. "Nothing too pressing since . . ." Her cheeks darken even further, her eyes averting to the floor. "Since the last time."

"You don't have to be embarrassed," I tell her. "It's just biology, remember?"

She nods. "I know. Still. I'm not exactly used to people fussing over me."

"You're going through an entire life upheaval," I remind her. "*Someone* should be fussing over you."

She tucks a stray lock of chestnut hair behind her ear, her neck flushing slightly. "I guess so."

"You can tell me if you start feeling strange again, okay? There's no reason for you to hurt needlessly."

"You mean tell you if I start feeling unbearably horny again," she scoffs, her voice low.

I can't help the way my mouth quirks. "Yes. That."

"Is this not incredibly weird for you? I mean, you didn't ask to take on my biological nightmare."

"It's fine," I assure her. "I want to help. We're friends, remember?"

"The weirdest friends," she snorts.

I grin fully then, noticing that her eyes linger on my mouth as I do so. "I'm fine with being weird friends."

"Hey, yo, Hunter!" Thomas calls.

My head swivels, and I find him looking at me expectantly. "We're all hitting the bar this weekend. You want in?"

I frown. That's no doubt Cat's doing. Honestly, the idea of piling into the crowded bar in town, surrounded by people who mostly look at me with pity, even so many years later, sounds like a chore.

"No thanks," I tell him. "Not really the bar type anymore."

Thomas shrugs. "Suit yourself."

I swear I hear a whispered mention of *vampire*, but surely I'm just imagining it.

"It'll be fun," Tess says quietly, studying her wood swatch intently as if she's not invested. "You should go."

That gives me pause. Is she saying that to be polite? Or is she saying that because she *wants* me to go? And why does that matter all of a sudden? This game we're playing becomes more confusing by the minute.

"I'll think about it," I say, knowing I most likely won't but not wanting to disappoint her.

Her lips curl slightly. "Sure."

I take one last glance at her brothers, making sure they're occupied before I gently touch her elbow and lean in. "I meant what I said. I want you to tell me if you start feeling . . . off. I don't want you to make yourself suffer."

I actually can't stand the thought of her suffering.

"Oh, I . . ." I notice her throat move with a swallow, and then she nods slowly. "Okay."

"Good," I answer, not missing the way she shudders slightly with the praise.

It's just hormones. That's all.

That seems to be the motto of my life lately.

"I'd . . . better get back to it," she says.

"Okay," I answer, letting go of her elbow once I realize I'm still touching her.

There's a slight blooming of her scent that threatens to distract me, and I feel a tension in my chest from breathing her in. Which is probably my cue to put some distance between us, something I've been trying to do whenever I'm not helping her practice shifting. Just in case.

I leave her to her work and return to my counter, knowing I have paperwork from the bank that's calling my name no matter how much I'd like to pretend it doesn't exist.

Still, as I settle back on my stool and start shuffling through the small stack once more, I can't help the way my eyes shift up every so often to take note of whatever Tess is doing in the other room. I glance her way *far* more times in the next hour than I'd like to admit, actually.

I can't help but think back to my conversation with Jeannie, once again wondering why it never occurred to me to seek out *her* help when Tess needed guidance. It was obviously the most reasonable answer, one that would have meant I could keep my distance, which would probably make for a much easier time for the both of us. For reasons I don't want to examine too closely . . . I realize that the idea of anyone else *helping* Tess leaves me feeling irritable and unsettled.

And I have no idea what to make of that.

13

Tess

"SO, HOW IS Nowheresville? Have you found the yeti yet?"

I don't make a joke at Hunter's expense about his strange imperviousness to the cold; I know that would mean getting into his slightly undone flannel and his sweat and his axe swinging—all things that would have Ada foaming at the mouth and asking too many questions.

I flounce back against my bed instead, jaw working as I stare up at the ceiling. "It's nice, actually. Quiet. I met a really nice girl in town too."

"Excuse me," Ada huffs. "Are you trying to replace me with a snow bunny?"

"Oh, shut up," I laugh. "You'd like her." I add, "It's been cool to sort of unwind. It's so pretty here. Nice and relaxing."

"And I'm sure the scenery is nice," she remarks innocently. "All that plaid."

"Don't even start."

"You told me you're staying with a sexy lumberjack. You've got to throw me a bone."

"I don't remember telling you anything of the sort."

"And you're all snowed in with him in some giant cabin," Ada says gleefully, ignoring me. "How tall is he? Paint me a picture."

"I don't know . . . maybe like six foot four? Six foot five?"

"And he has a beard."

"Yes," I sigh. "He has a beard."

"Have you wondered yet how that would feel between your—"

"Absolutely not."

Lies, my traitorous brain whispers. *You totally have.*

"And how is . . . everything else?"

I pause. I haven't told Ada about . . . everything. Not yet. I can't even pinpoint why. I don't know if I'm embarrassed or if it's just something I want to keep to myself for now.

"It's going okay. Hunter has been helping me practice shifting," I tell her cautiously.

"He *has*?"

"It's not a big deal," I say quickly.

"Wait, so you've been getting *naked* with him?"

"He never looks!"

He really doesn't, and I know that, because I check every time. I can't say why I'm always disappointed that he never tries to look.

Fucking hormones.

"Doesn't mean he doesn't want to. You should let him look."

I roll my eyes. "It's not like that."

Except it is, but then again, it isn't. It's all very confusing.

"There was . . . a moment," I admit. "Last week."

"Oooh, tell me more."

"We sort of . . . collided."

"Collided?"

"He was trying to help me get a handle on being on four legs, and he was chasing me, and then suddenly he ran smack dab into me, and we sort of . . . changed back."

And then proceeded to not-quite–dry hump the shit out of each other.

"Oh my God, so he *has* seen you naked!"

"It was an accident," I argue.

What happened next, not so much.

"I'm imagining sweaty, tangled limbs."

"Please don't imagine that," I groan.

"I can't help it," she huffs. "Apparently, you're trapped in some sort of Hallmark-level winter wonderland with a hunky lumberjack, and you're not even taking advantage of it."

"It was more of a straddling situation, honestly. And he's technically my boss, Ada."

"You were *straddling* him? Come *on*. Stuff like ethics doesn't exist in the mountains."

"I'm not sure that's true."

"Girl," she presses. "If anyone needs a hot sexcapade in the snowy mountains they can look back on fondly, it's you."

"Hey," I protest. "Speak for yourself."

"Bleh. The men in Newport are all either gym bros or entirely too into crypto."

"You just like to find something wrong with all of them."

"Shut up. This isn't about me. Explain to me why you can't let the hunky lumberjack split you like a log?"

I pull the phone away for a second to grimace at it as if Ada can actually see before bringing it back to my ear. "Well, that's beautiful imagery and not horrifying at all."

"Seriously. You can't give me a hot story like that and then tell me in the same breath you've been hiding in your room all day."

"I'm not *hiding*," I protest feebly. "I've been busy."

"Busy hiding," Ada accuses.

"I had some reading to catch up on."

"How is the world of Harlequin romance, anyway? Is it a laird this time? Or maybe . . . a lumberjack?"

"You're a menace," I groan.

"I love you too," Ada laughs.

"Talk to me about something else."

"I'd really rather talk about the possibility of you being able to feel the innkeeper's d—"

"Nope. Nope. Nope."

"But you were straddling him! Surely you must have felt som—"

"Something *else*," I urge, feeling heat creeping up my neck. I cannot let my brain even go where she wants it to. I won't get any sleep for the rest of the trip. "Tell me how my favorite pseudo nephew is doing."

"He's at home with Mom today," she tells me. "Probably goading her into buying him more Lego."

"Is he still into that?"

"Unfortunately," she huffs. "Do you know how expensive those damn sets are?"

"And you know your mom will fold," I laugh.

"Of course she will," Ada sighs. "She's weak."

"You're no better."

"That's fair. He's just so cute."

And he really is—Perry is a little carbon copy of his mom, with his auburn hair and freckles, and simply thinking about him makes me miss the pair of them.

Through the speaker I hear a loud rapping of knuckles against wood on her end of the line, then a shuffling of movement before she takes me off speaker, her voice clearer now that it's being spoken directly into the receiver. "Hey, the takeout guy is here at the gallery. Call you later?"

"Sure," I tell her. "I'll be here."

"In Nowheresville," she laughs.

"Yeah," I answer with a soft chuckle. "In Nowheresville."

She says her goodbyes just before the line disconnects, and I stay where I am for several moments after, chin perched on my folded arms as I stare at the opposite wall. I can't help but blush as I recall all the things she said about Hunter, unable to pretend I haven't been thinking about a lot of the same things. It's hard not to when I do, in fact, know what he looks like naked.

Which is to say good, I think idly. *Very good.*

I heave out a sigh as I roll on the mattress, pulling myself up to sit at the edge before I turn my face toward the window. It's been an extremely long day between staining the floors and helping Thomas, Chase, and Kyle bring in the rest of the stone to finish the fireplace, and for the first time since I got here, I feel like maybe I should take the night off and relax. I feel like I've earned it, with everything going on. The afternoon sun has already started to sink, casting a pinkish glow against the snow outside, looking serene and inviting. I groan as I drop down from the bed, telling myself to stop agonizing about the hot innkeeper.

And that's exactly what I'm going to do.

I KNOW A hot bath would probably do me a world of good, but given that my room only has a tiny walk-in shower, and the idea of even attempting to stand under the spray sounds like something

I'd rather die before attempting, I foresee a grumbly night right here on my bed.

At least until the knock at my door has me sitting upright.

"Yes?"

"It's Jeannie," she calls through the door. "You decent?"

"Oh. Yeah." I push up to sit cross-legged on the mattress as she pushes open the door, carrying a little tray with a cup of some steaming liquid.

"I thought you might want some hot chocolate. I make the good stuff. None of that packaged garbage."

"You have my full attention," I say with a smile. She hands me the cup gingerly as she takes a seat on the edge of my bed, watching with anticipation as I take a slow, careful sip. "Oh my God."

"Told you," she says smugly. "The secret is a dash of cinnamon."

"It's like Christmas in a cup," I tell her, taking another sip. "I needed this."

"It's nice to have someone to make it for," she says. "Hunter isn't so big on sweet things."

"I would have never guessed," I say, words dripping with sarcasm.

"He really has that old-man-trapped-in-a-young-man's-body thing down pat."

"Was he always like that?"

Jeannie considers. "He's always had a bit of seriousness to him that made him just a little different from other kids his age, but I'd definitely say it's gotten worse in the last decade."

"I guess running a business will do that to you," I muse.

Jeannie nods thoughtfully. "He's had a lot on his shoulders for a long time. Too much for someone his age, I think."

"When did he officially take over the place?"

I notice the way Jeannie's lips press together, considering for a moment as if I haven't asked a simple question. "Oh, it's been nearly ten years now," she says offhandedly.

"He was so young."

"Mm-hmm." She nods solemnly. "How's the room, by the way?"

"It's great," I tell her.

She cocks her head, watching as I rub my neck. "Bed do that?"

"No, no," I assure her, still rubbing at the crick that's forming. "It's just from bending over that floor all day. Has all my muscles hating me."

"I don't know if Hunter mentioned," she says, "but there's a hot tub out on the back deck."

I perk up immediately. "Oh my God, I forgot about that."

"Yep. Nothing fancy, but it's got jets and hot water at least."

"That literally sounds like heaven right now."

"Well, finish your hot chocolate and get your sore butt out there," she laughs. "Old thing would probably enjoy seeing a body other than mine and Hunter's."

"Hot chocolate and now a hot tub," I say almost giddily. "Starting to feel like vacation rather than a job."

"This is certainly a good place for it." She glances at the clock on the wall then, making a show of pushing up off the bed. "Oh, well, shit. I have to feed Reginald. He gets ornery when I don't feed him on time."

"Oh. Sure. Of course."

"You just leave that mug out on the hall table. I'll pick it up in the morning. Make sure you cover the hot tub when you're done using it. Last time I left it uncovered I found a damn squirrel swimming in it like he owned it. Don't know how that water didn't boil him alive."

I laugh at the mental image of that. "I'll be sure to cover it."

"I'd bring a robe too. It's gonna be colder than Jack Frost's balls when you get out of the tub. There should be one in the dresser over there."

"Perfect," I answer, still grinning. "Thanks."

I take another long gulp of Jeannie's hot chocolate when she leaves me, tipping it back to finish it off as it settles warmly in my belly. A hot tub sounds like the perfect thing after a day of hard labor.

Plus . . . maybe the hot water will make me forget all about the hot innkeeper.

THE ROBE IN the dresser that Jeannie mentioned isn't the most stylish thing I've ever worn—faded flannel (honestly, flannel should be on the state flag) that looks like it's seen better days—but it's warm and long enough that it covers my ankles, which is much more important than style as far as I'm concerned. I pair it with my fuzzy boots and my pom-pom–topped toboggan as I make my way down the stairs to the back door leading to the deck, wrapping it tight as I take quick steps to avoid the creeping chill that the old ducts of the lodge can never seem to ward off completely. I obviously didn't bring a swimsuit on this little adventure, but I figured my matching sports bra and boy shorts set would suffice. Even if I feel like I might be freezing to death.

Hot water, I remind myself. *There's hot water coming.*

I meet one very cantankerous Maine coon on the way to the back deck, the black mass of fur stretched out on the checkered couch with his belly up as I pass. I pause near him as I consider the consequences of a sneak attack, reaching quietly until my fingers skim the soft fur of his underside—for exactly two seconds. He hisses at me as he instantly pounces away, and I curse under my breath as I clutch my robe, watching him go.

"Mean ass," I mumble.

Whatever. It's too cold to worry about the grumpy old cat.

I'm doing something reminiscent of tap dancing and hopscotch as I barrel out through the deck doors, the frozen air taking me by surprise as the robe I'm wearing seems thinner than it did before I stepped outside. I'm only concerned with getting into the hot tub as fast as humanly possible to let the hot water warm me up, which means it takes me a second longer than it should to realize that I'm not alone on the deck.

Listen. There have been many moments over the last couple of weeks in which Hunter's flannel-clad shoulders have made themselves at home in my thoughts, there's no denying that. However, seeing them now—naked and broad and *wet*—that's a different kind of brain malfunction altogether, and seeing him naked isn't even a new experience for me. He hasn't noticed me yet—his eyes are closed as he lounges in the water with his head resting against the edge—and I don't immediately make myself known, because my brain is still trying to catch up to wet, naked shoulders and, what's worse, wet, naked *chest*.

Chopping wood has done wonders for Hunter, that much is obvious. His wide chest is defined in a way that some guys out in California kill themselves at the gym every day for. The dark dusting of hair smattered across his torso is a far cry from the waxed dudebros I encounter on a daily basis; it definitely completes the lumberjack vibe that Hunter's dark curls and dark beard set the groundwork for. It makes him look . . . *manly*, as corny as that sounds. My brain can't seem to form a more coherent thought than that.

I'm still openly gawking at him when I absentmindedly shut the sliding patio door, and the click it makes upon closing is what finally alerts Hunter to my presence. He looks surprised to see me when his head jerks up from the edge of the tub, obvious by the way his eyes widen enough for me to notice even by the dim glow of the old porch light a few feet away. I probably look ridiculous to him, standing there in the doorway in the freezing temperature while clutching my old flannel robe and clad in my fuzzy knit cap and fuzzier boots, and that thought shakes me out of my temporary stupor.

"S-sorry," I manage after what is probably an awkward amount of time. "I didn't know you were out here. Jeannie mentioned the hot tub, and I just thought—"

"Well, get in if you're going to," Hunter says with a lot more composure than I have. "It's cold as shit out here."

And then it hits me that I'm about to be alone with him in a hot tub, since my brothers went into town for the evening. I swallow thickly, eyeing his wet chest again and wondering how I'll survive the experience.

Painfully, I'd wager. Very painfully.

14

Hunter

I CAN TELL she's stalling; it's clear by her expression that she didn't expect me to be out here when she came. She clutches what looks to be one of Jeannie's old robes to her chest, eyeing me warily. Which seems silly, really, considering I've already seen her naked. Still, I look away to give her some sense of privacy so she can undress.

I hear the rustle of fabric as she no doubt discards her boots and hat, hear her slight hiss that must mean the robe has come off and the cold air has hit her fully. Her soft footsteps pad across the deck until she's just beside the tub, and only then do I glance her way again.

It shouldn't affect me like it does, seeing her in her forest-green sports bra and matching boy shorts—no doubt she didn't think to bring a suit when she came to this part of the country—but I can't pretend that noticing the way it molds to her body to accentuate every supple curve doesn't have my dick twitching in *my* swim shorts.

"*Shit*," she hisses. "That's hot."

"Hot tub," I remind her.

She sucks in air as she tries to settle in a little more naturally, sitting up a bit as she acclimates to the warm water. She sighs as she settles in front of one of the jets, a sound of contentment leaving her when she falls back against it.

"Oh God, that's perfect," she hums.

"Mm-hmm."

She finally glances over at me, finding me watching her quietly. "So, uh, a hot tub is definitely something you should mention on your website. It's a real perk."

"I haven't messed with that damn thing since it got up and running," I say with a shrug. "It gets the job done." I smile then. "Didn't you know? We're a real hot commodity. We got people coming in all the way from California, even."

"I mean," she says, laughing, "with the right marketing . . . this place could be booming."

"Yeah, right."

"No, really. Pretty spot like this? Seclusion factor? You spin it like some sort of secret getaway and people from LA and everywhere else would be all over it."

"I'll bet."

"Honestly? You just need the right exposure. My social media channels will help a little, but I *do* know this guy at *Travel Quarter* who covers smaller locations like this all the time. He'd probably wet himself over this place. He'd have the rest of California tripping over themselves to stay here. They'd want to plaster it all over their Instagram."

"Is that what the internet people call 'influencing'?"

She laughs loudly at that, the sound of it warming my belly. "You say it like a curse word. I don't think you have to worry about it anytime soon. You'd have to get Wi-Fi first, anyway, and apparently that goes against your moral code."

I roll my eyes. "Well, we snagged one, at least. No Wi-Fi and all."

"Yeah, well," she chuckles. "You could probably count me as a fluke, since you sort of hired me."

"Lucky us," I laugh.

"I could try to call my friend . . ." she says.

I shake my head. "I doubt they'd be interested. Probably isn't worth your effort." I gaze out at the snow wistfully. "Honestly, I keep finding myself wondering if all this reno is even worth it. If it will make any difference. For all I know, we might be closing our doors within a year." I blink a few times, shaking my head. "Sorry. I don't know why I said that."

"You can talk to me about it if you want," she says. "Sometimes it's good to unload to an unbiased third party."

"Unbiased third party, huh?"

"I mean, *mostly* unbiased."

"Right," I laugh.

I stretch my arms above my head then, and I notice that she eyes me, her gaze following the motion in a way that makes my alpha preen. So if I flex a little when I push my wet hair from my eyes after, well, that's no one's business but mine.

"We used to be so much busier than this," I tell her.

She nods. "Jeannie told me a bit about it."

"She told you about the new highway?"

Another nod.

"Well," I go on. "After that . . . everything slowed to a crawl. We bleed money every year now, and sometimes I don't even know how we're keeping the lights on. We had to get a loan just to pay you and your brothers."

Her mouth parts, and I immediately give myself a mental kick for saying that.

"Sorry," I say. "Again, I don't know why I told you that."

And I don't, really. For some reason, I find it easy to talk to Tess. Maybe it's because of all the *helping* I've been doing. It's hard not to feel comfortable with someone you half fucked in the snow.

"It's okay," she says gently. "I get it."

"I guess you could say all this"—I wave my hand aimlessly in the direction of the lodge—"is a last-ditch effort." I huff derisively. "Pretty pathetic, huh?"

She shakes her head. "I don't think so. You're trying to save something you love. That's admirable." She gives me a stern look. "And it's obvious that you love the place."

I cast my eyes down to the water, trying not to think of my parents. The last thing I need to do is get all morose on her. "I *do* love this place. My entire childhood was here, and the thought of changing things terrifies me."

"I get that," she answers. "I'm doing my best to revamp more than revise, if that makes sense."

"I can tell," I say. "And you have no idea how much I appreciate it."

Her answering grin is blinding, and I feel my gut clench with want that is sudden and fierce.

"So tell me more about you," I say, trying to take the focus off me.

"Well, you know what I do for a living and that I have three brothers."

"True," I say, "but there's gotta be more to Tess Covington than that. Did you always know you wanted to do this for a living?"

"For what feels like forever," she tells me. "It just seemed right."

"Seems like it's working out for you with all the social media stuff."

She looks sheepish then. "Actually . . . I'm in talks with HGTV for my own show."

"What?" My brows raise. "That's pretty fucking cool."

"It's . . . overwhelming. And there's a chance they'll pass, but . . . I guess it's cool just to be considered."

"Your family must be thrilled about that."

Her smile immediately falters, and she suddenly looks unsure. "Well . . . I mean . . . I'm sure they *would* be . . . if they knew."

"You haven't told them?"

"They have a lot going on." She fidgets in her seat. "I'm sure you don't want to hear about my drama."

"Unbiased third party," I remind her. "Remember?"

"Right," she snorts. "Well . . . I told you that my dad had a stroke ten years back, right?"

"I remember."

"Yeah, well. It was a rough time. The physical therapy and rehab he had to go through just to be able to get back to the eighty percent mobility he's up to now was gruesome. The medical bills were ridiculous." She reaches to rub at her neck. "It's why I changed majors to take over the business. I knew how much it killed my dad to not be able to continue it, and I figured I could kill two birds with one stone. Keep the business going and help out with the medical bills."

"That's really great of you, Tess," I tell her honestly.

She shrugs. "Yeah, I mean . . . I was happy to do it. I love this business. I love what I do."

"What did you want to be before you switched majors?"

"Hmm?" Her nose wrinkles. "Oh. I had some silly pipe dream about getting a degree in design. I thought I could sign on and help out my dad that way."

"So either way, you always planned to help your dad."

"I guess you could say that, yeah."

I get the sense that she really admires her dad and, what's more, that she really loves what she's doing, continuing his business and watching it thrive.

"So why haven't you told them about HGTV?"

Her face falls. "This last year . . . See, they put him on all sorts of medications after the stroke. He had AFib—that's atrial fibrillation. Basically, it means that the upper chambers of your heart don't squeeze right, so clots can form in your heart and move to your brain. That's what caused the stroke. For a long time, his meds kept everything managed."

"But this year . . . ?"

"Apparently, his medications haven't been doing what they should. He's still in AFib even with them. So his heart rate stays irregular. He's been having all sorts of fatigue and dizziness."

"You said 'apparently' . . . You didn't know?"

She shakes her head. "They didn't want to worry us, so they didn't let us know until recently. The doctors want him to get a pacemaker put in; actually, they said it's imperative that he does. They said that his life expectancy doesn't look good without one, but . . ."

"But?"

"But his insurance isn't great. Even with it, the damned thing will cost like twenty grand. They don't have that kind of money. And the business is doing well, but . . . *I* don't have that kind of money lying around. I'm hoping if I can land this HGTV deal, the signing bonus will help cover the costs so we can move forward with the procedure." Her lip trembles. "I *have* to land this deal."

I watch her expression crumple, and suddenly everything in my body screams that I give her something, *anything* to make her feel better. With that thought coursing through my body, I scoot closer to her on the bench under the water and gently wind an arm around her shoulders.

"Hey," I offer. "I'm sorry. I know I've only seen you work for a few weeks, but you're really great at it. They'd be stupid not to sign you on."

I remain perfectly still when her head tilts to rest on my shoulder, a sigh escaping her. "I hope you're right."

"I usually am," I deadpan.

That draws another grin out of her. "Somehow, I knew you'd say that."

"I think it's great what you do, Tess," I tell her honestly, because in these few weeks I've known her, I've seen her exude passion for something as simple as *floor stain* just for the sake of making someone—*me*—happy, and that says more about her than anything else, I think. It's clear she finds great joy in this, even more so in bringing joy to others through it. "And I think you're fucking amazing at it."

I hear the small catch in her breath, and I can't help but wonder if anyone has ever told her that. I can't say why the thought that I might be the first fills me with a sense of pride and satisfaction. Like in this small way, I'm taking care of her. It seems like Tess always makes sure to take care of everyone *else*—but does anyone ever really take care of her?

I find that lately . . . I like taking care of Tess a lot.

"I haven't told them about what's going on with me either," she says quietly.

"Why not?"

"I guess . . . I don't know. My mom has spent all this time taking care of my dad, and she's the only one working now, and she's always so stressed-out. I guess I've just gotten really good at being self-sufficient. It's easier not to be a burden that way."

"I don't believe your family would think you're a burden if you told them what's going on," I say. "Based on what you've told me."

"I know it's silly," she says. "But . . . with my dad's health being so bad for so long . . . I've always done my best to make sure I take care of myself as much as possible. It felt like I was making things easier on them that way. Like I was one less thing they had to worry about. I guess I *still* feel that way. With all this stuff happening with my dad's pacemaker and them worrying about money . . . it feels almost wrong to dump this shifter shit on them on top of everything else."

"I really don't think they would see it that way," I tell her.

She shrugs one shoulder, looking down at the water. "Maybe you're right."

I pull her closer to my side, leaning into the instinct to do so, to have her closer. She surprises me by curling her body, burrowing her head in my chest as my fingers tangle in her hair. I turn my head and bend forward so my nose can skirt along her shoulder, unable to resist the chance to breathe her in deeply, to revel in her warm scent, which never fails to make my mouth water.

I'm so wrapped up in it that I forget myself, forget to be careful. It takes me by surprise when the scent gland on her throat grazes mine, making us both gasp. I'm unprepared for the shiver that passes through her, despite the heat of the water. The effect is like adding gasoline to a flame, causing her scent to bloom and ripen, surrounding us in the small space, so thick I could choke on it.

"Hunter," she whispers hoarsely, shaking against me.

Shit.

My fingers tighten their grip on her hair, my face burying in her throat to try to breathe in more of her. "Tess, are you . . . ?"

"I think so," she whimpers. "I'm sorry."

"Fuck. *I'm* sorry. I didn't think. I didn't mean to—"

"It burns, Hunter."

"I know, I know," I soothe. "I can help. I'm sorry, I can help. I—*Fuck*, Tess. The way you smell."

"*Hunter.*"

"I need to—Can I taste you?"

She pulls back, her pupils blown and her eyes glazed. "Taste me?"

"You smell so fucking edible. I've wanted to taste you since that first night."

Her head whips around, noting how exposed we are. "Here?"

"Your brothers aren't here, and Jeannie will have already gone home." My hands slide to her hips under the water, urging her upward. "Let me make it better with my tongue. *Please.*"

Her nod heats my blood, and already I'm helping her scramble to the edge of the hot tub, tugging down her boy shorts as she goes. And when she's bare from the waist down, I waste no time diving between her thighs. No warning, no pretense—just my tongue in her pussy like I'm starving for her. With her scent thick in the air, threatening to suffocate me in a way I would say thank you for, I guess that I am.

"*Hunter!*"

I close my eyes as I lap at her slit again and again until the slight tinge of chlorine gives way to the heady taste of *her*. I grab her thighs and pull them over my shoulders, unable to stop tasting her for even a moment. She gasps and writhes against my face when my tongue touches her clit, and I swirl it around the little bud ravenously as I curl my hands over her thighs to hold her tightly against me.

My cock throbs in my shorts, swelling to the point of pain, but I can't stop what I'm doing. I'm dizzy with want and high on the taste of her, and I think distantly that I could do this for *days* without ever coming up for air if she let me.

Her fingers grip the back of my head to twist in my hair, and I relish the slight sting. I can tell this won't be slow, won't be drawn out; I'm too desperate, too keyed up by the scent of her heat. A dozen images flit through my head as I lap at her now-drenched pussy—of her riding me, of her stuffed with my knot, of me bending her over the side of this tub and fucking her until she screams loud enough to bring down the mountain—but none of that calls to me as much as the taste of her on my tongue at this very second.

Even as my cock swells to dangerous levels, so close to the edge that I can barely stand it, I grip her tighter. I lick at her soaked cunt. I suck on her clit until she's gasping my name.

Make her come, my alpha chants. *Make her come all over you. Mark her. Make her yours. Make sure everyone knows who she belongs to.*

"Hunter—*ohmygod, Hunter.*"

I hum against her, my nails biting into the soft flesh of her thighs as animalistic sounds rumble in my chest. I feel it when it happens, and it's far too late for me, but the sensation of her pretty pussy quivering on my tongue, of the gush of her slick that coats my mouth and chin—it's enough to have me licking a wide stripe down the center of her, slower now, like she's a treat to be savored. My eyes are heavy lidded and my body thrums with energy—and it almost feels a little like being in heat myself, tasting Tess.

I can hear her panting above me as she comes down from the furious orgasm I just gave her, her head thrown back and her chest heaving when I peer up the line of her body. And all the while, I'm still tasting her, almost as if I need to collect every drop of her orgasm so that it doesn't go to waste.

"What about—" She sucks in a breath. "What about you?"

"M'fine." I swirl my tongue slowly around her clit, enjoying the way she shakes from the aftershocks. "You taste too good."

Her eyes widen, her fingers tugging at my hair and forcing my head back to look up at her. "You came?"

"I did," I tell her with a dazed nod.

"Jesus," she breathes. "That's . . . that's fucking hot."

"Not exactly comfortable," I mutter, already feeling my knot swell because of the heat-like pheromones she's pumping out. "But worth it."

I'm about to dive in and give her another orgasm as quickly as possible, but Tess is already wriggling out of my hold. "Not comfortable? Are you okay?"

Her scent is already changing, the heat ebbing away now that she's been satisfied, but my knot is full and heavy, throbbing in my shorts with nowhere to go.

"Your heat," I say through gritted teeth. "It forces me to knot . . . outside."

She looks confused. "Knot?"

"Yes." It dawns on me then, that she likely has no idea what I'm talking about. "When an alpha and omega . . . have sex, the alpha . . . you see, his dick, it . . . swells."

Her brows shoot up. "Swells?"

"Fuck. It would just be easier if I show you."

I stand with effort, drawing my shorts down only low enough

THE MATING GAME

for her to catch a glimpse of the base of my cock, flushed with blood and swollen to a round mass that *should* be inside her, making sure she keeps my cum. As it is, it fucking hurts.

"That's . . . Wow. Why does it do that?"

"Well, at some point . . . it was to ensure conception. It's . . . part of our biology."

"So if we were having sex . . ." Her eyes look a little glazed now. "That would be . . . ?"

"Inside you," I murmur, watching the way her pupils dilate.

She lifts her hand as if considering, then looks up at me. "Can I?"

I nod shakily, the idea of her touching me making my head rush.

Her little fingers reach out tentatively, brushing against it, and I hiss as it throbs from her touch.

"It hurts?"

"When it happens . . . like this. Yes."

"Like this?"

". . . Outside."

Her mouth parts in surprise. "Oh. *Oh.*" Her teeth press against her lower lip, considering that. "How can I help?"

"Usually I just . . ." I reach down to grip it, squeezing it roughly, massaging the dull ache away. "Like this."

I watch as she licks her lips, her breath puffing out of her. "I could do that."

"You don't have to . . ."

She touches me again, and my knees almost buckle.

"I want to," she tells me.

And with the same fervor I showed her, Tess tugs at my swim trunks, freeing my cock, which is still half hard, and going straight for the swollen base to wrap both hands around it and squeeze it like I did. I have to lean back and grip the edge of the tub to keep my balance, my breath rushing out of me as if I'm being punched in the chest when she starts to massage my knot.

"Fuck. *Fuck*, Tess. Just like that."

She looks dazed again, and her scent burgeons slightly—not like when she's in heat, but enough that it makes my cock twitch with interest all over again. It makes me bolder.

"Harder," I murmur. "You won't break me."

She shudders with my command and does as I ask, squeezing me tighter. The relief is instant—I can almost imagine it's the warmth of her pussy gripping me, can almost imagine that my knot is safe and snug inside her.

Where it should be, something whispers.

And even as she's wringing the swollen flesh of my knot, she still takes me by surprise by leaning in, licking at the head to taste me too.

I hiss through my teeth, watching as she does it again, humming her approval.

"You want to taste me, Tess? You want my cum in your mouth?"

Her scent blooms, and I can smell it, how wet she is all over again. It's clear she likes it when I talk. If her scent is any indication, she fucking *loves* it.

"Suck me," I groan. "Please, Tess. Just the head. I'm—I just need—*Shit*."

Her lips close over the head of my cock, sucking gently even as she kneads my knot. It feels impossible that we've gotten here, that she's down on her knees with her pussy freshly licked and my cock in her mouth while she massages my throbbing knot—but I can't find an ounce of regret inside. Not with her looking so sweet, not with her being so *good* for me as she swirls her tongue around my glans, flicking the tip against the sensitive slit at the head.

And that's all it takes to have me careening over the edge all over again.

My eyes roll back, and my cock pulses, and another burst of cum spurts out of me, just enough to make the throbbing at the base of my dick start to quell, finally. My breath is ragged, and my limbs feel like jelly. Tess gives me one more kitten lick before pulling away, licking her lips as she does so.

"Feel better?"

I swallow, my throat dry and my voice scratchy when I answer, "I don't think there are words for how I feel." I slowly slide down to my knees, reaching to cup her face with one hand. "And you? Do you feel better?"

She gives me a slow, languid smile. "Much."

"We should . . . probably get out of here before your brothers come back."

She winces. "Yeah . . . Not a conversation I'm dying to have. Ever, maybe."

I don't know why that makes *me* want to wince—it's not as if I'm dying for her to tell her brothers about us either—and yet the idea of her keeping it a secret . . . irks me. Is that my instincts, residual feelings from my past experiences, or is it just . . . me?

"You go to bed," I tell her, trying not to dwell on it too much. "I'll clean up."

She nods as she finds her underwear and wriggles back into them, then climbs out of the tub, grabbing for her robe to hastily put it on. I watch all this, mostly because I can't seem to tear my eyes away from her. I'm fighting the urge to drag her back here and touch her some more. Something that is proving to be incredibly difficult.

"Good night," she calls from the door. She makes a face. "I feel like I should say thank you. Is that weird?"

A laugh burbles out of me. "No weirder than anything else that's been happening."

"Well . . . thank you," she says with a soft chuckle. "I'll see you tomorrow?"

I nod at her, watching her go back into the lodge as if she didn't just turn my world upside down in what was possibly the most gratifying sexual experience I've ever had—furious as it may have been.

But more pressing than the thought of what just happened, more urgent than wondering what it will mean if we keep doing it . . . is the overwhelming realization that I don't want to stop.

15

Tess

"I CAN'T BELIEVE you were in a hot tub with an actual mountain man with washboard abs—"

"I never said he had washboard abs."

"Of course he has washboard abs, Tess, but still I—"

"You've never even seen him, how do you know—"

"All wet and steamy and close together—"

"We were sitting across from each other I already told—"

"—and you didn't let him clean your pipes."

"Sorry for disappointing you," I huff.

"I'm kidding," Ada says. "I'm glad you got to relax. I just wish you would've done it, you know, naked. Preferably in the afterglow of some hot lovemaking. Maybe on a bearskin rug. Oh my God, is there a bearskin rug there?"

"I feel like it's not in my best interest to answer that question."

"*There is*," she hisses with glee. "So spill. Did anything salacious happen? I haven't had a real date in six years, Tess. You have to give me this."

I feel my face flush as I remember what happened in the hot tub. I still haven't told Ada *everything*—and at this point, I'm not even sure why. Maybe it's because I'm still figuring things out when it comes to my new life, or maybe I've just wanted to keep the bubble Hunter and I have made for a little while longer.

But I know I can't stave Ada off forever.

"Well . . . *something* might have happened."

"Oh my God. If you don't spill right now . . ."

I chew at my bottom lip. "Well . . . there have been some . . . weird things happening."

"Penis-related things?"

I roll my eyes. "You know, for someone so anti-dating, you sure do think about penis a lot."

"If you'd sworn off chocolate, you'd think about it a lot too. Now spill."

"I mean, the doctor said there might be some weird side effects, right?"

"Right."

"Well . . . there have been."

"I swear to God if you don't start making sense soon . . ."

"It turns out that Hunter is actually an alpha."

"You're kidding."

"I am not."

"That's gotta be hell on your hormones."

"You can say that again," I huff. "Not long after we met, I started having these . . . mini heats."

There is silence on the other end of the line for several seconds before: "*I swear, if you fucked the hot innkeeper and didn't tell me—*"

"I didn't!" I protest. "I mean, not really."

"Not *really?*"

"We may have done . . . some things."

"But not sex."

"Not sex."

Not yet, my brain taunts.

It's something that has been playing on a loop in my head since last night. Thoughts of how close we got, how much we *have* done—and what more we might do if this continues.

But mostly . . . I can't stop thinking about how much the thought appeals to me more and more every time I touch Hunter.

"Oral?"

"I'm not telling you that," I scoff.

"At least tell me you touched his penis."

"Please stop saying 'penis,'" I grouse. "But . . . yes. I did."

"Fuck me. That's perfect," she sighs. "Did you see his knot? That's really the only thing they have going for them in my opinion."

"Wait, you know about the knot thing?"

She goes quiet for a moment, her voice softer when she says, "Perry's dad was an alpha."

"Why didn't you ever tell me?"

"I don't exactly like talking about him. You know that. And it wasn't really relevant until now."

And I do know that. I feel guilty for bringing it up, even inadvertently. I know how sore a subject Perry's dad is for Ada. I try to steer the conversation away from him.

"I didn't even know knots existed until last night."

"And? How was it?"

I blush furiously, remembering the way I touched him.

"It was . . ." My face flames further, thinking about how unbearably hot it was to touch him like I did. "It was interesting."

"You're going to have to get me a picture of this guy soon. I need a face to put to the fever dream."

"Sure, I'll just ask my hookup shifter teacher for a selfie so I can show him off to my friend. That won't make me look like a weirdo at all."

"But a very cute weirdo," she teases. "You said you talked too, right?"

"We talked about the lodge a bit," I tell her. "I get the sense things aren't doing as well as they could be."

"I mean, I don't have to remind you that it's basically Nowheresville."

"But I was thinking about my friend Nate at *Travel Quarter*," I venture. "He covers places like Hunter's lodge all the time. Little hidden gems."

"And you're thinking of saving the day, huh?"

"I don't know . . . I just thought it's the least I could do. He and Jeannie are so great. I don't want to see this place fail. I don't think I'd be able to sleep at night if we did all this work and the place still went under."

"Out of the goodness of your heart, huh?"

"Well, yeah. What other reason would I have?"

"I think you *like* Hunter."

"Don't be ridiculous," I deny quickly. "We're . . . friends. Who help each other."

"Are you trying to convince me or yourself?"

I bite my lip briefly before I groan, "Maybe both."

"Fine, fine. You only want to *help*. So call Nate."

"I think I should."

"And when you land Hunter an interview, you two can celebrate with another romp in that hot tub. Preferably with more penetration next time."

"Don't say 'penetration' either."

"Seriously. It's got to be some kind of sexy serendipity that the same day someone tells you that you're suddenly an omega and your hormones go haywire, a bearded hottie alpha walks right off the cover of one of those romance novels you read to save your God-tier vagina."

"It's hard enough to look him in the eye after everything we've done without *that* in my head," I groan.

"Let him save you, Tess," Ada says dramatically. "Let him save you with his pen—"

"Liking you less and less by the second."

"Whatever. You know you lo—Shit." There's a bit of activity on the other line before: "Grace is looking for me. Call you later?"

"Fine, fine. Go kick ass. I'll still be here."

"Hiding, daydreaming, thinking about Hunter's huge—"

"*Go.*"

"Okay, okay."

I lean back against my bed's heavy wooden headboard and let out a sigh, eyeing the outfit I still need to put on to meet Cat and her boyfriend tonight. Despite my protests, I guess there's really nothing better to call what I've been doing today except *hiding*—feigning a headache to stay holed up in my room so I can avoid seeing the object of all my confused feelings.

Sleeping was almost impossible last night, given that every time I almost drifted off I would remember Hunter's hands and Hunter's body and just . . . *Hunter*, and I'd get flustered in a way that I've never been before in regard to a man.

I think back to my past relationships, and I cannot for the life of me remember feeling so . . . *giddy* over them. I feel like a damn teenager with the way I can't seem to get my hormones under control.

I think you like *Hunter.*

I mean, that really is ridiculous, isn't it? I mean, sure, I like him, but I don't *like him* like him, do I?

I snort at myself mentally. What am I, fifteen?

I think back to Nate and the way Hunter was so sure the lodge would hold no interest for him or the magazine, and it makes me question what exactly my reasons *are* for wanting to help. Is it simply for the sake of being nice, or do I want to help because it's *Hunter*?

Sometimes I don't even know how we're keeping the lights on.

I decide the why isn't important—or rather, I don't want to know the why right now—and before I can second-guess myself, I'm scrolling through my contacts in search of Nate's office number.

"Good morning," a receptionist greets me when the line connects. "Thank you for calling the business office of *Travel Quarter*. How can I help you?"

"I was wondering if Nate might be available to talk right now."

"I can check on that for you," she says sweetly. "May I ask who's calling?"

"Tess Covington."

"Hold one moment, please," she answers.

The seconds that tick past while I sit on hold feel much longer than they actually are, and each one that goes by only makes my heart rate pick up that much faster. Nate and I have always been on good terms; I've sent him plenty of material and photos over the years that he's used in past articles—and honestly, he's just a cool guy in general. He and his husband, Glenn, host a Christmas party every year that I never miss, but I've never called to ask him for a favor like this. Is it unprofessional somehow? Is he going to see right through me immediately and know I'm pulling strings for a guy I'm hooking up with?

Right as my anxiety is starting to get the better of me and I've nearly talked myself into hanging up the phone and giving up on this whole thing, I hear the line connect once again on the other end, and a familiar voice comes through.

"Tess. Hey. I'm so sorry I haven't checked in. It's been crazy over here."

I breathe out a sigh of relief. "No problem."

"How are you? I've been following your channel as best I can with work. Everything still good?"

"Everything is great," I tell him. "We've been talking to HGTV about a possible show."

"You're kidding," he says excitedly. "Glenn is going to lose his shit."

"How is he doing?"

"Oh, you know. Same old. Terrorizing my editorial department." Nate laughs. "Never work with your spouse."

I smile, remembering all too well how high-strung Glenn can be. "I miss you guys," I say honestly. "We need to get together when I'm back in California."

I ignore the sudden pang in my chest when I think about leaving Colorado.

That's new.

"We do," he agrees. "But wait, where are you? Are you not in Newport Beach?"

"Well, actually . . . that's why I was calling you."

"Oh? I'm intrigued."

"So I'm working on this little ski lodge in Pleasant Hill, Colorado . . ."

"Googling now."

"It's very small."

"I'll say," he laughs. "Jesus, you can barely see it on the map."

"It's so pretty here though," I assure him. "The lodge needs a little TLC—which we're already working on—but the area is gorgeous, and the town is practically Hallmark-worthy."

"People do love that seclusion factor," he remarks.

"It's the *picture* of seclusion," I urge. "I mean, seriously. It's basically the old country out here. A while back, they built some highway straight to Denver that bypasses the town, and ever since then, it's been like this little hidden gem tucked away in the mountains."

"What kind of reno are we talking?"

"Mostly cosmetic at the moment. We've already gotten underway on a lot of the main area—I think we could have it spruced up enough for pictures in another week, maybe."

"Hmm." I can practically hear Nate thinking over the line, a faint tapping sound coming from what I assume is his pen against his desk. "So, we're actually doing a piece in the next issue called 'Secret Getaways.'"

"Oh my God, that's perfect."

"*But*."

I frown. "Oh no."

"*Technically* . . . it's already getting ready for print. I don't know if I can squeeze in another location."

I get a sinking feeling in my stomach. "Damn."

"*But*," he says again.

I perk up. "A good 'but'?"

"*Maybe* I could convince my editor."

"Nate. You're an angel."

"I know," he laughs. "I mean, no guarantees, just in case—but I've been known to be pretty persuasive. Do you have any pics you can send me?"

"Yes! I can text them to you."

"That's perfect. I'll get it done, don't worry. Call it an I'm-sorry-I-haven't-checked-in gift."

"Don't even worry about it. I know how busy you guys are at the end of the month."

"I'll be sure to get back to you as soon as I can," he assures me. "Keep me updated about HGTV, yeah? We're rooting for you."

"I will." My face splits into a grin. "Thank you. Seriously."

"Talk to you soon, doll."

"Bye, Nate."

I squeal giddily when I hang up, flouncing sideways to lie across the bed as elation wells inside me. It feels so good to be doing something again, even if it's for Hunter's benefit and not my own.

I've got to tell Hunter.

I imagine he'll be excited, right? I think back to what he said last night and his attitude about the whole thing, and surely he'll be grateful to find that someone *is* actually interested in this place, right? Of course free publicity will do nothing but good for the business.

Unless he thinks it's none of *my* business, that is.

Oh shit.

I hadn't even considered that. What if he gets angry that I would try to do something like this without his actual permission? I mean, it's not like we're old friends. We're barely even friends with benefits. Is it weird that I would go out of my way to help him like this?

I think you like *Hunter.*

I roll face-first into the quilt and make a frustrated sound.

16

Hunter

WHEN NOON ROLLS around the day after Tess's and my . . . incident in the hot tub and I still haven't seen her, it leaves me anxious. I can't help but worry that I overstepped somehow, because when I offered to help her, it was about *her*, and yet when she offered to touch *me*, I couldn't bring myself to say no. The memory of her small hands wrapped around my knot and the head of my cock resting in her mouth will be seared into my brain until long after I'm dead, to be sure.

I work through my anxiety by spending the morning in my other form; being on four legs always makes it easier for me to think, and if it means I'm farther away from the lodge and not constantly checking the stairs to see if Tess appears, all the better. The snow under my paws is like a balm on my fevered brain, cooling the heat of the memories there.

It took every bit of my restraint not to ask for more from Tess, not to beg her to let me drag her up to my room and bury myself between her legs. Hands, tongue, cock—I'm not even particularly picky about how. I'm just finding that with every time I touch her, it only makes me want to touch her *more*. And deep down, I know that's dangerous. There's a risk to keeping up what we've been doing, one that could end in the same heartache I'm more than familiar with, and yet ... I can't seem to stop.

I tell myself I could, if it came down to it. If Tess came to me and said she was all better, that she didn't need my help anymore, I could put aside this aching want I seem to feel for her constantly and simply be her friend. But I know that the longer we keep this up ... the less true that will be.

I'm plodding back toward the lodge when the sun reaches the highest point in the sky, deluding myself with platitudes about Tess *not* being the reason I'm heading back. That I'm *not* returning early only to check on her.

But that would be polite, right? I mean, after last night ... wouldn't it be gentlemanly to see how she's feeling? What she's thinking? I don't know the protocol, and it's starting to drive me up the wall.

My clothes are in a small bag tied to a tree just out of sight from the back deck, and I quickly change back into them before stomping through the snow toward the lodge. I notice people piling out the back door as I approach—Tess's brothers stepping outside, without Tess among them, I immediately note.

As I climb the stairs, I nod my head at Thomas, who does a double take, pausing what he was saying to Chase and Kyle as he notices me approaching. "Oh, hey, man."

"Hey," I answer.

"Settle something for us," he goes on. "Who's hotter, blondes or brunettes?"

I feel like this is a conversation I *shouldn't* be having with the brothers of the woman I've been casually messing around with, but that doesn't stop my mouth from opening to immediately answer, "Brunettes."

"Told you," Chase says smugly.

Kyle rolls his eyes. "I think both of you are idiots."

"What about 'blondes have more fun'?" Thomas points out.

"I think that only applies when they aren't dealing with meatheads like you," Kyle scoffs.

"You're just still sore about Heather Jenkins," Thomas says.

Kyle's brow wrinkles. "Who?"

"That cheerleader from high school who called you a nerd," Chase supplies.

Kyle, who is definitely not as beefy as his brothers, turns a slight shade of pink. "She didn't call me a *nerd*."

"She said you were too smart for someone like her," Thomas reminds him.

"That's code for nerd," Chase adds.

I try to sneak past them, thinking that this conversation really isn't for me, but Thomas stops me. "Hey, you coming to Fred's tonight? Tess made a friend in town who invited all of us."

"That would be Cat," I tell him.

"Is she hot?" Chase asks.

My lips quirk. "She's practically married."

"Ugh, bummer," Chase sighs. "This town's too small. There are barely any women here."

"You'd have better luck in Denver, I think," I tell him.

Thomas nods eagerly. "We're going there tomorrow. Boss is giving us the weekend off so we can go sow our wild oats."

"And pick up supplies," Kyle corrects.

Chase waggles his eyebrows. "Yeah, but if we find a little strange on the side . . . Know what I mean?"

"Not really, no," I say.

Chase cocks his head. "You don't have a girl?"

Don't think about their sister. Don't think about their sister.

"Not for a long time, no," I answer. "My last serious relationship... It didn't end well. Haven't really had any desire to try to start over yet, I guess."

"You know what they say about getting back on the horse," Chase says.

Thomas nods with a shit-eating grin. "The horse you get on in this scenario being a hot—"

"Please don't finish that sentence," Kyle groans. "Tess would have your balls if she heard you talking like that."

Don't ask. Don't ask. Don't ask—

"Where is Tess, by the way?" I ask like an absolute jackass. "I haven't seen her this morning."

Thomas scratches at his neck. "Checked on her earlier. She said she had some dude to call. I can't remember who."

I feel my skin prickle, and I know that it's none of my business, but suddenly I'm dying to know who that might have been. Surely there's not someone back home she—

No. She wouldn't let me touch her if she was already involved with someone. I know she's not like that. She's not like Chloe. She isn't.

"You should come out tonight," Thomas presses. "You don't seem to get out much, dude."

"I'm more of a homebody," I tell him.

Thomas nods. "Yeah. Totally had theories that you were a vampire when I first met you."

"What?" I can't help it, I laugh. "Vampires aren't real."

"Dude, werewolves are real, why can't vampires be?"

"First of all," I say, chuckling, "'werewolf' isn't really the proper term. Shifters can change at will. A werewolf can only change during the full moon. I would know."

Thomas's mouth forms an O shape. "Oh shit. Tess mentioned that."

This gives me pause, wondering how much she's told them. Surely if she'd informed them about what she was, she would have told me, right?

"She did?"

"Yeah, she said you were talking about accommodations," Chase says.

"Dude," Thomas chimes in, his face lighting up with excitement. "Can you show us? I've always wanted to see that."

"You know I have to get naked for it, right?"

Kyle shoves Thomas's shoulder. "You basically asked him to strip."

Seeing a blush on the big man's face is sort of hilarious.

"I didn't think about that," he mutters.

"Maybe some other time, yeah? I just got back in from a run, actually," I tell him. "I have a few things to do."

"Sure," Thomas says with a bob of his head. "We're out here waiting on a call from Dad. My phone gets shit service inside."

This gives me pause. "Your dad?"

"Yeah. He's calling to check in on the project."

Despite it not really being my business, I can't help but ask. "How is he? Tess told me a bit about his health."

"He's . . . okay," Kyle says. "Or at least he pretends to be." A sigh escapes him. "He doesn't like worrying us."

"Typical dad behavior," I comment.

"Yeah," Chase says. "It drives Tess bonkers. She likes to mother him."

"They seem really close," I point out.

Thomas laughs. "Oh, Tess has always been a daddy's girl. I swear, sometimes I think *she's* his favorite son."

He doesn't say it with malice, more like with fondness that comes from them all being so close. It makes my chest hurt faintly, remembering what having that was like.

"How did she end up the boss of this operation anyway? Is she the oldest?"

Thomas shakes his head. "Nah, I am. Then Kyle, then Tess, then Chase."

"None of us really have a sense for business," Chase tells me.

Kyle shrugs. "We've always been better at taking orders than giving them. It just kind of happened that way."

"And it doesn't feel weird? Working for your sister?"

"Nah, she's a good boss," Thomas tells me. "She's got a great eye for that side of things."

"That's really cool of you guys to be so supportive," I tell them. Deciding it's best to extricate myself from the conversation before I say too much, I clap Thomas on the shoulder. "I'd better get inside. I have some paperwork to go over."

"Sure, man. If you change your mind about tonight, we're leaving at seven. We're all going to pile into my truck."

I can't pretend that the thought of Tess in a bar with other men doesn't leave a sour taste in my mouth, but I remind myself that it's none of my business what she does. She doesn't *belong* to me. No matter what we've been doing. Still, the surge of jealousy hits me so strongly that I almost cave right then and there.

"I'll think about it," I tell them.

"Cool," Kyle answers with a grin. "Might be nice to have another guy there whose sole focus isn't bedding the locals like these two."

A chuckle nearly escapes me, and I'm gathering that Kyle is a lot more like Tess than he is his brothers.

"Oh, hey, Hunter . . ."

I turn back, finding Thomas looking at me with narrowed eyes. "Yeah?"

He lowers his voice. "How do you feel about garlic?"

It takes everything in me not to burst out laughing, the seriousness of his expression making it even harder.

"You know, it's always burned my throat. Never really could stand the stuff."

Thomas's eyes widen, and when I turn away to reach for the door, I swear I hear him whispering, "See? Are we sure he isn't actually a—"

I leave them on the back deck, where I can already hear Kyle berating Thomas, and a quick sweep of the great room reveals it to be empty, no Tess in sight. When I reach the front desk in the foyer, I glance at the stairs, feeling that same urge to go and check on her but unsure whether it would be weird or not. I worry that *she* might feel weird after last night, and I worry that seeking her out might make it worse.

I tell myself that I should leave it in her hands as I settle on my stool behind the front desk, trying to distract myself with the bank statements I've been going through. There's plenty of stuff for me to do, and not thinking about a certain omega with big brown eyes and a mouth that literally haunts my dreams should be easy enough, given that.

Still doesn't stop me from glancing at the top of the stairs every five minutes. I also tell myself that I should shut it down, try to put some distance between us when I'm not . . . *helping* her—otherwise I'm just setting myself up for heartache.

I glance at the stairs again.

God, I am so fucked.

17

Tess

I THINK THE fatal flaw of avoiding someone is that the universe always seems to want to be a bitch about it. Because of course when I come down the main staircase to meet the boys to head to the bar, Hunter is waiting at the front desk, flipping through a notebook of some sort. I pause at the last stair right as he looks up at me, not missing the way his eyes travel from my knee-high boots to my red sweaterdress, all the way up to my face.

"Hey" is all he says.

I try to appear casual even though my heart rate has quickened considerably. "Hey. Hanging out?"

"Just going over some invoices," he tells me.

"You know, Excel would make that a whole lot easier."

"I like pen and paper."

I smile even as I roll my eyes. "Of course you do. Probably reminds you of better days when we used oil lamps."

His mouth twitches but only slightly. "You look nice."

I tuck my chin to my shoulder and bat my eyelashes exaggeratedly. "Oh, do I?"

"It's a far cry from the coveralls you were wearing yesterday."

Talk of yesterday only hurtles me back into hot tub hijinks that make my face flush, and I shift my weight from one foot to the other, hoping Hunter doesn't notice.

"We're meeting Cat and her boyfriend at Fred's tonight."

Hunter raises an eyebrow. "Oh?"

"Apparently it's the only bar in town."

His mouth quirks. "Does that shock you?"

"Not really," I laugh. "But I was promised the best cheese fries in the state, so . . ."

"Just don't ask how they make them," Hunter warns me, still smiling a little as he turns his attention back to his papers. "Your arteries might shrivel up."

"Do you *ever* go?"

He peeks up at me inquisitively. "To Fred's?"

"No, to Disneyland."

He rolls his eyes. "It's been awhile."

"Well, how can I trust your opinion on cheese fries if you haven't even been in a while?"

"Those things are pretty hard to forget."

He's reading again, not looking at me, and I bite the inside of my cheek as I consider asking him to go. That wouldn't be weird, right? I mean, with everything that's happened between us . . . it would be almost rude not to at least *invite* him. The worst he could do is say no, so what's the harm?

He could say no.

Right. That might be a bummer.

Come on, Tess. Don't overthink it.

"You could come with us," I say as casually as I can. "Give those cheese fries another try."

Hunter's expression is unreadable when he looks back up,

eyes locking with mine for a few seconds as he (at least I hope) considers.

I can tell the moment he decides to shoot me down. "I've got a lot of stuff to do around here tonight." He's nice enough to give me a teasing smile so I don't completely want to disappear. "We don't have Excel, after all."

I try to smile back, but I'm not entirely sure it hides my disappointment. "That would be too easy."

"I like doing things the hard way," he tosses back with a laugh.

Now why does *that* make my stomach flutter?

Am I actually a horny cartoon wolf and simply unaware?

"Just thought I'd ask," I tell him breezily. "No big deal or anything."

There's a stretch of silence as I fidget, trying not to be embarrassed about being shut down. I bite at the end of my thumbnail absently while I try to appear as if I'm not watching him work. It's only that his dark curls sort of fall into his eyes with his head bent like it is, and the way his flannel shirt (green this time) is rolled at the sleeves . . . I'm just saying. Forearm porn could be a thing if we believe hard enough.

"So, um," I start nervously, averting my eyes to my lap as I attempt a casual tone. "I called my friend today. The one from *Travel Quarter*."

Hunter tenses, his hands going still on the paper as he looks back up at me. "What?"

"I thought . . . I don't know. I just wanted to reach out to him. It really stuck with me, what you said last night, and I know that this place could do well if someone gave it half a chance."

His expression remains blank, eyes flicking down to the wooden countertop as if thinking. "Huh."

"Are you mad?"

"What?" He seems confused when he looks back up. "Mad? I mean . . ." His mouth opens and closes briefly as if considering his words. "I'm not mad. I just . . . Why do you want to help so much? Or I guess I mean . . . more than you already are."

Don't start asking questions that I don't even know the answers to myself, buddy.

I shrug as nonchalantly as I can manage. "It's not a big deal," I say weakly. "It was just a phone call."

"Uh-huh." I can feel him looking at me even when I'm still too afraid to look up. "And what did your friend say?"

"After he saw the photos, he said he thinks this place has real potential. He's talking to his editor about getting it a page in the next issue for this 'Secret Getaways' segment they're doing." I realize how presumptuous I sound. "I mean . . . that is . . . if you even *want* that. It would mean we'd have to do an interview. Plus, we'd have to really speed up the timeline to get the foyer done next week. And then we would need to make sure you own something that isn't flannel. Actually, maybe people would dig the flannel. We could—" I *do* look up then, catching the strange expression on his face. "What?"

"You keep saying 'we,'" he says, almost like a question.

"Oh." I feel my neck heat. "Well . . . of course I wouldn't mind helping you get ready for it. You've been helping me out—"

"I didn't offer to help you to get anything in return."

"—and Jeannie has been cooking for me this entire time—"

"That's part of your stay."

"—and I just want to help, okay?"

He looks at me again with that expression I can't make heads or tails of, causing me to question everything I've done as I start to worry all over again that I've overstepped. He doesn't say anything in response to the things I've said, and I can feel myself about three seconds from beginning to squirm before I blessedly hear the horn honk outside.

"Oh shit. That's my brothers," I half sputter as I push up from the chair. "Just . . . think about it, okay? He's supposed to call me back soon, but if it's not something you want, I totally respect that. But I thought it couldn't hurt to call."

Hunter nods as he watches me go, and still I can *feel* his eyes on me, even when I don't look back. Outside the cold air seems extra icy as I shrug into my coat, and I can only imagine that it's because my face is most likely as red as my lipstick. Thomas is leaning out the window of his jacked-up Chevy, waving me over, and I pick up the pace as I try not to think about the innkeeper I'm leaving behind. Mostly trying not to be embarrassed about the way I just railroaded his life and, even worse, the way he flat out rejected my attempt at sort of somewhat asking him out.

Told you he could have said no, my brain mocks.

As I climb into the truck, I think to myself that it really is a bummer.

"—AND I WAS telling Jarred about the time you renovated that cabin in Wyoming," Cat is rattling off as we step inside the bar, tapping snow off our shoes. "That kitchen lives rent free in my brain. Not to mention flooring! One day I definitely want to—"

"Babe, take a breath," Jarred laughs. "You're going into overdrive."

Cat looks sheepish even as her boyfriend throws an arm around her. "Sorry."

"It's fine," I assure her as I follow them toward a booth against the wall. "I really loved that project."

Fred's is both everything and nothing like I expected—scuffed wood flooring that's seen better days, a massive hand-carved bar that stretches down one side of the entire room parallel to a line of red leather booths on the opposite wall, and an array of sometimes-cracked neon signs that range from beer brands to half-naked ladies.

It's sort of amazing, actually.

Cat and Jarred pile in on one side of the booth as I take the other, his head coming a good foot above her petite frame even when sitting. His hair is tied back with an elastic, and his light brown skin complements her olive tones in a way that has them looking like some sort of model couple. He throws an arm around her shoulders as he stretches out, scratching at his neat beard absently as he turns to crane his neck toward the bar in search of a waitress.

It strikes me how good they look together, but it also makes me more painfully aware of the fact that I'm a third wheel here, since my brothers immediately disappeared into the crowd.

I lean forward on my elbows right as Jarred is waving over a waitress. "So how long have you been dating?"

"Almost . . . eight years now?" Cat looks over at Jarred slyly. "Took him awhile to notice me."

"Probably couldn't see your short ass until then," Jarred quips just before she elbows him in the side.

"I had the biggest crush on him in high school," Cat barrels on. "But then again, everyone did. He and Hunter sort of had a monopoly on dates back then."

"Wait, Hunter?" I have a hard time keeping the shock from my voice. "*Hunter* had a monopoly on dates?"

"Right?" Cat laughs easily. "I know it's hard to imagine now since he's constantly playing the quiet game with himself, but he used to be sort of a flirt back in the day." She makes a face at her boyfriend. "Not as much as *this* one, mind you."

Jarred rolls his eyes. "I didn't date *that* much."

"Do you know how many girls I had to watch you and Hunter bring through the movie theater? My poor little teenage heart was just wishing you'd look my way when you bought your popcorn."

Cat sighs heavily, and Jarred simply shakes his head, smiling. "Did she tell you she was head of the drama club back in school?"

"Whatever." Cat shrugs. "Anyway, so I'd been working at the store since I graduated when Jarred came back to town from college, and he came in looking for a sweater—he wanted this *horrible* argyle number I'd ordered completely by mistake—and I managed to talk him into a different pullover instead." She looks smug then. "He was *totally* staring at my chest the entire time. Practically begged me for my number."

Jarred makes a face. "I wasn't staring at your chest the *whole* time."

"Needless to say," Cat continues, ignoring him, "teenage Cat was fist-pumping."

"Okay, but opening a boutique practically right out of high school and keeping it up and running this long is pretty impressive," I note, changing the subject.

Cat waves me off. "It was my mom's store before I took over. I can't take all the credit."

"Bullshit," Jarred scoffs. "That place was going under when you took over." He gives me a pointed look. "She brought that store out of the red in, like, the first year."

"That's amazing," I say, genuinely impressed.

Cat tries to look modest, biting back a grin as she shrugs. "I like clothes."

Jarred leans in to press a kiss to her hairline, and even despite their teasing and pseudo bickering, it's obvious how much they love each other. It's enough to make anyone a little jealous. I know—because Cat told me—that they're a human beta couple, and I can't help but think back to a time when my life was as simple as that. When I wasn't constantly searching the air for notes of sunshine and rain and going through fits of need that feel like they could consume me from the inside out. Not to mention the days when I *didn't* turn into a wolf at will.

I wait for the moment to pass before asking Jarred the staple conversation starter. "So, what do you do?"

"I manage my dad's car lot," he tells me. "It's not a giant cabin in Wyoming, but it pays the bills."

"Hopefully it pays the bills to build our own giant cabin," Cat mumbles.

Jarred laughs, shaking his head at her before he gives me his attention again. "My grandpa built the lot back in the seventies when this place was still dirt roads and wooden buildings. My dad took over when he retired, and I guess I just never thought of doing anything else. Went and got my business degree to try to bring the place into the twenty-first century, you know?"

"I hear that," I say with a smile. "I actually did the same thing."

"Really?" Cat asks. "I knew you'd been doing it for a long time, but . . ."

I nod back at her. "My dad had a stroke the summer before I

went to college. It was clear pretty quickly he wouldn't be able to return to work. He was so bummed out about the business. My brothers are great at what they do but never had any interest in running the place—well, maybe Kyle, but he's never really been the boss type. His words, not mine."

"That's so badass though," Cat says. She swivels her head. "Where are your brothers, anyway?"

"Probably talking to anything with tits and legs, if I had to guess," I snort. "They're kind of predictable that way."

An older woman interrupts us at the table before I can add anything else, taking our drink orders and jotting them down on a little pad before making her way back to the bar.

"So," Jarred asks after the waitress leaves. "How's my buddy the hermit? Is he coming out of his cave?"

My brow furrows. "Hunter?"

"I tried to get him to come down from his mountain," Jarred says. "Gave me some bullshit about being busy."

I press my lips together briefly. "He told me the same thing."

"At least he's talking to you," Cat laughs. "Pulling conversation out of him is like pulling teeth sometimes."

I consider all the quiet teasing and the dry jokes over the last few days—not to mention everything *else* we've done—and I don't know if I can fully agree with that. "I don't know," I say nonchalantly. "He talks occasionally." I give a noncommittal shrug. "He's been helping me a lot since I got here."

In a lot of ways, I think.

Cat and Jarred share a look of incredulity, turning back to me with matching expressions of disbelief. "Hunter?" Jarred's voice holds actual surprise. "Hunter Barrett? Mountain man–looking dude? Smiles, like, never?"

I'm laughing at Jarred's description, finding it not much different from my own first impression of Hunter. "I mean, he can be kind of quiet sometimes, but once you get him talking, he's really—"

"Are we talking about me?"

My words die on my tongue, my heart doing this Pavlovian thing where it picks up a few dozen beats all at once. Jarred's face splits into a grin as he slides out of the booth to embrace the newcomer in a hug, and it takes me several more seconds to peek up and confirm what I already know.

That Hunter has taken me up on my invitation after all.

"Hunter? What are you doing here?"

Hunter pulls away from Jarred's hug to look at me. "I was invited, remember?"

"I thought you said you were busy," I accuse, still mostly just surprised to see him here.

He slides into the booth next to me, his big body now flush against my side in the small booth as he eyes me with that quiet expression that never tells me anything he's thinking. His scent washes over me, calming me and yet lighting me up all at once, and I have to resist the urge to lean into it as he settles.

"Took less time than I thought it would," he says easily. He flashes me a grin. "Found my oil lamp."

Jarred looks ecstatic that he's here, leaning in with his palms flat on the table to get our attention. "We already ordered. What are you drinking? I'll go tell the bar."

"Beer is fine," Hunter tells him. "Whatever you're having."

Jarred snaps his fingers, then points at Hunter with enthusiasm, still looking gleeful. I laugh as he walks away, regarding Cat. "Someone's excited."

"Well," Cat says pointedly with a sly grin. "*Someone* only sees us on holidays." Her eyes find mine as she makes a face, hitching her thumb in Hunter's direction. "This is basically like seeing a unicorn or Bigfoot or something."

Hunter makes an indignant sound. "You're exaggerating."

"Oh, really?" Cat laughs. "I'll buy your drinks for the entire night if you can tell me when we last hung out that wasn't a holiday."

I turn my head to watch Hunter's lips purse in thought as he frowns at the table for a good number of moments before Cat begins to cackle.

"*Yeah*," she says with amusement. "Like I said."

"Whatever," Hunter mumbles. "I'm here now."

I don't miss the way Cat eyes me with that same sly grin. "I wonder why that is."

"Just decided a drink sounded good," Hunter says casually.

"Yeah, yeah," Cat quips. "Well. Whatever. I'm glad you're here. Now you can suffer Jarred's fantasy football updates and leave me to have an actual interesting conversation with Tess."

Jarred approaches the table at that exact moment, sliding back into his spot. "What are we talking about?"

Cat's smile is innocent now. "Oh, nothing."

"Dude," Jarred tells Hunter. "I'm so glad you decided to hang."

"Yeah, well." Hunter gives another shrug. "Tess told me how much you guys were crying about missing me, so . . ."

"I absolutely said no such thing," I laugh.

Hunter's eye catches mine, and he actually *winks*.

Is he trying to kill me?

"I just got bored," Hunter tries again. "No big deal."

Cat looks unconvinced. "Mm-hmm."

I won't pretend I'm not wondering myself what he's doing here, but at the same time, I can't ignore the fact that it almost feels like he... came for me? That's probably so conceited of me, but, I mean, he did, right?

Listen to you. The guy had his tongue between your legs last night, and you're giddy over him showing up to a bar.

Hunter and Jarred are talking when the waitress brings our drinks to the table, passing them around before leaving us to it. Jarred raises his beer bottle in a toast as he waits for us to do the same, and all the glasses and bottles clink together.

"Here's to our very own mountain man coming down the mountain," Jarred says all serious-like. "May it mean six more weeks of winter this year or something."

Hunter laughs as he pulls his bottle to his lips. "Shut up."

I don't miss the way he looks at me as he takes a slow sip of his beer, and I definitely don't miss the way my belly erupts in full-on fluttering in response.

This is going to be a long night.

18

Hunter

THE FUNNY THING about alcohol is that it makes everything seem funnier, makes everything taste better (because yes, the cheese fries at Fred's are as good as I remember), and—in this instance—makes one already very appealing contractor somehow *more* appealing. Only one drink in, and I'm noticing the way her mouth curves around the lip of her bottle, I'm appreciating how nice her laugh sounds when someone catches her off guard. And by my second—probably one more than I should be having in the span of two hours—I'm leaning close enough into her that I'm noticing, not for the first time, how *good* she smells.

The scent of her—warm apples and baked cinnamon and something that is just inherently *her*—is intoxicating. I think I've leaned into a laugh a little harder than I needed to on at least two occasions now, just to have the chance to press my face into her shoulder for another whiff.

Yeah, that's creepy, I know, but sue me.

"Okay," I say, cutting into our loud conversation. "I don't think Tess wants to hear anything about that."

"Oh, on the contrary," she protests. "Tess wants to hear *all* about this."

"I'm telling you," Jarred barrels on loudly, a few beers in himself. "Picture the same lovable Hunter you know now, but, like, maybe fifty pounds lighter—you were a wiry little thing, weren't you?"

"You're one to talk," I snort. "Your lanky ass had to cut extra holes in your belt. Made your ears look huge."

"Oh my God," Cat gasps. "You *did* have those huge ears!" She pats the table excitedly in my direction. "Tess. *Tess*. Jarred used to braid his hair for football, and let me tell you, those things were like satell—"

Jarred claps a hand over his girlfriend's mouth. "Let's not distract ourselves from my story," he chides. "So anyway, imagine baby Hunter. Seventeen. Starting tight end for the Pleasant Hill Panthers. Hot shit, right? So we all make this bet. We said, didn't we?" He laughs at me when he catches me shaking my head. "We said the loser would have to do it, didn't we?"

"You're *killing* me," Tess groans. She snaps her fingers in Jarred's direction. "Focus. What did baby Hunter do?"

"So the coach, like, had the same routine after every practice. Five laps around the field at the end. Every time. Like clockwork. So it's our last practice of senior year; we've got one more game left, and we all make this bet, right? Last person to the showers has to streak naked across the field after the final game."

"Shut up!" Tess gasps.

Jarred is already cackling, his arm around his middle to steady himself. "People talked about Hunter's *tight end* for years."

"This might be the best night of my life," Tess sighs. She pokes me in the ribs. "Make any bets lately?"

I eye her from the side, my mouth curving upward. "I learned my lesson."

"Tess," Cat half shouts. "You have to take a picture with me. You probably *are* the most famous person who's ever come here. I need to document."

"Oh." Tess starts digging in her pocket. "I want one too, actually."

She hands her phone to me, grinning. "Do you mind?"

I smile as I take it from her, and she and Cat lean closer together over the table to smile for the pictures. Cat is gushing over hers when Jarred hands her phone over, and I notice Tess studying the one I took when she gets her phone back.

"Not bad," she tells me. "You might have to change careers."

"Any day now," I chuckle.

"We should take one too," she says suddenly, her eyes a little glazed with alcohol. "Can we?"

This makes me pause for a moment, but after a second I collect myself when she motions me closer. With my head tilted toward hers and her body pressed against me, I am assaulted with that nice, warm scent of hers, and I try not to make it obvious that I'm breathing it in as she holds out the camera selfie-style. Her scent reminds me of all the things that happened last night, and it takes all I have not to pop a boner right here under the table, my inhibitions lowered by the beer.

She elbows me lightly. "Smile, Grandpa. Think about whittling."

"You can't see half your face," I toss back. "Let me just . . ."

I snake an arm behind her back, curling it around her body to pull her in closer to my side. My limbs are warm and heavy enough against her that touching her feels somehow . . . *more* than it actually is. It makes me think of all the other places I've touched her. And all the places I *haven't* yet.

"There," I murmur quietly, so close now that I'm practically speaking directly into her ear. "That's better."

She smiles at the camera even as it takes me a second or two to catch back up to reality and rouse myself from the Tess-related la-la land that I've descended into with her touch. Mirroring her smile, I try not to look too out of sorts when I snap a picture of the two of us. I study it after, grinning like some sort of idiot, only a little fazed when Tess leans in again to peek at it over my shoulder.

"Cute," she says.

"One of us, maybe," I counter.

She laughs at me as she gives me another elbow, and I teeter to the side good-naturedly as if she could actually move me. She seems to notice then that we're alone at the table and cranes her neck over the small crowd milling about the room in search of our friends.

"Where did they go?"

I nod toward the dance floor at the back of the bar. "Never takes them very long."

Sure enough, I can just make out Jarred's ponytail bouncing to the beat of the old country song blaring from the jukebox. He's doing some sort of variation on a line dance as he kicks his feet in time with his much tinier girlfriend, who I can barely make out through the crowd.

"That looks like fun," Tess says in my ear so I can hear her over the music.

I shrug. "Not much of a dancer."

"How do you know?" Her smile is flirtier now, and I can't pretend it doesn't make my heart rate pick up. "Maybe you just haven't tried it in a while."

My brow arches as I turn toward her in the seat. "Are you asking me to dance?"

She bites her lip, shrugging a little before saying, "Maybe. What if I was?"

"Maybe I'd be inclined to give dancing another go," I say huskily. "If you were asking."

Her smile is wide as she shoves me from the booth, and I move to stand without any kind of protest to let her out. She grabs my hand wordlessly as she leads me through the little crowd, and I catch myself enjoying the warmth and weight of her hand holding mine. I *definitely* don't fail to notice the way she curls it slightly to envelop mine a little tighter.

The song is ending when we step out onto the wooden dance floor, bleeding into something slower, something with a twanging guitar and a crooning voice. She reaches up tentatively to wind her arms around my neck, holding them there as if waiting to see what I might do. I don't leave her waiting long, my hands coming up to rest on her hips. Just the simple touch has my stomach clenching with want. I catch a burst of her scent when I touch her, letting me know she likes it too.

We're both quiet when our feet begin to move across the floor, keeping it to a slow shuffle in time with the music as we sway back and forth. It's admittedly a little difficult, given that I haven't danced in years, but I concentrate on the music and my hands on her as I continue to move. I watch as Tess peers out into the crowd to see Jarred dancing closely with Cat, Jarred leaning down to kiss her as they move, and she smiles at the pair of them, her lips only falling when she turns back to notice that I'm not looking at them anymore.

I'm only looking at her.

"See?" she says sweetly. "You're not so bad."

"Only with you, apparently," I answer quietly.

Her smile really does do something wicked to my insides, and I realize that it has nothing to do with the ways I've had her, or even the ways I haven't yet. No, I'm realizing that when Tess smiles . . . it almost feels like things might be all right in my world. Which is insane given that I've only known her a few weeks.

"So, I'm curious," she prods. "Why did you decide to come? Really?"

That's not an easy question to answer. It involves me going back and forth a million times—imagining all the people who might make her laugh, all the ones who might touch her and dance with her—and recognizing that I hated the idea of any of them not being me.

But I can't tell her that. Not without sounding like I've lost it.

"I didn't thank you earlier," I say instead. "For calling your friend. I probably seemed ungrateful."

"I was thinking maybe you thought I needed to mind my own business," she admits.

I shake my head, not wanting her to feel that way at all. "No. It was . . . really amazing of you to do that for me." I clear my throat, feeling embarrassed. "I mean, for the lodge."

"Right," she answers back with a smile. "For the lodge."

"Plus, it seemed dangerous, leaving you to fend for yourself at this rowdy old bar when you're dressed like that."

"Oh? When I'm dressed like this?" She bats her eyelashes playfully up at me. "You flirting with me, Mr. Barrett?"

That makes me chuckle because: "I don't think I would know how to even if I wanted to."

"Kind of sounds like you're doing a pretty good job of it right now," she says, shrugging one shoulder.

"I think you're kind of drunk," I laugh.

"Oh yeah?" Her smile turns Cheshire-like. "You know what I think?"

Her eyes crinkle at the corners, her scent blooms around us so sweetly, it makes me dizzy despite the ebbing of my buzz, and she looks downright *sinful* when she says, "I think . . . you kind of want to kiss me."

Holy hell, I think, the last rational part of my brain watching as if from a distance. *Tipsy Tess is bold as hell.*

But I do, I realize. Terribly. It's something I haven't done, even with all the ways I've touched her, and I'm just now realizing how much of a travesty that is. Especially given that her mouth looks soft and plump, like it's begging for the imprint of my teeth. I get flashes of images—I see her fingers in my hair and my tongue teasing hers—and I want it so badly at this moment that it feels like a tangible thing, my need.

Maybe it's naivete on my part, the way I'm completely ignoring the distant alarms blaring in my head about the dangers of being so close to her like this, understanding it could trigger another mini heat—but for some reason, I can't find it in me to worry right now. Maybe it's because I'm aware that if it happens, I'll be here to take care of her. That I'm the *only* one who gets to take care of her like that. It's a heady thing to realize.

All I know is that her eyes seem bigger and brighter when she looks up at me under the pulsing lights, that my hands on her waist make my palms burn as if I'm touching her skin directly, and most importantly, that her mouth looks so *soft*. I watch as she starts to press up on her toes gently, and I know I could let her, that her lips on mine would be a revelation I might not recover from—but something holds me back.

Not like this, I think.

"I'd better get you home," I say abruptly, startling her.

Her lashes flutter, not quite processing what I've said at first. She rears back in confusion. "What?"

I can't look at her now; my eyes are scanning the room for Jarred and Cat, then I signal them over. "It's getting late. There's supposed to be a storm this weekend. We should leave before the snow gets bad. Plus, I caught Thomas on the way in. The three of them are moving to a private party at some girl's house. I told them I would make sure you get home."

"I—What? Wait, it feels like you just got here!"

But I'm already pulling her by the hand across the dance floor, finding my friends to offer our goodbyes, watching a dazed Tess accept a hug from Cat.

"This was so fun!" Cat squeezes her tight. "Don't you leave without seeing me again!"

She manages to smile even though she still looks a bit bewildered, and who could blame her? I feel sober now; my brain is whirring instead with how much of an idiot I must be, turning her down like that—but between her being so buzzed and my own insecurities about what that kiss might do to me, what it might mean . . . I feel myself devolving into bit of a mess.

But she's still letting me hold her hand, oddly enough, and I weave her through the crowd until we're out in the cold, then I drape my coat around her shoulders before I shepherd her to the Bronco. The cold air is good for my raging thoughts, and I can tell Tess is switching from confusion to irritation as she snatches her hand away, electing to climb into the car on her own.

Shit.

I can tell she wants to ask me what my deal is as she watches me fold myself into the driver's seat and crank the engine, but she remains quiet, leaning against the passenger window with a slight pout that I would find adorable if I didn't know I'd put it there.

I fiddle with the heat. "Cold?"

I can tell she is, but she's still sulking, so she shakes her head.

She curls her arms around her middle as she leans on the door, watching the lights go by as I drive us out of town and toward the snowy trail that leads to the lodge. The pouting gives way to her inevitable drowsiness after about ten miles, and I notice her eyelids growing heavy when I glance at her again as we leave town.

Even as she drifts off to sleep, I still can't fully say what the hell just happened back there.

SHE'S DISORIENTED WHEN she wakes again, leaning into me as I hold her up to help her inside. She's still wrapped in my coat, and scenting myself on her feels so *right* in a way that terrifies me because it makes me want to mark her up more. I don't really know what's happening to me when it comes to her.

"Almost there," I murmur. "Come on now."

"You're so confusing," she mumbles sleepily. "Where are we going?"

"Putting you to bed," I tell her. "Think you had a little too much."

I tighten my grip around her waist as we stumble into her room, and she falters slightly when we near the bed, clinging to me tighter.

"I'm sorry," she groans. "You're having to take care of me again."

I don't tell her how much I've begun to *like* taking care of her.

"I'm starting to think you're kind of clumsy," I chuckle.

She blows a raspberry. "If you didn't make me so *nervous*."

"Oh yeah?" I can feel myself smiling, but I doubt she sees it with the way her eyelids are drooping again. "In you go now."

I pull off her boots one by one as I tuck her into bed, tossing them to the floor before I pull the covers up and over her. She snuggles into her pillow, and as I shift to leave, I make out the disgruntled sound she makes, her eyes still shut.

"Should have kissed me," she mutters into her pillow.

She's probably right, but even now, my head is a bit messy. I'm thinking about the last time I kissed a woman I cared about, how I thought she was going to be my everything, only for me to learn that I was really nothing to her. For nearly a decade I've avoided ever finding myself in that situation again, and yet here I am, torn up over a woman I barely know. I can blame hormones and biology all day long, but in the end . . . I think it might just be her. Every new thing I learn about her only endears her to me further.

"You're probably right," I answer softly, knowing she can't hear me since her breathing is already starting to even out.

I brush her hair behind her ear, tracing a barely there stroke of my thumb down her cheek. She sighs with contentment as she sinks deeper into the bed, and I finally ease myself away from the mattress to let her sleep.

Reginald's massive form pushes past me when I open the door, jumping onto the foot of her bed and blinking at me with a bored expression. I watch as he curls up in a more comfortable lounging position near her feet, still watching me as if saying, *Yeah, you should have kissed her.*

I snort to myself as I close the door behind me.

Even the cat knows I fumbled this evening.

19

Tess

"FIVE MORE MINUTES," I mumble into my pillow.

It takes me several seconds to realize there's no one actually calling for me, but rather someone *yowling* at me—Reginald, sitting up straight a foot away from me on the bed and making disgruntled sounds. I lift my head to peer over at him, trying to remember how he got in here. Did he sleep with me all night?

At least the cat is starting to like me.

I stretch under the covers as my mouth opens with a wide yawn, blinking away the lingering sleep from my eyes. I feel mostly okay, even though I overindulged last night, but I could have definitely used another hour of sleep.

It takes a little bit for the events of last night to start bleeding back into my thoughts. Lying in bed, I can start to remember laughter and drinks and slow dancing with big, warm hands at my waist—but I can also remember a very embarrassing failed attempt at a kiss, unfortunately. I definitely don't think I misread things, given that Hunter had been so obviously flirting with me—because he *was* flirting with me, wasn't he?—so that means I have no idea as to why he would so blatantly turn me down when I attempted to move things along.

There's a very clichéd warm and fuzzy feeling inside me when I remember him tucking me into bed after bringing me back to my room and even a vague phantom sensation of him touching my cheek that suggests perhaps I wasn't off base at *all* about the flirting.

So what gives?

My window rattles slightly as a howling wind slams against it, breaking me out of my early morning musings, and I sit up in bed and frown when I notice the way the snow is coming down outside. I vaguely remember Hunter saying something about a storm rolling in this weekend, but at the time I thought he'd just been making excuses to get us out of the bar and get his mouth far away from mine. Judging by the size of the snowflakes outside though, I'd say it turns out that part was true.

Which probably explains why it's a little colder in my room than usual. I shiver when I pull the covers away, hopping out of bed and moving to the closet in search of a hoodie and some thick sweats. It's then I notice the lone glass of water and tiny tablets that look to be ibuprofen, and I have to bite back a grin, knowing it was most likely Hunter who left them there.

I don't know what to make of it, the way he takes such care of me, doing so more and more often. In fact, it seems like all he *does* lately is take care of me, and what's more, he might even enjoy doing it. So why did he turn me down last night after everything we've already done?

I settle for grilling him later (maybe, if I can work up the courage), then take the pills and swallow them quickly before resuming my task of finding some sweatpants that don't leave goose bumps on my legs. I'm shoving my feet through the ankle holes when my phone begins to ring, so I stomp across the room while still trying to pull my sweats up and snatch my phone from the bedside table.

"Hello?"

"Hello, Ms. Covington. This is Alisha with Mr. Cole's office. Do you have time for me to put you through for a call?"

Nate, I think excitedly.

"Sure," I tell her quickly. "I have time."

I hear the line go quiet for only a brief moment before: "Hey, Tess. Did I catch you at a good time?"

"I'm staying in a town with barely ten thousand people in it," I say dryly. "Literally all the time is a good time."

I hear Nate laugh on the other end. "Well, maybe this will liven up your day a little. My editor gave me the green light to fly out and do a scoop for the lodge you're staying at."

"Shut up."

"I know. She loved the pictures. Said it reminded her of her favorite Monet painting."

"Which one?"

"I have no idea, but at least she loves them."

"Right." I squeal a little as the realization sets in that some things can still go my way. "This is amazing. When are you flying here?"

"Hmm. What is today . . . Saturday? I'm showing a winter storm scheduled through the weekend that's not supposed to break until Tuesday—so let's say I fly out Wednesday just to be safe? I can probably be there around lunchtime. Do you think you can clean up enough of the main space to get it done?"

We're nearly finished with the great room, but I'm already compiling a mental note of tiny projects that would make a world of difference.

"We can do it," I assure him.

"I'll want to interview the owner . . . What's his name?"

"Barrett," I tell him. "Hunter Barrett."

"Great. It won't be too extensive. Just a little history on the lodge and the area and maybe some info on the best times to visit. The standard stuff."

"That sounds great. This is all so great. I really appreciate you doing this, Nate."

"Of course. It's not like I don't owe you a dozen times over."

"I'm happy to be able to finally cash in," I laugh.

"Well, be careful out there. Forecast is showing this storm is gonna be a doozy. Don't freeze before I get there."

"No promises," I chuckle. "I'll see you next week."

"See you then."

I think I'm actually beaming when I hang up the phone, doing some strange little dance number in place. I already can't wait to see the look on Hunter's face when I tell him.

Thinking of him gets me excited all over again, and I rush out of my room, still pulling on a fresh pair of socks, to bound down the stairs. I don't see him in the main entrance at his desk when I step off the landing, so I start to wander through the rooms at a quick pace, shouting his name excitedly as I move throughout the lodge.

It takes a few minutes for him to appear from the back door that leads out to the deck where the hot tub is. He's rushing inside with a concerned expression when he finds me running around and shouting his name. I'm only a *little* distracted by the sight of him in black coveralls and a thick buffalo plaid coat that makes his dark hair seem darker and his big body seem bigger—but seeing him look distressed brings me out of it.

"Tess? What's wrong? Are you okay?"

I grin even wider, rushing up to him and grabbing his hands. "Nate called me back!"

"Nate?" Hunter glances down between us where I am still gripping his hands, raising an eyebrow before finding my eyes again. "Who is Nate?"

"Sorry, sorry." I shake my head to clear away my excited energy. "My friend. The one from the magazine. He wants to interview you! They're going to fly him out next Wednesday, after the storm passes so he can get pictures of the place."

Hunter's mouth parts in surprise. "Wednesday?"

"Okay, I know that's sort of short notice, but we can totally spruce things up around here with very little effort. We just need to clear out the paint cans and stuff . . . fix some of those railings outside, polish the wood surfaces a little—oh, and we definitely have to give this place a *major* dust-over. I'm talking top to bottom. And those Santa hats should probably come down from the elk head until he leaves, at least. Also, I think we should—"

I finally notice the way Hunter is looking at me—sort of a mixture of shock and confusion as his eyes move from my face to our joined hands and back again—and it's then I realize that in my excitement I marched down here and rushed him with this wild news, the memory of the kiss he rejected only last night momentarily forgotten.

But I'm remembering it now.

I release his hands quickly and let mine hang limply at my side, unsure for a moment what I should do in this situation.

"I'm sorry," I offer, feeling shy now. "I didn't mean to bombard you first thing in the morning."

Hunter shakes his head slowly. "No, it's fine. I thought you might be hurt or something."

"I just got so excited when he called . . . I didn't think. You might not even want all this. God, I'm such an idiot. I didn't even confirm that you wanted all this to happen before I just set up a damn interview for you."

"No, I appreciate it. I . . ." He still looks a little stunned. "He really wants to come out here?"

I nod emphatically. "His editor *loved* the pictures I sent. Said this place reminded her of some old painting or something or other. I don't know. The point is, yes, they want to come if you want them to."

Hunter's brow furrows as he looks down at his feet, thinking. His hands come to rest on his hips as his jaw works subtly, and now I notice the bits of snow clinging to his hair. I reach unconsciously to brush them away, but his head snaps back up right as my fingers slide against the dark curls near his temple.

"Sorry," I squeak. "You've got some . . ."

"Oh." He runs his own hand through his hair to shake away the snow. "Yeah. It's really coming down out there. I was making sure we were going to have enough wood if the power goes out."

"Does that usually happen?"

He turns to grimace at the patio door and the increasingly thick flurry that continues to come down. "If it gets any worse than this . . . I wouldn't doubt it."

"Awesome," I deadpan. "I've always wanted to freeze to death."

Hunter laughs enough I can see that dimple hiding behind his scruff, and I have the odd urge to touch it.

"So," I prod gently. "What do you think? I can cancel this whole thing if you like. I don't want to overstep."

"I just . . ." He reaches to rub at the back of his neck. "Are you sure you want to be wasting your favors on me? I mean . . . on this place?"

"I told you last night," I remind him. "I want to help."

"You never said why though."

I shift my weight from one foot to the other, shrugging. "I know it sounds silly, but when you said you didn't know how long you might stay open . . . I guess . . . it made me sad to think about something happening to it."

"It doesn't sound silly," he says quietly.

"So . . . does that mean you want to do the interview?"

He doesn't answer for a moment, and I keep quiet as I let him mull it over. I can sort of tell when he reaches the decision, nodding to himself as he breathes in deep, then expels a sigh noisily between his lips.

"Okay," he says.

"Okay?"

"Okay. I'll do it."

"Yes!" I half shout. I'm beside myself all over again as I awkwardly hug him without thinking, my arms barely reaching around his middle just as his come up in surprise to make room for me. "It's going to be great," I say against his coat as I give him a squeeze. "And I will totally help you."

Shit, I think, Hunter's scent assaulting my senses as I realize I've gotten ahead of myself again. I pull back carefully, feeling embarrassment heat my cheeks and my neck and even lower in my chest.

But Hunter doesn't look embarrassed.

In fact, Hunter is sort of looking at me like he was last night. He's looking at me like he wants to kiss me.

And that only raises more questions.

Questions I'm still afraid to ask, if I'm being honest. I think there's a part of me that won't like his answer if I prod him about why he doesn't kiss me. I've had my fair share of heartache and disappointment and downright *bullshit* in the men department over the years, and adding *not the hot lumberjack's type* to the list might actually be the thing that pushes me over the edge.

But apparently the universe still hates me—or loves me, depending on how you look at it. The loud sound of a tree limb banging against a window robs me of any chance to ask Hunter anything, even if I *could* find the courage to do so. We jolt apart as the branch gives another loud bang, and Hunter curses under his breath as he scowls at the glass.

"I have to take care of that," he sighs. "Don't want another broken window. I need to finish bringing in the wood anyway before the snow gets too high."

"Right," I say airily, weirdly feeling like pouting all over again. "I'll just . . . go shoot Nate a quick confirmation text."

"Okay." Hunter's eyes linger on mine for a moment as if he wants to say more, but he finally nods. "I'll find you later?"

"I'll be here," I say. "Nowhere else to go and all that."

His mouth quirks. "Right."

He turns back to leave and is nearly through the patio door before I call after him, "Oh, hey, where's Jeannie, anyway? I want to tell her the good news."

Hunter looks at me pointedly, with one hand gripping the doorframe and the other on the handle, his brown eyes seeming to darken a little as they lock with mine. "Jeannie went back down to her place in town this morning. She's riding out the storm there."

"Oh." I feel a bit dazed by the implications of that, especially since even in my hungover state . . . I'm remembering my brothers were supposed to head to Denver early this morning. "So it's just . . . us?"

Hunter nods. "Until the storm passes."

I nod back because that's all my brain can seem to manage, and

Hunter gives me one last lingering look before he disappears outside. He leaves me standing there as I try to remember how to take steps, the reality of what he just said beginning to set in.

Because until this storm passes . . . I'm all alone on a mountain with a hot lumberjack.

One who may or may not want to kiss me.

"FUCK," I HUFF, pulling off my goggles.

The last of the old carpet I've torn up has yielded a nasty surprise, and I stare down at the gaps in the original wood with a frown. Of course, I should have been skeptical when we made it this far without a hitch. Thankfully, I've already filmed a short TikTok highlighting the wood *before* I found this problem. Usually this far into a project we're up to our eyeballs in issues, so I suppose I should be grateful that this is our first one.

The only problem is . . . I'm not entirely sure how to proceed. I wrestle my cell from my pocket, muttering obscenities under my breath as I scroll through my contacts. There's a fifty percent chance he'll just let it go to voicemail because he's lost his phone again, and I wait patiently to see what type of day he's having in that regard.

Fortunately, he picks up on the third ring.

"Hello?"

"Hey, Dad," I say, feeling warmth bloom in my stomach at the sound of his voice. "What're you up to?"

"Same old," he grunts. "Watching *Pawn Stars* reruns."

"Anyone bring anything good?"

"Some rip-off of Elvis's signature."

"Ah," I answer. "I've seen that one, actually."

"Pretty sure we've seen most of them," he chuckles. "Did you need something, kiddo?"

My brow wrinkles as I stare down at the problem at my feet.

"Right, yeah . . . I'm restoring some original hardwood here at the lodge, and I had a question about some gapping."

"Gapping," he echoes.

"Yeah. Some of them seem too wide for filler. I wasn't sure of the best way to move forward."

"If they're that bad, might as well just rip 'em up."

I frown. "The owner wants to keep everything as original as we can. We can't just rip them up."

"Sounds like the owner is kind of fussy," he laughs.

I smile despite myself, finding it mildly hilarious that my dad could be so spot-on about Hunter without ever having met him.

"Maybe a little," I say. "But you'd like him. He's just as ornery as you are."

"I'm nothing of the sort," Dad scoffs.

"Sure you aren't," I laugh. "So do you have any suggestions?"

He hums as he considers, and I hear the creaking sounds of his old recliner as he situates himself. "I reckon you could make a patch out of glue and thin strips of wood."

"Have you done that before?"

"A few times," he tells me.

"Okay, that could work." I clear my throat. "It's looking pretty good so far. We've nearly finished the flooring, and the paneling has been refinished. The boys are in Denver today picking up some more supplies, and once they get back we'll—"

My voice cracks, and my dad doesn't miss it.

"What's wrong?"

I stand there, clutching the phone too tight, feeling my eyes prickle for reasons I can't pin down. "I don't know," I say. "I just miss you, I guess."

"Oh, hon," he sighs. "You can come visit anytime, you know that."

"I know," I tell him. "I will. As soon as I finish here." I hesitate, knowing he doesn't love talking about it, but I can't help it. "How are you feeling?"

"I'm fine," he snorts. "Healthy as a horse. Those doctors don't know what they're talking about."

"Dad," I chide. "You're doing what they say, right?"

"I'm being good," he huffs.

I nod to myself. "And when is your next appointment?"

"Next Tuesday," he tells me. "We're supposed to go over options."

"You let me know what they say, okay?"

"Yeah, yeah," he chuckles. "You're almost as bad as your mother."

"I just worry about you," I admit.

"I'll be fine. I've got some more good years in me, don't you worry."

"Sure, Dad," I manage. "I'll call you later?"

"Sounds good, kiddo. Be safe out there."

"I will. Tell Mom I said hi."

"Can do."

The line goes dead, and I stare at the phone in my hand for a few seconds as I think back on the conversation. He sounded . . . tired. He always sounds tired lately, and that does nothing but worry me. I know from my own research that he *does* have options besides getting a pacemaker put in, but none of them will give him the same life expectancy. Which is why I need to get back to work.

I glance at the gapping wood in the corner I've been working myself into, staring at it like it's the enemy, and maybe it is at this moment. At the very least, it's a good outlet for my frustrations. Deciding that this thinking isn't something I have time for, I pull my goggles back down into place and do what I always do when I'm avoiding my feelings.

I get back to work.

IT MIGHT BE all the nervous energy I'm still carrying after having been told I'll be alone for the weekend with Hunter in a snowy cabin like some sort of cheesy Hallmark movie—only with a heavy dose of sexual tension—but I'm almost grateful when Hunter keeps busy throughout lunch, getting ready for the storm. I scrounge up a sandwich that I eat in my bedroom as I text back and forth with Ada, doing my best to resist the urge to peek out my window every so often to see if I can catch a glimpse of my quiet innkeeper.

Not my *quiet innkeeper*, I mentally correct.

Even an hour after lunch, Hunter is still outside doing this and that (how he isn't freezing to death, I'll never know), and I decide my energy would be better spent doing something productive rather than sitting around.

It takes me a little while to locate what I'm after, but I find a stash of cleaning supplies in a closet just off the kitchen and then a ladder stored away in another on the opposite side of the house. I get to work in the main entry first, ridding the old elk head of his Santa hats before I start dusting and cleaning all the cobwebs from the walls and ceilings. And there are a lot of both, it turns out. I'd wager no one has done this in years, and it takes me a good hour and a half to finish this room. Granted, I polished and organized the front desk after I finished with the walls, then gave the floors a good mopping and the staircase banister a thorough wipe-down. The room looks like a whole new place by the time I'm done.

I figure if we can clean the main rooms and the best bedroom in the place for pictures, that will be more than enough for Nate and his team to print up in the magazine. We can worry about the rest when the interview is over and we have more time.

I notice I'm definitely still thinking *we*. Is that weird?

Probably best not to analyze that one too much.

After a few hours of working up a sweat, I notice it's getting dark outside, the chilled gray of the day deepening into a dusky bluish-black as the sun goes down, and I reckon I could use a shower before dinner. I smile a little to myself as I think about Hunter coming back to a (mostly) clean lodge. I'm smiling at just the thought of Hunter, to be honest.

I peel off my hoodie and sweats and everything else when I'm back in the attached bath off my room, cranking on the shower and sighing in contentment when I feel the hot spray splash across my palm before I step in. My arms are a little sore from reaching to clean the walls for so long, and the hot water feels like heaven against my shoulders, so I stand under the showerhead for a solid minute or two before I finally start lathering shampoo into my hair. The sweet scent of tangerines fills the shower as the steam clouds around me. I close my eyes as I work my fingers through my hair to coat the entire length, spreading the shampoo from roots to ends, taking my time with it.

Which quickly reveals itself to be a massive mistake when all the lights go out.

A lot of things happen all at once when the power is cut. The water keeps running, so that's a plus, but I let out a scream, and the way I push myself against the back wall somehow causes the thick lather I've created in my hair to gloop right into my eyes. Instant burn. And if that's not enough, I do a panicked little dance, still squealing over the sting as I frantically try to wipe the bubbles from my eyes with already-sudsy hands (reason went out the window with the lights, apparently), which means that my feet aren't as steady as I'd like them to be, and I'm a little more off-kilter than I should be when standing under an active spray.

So I find myself falling right on my ass.

Well, more accurately, my ankle, I guess. The pain is instant, the scream is delayed, and the water is constant, spraying down somewhere on my thighs as I continue to yelp from the sharp throbbing just above my foot. And I might think that my bad luck would end there—probably, given that there is little else I can imagine could happen in this tiny little window of five minutes or so—but I would be wrong.

"Tess?" Hunter's slightly panicked voice is in the other room. I can hear it over the shower. "Are you okay? I heard screaming."

"I'm naked!"

Probably not the most pertinent information, but it feels like it at the moment.

I can hear him right outside the door now. "Power is out. Are you okay in there?"

"I slipped," I whine, eyes shut tight and still stinging from shampoo. "I think I might have messed up my ankle."

"Can you move it?"

I give it a try, and I'm able to move it back and forth, but doing so causes a major ache. "Yeah, but it hurts like hell."

"Probably just sprained then. Can you stand up?"

"About that . . ."

"Do you . . . I mean . . . I can help. I won't look."

Oddly enough, I'm more worried about him seeing me in this clumsy state rather than him seeing me naked. *Again*, that is. But he doesn't need to know that.

"I can't see. I have shampoo in my eyes."

I hear the handle click before the door squeaks open, a bit of cold air creeping into the warm bathroom. "Yeah, it's pitch-black in here anyway. No worries."

"Can you get me a towel or something? My eyes are burning."

I can sense him rummaging around in the cabinets for a second before I hear the rustle of the shower curtain. I reach above until my fingers collide with terry cloth, and I yank down the little hand towel he's given me and rub the suds from my eyes. Then I reach up again to grab one of the corner shelves to try to hoist myself up afterward, but my ankle throbs sharply, making me yelp.

"I don't think I can get up by myself," I groan. There's a moment of silence on the other side of the shower curtain. "Hunter?"

"Yeah," he says finally. "Okay. I'm just—Just raise up your arms, okay? I don't want to . . . I just want to make sure I get your hands."

I do as he says, feeling about as mortified as I possibly can at this point, but after a second I feel his hands curl around mine, and he gently starts to tug me upward. It takes a little maneuvering to get me on my feet, and even then I have to sort of stand on one foot while he supports my weight by holding on to my hands. After that we stand there for a bit, neither of us knowing what to do next.

"I have to get this shampoo out of my hair," I say resignedly. "Before the water goes cold."

"Okay," he says a little roughly. "I'll just—Maybe I can—Okay. I'm going to keep hold of your hands, okay? Hop a little to your . . .

right? I think? Just hold on to my hands and lean back to rinse your hair. I've got you."

This too, proves difficult, given that I can't put a lot of weight on my foot, but I manage to sort of sideways moonwalk under the spray like a hobbling magician and finally feel the warm water pouring over my face. I tilt my head back to let it rinse the lingering shampoo from my hair, keeping my eyes shut tight until I'm almost positive I've gotten it all out.

"Okay," I tell him. "I think I've got it. I had a towel on the toilet. Do you think you could . . . ?"

"Yeah," he answers quickly. "Grab one of my hands with both of yours. Keep steady."

I do it, gasping a little when I feel the brush of his hand against my hip.

"Shit," he hisses. "Sorry. I'm just trying to turn the water off."

"I-it's fine," I manage, my skin feeling too warm where he's touched me. "Hurry up with the towel. It's cold in here now."

"Okay, I've got it." He gives my hands a tug. "Can you step out?"

"Maybe? Let me just—*Fuck*."

He catches me, because of course he does. I'm fully aware that my naked, wet boobs are pressed to what I think is flannel (let's be real, of course it's flannel), and I can feel the bite of a shirt button pressing into one of my nipples. One of his hands is still wrapped in both of mine, but the other—the one that was holding the towel—is now wrapped around my upper arm, holding me steady against him.

God, and his *scent*. It's not a combination that should be mouthwatering, but I find myself wanting to lick him all the same.

Neither of us speaks at first—hell, I might not even be breathing—but it really is getting colder by the second, and a cold, wet ass is one heck of a motivation to not let awkwardness get the best of you.

"Don't say one word about me being clumsy."

His hand might flex at my arm, but I'm not sure. "I wasn't going to say anything."

"The towel," I mumble, my voice still sounding too loud now that the water is off. "Can you wrap it around me?"

"Yeah," he breathes. "Just . . . hold still."

No trouble there, I think. Even though when I'm standing this close, I'm assaulted again by the warmth and scent of him. So much so that it makes something pulse low in my belly. Makes me even more aware of the fact that I'm naked with him. *Again.*

His hands move over me carefully when I release my grip on him, and I feel the terry cloth gingerly meeting my skin as he slowly works the towel around my body. I replace his hands with mine as soon as my fingers can find the towel's edges, quickly covering myself with it for some semblance of modesty as I attempt to straighten.

"I can help you to your room," he tells me. "Just grab my hand."

Once again I find myself holding Hunter's hand, but this time he pulls my arm up and over his shoulder to tuck me into his side, no doubt trying to support my weight so I can hobble to my room. If I weren't so painfully aware of how close my naked body is to him, I might actually die from embarrassment.

But I am aware. I am *very* aware.

It's hard *not* to be aware when the thin light of dusk is still spilling in from my bedroom window, less so now than it was when I got into the shower, but still enough that I can make us both out as Hunter guides me to my bed. I peek up at his face to find it dutifully trained upward at the ceiling, his lips pressed into a tight line as he helps me along.

"I'm not looking," he assures me.

A childish part of me pouts somewhere in the back of my mind.

I mean, doesn't he *want* to look? Even a little? It's not as if he hasn't already seen it. I quickly squash that ridiculousness though. Mostly because I'm still hobbling and growing increasingly colder by the second—it's hard to feel indignant when your nipples could cut glass.

"My clothes are on my bed," I tell him. "If you could help me sit down, I think I can—"

"Right," he cuts me off, guiding me toward it.

He gently helps me into a sitting position on top of the quilt, quickly turning his broad back to give me privacy. "Do you want me to step outside?"

"Um." I've got one foot in my underwear at this point and am struggling to get them on with my throbbing ankle, and I know the pants are going to be twice as difficult. "I might . . . need your help. But stay turned around. Just in case."

"Okay."

I manage to get my underwear on after a minute of huffing, and I grab for my sweater next, figuring it will be an easier task to tackle. I shrug into it sans bra, thinking that the material is thick enough to hide that fact. Not to mention it's growing darker by the second. The pants do indeed prove to be a problem—it's hard to pull them up while I'm in a sitting position. I have one pant leg mostly to my knee, but the other—the one that goes over my injured ankle—is being a little bitch about it all.

"Hunter," I whine. "I can't get my pants on."

I think he makes a sort of groaning sound in the back of his throat, but I might be imagining it.

20

Hunter

"OKAY," I TELL her, turning my head ever so slightly. "I won't look, all right?"

"I'm mostly dressed," she points out. "It's fine."

I turn and immediately crouch, my fingers brushing along her calves as I try to locate the waistband of her sweats in the half-dark room. My knuckles brush against her skin when I find it, and my fingers curl into the edge as I slowly start to pull her pants up her legs.

Now, I know this is probably one of the most awkward, ridiculous moments of my life, and I *shouldn't* feel a rush of adrenaline and a quickening pulse as my knuckles inadvertently glide against her knees and then higher over her thighs as I work the material up to where it's supposed to be, but my body doesn't seem to have gotten the memo.

"Lift up," I murmur, my voice rough.

She raises her hips as instructed so that I can work her pants to her waist, then she lets out a quiet gasp that makes me still for half a second when the backs of my fingers graze her ass on the way.

"There," I rasp, quickly pulling away from her. "All done."

"I can't find my socks," she mourns. "I think they got knocked off the bed."

"Oh. I have . . . Just a second."

I move to the other side of the room, knocking my hands against the things on the dresser, the sound deafening in the quiet space, right before a bright beam of light illuminates the entire room.

"You had a flashlight that entire time?"

I can only hope she can't make out my sheepish expression in the glow of the flashlight. "I didn't think you'd want me to bring it into the bathroom. Didn't think you'd want me shining it on you when you were naked."

The flashlight is pointed right at her, so I clearly see the way her lips part slightly and her eyes go wide, no doubt realizing that fact herself. If the sudden burst of her scent is any indication, I almost think she might not have minded.

Hopefully the bright light of the flashlight is washing me out enough that she doesn't see my face flushing.

I move the beam to the floor in search of her socks, quickly finding them under the edge of the bed where they've fallen. I grab them before I set the flashlight upright on the ground beside me, looking at her from where I've knelt and holding out my hand in a quiet request. She gives me her foot while I barely breathe, unsure how putting on her socks could be so hard on my heart. It's practically dancing in my chest right now.

I slide one sock over her good foot before moving to the sprained one, cradling her heel gently as I carefully pull the material over her toes and upward to slide it onto her foot. Again, the backside of my finger teases her skin as I work, but there's an added bonus of my palm half curving against her calf as I tug the long sock all the way up.

"Done," I tell her, looking up at her from the floor.

There's probably something wrong with my face—maybe it's blue or something, given that I stopped breathing about thirty seconds ago. Maybe that's why I linger on the floor for a moment, just staring at her and breathing in her sweet scent. It's brighter like this, fresh from the shower, and the urge to rise and press my tongue against her skin is stronger than it should be. I don't know how long it is before I remember myself, clearing my throat and pushing up from the floor to return to a standing position before grabbing her towel from where she dropped it on the bed and handing it back to her.

"Dry your hair," I order gently. "Don't want you to get sick."

"Right," she answers, taking the terry cloth from me. "What about the power?"

I shake my head. "I texted my friend at the co-op. He hasn't texted me back yet."

"Are we going to freeze to death? Is this how we die?"

I can't help but chuckle.

"I'm going to build a fire downstairs. It'll warm the room right up, don't worry."

"My hero," she laughs.

I reach to rub at my neck. "But . . . we'll probably need to sleep down there. This upstairs is going to freeze after a bit."

"Together?"

It's an innocent question, but what it does to me is less so.

"There are extra blankets and pillows in the storage closet downstairs. We can make pallets near the fire."

It's not quite an answer to what she was inadvertently asking, but only slightly, as far as I'm concerned.

"My phone," she says suddenly. "It's on the bathroom counter. Can you grab it?"

"No way to charge it," I point out.

"I just want to let my brothers and my friend Ada know what's going on," she tells me. She laughs then. "Want to make sure she knows who to blame if you murder me out here."

I snort out a laugh of my own. "More likely that a bear finds its way in looking for warmth and makes a meal out of you."

"*What?*"

I flash her a sly grin in the glow of the flashlight. "Kidding."

"Hysterical," she grumbles.

"Come on," I say, reaching out my hand to help her stand after picking the flashlight off the floor. "Let's get you downstairs and warmed up."

I don't think it really hits me, not until she's once again tucked against my side with her arm around my neck and her hand clasped around my waist to steady herself as we work our way out of her room toward the stairs. It takes that long, at least, to fully sink in.

That we're all alone. That we're trapped in the lodge without power and with only each other for warmth.

Okay, maybe that last bit was a stretch . . . but tell that to the sense of anticipation clenching in my gut.

"OUCH, OUCH, OUCH."

I give her a stern look from the floor. "I told you to be still."

"It *hurts*," she whines.

I shake my head as I continue to wrap her ankle with some gauze from the first aid kit. "I think it's just twisted. It's not even swollen. You'll probably be fine by tomorrow. Better keep off of it tonight though."

"Well, there go all my pressing appointments," she remarks dryly.

I grin as I work, the warm light of the fire I built flickering across her face and my hands as I continue to gently wind the cotton gauze.

"There," I say finally. "That should be good. Not too tight, is it?"

She curls her toes to test before shaking her head. "Feels good."

I'm all too aware that my hand is still cupping her heel, her skin somehow warmer than the nearby fire. Her natural scent is intoxicating—and something deep inside me feels immense satisfaction at being able to take care of her like this. Even if the thought of her hurting makes me feel the opposite.

"Want some ibuprofen?"

"Please."

I disappear from the room with my flashlight, quickly finding what I need and returning to her so I can hand her two pills and a glass of water. She downs them quickly, and I watch her wince as she tries to put a little bit of weight on her foot.

"Be careful," I tell her. "You don't want to hurt yourself more."

I know that if she does, it will be hell getting her any sort of help with the storm beginning to rage outside, which only makes it more obvious how alone we are up here. How I'm trapped in the lodge with no one but her and her delectable scent and the memory of her leaning into me only last night.

I think . . . you kind of want to kiss me.

I've been trying to reconcile why I didn't—why the thought of doing so sent a shock of terror through me—and all I can come up with is the fear of being so intimate with someone again. And yes, I'm aware that she and I have been *intimate*, but there's something about kissing that brings everything to a new level. It's a connection, a promise almost. One I'm not sure I can give her.

"Did your friend text you back?" she asks, breaking me from my reverie.

I nod. "A couple of downed trees on the line. He says they won't be able to get up the trail to fix it until the snow stops. We might be out for a day or so."

"Awesome."

"We're really roughing it now," I joke.

"I bet this is your regular Saturday night," she teases back, tucking a blanket all around herself. I notice sweat beading at her temples despite the way she's bundling herself up and worry that she might be getting sick somehow.

I touch my fingers to her water glass, urging her to drink more. "All that's missing is my whittling knife."

"And an oil lamp." She takes another gulp. "Can't forget the oil lamp."

I shake my head as I turn away from her to rummage in a pile of things I brought back with the first aid kit after I built the fire. I grab two cans from the pile before I turn back to her with one cocked brow, holding them out for her to see.

"Would you rather have chicken noodle or . . ." I squint to read the other can. "Creamy wild rice?"

She wrinkles her nose. "Cold soup?"

"I'm going to heat them up over the fire," I tell her. "Which one?"

She gives me a look that says she doesn't find this possible, but points to a can all the same. "Chicken noodle."

"I was hoping you'd say that."

"Sure you were."

I actually *do* pull out a knife then, ignoring her follow-up whittling joke with a roll of my eyes, instead popping two holes in each can's lid before I tear the wrappers off both.

"This feels like I'm watching a live National Geographic documentary," she comments.

I grin as I place both cans as close to the fire as the hearth will allow. "It's something my dad taught me when we would go camping."

"Did you do that a lot?"

"Every summer when it got warmer," I tell her. "Until I went off to college, that is."

"You went to college?"

I frown. "Only for a year. Not even that, really."

"Why did you leave?"

I can't bring myself to look at her, shrugging as I keep my attention on the cans near the fire. "Parents died."

"Oh." She gives me a look akin to pity. "Right. I'm sorry."

"No reason to be," I say quietly. "Where did you go?"

"I got my bachelor's at UCLA."

"I bet your parents are proud," I say.

Her expression turns soft. "They are. My dad worries a lot that I gave up my own dreams to live his, but I really didn't. I've always known I wanted to carry on things in one way or another."

"That's really special," I tell her wistfully. "I imagine your dad thinks so too."

She smiles shyly. "It's nothing glamorous, really—or, well, it *wasn't* before the social media aspect of it all . . . but still. I like it. I like knowing that something my dad built will go on even if he can't go on with it, you know?"

Her phrasing tugs at my heartstrings, and I can't help but think of my own situation. Sure, it's not something I chose on my own, but there really *is* something special about knowing that something my parents built will go on . . . even when they can't go on with it, just like she said.

"Your brothers said you were a daddy's girl," I tease, trying to change the subject before I get all forlorn.

"Terribly," she tells me with a laugh. "He used to bring me to jobsites when I was younger. I loved watching him work. He focused more on home renovations back then." She chuckles softly to herself. "My dad isn't actually big on the outdoors."

"That's surprising somehow," I state.

"Kind of," she responds. "Needless to say, this is as close to camping as I've ever been."

She looks down as she says it, which eats at me a little.

"Then I guess I'll have to give you the full experience."

I turn my attention to the cans by the fire, grabbing a small towel and folding it lengthwise before wrapping it around one of the cans to bring it over to her. I murmur that she should be careful as I hand it over, leaving and coming back in an instant with a spoon, which I use to open the pull-tab top before relinquishing it to her. I don't speak while I prepare my own soup, not until I carefully carry it over to the couch to sit down beside her, my shoulder touching hers as I stir the soup without looking at her. The silence in the room is an ever-present reminder of how alone we are, and the heat emanating from her body makes me shift slightly in my seat. Not to mention how her scent fills the space, threatening to suffocate me in a way I would be grateful for.

"So . . . I get that I don't know a lot about what you do," I say. "Or much about any of that stuff, really, but I think it's easy to tell how much it means to you. I don't know you as well as your brothers or your parents—hell, I don't know that much about you at all, if I'm being honest." I bring my spoon to my lips to blow on it gently, watching from the corner of my eye as she gapes at me with an open mouth. "I think anyone with half a brain can see that you're passionate about it and that giving up on whatever your life might have been to help your dad is admirable." I shake my head. "I can't say that if I had been given the choice, I'd have done the same."

I hear her small intake of breath, my pulse quickening as her scent blooms deliciously. Something about it makes my skin prickle, but I keep my eyes on the fire as I continue to slowly bring the spoon back and forth between my can and my mouth, mostly because I don't know what else to say after uttering something so embarrassing. I sense the way she's still gawking though and give her shoulder a slight nudge.

"Eat your soup before it gets cold."

She does as I say, her brow wrinkled in thought as she tucks into her food. My mind lingers on what I've said, realizing how much truth there is to it. Tess really *is* passionate about her job, and it's clear she shares that same passion for her family. It makes me feel like a bit of an ass for the way I treated her when she first showed up here.

"How is your ankle?"

She turns her head to catch me looking down at the bit of her toes that has slipped out from under the blanket and pushes her foot out farther to reveal the ankle in question. "I think it's a little better," she tells me. "Ibuprofen must be kicking in."

She slowly tilts her foot from side to side to show me that it is indeed getting better, and I nod in approval before I take another bite of soup.

"Good."

I can hear the scrape of her spoon as she stirs it in her can, and when I peek over at her from the side, I can see her white teeth pressed against her soft lower lip.

"What is it?"

"I didn't thank you for taking care of me last night," she starts quietly, and I feel my heart begin to pound in my ears a little with nerves. "You know . . . getting me back here . . . tucking me in . . . all that."

"No reason to thank me," I answer, turning my face away. "Just the decent thing to do."

"I told you I'm not used to people fussing over me," she mumbles.

I smile. "And I told *you* that you should let people fuss over you more."

She goes quiet again, and I can practically hear the question on her tongue as she obviously struggles to ask it, my body tensing in preparation for the conversation I knew we would need to have eventually.

"You know . . . about last night . . ."

There's a sound of metal against metal that signals my can is empty, but I continue to absently scrape my spoon around the bottom. "Last night?"

"Don't play dumb," she huffs. "Did I misread things? It felt like you . . . I mean, at least, it *seemed* like you wanted to—"

"You didn't," I say evenly. "Misread things."

"Then why didn't you . . . ?"

I experience a familiar panic and the echo of old wounds throbbing deep inside, feeling silly all of a sudden. Like maybe I'm reading too much into it. Maybe it isn't a big deal to her, and after everything we've done, maybe it shouldn't be a big deal to *me*. For the life of me, I can't quite figure out why, but it *is*, I'm realizing. It feels like the start of something. Something that, deep down, I'm afraid might break me all over again.

"There was a girl back in college," I start, wincing at the thought of her name. "Chloe."

Tess is quiet, seeming to sense that I need to get this out all at once, and she nods softly for me to go on.

I drop my spoon into my can and let it rest in my lap, eyes downcast as my jaw works and I consider what to say.

"We met during freshman orientation," I tell her. "She was an omega, like you, and she was open about it. I'd always felt so . . . different after discovering I was an alpha when I was just a teenager, but she made me feel . . . normal. For maybe the first time."

"Did you . . . ?"

I nod. "We dated. You might have guessed that it got intense between us very quickly because of what we were, but I didn't care about any of that. I was so gone for her, all I could focus on was how it felt like she was the *one*. We hadn't been together long, but I was already planning our future. I wanted to make her my *mate*."

I see Tess wince from the corner of my eye, and I imagine it's strange to hear things like this considering the way I've been . . . helping her lately.

She clears her throat. "What happened?"

"My parents wanted me to come home. We had this tradition . . . and I . . ." I shake my head, the memories still too painful after all this time. "I made plans with Chloe's parents instead. We went to the beach. I was on a *beach* when they ran their car off the road."

"Hunter . . ."

I feel her small hand curl around my forearm, and that gives me courage to keep going. "It felt like my fault. Like maybe, had I been there, they wouldn't have . . ."

"Of course it isn't your fault," she says firmly. "You weren't even here."

"That's my point," I tell her. "I *should* have been here."

Her lips purse, but she doesn't comment, asking instead, "So what happened then?"

"I felt like I needed to be back here. I felt like I owed that to them, to make sure this place kept going. They loved it so much, I just..." I let out a sigh. "Regardless, it didn't fit into Chloe's plans."

"She left you?"

"Brutally," I say with a bitter laugh. "Not only did I find out I wasn't the only person she was seeing, when she realized I was serious about quitting school to come back home, she told me she wasn't going to waste her life taking care of some dingy little lodge. She had *plans*, and I obviously wasn't meant to be a part of them. I was just... something for her enjoyment. Something to pass the time."

I don't miss the way she makes a face at Chloe's echo of her own word for the lodge, and I can't bring myself to look at her as I say it.

"I'm so sorry," she says. "What I said when I got here..."

I shake my head. "It's fine. You didn't know." I draw in a deep breath, letting it out slowly. "I learned back then that sometimes the only person you can rely on is yourself. And I guess I learned that soulmates don't exist."

"So you didn't kiss me because..."

"Because you're leaving," I say. "And I don't know if I can let myself be that vulnerable again."

Her mouth opens as if she's going to say something, then quickly closes again, as if she thinks better of it. The silence is so thick it threatens to swallow me, and I stand from the couch before she has the chance to respond.

"I need to get more blankets, I think," I say. "That floor can be brutal."

I stalk out of the room like the coward I am, stomping into the next room to gather some blankets from the linens closet as Tess's delicious scent closes in on me from all sides, permeating the room and beyond. It occurs to me again when I'm bringing back piles of blankets to drop onto the bearskin rug that I will be sleeping in close proximity to this woman, that her scent and the waste of a promised kiss will linger between us intimately for the entire night—and who knows how much longer with the storm—and suddenly the thought of coming out on the other side of this unscathed seems harder than it did before.

I don't know what it's like to kiss Tess, even if I'm too afraid to let myself have that, but I *know* what it's like to touch her. And I already believe it's something I'm wholly addicted to. Being forced to share warmth with her for the entire night without doing so seems almost impossible. But this is a game we're playing here, one that has a certain set of rules. She only wants my touch when she *needs* it, and wanting it aside from that isn't something we agreed to. As I try to ignore the subtle way her eyes follow me while I set up our bedding, it hits me just how *long* of a night I'm in for. Because even if I can't bring myself to kiss her, despite how much I desperately want to, the urge to touch her is something I'm realizing never really goes away.

And with the recognition of how much I'd *like* to kiss her, consequences be damned . . . I'm realizing I really might be utterly fucked.

21

Tess

GOING TO BED with someone you tried (and failed) to kiss the night before is about as awkward as you might think. I watch with growing nerves as Hunter makes two—yes, two, and my brain can't decide how to feel about that—makeshift beds on the bearskin rug (a *bearskin rug*, for goodness' sake). My thoughts race like it's Christmas Eve, except Santa is hot, and I really want to kiss him but can't figure out if he wants to kiss me back. Also, in this horny waking nightmare, Santa is practically six and a half feet tall, with shoulders that stretch his black T-shirt to mind-boggling proportions, and he wears flannel pajama pants (has flannel just become a sexual trigger for me?) and no socks, so my brain has to deal with the oddity of trying to figure out why a man's bare feet are suddenly attractive.

"Do you need help getting down here?"

I blink back at him from the couch, still thinking about the way his arms flex when he pops a quilt to straighten it out. "What?"

"The floor," he clarifies. "Do you need me to help you get into bed?"

Logically, I know that what my brain is doing to that sentence is not at all what he intended when he asked the question. My ankle actually feels much better than it did, and if I'm being honest, I can probably get into the little pallet he's made me on my own with very little trouble if I want to. In fact, part of me is appalled by how much he's had to coddle me already, but that part of me is effectively silenced by the part that wants him to touch me again.

"If you don't mind," I answer sheepishly.

He's right in front of me, his body looming over mine as he takes my hand to help pull me from the couch, and sure, maybe I lean into him a little more than I need to—but who can blame me, really?

Hunter is careful with me, letting me cling to his arm as I gingerly cross the floor to the bed of quilts he's laid out for us side by side, never letting go as I lower myself to the floor.

"Easy," he murmurs. "Don't hurt yourself again."

I roll my eyes, my grip moving from his forearm to his hand, which curls around mine as I adjust myself to sit with my (sort of) injured ankle slightly suspended. "I think you're enjoying that joke."

"Me?" His lips curl a little at the corners as he tries for an innocent look. "Just concerned for your well-being. You only have so many ankles."

He keeps hold of my hand as I lower my leg to the blankets, settling in as he steps to the side a bit to make room for me. "Yeah, sure," I scoff. "If I didn't know any better, I'd say you—"

Okay, I'll be honest. I've always thought serendipity was bullshit. I mean, divine luck coming together to create happy accidents that seem to right all the wrongs in the world? It always sounded like a hokum informercial to me. But what happens at this exact moment, what causes me to stop short midsentence and lose my train of thought in a matter of seconds . . . Well. I *might* be tempted to rethink my stance.

It happens so fast I don't even realize it *is* happening at first. It's not like any of my recent mishaps; things don't move in slow motion or feel like they drag on forever. No, when Hunter's foot slips on the edge of one of the quilts, when he loses his balance and tumbles forward, that seems to happen so quickly. He's upright and standing and perfectly stable one second and simply . . . *there* the next. And by *there*, I mean right over me. I mean his hands are braced on either side of my head to keep himself from completely smothering me. I mean his frame is so close to mine that I can feel every inch of his body heat radiating over me.

I had a lot of thoughts in my head a second ago, but right now I sort of can't remember how to even form them.

"Now who's clumsy?" I breathe, feeling dazed.

He's so close that I can see every little movement of his Adam's apple when he swallows.

"Maybe . . . you're rubbing off on me," he answers, his voice much rougher than it was a second ago.

He's looking at me like that again. It's the same look from the bar, the same one he gave me after I told him the good news about Nate—the one that looks like he's holding himself back when I don't *want* him to. A look like that is enough to make a girl brave.

"I still believe you want to kiss me," I whisper.

He laughs, I think, but it's more of a rasp, really. Like it's choked.

"Only a very, *very* stupid man wouldn't want to kiss you, Tess."

My throat feels like sandpaper, but somehow my tongue is very wet. Heavy, even. Maybe it's swollen. Maybe that's why Hunter's eyes look so transfixed on it when it slips past my teeth to wet my bottom lip. I try swallowing, but it feels useless. Maybe it's because I'm breathing so hard.

"But you won't."

"For a few reasons," he murmurs.

I wonder if it's difficult for him to keep himself suspended like he is. He's so *close*, and yet somehow there's still that tiny fraction of space between us, just enough so that he isn't touching me. I mean, surely his arms must be hurting, right?

If I only slightly move my hand, my fingers can graze the cotton of his T-shirt. "A few?"

"I told you about Chloe." He makes a strained sound in his throat when the tip of my finger finds the space between the cotton and his bare skin. "That's a big part of it."

"But not all of it," I press, curling my finger around a bit of his T-shirt.

"You also barely know me," he breathes. "I don't want you to do anything you might regret. You've already had a ton of things out of your control lately."

"I wouldn't," I assure him, an urgency building as I notice he isn't even looking me in the eye now but at my mouth. Only my mouth. "Regret it."

"I can smell you, Tess," he rasps. "Your scent . . . You smell like . . ."

His knee is between my legs. I can feel the heat of it against both my thighs. I think his thumb just touched my hair.

I nod dazedly, feeling my head start to swim but not so much that I don't know that I want whatever he's willing to give me right now, regardless of what's happening to my body. Realizing that I want it for *me*, not simply for the demands of my newfound designation.

"Also," he says distractedly, as if he's having a hard time figuring out his thoughts too. "You'd been drinking."

That one throws me off a little. "So?"

And maybe he's figured out how to make thoughts before I have—in fact, I highly suspect he has—because he isn't looking at my mouth anymore. Maybe it's because it's too hard to look, since his face is so close to mine now. The deep brown of his eyes seems dark and bright all at once, so much so that I can't look away as they bore into mine.

"If I ever kissed you . . . I'd want you to damn well remember it tomorrow."

All the air just . . . leaves my lungs. That can't be normal, right? Regardless, I might not be breathing. Speaking still seems to be possible, but only barely.

"I haven't . . . had anything to drink today."

"Tess," he growls. "Is it happening again?"

"Maybe," I admit, feeling that familiar surge of heat pooling in my belly that is somehow *worse* than before. "It feels different."

"You smell different," he tells me. "You smell like . . . like . . ."

"What do I smell like?"

"Like you need me," he says, echoing the same shiver-inducing sentiment from weeks ago. "Do you?"

"No," I say, mustering my courage even as the heat builds and builds inside me. "I *want* you, Hunter."

He looks hesitant for a moment, his gaze moving to my mouth as he studies it for a long span of seconds like he's considering, and I watch with bated breath. I watch his jaw tic as his tongue darts out to wet his lips, and then his eyes collide with mine, an intense heat in them that looks exactly how I feel.

"Fuck it," he practically growls.

And just like that, the tiny bit of space between us is nonexistent.

I've been wondering all day if Hunter Barrett wanted to kiss me.

I've been playing a torturous game of Does He or Doesn't He in my head often enough since last night to drive myself crazy. But there isn't any doubt now. Now it's *very* obvious that he does.

I mean, it's sort of hard to doubt when he's whispering against my mouth, urging me to open it.

I gasp as his tongue slips inside, licks mine with a desperation that is only outmatched by the way his hand wraps around my hip. His scruff tickles the place above my mouth, enough so that I giggle a little when he turns his face to deepen the kiss.

"Is something"—the words are sort of muffled when he speaks them to the corner of my mouth, and he licks gently, pressing his lips there after—"funny?"

"Your beard," I laugh. "It tickles."

"Does it?" My breath catches when he rubs his cheek against mine, his mouth ducking below my chin to lick there, to chase after his tongue with a kiss. "Does this tickle too?"

"Hunter," I sigh.

His hand is touching my skin now, tucked under my sweater as he traces idle circles with one of his fingers. His mouth, however, is still wandering, still tasting.

"I like your freckles," he murmurs along my jaw. "I keep thinking about everywhere else you have them."

I smile as he kisses my cheek. "All over."

"I know." I can feel his hand moving to glide over my bare stomach, his thumb brushing my belly button as my skin trembles. "I like it."

His mouth trails down my throat until he stops to suck at a spot near my collarbone—which I didn't even know could make my stomach flip until this very second—while both hands pushing at the fabric of my sweater as it moves up and over my belly until the warmth of the fireplace glowing nearby licks at my exposed skin. I make an embarrassing sound when I feel his thumbs sliding back and forth across the sensitive swell of my breasts (my God, his thumbs are so large they barely even have to move to span the underside), his breath releasing raggedly at the base of my throat as he lingers there for a moment.

"Tess." He gives one side a gentle squeeze, making a sound of his own that makes me less embarrassed about mine. "Is this okay?"

I don't have the ability to tell him that this is spectacular, that this is fireworks and cotton candy and every good sensation I've ever felt, but I manage a nod and a quiet *Yes* at the very least. Even as the familiar heat and cramps threaten to overtake me, some part of my brain is so fixated on his touch that it almost seems to keep those sensations at bay, even if only a little.

His hair, mussed and wild from where my fingers have been digging into it, is falling in his eyes when he pulls away from me, and his eyes are so dark now they appear almost black as he looks down at my rumpled state. There's something about his mouth that seems hungry somehow, a rise and fall of his chest that feels impatient while he looks at me.

"Fuck, Tess," he rumbles, the tip of his finger reaching to trace the bare skin of my breast that just peeks out from my rucked-up sweater. "There's one here." His head dips to press his mouth there, and my back bows instinctively when I feel warm air kiss at my nipples as he pulls my sweater higher. "And here." His tongue flicks along the swell, sucking gently at the spot. "Even . . . here."

His tongue is light at first against my nipple, teasing at the spot he's found before he swirls around the entire thing in a slow circle—but then his entire mouth covers it, sucks it inside, making me moan, and then he just . . . keeps going. I can feel him growling against me, actually *feel* it like a deep vibration that hums along my skin, and my fingers push into his hair again—to bring him closer or to push him away, I really can't be sure. It feels so good, I can't decide what I want.

"Raise your arms," he urges, turning his head to pay attention to the other side even as he tugs harder at my sweater. "Want this off you."

And who am I to argue with that, really?

My sweater winds up somewhere across the room, but I have no idea where. Hunter doesn't really give me time to consider it, since he decides his shirt should join it immediately thereafter, robbing me of all coherent thought.

My fingers skim up the dark line of hair from his navel to his chest. "We should put *you* on the website. Make some sort of influencer out of you."

I can make out the dimple in his beard. "I don't think I'm cut out for influencing."

"You're influencing *me* a whole lot right now."

"Am I?" He turns his face to let his eyes roam over my naked chest. "Fuck. Look at you." His hand reaches to curl around my breast, his thumb flicking lazily against my nipple. I'm vaguely aware that his hand can cover the entirety of my breast with very little spillage, and my boobs are in no way small. "I thought I was going to lose my mind earlier," he admits. "I felt like I was some sort of asshole for being so fucking turned on helping you out of the shower when you were injured."

"Does it help to know that I *probably* could have gotten my pants on by myself?"

"You're gonna kill me."

I don't really think that's a fair accusation, considering a second after he says it, he's ducking his head again to wrap his lips around one of my nipples, making me cry out. I can feel a delicious graze of teeth that seems to draw warm pulses from between my legs with every pull, making me unconsciously try to press my thighs together, only to be foiled by Hunter's leg, which still rests between them.

Hunter seems to remember this too, since I feel one of his hands tickling down my stomach to let his fingers tease the waistband of my pajama pants. They simply . . . hover there, not really dipping beneath and not really touching, and he turns up his face to look at me from between my breasts with glazed eyes. "Can I . . . ?"

"Stop asking me for permission and just touch me," I practically growl, feeling that need swirling inside.

I mean, a girl can only take so much edging, really.

He watches my face as he lets his fingers slip inside the front of my pants, tucking them under the elastic band of my underwear—which I'm remembering have pictures of cartoon kittens holding little fish on them, but I'll worry about that later. Right now I'm just trying not to let my eyes cross as I feel the calloused pads of his fingers dip into the already-too-wet crease between my legs. I bite my lip as he lets the thick length of his index finger part me. He circles my clit experimentally before he dips lower to do the same thing to the opening, where slick is already starting to stream from me copiously.

"I'm not"—he pushes only hard enough to let the tip of his finger dip inside me, and I feel my skin thrum as I shiver—"prepared. For this." He looks sort of pained as he says it. "I don't have anything."

"I take the pill," I tell him a bit too quickly. "Like, religiously. Like, you could set your watch by it. I'm *so* prepared." He cocks an eyebrow at me, but there's humor to it, and I know he's silently teasing me. "Shut up. Not in a weird way. In a totally normal way. And my last panel was all clear. I haven't been with anyone since."

Hunter actually laughs a little. "You're the first woman I've touched in . . . a very long time. So it's safe to say the same."

"It's been a long time for me too," I manage. "I mean, not that I've ever touched a woman, but—*Ah*."

My hips cant upward when he pushes as deep as his finger will reach, twisting a little as he withdraws, only to do it all over again. "You're so slick for me," he practically hums. "Tell me how to touch you. I want you to feel good."

"I mean, you're off to a stellar start," I pant. "*Oh*. Keep doing that."

He presses the heel of his hand against my clit again, rubbing it slightly as his finger continues to pump in and out of me. When he adds a second, I think I actually shout a little. I can't be sure, since Hunter chooses then to slant his mouth across mine, swallowing down the sound.

I can feel his cock pressing on my stomach, hard and positively *throbbing* through the soft flannel of his pants, his hips tilting back and forth a little so he can rub himself against my skin. It's a little clumsy, the way I grab at his waistband to try to pull him free, and it definitely takes a second longer than it probably would if his tongue weren't occupying my mouth and his fingers weren't occupying . . . other places, but somehow I manage to wrestle him out of the confines of his pants to feel the hot, velvety length of his cock as it thumps (yes, I said *thumps*) against my belly. There's already a sticky wetness at the head that dews well above my navel, and my hand is unable to fit around all of him, so I settle for running my palm along the underside before fisting the tip.

His hand stills as I feel his arm shake against me, his entire body shuddering as his lips trip across mine, like he's forgotten what he was doing. "Don't—I don't—Jesus, Tess. I want to come already. I could come all over you."

Wow, okay.

I love that when he touches me, it's bye-bye to the quiet, reserved Hunter.

Hello, axe-wielding sex lumberjack.

His head falls to rest on my shoulder as he pulls his hand from my pants, and I whine in protest, which he effectively ignores. When he wraps his fingers around my wrist to pull me away from him, I can feel my own fluids all over his fingers.

"Give me a second," he grunts into my neck. "I want to be fucking you when I come. I want to feel you on my knot."

The cartoon wolf inside me is beating the table right now. It's howling at the moon. It's hitting itself over the head with a comical-looking mallet. Because I want it too, I realize. *Desperately.* I haven't the faintest idea what it feels like to have his knot, but something in my hindbrain is *begging* to find out.

I squirm impatiently—because let's face it, I *am* impatient—shifting my weight to try to entice him to hurry up. My bad foot taps against his and makes me wince during all this, and I hiss out a breath as I mutter a quiet expletive.

"Ow." I bend my knee to bring my foot off the floor. "My foot."

"Shit." He's already pulling away from me, and now I sort of wish I'd just borne it. "I forgot. Are you okay?"

"It's fine," I assure him. "It's not bad. Don't you dare stop."

There's an impish quality to his grin, making him seem younger, like a hormonal teenager doing something he shouldn't. "I'm not stopping. We'll just have to be a little more careful." His eyes rake up my body hungrily. "This time."

He's gentler now when he starts to tug my pants over my thighs, gingerly working them down my legs and over one foot at a time, taking extra care with the one that's wrapped. He notices my underwear when he comes back for them, cocking an eyebrow up at me as I roll my eyes. "They're cute."

"They are," he agrees. His fingers curl purposefully on either side of them, hooking into the elastic before he looks up at me again. "But they're coming off."

Getting my underwear off has me spreading my legs a little to help him, and no sooner am I rid of them than he has his hands running up the insides of my thighs to keep me that way. He holds me open so he can curl his body and press a kiss right above my crease, brushing his nose back and forth along the soft, neat curls there.

If I weren't so horribly turned on, I might even be embarrassed.

"If I didn't need to come inside you so badly," he says against my core, lowering to give me one broad lick directly up the center with a rumbled sound that seems to come from deep in his chest and has my back arching and my breath catching, "I'd be down here all night."

"*Hunter.*"

"Next time," he promises quietly, pressing one last kiss between my legs before he pushes back up again.

I can't do anything but watch as he starts to shove his pants down broad thighs that are dusted with the same dark hair that covers his chest, thick and corded with muscle that he surely got doing wilderness tasks that make the cavewoman part of my brain purr. But none of that really compares to the shocking size of him—long and so heavy that even fully hard it sort of hangs between his legs instead of jutting upward. I didn't have time to fully appreciate it last time with how frantic we were, but I sure as hell do now.

I'm not a virgin by any means, but that doesn't mean I'm not equal parts excited *and* nervous when I see all of him, knowing that this is really happening. That he'll be inside me. Not that I have any real time to dwell on it, given that Hunter seems to be single-minded right now.

He crawls up next to me only to urge me to turn onto my side, then wraps an arm around me to pull my back against his front as easily as if I were some cotton-filled doll rather than a fully grown woman. His hand makes my thigh seem tiny when he curls his fingers around it, lifting and pulling it back to drape over his so that my injured ankle hangs safely behind his calf.

At first I'm a little put out by the fact that I can't see his face in this position, but then Hunter starts to lick at a spot where my shoulder meets my throat, and I sort of forget where I am. I feel his fingers skimming back up my thigh before he reaches between my legs to tease my swollen, slick folds, running his knuckles between them in a slow up-and-down motion that's only interrupted by the periodic rubbing of my clit, which makes me squirm against him.

"Talk to me," he says into my neck. "Can you take my cock now? Tell me what you need."

I *don't* say that if it weren't for my somewhat busted ankle I would be pushing him to the floor and taking advantage of him in utterly obscene ways, forcing a nod instead, because I am so *wet* already with the climbing heat threatening to take over me.

"You can—I can—*Hurry*."

Oh.

The head of his cock is so broad and so *hot*, but in a way that makes me want to sink down farther, to feel his heat deeper. I would too, if it weren't for the sheer fucking *size* of him. I can say with utter confidence that I have *never* experienced anything like it.

I reach behind me to tangle my fingers in his hair, pulling his face closer to my throat to encourage him to keep going. His kisses are sloppier now, with a staccato rhythm, as if he loses just a little more focus with every inch that he gives me. I can feel warm breath puffing against my skin from his nostrils in that same sharp rhythm as he holds his breath again and again like he's simply forgotten how to breathe properly, and I tilt my head back in pleasure as he fills and fills and *fills* me until it feels like he's touching every part I knew about and a few that I didn't know even existed.

"*Fuck*." His entire palm flattens between my legs to cup me, and he slides a finger on either side of where we're joined. "You're so tight."

"I can handle it," I urge.

He tenses above me. "I don't want to hurt y—"

I let my hand slide down my body to circle him, feeling the throbbing length of him between us as I urge him forward. He hisses when he bottoms out, and I can't help the whine that escapes me at the feeling of being so full of him.

"It's . . . *Fuck*. I don't want to come yet."

That is the *opposite* of what I want to do. I would like to come very much. I even press back against him to try to wordlessly let him know, but this only makes him groan into my hair as he shivers.

"Hunter," I practically beg. "Can you—? I need you to—"

"I could come just like this." His hand slides back up between my legs, only enough so that he can press his fingers against the swollen bud of my clit, rolling it in a steady pattern as I sort of rock into it. "But I want to fuck you. I wanna feel you come."

"I'm—Keep doing—Yes, yes, *right there*."

Honestly, this alone would probably be enough for me if he keeps touching me like that, but then I would be robbed of the utterly decadent sensations that spark inside me when he starts to *move*. Even with the extreme fullness, it's an easy glide in and out, given that I'm probably more aroused than I've ever been, and I find myself chasing after each thrust, trying to push down onto him even when he's barely pulled out. Not to mention the subtle swell of his knot inside me, something I never could have anticipated would feel so good. Right now it's only a hint of what it could be, but still, something inside me *wants* it more than my next breath.

"Don't move," he grunts. "You're going to make me—*Fuck*. I just want to feel you a little more."

Another thick arm works its way underneath me to wrap around my middle, effectively trapping me and holding me in place as he continues that same dizzying circling of my clit that has me fighting to chase after more.

"Be good," he coos. "Be still for me." I feel goose bumps pebble over my skin despite the warmth of the fire and the heat of his body, his lips finding my ear so he can nibble at the lobe as he whispers praise that has me half out of my mind. "You feel too good," he huffs. "Can you come like this?"

"So close," I manage. "Just—Don't stop—Just keep—"

His mouth goes a little slack against my neck when he pushes a little deeper, a little faster, a little *harder*—hitting some spot inside me that has hot, liquid pressure swelling deep in my belly and between my legs, even bleeding warmth down my thighs as everything seems to tighten like a coil that's being wound too tight.

"Hunter. *Hunter*."

"You're squeezing me so much," he groans. "So *wet*. Can you take my knot, Tess?"

A tremor of unease runs through me at the unknown of it all. "Will it hurt?"

"You're so slick for me," he says, rolling his hips so that his cock glides in and out to accentuate his point. "Feel that?"

"Uh-huh," I breathe.

"It's going to feel so good when I knot you," he promises, and the feel of him has my eyes rolling back. "You were *made* for me. You can take it, can't you?"

"Oh. *Oh. Yes.* I can." I'm babbling, not even sure if that's true but *wanting* it all the same. My body seems to be on board for it, in any case. "Just like that. *Please*."

I've read about "toe-curling orgasms" since the summer of my fifteenth year when I would hide downstairs at my grandmother's and sneakily read her Harlequins. I'm well acquainted with the phrase; I simply thought it was a crock of shit until now.

But when that coil stops winding, when that pressure inside spills to give way to the all-over rush that seems to explode inside . . . my toes *actually* curl. Hell, if it weren't for the way Hunter is holding on to me, keeping me pressed tightly against him, I suspect my entire *body* would curl. I shake and shiver and make noises that are probably going to haunt me later when I recall them—but I don't think Hunter will notice anyway. Not with the way he practically shouts against my skin before biting down on my shoulder, shaking a little himself.

I'm so full of him that I can actually *feel* it when he lets go, the pulsing warmth as he fills me seeming to last forever. I feel everything when it happens—when his knot swells to proportions that I've only felt with my hands—and the fullness nearly steals my breath as it thickens inside me. As it touches me in ways I've never dreamed of being touched. Like I've spent my entire life missing something and now I'm complete.

"*Oh*."

"Does it hurt?"

I shake my head. "Feels good."

"I don't . . . I don't smell your heat dissipating."

"What?"

"Normally, after you . . . Well. Normally it starts to fade after."

"What does that mean?"

He inhales deeply from my throat, sighing softly. "That it might not be over this time. This might be the real thing."

"So I'm . . . ?"

"Going into heat? It's possible."

"But you'll . . ." There's a sudden flash of fear at the unknown, but his arms around me keep it at bay somewhat. "You'll help me, right?"

His fingers find my chin to tilt my face back so I can meet his eyes, his gaze intense and singular. "I'm not going anywhere." He shifts his hips so that his knot tugs a little, and I whimper as sparks of pleasure flit through me. "I want you right here on my knot for as long as you need me."

"Good," I tell him with a relieved sigh. "That's good."

He places lazy, sporadic kisses against my neck that feel impulsive, like he doesn't even realize he's doing it, and lying in the afterglow of what we've just done might be one of the most singularly satisfying moments of my entire adult life. I couldn't have known how complete I would feel with his knot swollen inside me, my back tucked against his front, fitting like I'm *meant* to be there. Even if I feel so full that I might burst with it.

God, Ada wasn't too far off with the splitting analogy.

That makes me laugh without being able to help it.

"Something funny again?"

I shake my head even though I'm grinning like an idiot. "I knew you wanted to kiss me."

Hunter snorts as he nuzzles my hair, seeming to be in no hurry to pull out of me. "Give me a minute, and I'm going to do it again."

"Wow, again? At your age? What if you mess up your whittling arm? Maybe we should—"

His hand at my chin and his mouth over mine don't really leave room for jokes.

I absolutely forget what I was going to say anyway.

22

Hunter

IT'S MUCH COLDER in the gray light of morning, even under the pile of quilts from the two makeshift beds—which became one makeshift bed in the course of the night—and I stir, feeling Tess shiver as she burrows deeper into my side. She still smells faintly of heat; it's slight, nowhere near what it will be when it fully hits her, and based on her scent . . . we have some time.

She shudders again when I slip out from beneath her, immediately curling deeper under the covers to retreat back into the warmth. It doesn't take long to find what I'm looking for, and as quiet as I try to be, I hear a rustling under the blankets after another thirty minutes or so.

"What is *that*?" I look at her over my shoulder, watching her eyes move down my naked torso to my plaid pajama bottoms. "Aren't you freezing?"

"It's not that cold," I tell her, a tone of excitement in my voice. "Come look at this."

She only grumbles a little as she wraps her naked body in the thickest quilt she can grab from the pile, then shuffles over to the polyester dome that I've been assembling while she slept. "Is that a . . . tent?"

"Yeah . . ." Her astonished tone has me feeling a little embarrassed now. "You said last night you'd never been camping . . . and we had this sitting in the storage closet, and I thought . . . I mean, *technically* this is what you're supposed to do in this situation and all, and I just—" I press my lips together, as I realize I've started to babble. "This was stupid, wasn't it?"

She smiles softly before crouching down to look inside, noticing I've deposited all the blankets that would have been my bed inside the tent along with a plethora of assorted pillows, ranging from couch cushions to ones that I've stolen from some of the upstairs bedrooms. It occurs to me that I may be nesting, that I'm subconsciously trying to make things more comfortable for her heat—something that usually only mates do. It's a strange thought, but not an altogether unpleasant one, if a little worrisome.

She crawls inside, blanket still wrapped tightly around her as she plops down in the center of all the bedding materials. "Well," she says expectantly. "Give me the full experience."

My lips tilt up in a grin as I crawl in after her. "Now when the bear breaks in, it won't be able to find you."

"That joke gets more and more hilarious every time you tell it."

I look around the tiny space, thinking it would probably be a lot grander out under the stars somewhere, but I suppose it's the thought that counts. I'm almost too big for the damn thing, my head nearly touching the ceiling even with the way I'm sitting, leaning back on my hands with my legs spread in front of me to spill out through the unzipped opening.

"How is your ankle?"

She wiggles her toes. "Better. Just a little sore now."

"Good."

"I bet you take all the girls here," she teases. "Is this how you would have wooed me if I'd grown up here?"

"This is *definitely* how I would have wooed you if you'd grown up here," I say seriously.

"Oh?" She shifts so that she's turning to face me, still wrapped in her blanket. "Tell me what that would look like."

I keep myself propped on one hand even as I reach up with the other, tucking a stray piece of hair behind her ear. She looks so soft like this, and her scent is much thicker now, making every breath almost painful in the way it has me burning for her. It takes everything I have just to keep my hands off her. Does she know how enticing she is right now?

"I'd build us a fire first," I say.

"Check," she notes. "Although, maybe you should poke it or something. It's freezing. Anyway . . . And then?"

"Then I would impress you with my spectacular tent-pitching skills."

"I am thoroughly impressed," she assures me. "Then what?"

"Then maybe I'd show you where all the constellations are."

"Wow, astronomy nerd."

I roll my eyes. "Trust me, you would be thoroughly wooed."

"Oh, I have no doubt. Fire, tents, stars . . . sounds like you were regularly getting laid with this foolproof tactic."

I shrug. "Never took anyone camping till now."

"Really?" She feigns shock as she brings her hand to her cheek, the blanket slipping a little off her shoulder. "I feel so honored."

I'm watching her face now—her full lips, her pert nose that is awash with freckles, her wide eyes that seem to sparkle—my expression softening a little. "I'd probably tell you that you're so beautiful it hurts to look at you sometimes."

"Wow." Her cheeks tinge pink. "You tell all the girls that?"

"Just you," I say quietly.

She bites at the inside of her lip, holding back a smile before telling me, "A line like that would *definitely* get you a make-out session."

I kiss her softly then, closing my eyes as she leans into me. She's so warm, so soft and sweet—it's hard not to pull her closer, to let her warmth bleed into the coldest parts of me, thawing them, making them come back to life.

I haven't felt as alive as I do with Tess in a very long time.

"I'm sort of jealous I didn't grow up here," she murmurs. "Seems I missed out on a lot."

"Well," I tell her, gathering her in my arms and pulling her down into the blankets, "I could show you a thing or two."

I reach up to trace my finger against the polyester ceiling of the tent, drawing shapes. "That's Ursa Major right there."

"Oh, is it?"

"Mm-hmm." I move my hand, drawing another shape above her. "And that's Andromeda."

"You really are a nerd," she laughs.

I eye her from the side. "You got something to say about that?"

"No way," she teases. "I think it's pretty hot."

"Sure you do," I murmur.

She cuddles closer to me. "Show me another one."

"Well. This would be Orion," I tell her. I draw a line across where its middle would be. "And this would be his belt."

"Sure, sure," she says.

"And then there's Lupus," I point out, drawing it on the polyester with my finger.

She cocks her head. "There's a constellation called Lupus?"

"The wolf," I say. "Yeah."

"Huh. I bet I would have known that if I'd grown up like this."

"Maybe," I tell her. "Maybe not."

"It's still so weird."

"I can only imagine."

"One day I'm one way, and then the next . . . *Poof*. Something else."

"Do you regret it?"

She looks up at me, smiling softly. "Not really."

Her soft look does something to my insides, like she's saying without words that *I'm* the reason she doesn't regret all the changes she's going through. It's like a knot that's been tightly wound for ages slowly starting to unravel. That's a heady thing for someone who isn't sure they're worth all that.

She shifts beside me, squirming a little as her face scrunches up. "Are you okay?"

She looks sheepish. "Just a little sore."

"I'm sorry," I tell her.

"Don't be," she sighs. "You're just fucking huge. My poor vagina's eyes are bigger than its stomach."

"That's horrifying," I laugh.

"But not untrue."

She looks up at me then, her eyes shining a little. "Hunter?"

"Hmm?"

"I'm glad it was you," she tells me. "I'm glad that you're the one here with me."

And the knot that's inside unravels a bit more, turning me into this loose, lax thing, and I might *actually* believe I'm worth all the fuss. I've *never* felt the way I do when I'm here with her, doing something as simple as this.

It makes it impossible not to lean down and capture her lips, my tongue sweeping through her mouth, my lips lingering at hers, my voice rougher than it was before. "Still cold?"

"Nope," she sighs.

My lips curl against hers. "Good."

"You know . . ." She shifts a bit, looking mildly uncomfortable. "No one's ever done anything like this for me."

Something squeezes in my chest, and I wind my arms around her as I pull her tighter against me. "That's a real shame."

"I think I like camping," she says softly, looking almost shy.

"I haven't even shown you how to make breakfast over the fire."

"That might be hotter than anything you've done so far."

"Oh?" I make an indignant sound. "I don't know how I feel about that."

"I might need another point of reference," she says seriously. "Just to be sure."

I huff out a laugh. "Greedy thing."

"Maybe," she says. "But after last night . . . I don't think anyone can blame me."

She wraps her arms around my neck and pulls me in for another kiss, and I can feel it happening—the last of my walls crumbling and giving way to the vulnerable center of me, laid bare for her to do with whatever she might want. It should terrify me, but right now . . . I can't find it in me to feel that. Not with her warm and sated against me.

I hold her a little tighter as I steal one more kiss, telling myself that this time might be different—that Tess is nothing like Chloe—

even as some part of my brain tells me it's impossible to be sure of that after knowing her for such a short time. Which is true, really, and I'm aware of that. But the problem is, now that I've started?

I can't seem to stop wanting to kiss her.

Something deep inside me worries I never will.

23

Tess

"I'M JUST SAYING," I tell him after eating the last bit of fireplace bacon. "There's an argument to be made here."

Hunter snorts. "Are you complimenting my cooking or insulting me in . . . other ways?"

"Maybe I'm goading you," I suggest, waggling my eyebrows.

He shakes his head, stowing his plate away. "I've got to check the windows after the storm last night. Need to make sure there aren't any cracks."

I don't tell him that he's really putting a damper on about a dozen different sexy ideas I dreamed up during breakfast, but since I *am* the one who got the whole revamping ball rolling, I guess I don't have any right to complain. I've already suffered through him redressing as it is, and if I can survive being robbed of shirtless Hunter after having intimately experienced it for twelve hours straight, I guess I can survive this as well.

"We could totally fix the railings today too."

Hunter raises one eyebrow, the ghost of a smile at his mouth. "'We'?"

"Yeah, I can put you to work." I can see that he's seconds away from laughing. "You can be Mr. Fixit for a day."

"You don't need to be on that ankle of yours," he says sternly. "And you still smell like heat. It could hit you anytime. You need to rest."

"It's not even bad today," I argue. "I'm just a little sore. And I feel mostly fine otherwise. So we might as well do what we can while we can."

"It's too cold," he counters.

"Okay, Grandpa." I tsk. "I'll dress warm."

"You keep calling me Grandpa," he warns with a low sort of laugh, "and I might have to do something about it."

Warmth pools low in my belly. Now, *that's* what I'm talking about. "Oh? Like what?"

"Hmm." He eyes me up and down in a slow, lazy way that has my toes curling again (and there aren't even any orgasms involved this time, go figure), his brown eyes hooded and thoughtful, as if he's imagining *exactly* what he might do. God, I would eat a hippo whole to read minds right now. "Guess we'll see."

Damn it.

He pushes up from the floor to stand, retrieving his plate, and I realize that he's really not planning to indulge in a little secluded sexcation with me. Cowabummer.

"Fine, fine," I sigh. "We can do responsible things today."

He crosses the minimal space, stepping over the still-rumpled pile of blankets that made up our personal love nest last night, and if that memory isn't enough to have me blushing, the way he bends to kiss my cheek as he takes my plate from me definitely finishes the job.

"At least for a little while," he murmurs, a silent promise of much-less-responsible things to come later.

Now, *that* I can work with.

I HAVE TO make the trek back up to my room after breakfast. Hunter was completely right about the upstairs freezing over when the power went out—I can barely stand to be up there for the five minutes it takes me to grab fresh clothes and some washcloths from the cabinets so I'll be able to take some semblance of a bath with the water Hunter is boiling over the fireplace (it'll be more of a rub-down situation, from the way he described it, but he did allude to helping me, so I'm letting it slide).

I can dress myself now, thankfully (or not, depending on how you look at it), and even though my hair is still a disaster—the sex-mussed mess hastily thrown into a bun without many other options—I feel much better in new clothes and slightly more prepared to tackle a bit of light reno by the time I come back down the staircase to find Hunter.

He appears from the dining room with a befuddled expression, looking from me to the ceiling as if trying to figure something out. "Did you . . . clean?"

"Yeah, yesterday." I cross my arms when I step off the staircase. "You're just now noticing?"

"I was a little distracted yesterday, if you remember. You know, the snow, the shower . . . other things."

He purposely leaves out the other *s*-word from last night, but it doesn't keep me from remembering. He really has a way of getting the upper hand with minimal effort.

"Well, yeah," I say, a little red-eared. "I cleaned. Figured I'd get a jump on the easy stuff since I had time, you know?"

"You didn't have to," Hunter tells me. "That's not part of your job."

I shrug, going for unbothered as I tuck an escaped tendril behind my ear. "No big deal. I just wanted to."

Hunter surprises me with a wide arm sweeping around me to pull me in close, his hand tipping up my chin as his lips press to mine for another stomach-swooping experience. I close my eyes as I melt into it, feeling a little dazed when he pulls away.

"What was that for?"

Hunter smiles as he gives me that same sort of unbothered shrug. "Just wanted to."

I curl my fingers into the hem of his flannel shirt (it's blue today). "Are you sure you don't want to . . . ?"

"Come on," he says with a sort of wizard-like move that has me turning on my heel at the gentle urging of his hands on my hips. "Put me to work."

"SO EXPLAIN TO me what we're doing here again."

Hunter's stained towel continues to swipe back and forth across the wooden counter where the computer and other things have been cleared away for the moment, and his lips press together in a line.

"It's like . . . a cheat varnish. A refresher. It's supposed to restore the old finish so you don't have to sand and stain again."

"Do you always keep cheat varnish on hand?"

"For emergencies," I tell him. I can see the way his brow wrinkles in concentration from across the room, his lips turning down in a frown as I say with a chuckle, "Just focus on your counter."

"Sure thing, boss," he grunts. "It seems to be working, at least."

"It'll do in a pinch," I say. "We'll make sure to do it properly after this whole thing pans out."

He makes a quiet *hmph* sound that I don't miss. "You mean *if*."

"Don't be such a downer," I chide from the staircase where I'm working on the banister. "Positive thoughts manifest positive outcomes."

"Did you just think that up?"

"No, someone wrote it on a wheatgrass smoothie I got from a café once."

Hunter makes a less-than-pleasant sound, and when I peek over at him he looks positively disgusted. "*Wheatgrass?*"

"Yeah, it was about as good as it sounds." I laugh. "My friend Ada was on this health kick, and for like two seconds I let her take me along." I stick out my tongue. "No thank you. It would take a hell of a lot more than positive thoughts to get me to drink that stuff again."

Hunter shakes his head, muttering something under his breath that sounds suspiciously like *Californians*. One of these days I'm going to have to take him back there simply for the comedic value of seeing him so out of his comfort zone.

There's a bit of quiet that settles as we both continue working our way through the main room, approaching this project with a divide-and-conquer attitude as we try to focus on the rooms that will most likely be included in Nate's article.

"So, besides practicing your camping seduction tactics and streaking across football fields," I say good-humoredly to break up the silence. "What else did baby Hunter like?"

"I don't know . . ." Hunter seems to have to really dig hard for an answer to this question, his expression one of puzzled concentration. "I liked music, I guess. I mean, I still do, but I always liked listening to my dad's old records. I still have them up in my room, actually."

"No Taylor Swift, I imagine," I say with a sigh.

He sighs, feigning actual regret. "Unfortunately, no."

"Damn. You totally look like a Swiftie too."

"Right. I realize how misleading that must be."

I shake my head, holding a closed hand near my head and opening it as I pull it away to mimic an explosion. "So hit me with your favorite song."

"I don't have a favorite song."

"*Everyone* has a favorite song."

"Then what's yours?"

"'Summer Girls' by LFO," I tell him without missing a beat.

"I don't even know what that is."

My hand stills, and I stomp down the stairs to give him an incredulous look. "Excuse me? Everyone knows that song."

"*I* do not know that song."

"It's like a nineties classic," I exclaim.

"Okay, but I don't know it."

"'Hip hop, marmalade, spic and span'?"

Hunter wrinkles his nose. "What?"

"Oh, come on." I throw up my free hand in disbelief. "'Call me Willie Whistle 'cause I can't speak, baby'?"

"Okay," he chuckles. "You're making this up."

"It was like the weirdest song to come out of that decade! It's full of all these ridiculous one-liners that don't really make sense. That song is like trying to get a straight answer out of a Dr. Seuss character who's done shrooms. It's fantastic."

Hunter is full-on laughing now. "I'll take your word for it."

"You'd better be glad the power is out," I grumble, stomping back up the stairs to continue with my own varnish brushing.

"I honestly never really got away from music from the seventies and eighties," he admits. "The Bronco still has an eight-track player in it. So that's kind of what I'm working with."

"You're like a lumberjack version of Captain America when he came out of the ice seventy years later." I snort.

"Captain America? Is that a politician?" I wheel around with an open mouth only to catch his sly grin. "Just kidding."

"You're lucky you're so pretty," I threaten.

Hunter does his best impression of me batting my eyelashes. "You think I'm pretty?"

I giggle as I shake my head, having no idea where this playful Hunter came from or what he did with the stoic giant I met a few weeks ago, but I'm not hating a single second of it.

"*Fine*," I concede. "So you like oldies. That tracks, if I'm being honest."

"Tracks?"

I often forget I'm dealing with a man who is still using a flip phone in the year of our Lord 2025. I shouldn't expect him to be up to speed on social media lingo that I started using ironically and now can't seem to stop. "It basically means it makes sense."

"Really? Who comes up with this stuff?"

"Must be all the young folk," I deadpan.

"Are you being smart right now?"

"I would never," I say seriously. "So, oldies? Is that part of your solitary lumberjack aesthetic?"

"It's Dad's fault," he says with a quieter laugh now, watching his hands wipe on the refinisher with a faraway look as if remembering.

"Pretty sure he was blasting Creedence Clearwater Revival to me in the womb."

"He sounds like a cool guy," I comment. "So what would baby Hunter be doing in this situation?"

"A snowstorm? As a kid? If the power was on, I was definitely in my room playing a video game or something." He chuckles softly. "My dad would whip out his famous homemade hot chocolate."

"What made it famous?"

"That he managed to convince us it wasn't out of a packet, I'd wager."

I bark out a laugh. "He sounds like he was a lot of fun."

"He was." I notice then that Hunter's hand has stopped moving, and there's a wistful sort of smile at his mouth. "They both were, really. It was . . . hard. Losing them."

"You were so young," I offer. "I can't imagine."

He still isn't moving, staring at the half-done counter as his tiny smile slowly morphs into a frown. "I told you about our tradition, right?"

"You mentioned it," I say.

"Every year my dad would take us out the day after Thanksgiving to pick a tree."

"The *day* after Thanksgiving?"

Hunter shrugs, one corner of his mouth tilting. "I know. My mother was obsessed with Christmas. She wanted to put that thing up the second the turkey leftovers were stowed away." He absently makes a slow swipe over the counter with his towel as he remembers. "We did that every year. Every single year. I *always* went with them . . . until I went to college."

I notice there's something pained about his features now, something about this story that's obviously causing the hurt reflected there. "Hunter?"

"My mom begged me to come home for Thanksgiving," he tells me. "But Chloe's parents had invited me to go on vacation with them, and I . . ."

I drop my rag and take slow steps down the stairs. "Hunter . . ."

"I should have been there," he half whispers. "If I'd come home . . ." He shakes his head. "It was snowing so hard that day. Maybe if I'd been here I could have talked them into holding off, or maybe I could have driven them, maybe they wouldn't have . . ."

I think I surprise him by how close I am, and his words die on his tongue as he watches me approach. I think a lot of things about Hunter and this place are starting to make more sense than they did when I first came here, painting a picture of a man still carrying regret and letting it rule his entire life. His solitude and his surliness feel like they have built up from years of blaming himself for something that absolutely wasn't his fault—which is obvious even to me.

I'm right in front of him now, definitely getting the refinishing liquid on the wool of my sweater and more on my hands as I scoop up both of his hands, rag and all. "Hey."

He looks at me now, his eyes a little glassy. "Sorry, I don't even know why—"

"Stop it," I cut in. "Don't apologize."

"I never talk about this," he admits.

"Then maybe it's a good thing that you are," I answer. "It seems like you've let yourself be swept up in this guilt. Like it's still got a hold on you. I get why you were so against the reno now."

He nods slightly. "It felt like an insult. Changing things. This was their entire *life*, you know?"

"I didn't know them," I say, "but I'd feel confident in betting that *you* were their life, Hunter. They sound like good, loving people. I'd go so far as to guess that they'd be more concerned with *you* being happy than the state of this building."

His mouth turns up, but only a little. "Maybe."

I lean over the counter, making a bigger mess of my sweater but not caring in the slightest as I pull him in by the collar of his flannel shirt to cover his mouth with mine. I linger for a second longer than I should, probably, but I'm getting a little addicted to the soft-to-scruff ratio that comes with Hunter's kisses. More truthfully, I'm sort of getting addicted to Hunter Barrett and all the layers of him that keep getting peeled away.

"What was that for?" he asks when we finally pull apart.

I smile against his mouth. "Just wanted to."

"You make it very hard to get work done," he murmurs.

"Just trying to motivate you to hurry up and finish," I say with a smug expression as I push away from the counter. I look at the mess on my sweater then, frowning as I pull the material away from my body. "I'll have to change again." I give him a sly grin, doing my best to draw him out of his mood and back into the cheerful Hunter who batted his eyelashes at me only a few minutes ago. "Probably need another one of those wipe-down fireplace baths after we're done."

And as I saunter back up the stairs to finish my work, his answering groan makes me think that maybe he isn't the only one who knows how to get the upper hand.

24

Hunter

"I COULD GET used to this," Tess sighs.

She looks like a quilted armadillo with the blankets wrapped around most of her body, save for the lone ankle that pokes out for my inspection. My fingers press gently into her skin to work out the soreness that's crept in after a day of whipping this old lodge into better shape. We're bundled up in our cocoon of the tent, and after spending so many hours trapped here with her, I don't know how I'll go back to the real world when all this is over.

In the nine or so hours since we pulled ourselves from the sex-bed-and-breakfast we made for ourselves in the main living room, we've managed to shine up the walls of most of the major rooms, clean away the dust and such that she wasn't able to get to the day before, and even fix the broken railings on the front deck.

Okay, so that one was mostly Tess, but I don't even feel emasculated by it. Watching Tess with a hammer is kind of an aphrodisiac for me, as it turns out.

We've gotten a lot done in a minimal amount of time, and that's extra impressive considering we'd both (I think both, at least, if her scent is any indication) rather be doing . . . other things.

"Yeah?" I answer finally. "Should I put this on the website too?"

She cracks open one eye. "Did I say that out loud?"

"Sort of moaned it, really."

"There is a definite market here for some sort of VIP service. Especially if we put you on the page like I suggested."

"Yeah, no thanks," I say with an amused huff of air.

"We could do a Hunter-of-the-month calendar," she counters. "How do you feel about Santa hats?"

"I think they're better left for the elk head."

She clicks her tongue. "I'm going to need to see a little more dedication from you, Mr. Barrett."

My hands still on her ankle for only a moment, resuming their slow ministrations when I catch back up. "I don't think I should feel the way I do when you say that."

"'Mr. Barrett'?"

I go still again. "Careful."

"Interesting." She grins wide. "I'll have to tuck that away."

I shake my head again as I bite back a smile. "You might be a little diabolical."

"It's probably the grandpa in you," she says seriously. "All that whittling has given you these old-man kinks."

I roll my eyes, releasing her ankle before crawling over her legs and pulling open her quilt to snuggle into it with her. "Scoot over."

"So bossy," she laughs.

I adjust her until she's sitting between my legs with her back to my front, then settle against the back of the couch as I rewrap the quilt around us both before nuzzling my face in her hair. "You smell good."

"What?" She snorts. "I probably smell like wood finish and leftover sex sweat."

I grin against her throat. "I like it."

"Weirdo."

"Are you hungry? I could cook something."

"Just sit like this for a bit," she hums, snuggling deeper into me. "You can impress me with your fireplace-food skills in a minute."

"Okay." I shift a little, the movement slotting her more easily between my legs. "I turned my phone on today. My friend at the co-op said they've started working on the downed power lines. We'll probably be the last ones to get power back, but hopefully by tomorrow we'll have heat again."

"You mean to tell me I have to stop being personally warmed and go back to central heat and air like some sort of regular person?"

"You'll survive."

She lets out an emphatic *hmph*. "Will I?"

My arms come around her to hold her against me in answer, and when I glance down I notice her eyes closing as she lets her head fall back on my chest.

"I really *could* get used to this," she mumbles lazily.

"Could you?"

I kiss her hair. Her scent is stronger now, and in it, I can smell everything that's been building for the last twenty-four hours. It's slower than the other times, but no less potent. I worry about how she'll feel when it comes, if she'll be afraid, if I'll be able to do everything right to help her . . . It's been so *long*, after all.

"I don't think you have much time until your heat," I tell her. I pull her in even tighter against me. "It's fucking sinful the way you smell, Tess."

She wiggles slightly. "But you . . . you like it?"

"Like it?" I snort. "It's taking everything I have not to tear this blanket off you and fuck you until sundown."

Her breath catches. "And this is a bad idea because . . . ?"

"You're too close. You should rest. Before . . ."

"Before you fuck me until sundown," she laughs.

My cock twitches, and I have to give it a strong mental talking-to. "Yes," I answer hoarsely. "That." She's quiet for so long that I can't help but add, "Are you scared?"

"I . . ." Her lips close as she considers this. "Weirdly no? I mean, it's been okay so far, right? And plus . . . you're here."

My chest swells with her faith in me, and I hold her even tighter, so tight that she would be well within her rights to complain. "I'll take care of you."

"Yeah," she chuckles. "It's funny . . . Normally I would revolt at that."

"At what?"

"Letting you take care of me."

"You can't be strong *all* the time, Tess," I tell her, feeling something soft in my chest for this headstrong woman.

"Maybe," she answers softly.

I kiss her temple. "You're worth being fussed over."

"You probably say that to all the girls," she teases.

"No," I say seriously. "Just you."

I'm rewarded with a sharp intake of air, her fingers sliding over my forearms and gripping there as if holding me back. My lips curl even though I say nothing, letting my chest rise and fall in the same pattern as hers as we both settle into a contented silence. When I let my eyes drift open, I can see that the sun has finally started to shine after the hazy gray of the storm yesterday, and I take that as a good sign. It's just begun to sink toward the glittering white horizon farther up the mountain, and from where we're sitting, the light of it seems to make the freshly fallen snow sparkle.

"I wish I had my phone," she complains after a while. "That would be a pretty picture."

"It's still pretty," I tell her. "Even without the picture."

She rolls her eyes. "I forgot your ongoing vendetta with modern technology."

"It's not a vendetta," I argue. "Just never really got the obsession with being so . . . *connected* all the time." I laugh a little under my breath. "That's probably my dad's fault too."

"Was he boycotting fax machines in the nineties?"

My chest shakes against her back as I try not to laugh out loud. "I don't know . . . He just . . ." I go quiet for a moment, thinking. "He always used to say that people need to *live* in moments more. I remember being a teenager and asking for a cell phone for the first time—"

"Is it the one you're still carrying? Because I could make a *strong* argument that you bought a cell phone as a teenager and never—"

I pinch her hip, making her squeak, but it effectively quiets her.

"*Anyway.* Facebook was just becoming a thing, and phones with the internet were everywhere, and all my friends at school were getting them, and I *begged* him to get me one, but he said no. He sat me down and told me that the obsession with being dialed in *all* the time was going to be the thing that ruined real-life relationships. He told me I should try to focus more on *living* in moments instead of obsessing over sharing them with everybody."

"Ah. So you adapted this whole cyberphobia aesthetic at a young age."

"Not at all," I assure her. "I was mad as hell. I went behind his back and did a ton of odd jobs until I could buy my own."

"Oh my God, you little rebel."

"I haven't even told you about my biker gang yet."

She elbows me. "So then why are you carrying a phone that's one step up from those eight-inch monstrosities with antennas?"

"It's funny." My chin tucks against her shoulder. "It had been years since I'd had that conversation with my dad, but when they died . . . it was the first thing I thought of. I guess . . . when you lose someone . . . you regret all the memories you didn't get a chance to create. It just makes you reconsider all the things you used to think were important."

"God." She takes a deep breath, then blows it out loudly. "Now I feel like an asshole."

"It's okay," I urge sweetly, rubbing her arm with my hand. "I'm sure you didn't mean to make fun of my poor departed father's imparted wisdom."

She pulls away to wheel around and face me, her mouth hanging open as she slaps my shoulder, and I'm seconds away from bursting out laughing. "Oh my God! You can't joke about that, you jerk." She rearranges herself until she's facing me with her knees on either side of my hips, my hands finding her waist to settle there as she crosses her arms. "Now who's being diabolical?"

"I guess you're rubbing off on me," I say with a smile.

She unwinds her arms so she can press her hands against my chest, sliding them across the flannel appreciatively as she lets out a deep hum that makes me squirm. Her hands push higher until her fingers graze my throat to tease at the curls clinging to my nape, then she breathes in deeply before releasing a satisfied sigh.

"I have to admit, it's been . . . kind of nice," she tells him. "Being unplugged like this."

"Has it?"

"Mm-hmm." She twirls one dark strand of my hair around her finger. "It helps that I've had a good distraction."

"If I had my way, you'd be too distracted to ever turn that phone on again."

"I can see the headlines now," she chuckles. "'Tess Covington Abducted by a Mountain Man, but She Isn't That Mad About It.'"

"I'd be happy to abduct you anytime," I tell her, meaning it despite my playful tone.

Her eyes are softening now, moving across my face slowly as if memorizing my features. I feel my pulse quicken when I reach one hand out to cup her jaw, my thumb stroking back and forth across her cheek as I study her. I remember thinking she was pretty when I first saw her, and knowing her hasn't diminished that. Now that I understand she's a little quirky and a lot wonderful, with her desire to help others and her love of silly songs, she's fucking beautiful. It's hard to even tear my eyes away from her.

"Now this would make a pretty picture," I murmur.

She bites her lip. "You're getting good at this flirting thing."

"Who would have thought?"

"I bet the camera on your phone is terrible."

"I'm not even really sure it works."

"Why does that not surprise me?"

I grin, leaning in to press my lips to hers in a slow, lazy way, as if only to test the softness of them. There is a tease of tongue and a trip of her breath as I raise my arm from where it was resting at her waist to circle around and pull her in tighter. I give a contented sort of rumble in my chest before I lean back to take in the dazed expression on her face now. One that *I* put there. Her eyes are half-lidded and her lips are kiss-bitten, her face flushed with color.

My alpha is practically beating his chest at the sight.

"Beautiful," I whisper.

I lean backward on a whim, bringing both of my hands in front of my face to make a square shape with my fingers. Then I make a clicking sound with my mouth as I pretend to take a picture, watching her blink in surprise as she cocks her head.

Her face breaks out into a smile. "What was that?"

"A mental picture," I tell her. "So I can remember."

"Oh?" She presses a finger to one of the buttons of my shirt, tracing it lightly. "So this is something you definitely want to remember, huh?"

I look at her then—*really* look at her, at the way her freckles spray across her nose like lightly dusted sugar, the way her bangs perpetually hang into her eyes, giving them a sort of sultry quality, the way her nose is so petite that it wrinkles with almost every emotion that plays across her face—and, well . . .

"I think everything about you is something I want to remember," I answer quietly.

Her nose does in fact wrinkle with her wide grin, her arms looping around my neck as she pulls me in for a kiss. I can't seem to remember the time when I was afraid of this, of giving her this piece of me, worrying that if I did, I might not get it back. Now I seem to be content with throwing her every piece she can hold, consequences be damned.

Her tongue tangles with mine as she buries her fingers in my hair, and I can almost taste the sweet scent of her blooming in the air around us, so thick it threatens to suffocate me, but I would happily let it. I trace the curves and planes of her with my hands as I plunder her mouth, my lashes fluttering closed as I try to memorize every slope, every dip with my fingers. I feel the way she starts to rock in my lap, asking for something without words, her kisses becoming just a little more frantic, her touches just a little more eager.

I think I don't recognize it at first, because the scent and taste of her are hypnotizing, consuming. I don't see it for what it is until I feel the heat between her legs pressing against my flannel pajama bottoms, so hot it threatens to melt me. I hear a whimper in the back of her throat that I catch with my tongue, and I feel her body stiffen when she makes that sound again, pulling away from me with that dazed look, but it's sharper now. More in focus. Or maybe it just feels that way, because she looks . . . hungry.

"Hunter," she rasps, rocking her hips again. "I feel . . ."

I take a deep breath, the scent of warm cinnamon and baked fruit reaching so deep into my senses I seem to be drowning in them, and I know at this moment that we don't have any more time. Despite the fact that everyone will most likely be returning soon, even if I share this with her, and there's a good chance I'll have to let her go . . . none of it will stop what's coming.

"I've got you," I tell her. "I'm not going anywhere."

There's not a place on this earth that could entice me away.

25

Tess

I THOUGHT I knew what to expect when it came to all this heat business, but I'm quickly realizing that every incident before this one was . . . mild. They must have been, because it suddenly feels like my body has caught fire. I gasp for breath as the inferno rages through me, my pajamas feeling like they're too tight, too scratchy, like I need to get them *off*.

"Need these off," I hiss, tearing at my top.

"Shh," Hunter soothes, taking over my futile efforts and easing the cotton over and off me. "You're okay. I'm here."

"It burns," I groan, clasping my arms around my middle. "It *hurts*, Hunter."

"I know, sweetheart," he says gently. "I'm here."

He seems too calm for this, considering I feel like I'm bursting at the seams, but when I catch sight of his eyes as he urges me to sit up so he can start helping me out of my pajama bottoms, there's a wildness there that betrays his placid demeanor. Almost like he's holding back for my sake.

When I'm blessedly naked, I become wholly irritated that Hunter isn't in a similar state, so I shove at his shirt to try and force it off of him, but he takes over that task too. My eyes feel heavy-lidded as he pulls away from me to continue stripping down to nothing, and it isn't until he's fully bared to me that I get some relief from the frenetic energy that's pulsing inside me, my body seeming to take this as a sign of impending relief.

"Hunter," I whimper, barely recognizing my own voice as a cramp tears through me. "I need you."

"I know you do," he hums, gathering me in his arms and pulling me against him before turning to spread me out over the mound of blankets and pillows lining the bottom of the tent. "I know exactly what you need."

His kiss is gentle when he curls his big body over me to press his lips to mine, but in my current state, it feels like that isn't enough. I nip at his lower lip like some sort of animal—and under different circumstances I might find that funny—but right now, all I can think about is the ache between my legs and deep down in my belly, begging for some sort of satisfaction. Satisfaction that I'm starting to understand only he can give me.

I gasp when I feel his cock slot between my legs, so thick and hard already that it steals my breath, I want it so much. "Please," I beg, hardly even recognizing my own voice. "*Please*, Hunter."

"Fuck, Tess," he rasps. "The way you smell right now..." He lifts his head, that same wildness in his eyes, the pupils so enlarged they nearly swallow his irises. "You need my knot, don't you, omega?"

"Please," I plead again, my nails digging into his sides as I try to pull him back down to me. "Need you."

"I told you," he says, his voice gravelly and low and seeming to reach right between my legs like a caress. His large hands circle my waist, gripping me tight as his thumbs span across my belly, stroking there. "I know *exactly* what you need."

My head tilts back and my mouth gapes open when he starts to push inside me, stretching me with a wonderful burn of a different kind—one that is almost enough to distract me from the fire licking at my skin. Almost.

Hunter takes his time inching inside me, his pace too slow for my liking, but if I close my eyes, I can focus on the hot length of him filling me, and he bites at my lower lip roughly as I cling to his hips. He never takes his hands off my waist, keeping a tight hold on me and almost pinning me down as he goes just a little deeper.

"So wet," he says on a sigh, and when I open my eyes, I catch him staring down between us as he bottoms out. "So fucking *hot* inside."

"Feels so good," I whine. "More. I need more."

"You need more?" His thumb skims along my belly as he stirs his hips. "You need me to fuck this pretty pussy?"

"Please," I mewl, my vision blurring and my embarrassment at begging flying out the window. "Please move."

Hunter's teeth press into his lower lip as he looks down at me from beneath hooded lids, holding my gaze as he slowly pulls out of me. I feel every inch of him, can feel the slight bulge of his knot as it eases out of me, the press of it against my inner walls sending a flurry of sparks through my system that threaten to steal my breath.

"Look at you," he breathes, his voice shaky. His breath catches when his knot slips inside me again, a flush creeping down his neck. "You look so pretty when you're full of me. Fuck, Tess. You look like a goddamn daydream."

I gasp when he thrusts *hard*—the sudden fullness so intense that I feel fit to burst. It's too much and yet not nearly enough, and I reach above myself to grip the pillows scattered about our tent. He rocks his hips in a smooth motion when he withdraws this time, never slowing as he pulls out to the tip only to glide back inside.

The sounds in our tiny space—wet, slick sounds that only betray how needy I am—add to the frenzy building inside me. I need his next thrust more than air; I don't think I knew what need really was until this moment.

I feel like I'm burning when he pulls one hand away from my waist to lick the pad of his thumb, then brings it between us and rolls it against my clit. The simple touch sets me off like a firework, and I claw at the bedding above my head, trying to get closer or to escape—I'm not even sure which.

"That's it," he hums. "That's a good girl." He paints a circle against the swollen bud, each touch making me clench around the hard length of him as he rocks in and out of me. "You're going to take everything I give you, aren't you? You're going to take it because you need me, don't you?"

"Yes," I hiss, my eyes rolling back. "Need it. Need you."

Through the haze, I don't miss the slight edge to his voice, and something primal inside me preens at the knowledge that this is satisfying to him, that maybe he needs me too. His hand is still on my belly, so I cover it with mine, urging it upward, and he lets his palm slide over my sternum and between my breasts. I hold it there over my heart, clutching his fingers in mine as I push down on his still-thrusting cock.

"I do," I say again. "I need you, Hunter."

His pupils flare, his jaw clenching for only a moment before his arms wind around me, urging me off my back. He gathers me up in his embrace like it's nothing, like it's *easy*, and holds me to him as his mouth covers mine. My thighs bracket his hips as I straddle his lap, the angle forcing him deeper, forcing his knot to press into a place inside me that has me seeing stars.

"*Hunter*," I cry against his tongue.

"I've got you," he growls. "You're *mine*."

In my current state, those words do funny things to my brain, making me shiver all over as I wrap my arms around his neck to cling to him more tightly. My tongue tangles with his as he bounces me on his lap, my slickness leaking out to wet his thighs in a way that might embarrass me any other time. But right now? Right now it only makes me burn hotter, knowing that I'm marking him this way. It makes me feel like—for right now, at least—he's mine too.

His kisses move to my jaw, then across my cheek, farther still to my throat, and I can feel the sharp press of his teeth against my ear before he rasps, "I own this pretty pussy, and I'm going to knot you until neither of us can walk."

And that sounds like heaven, like *bliss*, and the raging inferno inside me climbs to new heights, threatening to carry me away. I cling to him like he's holding me down, and in a lot of ways, he is. His arms keep me rooted on his lap, his cock fills me in a way that makes me feel desperate, and his scent dizzies me but in the best way. I bury my face in his neck to draw in more of it, a choked cry escaping when he fills me just right.

I feel his fingers in my hair, winding through the strands and gripping them tight enough to urge my head back, forcing me to look at him. He holds me there as he thrusts up into me roughly, baring my throat to his gaze as he studies it intently. I don't know what he sees—can't fathom what he's looking at—but in the next second his lips follow the path of his eyes, and he puts his mouth on the tender skin there, his tongue licking at a place near the bend of my shoulder, making me seize up.

"*Oh*."

"Do you know what this is?" He licks there again, nibbling with his teeth gently. "This is your mating gland," he explains. "If someone bites you here, if you bite them back . . . it binds you. Did you know that?"

And he makes no further moves, and deep down beneath the haze I know that this isn't something for us—it's too soon, nonsensical even—but amid my fevered thoughts, the explanation still makes me shiver.

His nose is buried in my throat. "You smell so fucking good. You *feel* so fucking good. It's too much." He nuzzles that gland, and I tense up in the most delicious of ways, his cock swelling, feeling a bit thicker than before. "I need you to come, because when you do, I'm going to fill you up. I want you so full of me that you feel me for *days*."

I realize all at once how much I want that too, and when his fingers dive between us, skimming just below my belly button, I find myself nodding eagerly even as their tips collide with my clit.

"Right there," I breathe. "Don't stop."

"Not stopping," he hums. "Never stopping."

He rolls the sensitive bundle between his fingers expertly, applying exactly the right amount of pressure, enough that the fire licking at my skin seems to take on a singular purpose, pooling low in my belly and even deeper as the pleasure climbs higher and higher. My nails bite against his shoulders—they're surely going to leave a mark, and I like that too. I want to mark every inch of him. I want to sink my teeth into his skin until he bruises. I want *so many things* that have never occurred to me in the slightest, and I can't say how much of it is my heat or just . . . him.

"Oh," I gasp suddenly as he touches me perfectly. "Right there. *Right there. Oh my God.*"

I cry out loudly when I start to shake with my orgasm, and the rush of slickness between us has the sound of his skin slapping against mine sounding downright filthy. I throw my head back, oblivious to anything and everything except the feeling of his cock sliding along my sensitive inner walls. Distantly, I can hear Hunter let go also, and I close my eyes when his knot starts to swell, feeling it press against my insides tighter and tighter until he can barely move, until he's forced to slow. Even then, he continues to rock his hips in tiny thrusts—like he simply can't bear to stop.

I don't know how long we stay like that—clinging to each other and trapped in our current position—but when the pounding of my heart finally slows, when I can finally let my eyes flutter open, I find Hunter watching me through hooded eyes, his expression awestruck.

"Are you . . . okay?"

I blink slowly, trying to make sense of the question, and when I do, a laugh burbles out of me. "Am I *okay*? I'm fucking fabulous. I mean, I feel like Jell-O, but I'm *great*."

"I didn't . . . hurt you, did I?"

"Not at all," I assure him, tucking my head against his shoulder. "That was perfect."

His fingers comb through my hair, and I hear him slowly inhale at my temple, hear the soft sigh that follows.

"*You* were perfect," he says quietly.

My mouth curves into a smile. "I was?"

"Mm-hmm."

"So were you," I assure him.

He moves to situate himself, the action making his knot jostle inside me, forcing a soft whimper out of me.

"*Oh*."

"It'll pass," he assures me. "In a little while."

And instead of feeling put out by the fact that I'll be here for the foreseeable future, I feel oddly morose that it won't be longer. I know it's probably simply the hormones, but something deep in my brain mourns the fact that we can't stay like this forever, as silly as the thought is.

"But this will happen again?" I ask, trying to sound curious and not desperate.

He nods against my hair. "It will. For a couple of days, most likely. I can't be sure since your cycles are so irregular."

I don't want to think about what that might mean for when my brothers return or when we're forced to go back to the real world, so I choose to live only in this moment. It's a really nice moment, after all.

I can't help but shudder with pleasure as I remember the intensity in Hunter's eyes when he fucked me, when he uttered dark promises of *owning* me, and I let them replay over and over in my head as his hand starts to rub soothing circles against my back. I hold him close and wonder what it means—how much I liked hearing it, how much I want to hear him say it *again*.

The things I'm feeling right now could be just hormones, just some product of biology—but I *feel* them just the same. And what does that mean for us? Can I really let him take care of me like this, knowing what I do about him? What will happen when this is over? When we're forced to return to reality? Will I still feel this way? Will *he*? The uncertainty of it all has my stomach twisting into knots. Because given that this is temporary, given that we're only supposed to be "friends who help each other" . . . I have no way of knowing what all this means.

If Hunter's contemplative silence as he touches me is any indication . . . I have a feeling he doesn't either.

26

Hunter

IT'S BEEN TWENTY-FOUR hours since her heat hit her fully, and Tess is still just as needy. Not that I mind. I'm realizing, much to my surprise, that I *like* her this way. In fact . . . I might like it a little too much.

"Look at you," I croon. "Making a mess of the blankets. So *messy*."

She bites her lip. "I'm sorry, I—"

"No," I say with a shake of my head. "I want more. I want you to make a mess of *me*."

I've never been as hard as I am for Tess right now. It's like my cock *knows*. It knows what's coming. It's almost painful, how hard I am for her. That voice inside me that seems to be running the show screams for me to take her, to bury myself inside her—but not yet. Her scent has been waning the last few hours. Not significantly, but enough to let me know this won't last as long as I thought it would. And I want to savor her a little more first.

I reach to curl my arms beneath hers, pulling her against me and rolling so I can drape her across my abdomen. She's moving—

tiny shifts of her hips as her slickness drenches my skin—and *fuck*, I need more of that.

I press two fingers to my lips, looking up at her. "This is where I want you. Come here."

"Please," she says pouting. "I need—"

"I know what you need. Come *here*."

She is hesitant as she moves up my chest, a trail of slickness left in her wake, and I'd be happy to let it cover my entire body. When her thighs are around my head, I pull her close, my hands gripping at the rounded curves of her ass until the wet center of her pussy is just where I want it.

Fuck.

I could live like this. Survive on her alone. Breathing her in. Tasting her. I can see *everything* from this angle, the way her slickness trails out of her at a steady pace, the way her pussy clenches at nothing.

Soon. Soon I will give her more than enough to fill it.

I tease at her entrance, enjoying the way she watches me as I do so. I like the way her lashes flutter when I push a finger inside her, wetting it, slowly pumping it in and out until her breath catches.

"Lean back," I urge. "Put your hands on my stomach."

She does so without question, and her obedience speaks to something inside me that I haven't allowed myself to touch for a very long time. I'd almost forgotten it, it's been so long.

"That's my good girl. I want you to brace yourself. Don't let go."

"*Hunter.*"

"I know, I *know*. I'm going to take care of you. Just take the edge off a little." I curl my fingers around her hips, gripping the soft swell and tugging her even closer so I can lick a long stripe up her center.

I hum against her slick core, loving the way it forces a gasp out of her. "You made such a mess, after all." I let my tongue linger at her opening, teasing her there. "All over the tent. So *wet* for me."

"Hunter, *please*."

I feel her hands slip a little along my stomach, and I turn my head to nip at her inner thigh with my teeth. "I said *brace* yourself, Tess. If you let go, I stop. Understand?"

"I understand," she says with a fervent nod. "I'll be good."

Fuck, I love the edge in her voice. Breathy. Soft. *Desperate*. I want her that way.

I want her out of her *mind*.

My chest is so wet now that she slides against me, and I have to physically *hold* her to my mouth to keep her from falling away. I *love* it. Love being so coated in her that I'm not sure if it will ever wash off. I imagine still being able to scent her on my skin tomorrow, keeping her with me. And I *want* that. I want to take her again tomorrow, and the next day. I want to knot her for *days*.

But first things first.

She rolls her hips over my face when my tongue meets her pussy again, and I pull her even closer until the only thing I can breathe in is her. I lick through her drenched folds and pull her clit between my lips to suck as I let my tongue swirl over it. Her slick continues to stream out of her, coating my chin and more, even as I drink her in from the source.

Her pussy clenches around my tongue as I slide it into her, and if I could, I would crawl inside her fully. Her flavor is enough to drive me *mad*—I don't think I've ever tasted anything as sweet as Tess.

Her thighs shake as she struggles to contain herself against my mouth, and I paint circles around her clit, even grazing it with my teeth. When she bucks against my face so hard that I have to force her still with my hands, she makes the softest sound, one that rings in my ears and makes me feel hot all over.

When she begins to tremble, a soft cry escaping her as her head lolls forward in pleasure, the flare of contentment in my chest is overwhelming. *I did this to her. I know what she needs.*

It's only when she's still that I allow her to sit back against me, shifting so that she settles over my stomach as she struggles to catch her breath. I'm left with a mess of fluids in her wake, and I let my fingers trail lazily through them to gather them up. She watches with wide eyes as I bring them to my mouth and suck them clean without looking away.

When I move to do it all over again, I instead let my fingers hover, holding her gaze before offering the slicked digits to her instead.

"Open." She obliges, letting her lips part as I push my fingers into her mouth. "Taste."

She sucks softly, pupils blown wide to the point that her eyes appear black. Her lashes flutter somewhat as she tastes herself on my fingers, and it only heats my blood further.

"Do you need more, Tess?"

She nods dazedly, still sucking my fingers. It makes my insides clench up with want, and in an instant I'm wrapping my arms around her, rolling us so that she's beneath me. I spread her across the blankets like an offering, her hair fanning out like a halo as she looks up at me with complete trust in her eyes.

"So pretty." I run my hand down her belly, causing her to wince slightly as her body tenses, and I reach to let my thumb brush across her lip. "Does it hurt?"

She nods, her eyes glassy as my hand cups her cheek, and she turns to nuzzle into my palm. "Please."

She squirms, her legs falling apart to welcome me, stirring up her scent that robs me of rational thought. I can hear my pulse in my ears, my instincts chanting for me to *take, take, take*—but I don't have to. There's nothing to take because she's *giving* it to me.

I curl my body so I can brush my lips against her throat, and my tongue traces the heated flesh just below her ear. I press my lips there, sucking softly as a rush of her scent overwhelms me, so potent I can taste it. My cock slots along her core, and I thrust lightly as I drink in her scent and taste, feeling them cloud my mind.

"Such a tiny thing," I murmur. "I'm going to fill you up, omega. I want to feel you taking everything I give you." She whimpers, and I let my cock slide heavily along her slick center. "Want to feel you stretch around me."

"Yes," she breathes.

I hear a slight growl in my chest, and I can't pinpoint where it comes from. "Yes what?"

"What?"

My jaw clenches as I take in her confused expression. She hasn't called me it since that first time, weeks ago, and even then, it was no more than an accident. I can't say why I'm so desperate to hear it again, the need building inside me at a constant pace since she first went into heat.

"Alpha," I tell her, nipping at her earlobe. "I want you to call me alpha."

And she doesn't hesitate, gasping when I tease the sensitive flesh between my teeth as she utters, "*Yes*, alpha."

I feel the word as if it's reached out and caressed me, my chest swelling and my cock doing something similar as I thrust against her again. I let a hand slide down the length of her side and wrap it around her hip to steady her squirming body as I dip into her.

The first press of my cock against her entrance actually takes my breath away. I brace myself on my hands when I begin to push into her, needing to see her face. Needing to watch every expression as she takes me. To commit them to memory. There's a kernel of fear deep inside me that grows each time I touch her like this, because I have no way of knowing what comes after. I can tell myself it's just hormones making me feel this way, that her heat is triggering my more possessive instincts—but I don't think that's true. How can it be, when I spend most of my waking moments lately thinking about her?

I'm distracted by the way she clenches around me—she's so tight, so *small*. I feel every inch, every ridge of her, gripping me, *holding* me. Her mouth parts in a silent cry, and she watches my face as I push deeper. She tenses, and I reach down to hold her face as my thumb strokes her cheek. "Relax, sweetheart. You have to relax. You can take me. You already have. You were made for me. For this."

She blows out a breath, and I feel the tightness of her pussy relax a fraction as she tries to obey. I press my lips to hers, gripping her tight as I sink farther. Every time I'm inside her, there's a slight resistance at first—I'm so much larger than her, I'm not sure if there will ever be a time that there isn't—but there's relief in knowing that she *can* take me, that she was meant to.

My body acts on its own now, taking what she's offering—*claiming*. When I surge deeper, the quietest of sounds escapes her, and I cover her face with kisses over and over as I seat myself inside her fully.

It's torture.

It's *bliss*.

It takes everything I have not to move.

My chest is tight with some primal satisfaction, and the sound I make can only be described as a purr. "You take me so well, Tess. Such a *good* girl for me. You feel incredible, do you know that? So wet, so *warm*—I don't ever want to do anything else but this."

"*Alpha.*"

"Tell me how you feel."

"Full. So *full*." She shifts her hips, pressing closer as I hiss out a breath. "I need you to move. Please, move. *Please, alpha.*"

Pulling out of her is sweet torture. Every inch of her tight channel grips me as I withdraw, my cock wet with her fluids and yet still *snug* inside her. "You're so perfect," I groan into her skin. "Made for me. This pussy was *made* for me."

"*Hunter.*"

I love the way even my name sounds as if she's begging for me. "I'm going to knot you, Tess. Do you understand?"

"*Yes.*"

I thrust back into her a little harder. "I'm going to knot you because you need it. Because *I* need it. I'm going to knot you because you *belong to me*."

And I don't know if that's true, but I can't seem to stop asserting that it is. She might not be mine next week or even tomorrow, but right now? Right now she absolutely *is*.

"Say it, Tess," I urge. "Who do you belong to?"

"*You*," she whines. "You, Hunter."

I'm driving into her now, abandoning my feeble attempts to be gentle. She doesn't protest—only wraps her legs around my waist as she clings to my shoulders, taking everything I give her. Her breathy sounds wash along my throat, her face buried in my hair. I feel her lips as they find my skin, the light flick of her tongue along my gland, and I'm lost, utterly *lost* in her.

I don't know what comes after this, don't know what it will mean for us when it's over—and I realize all at once that it terrifies me, the not knowing. I told myself I would never feel this way about another person, not again, and yet here I am, wanting to own this woman like she was made for me, because right now . . . it feels like she was.

"That's it," I huff. "*That's it, Tess.* Do you feel that? The way your body accepts me? Welcomes me, even?" I roll my hips and bottom out, feeling that flood of heat building at the base of my spine as my balls draw up tight and my cock hardens further. "Because it's *mine.* Your body, your mouth, your sweet little pussy—every inch, every curve, every fucking piece of you is mine. Do you understand?"

She's nodding against my skin, her little tongue at my gland until my vision is nothing more than a blur of colors and the world a haze of sounds and there is *nothing*—nothing but her and this moment.

My breath comes out in labored pants as I surge into her with such a force that her entire body jolts with every thrust. She's clinging to my shoulders, holding me as tight as she's able as I fill her again and again and *again.* I'm so close—so fucking *close*—I need her to come. Need to feel her quiver and shake around my cock knowing I did that, *I* made her fall apart.

I can feel it—how close she is—in the way her body tenses beneath me, in the way her fingers grip my skin, even from the quiet gasps that stream continuously from her mouth.

"Want to feel you come, omega. Come for me. *Come.*"

She does, after seconds, minutes, hours—I can't be sure. Time is irrelevant when she's beneath me. It's beautiful when she falls apart, her back arching to bring her closer and her eyes shut tight as she trembles around me. It's enough to push me over the edge, and I'm far less quiet when I thrust into her that final time.

There's a distant roaring, and I vaguely recognize that it's me making the sound. I pull her so close I wonder if I might crush her—I want to imprint her shape into my skin so a piece of her is always with me. A thought that, were I more coherent, might worry me.

When my knot begins to swell, it's almost a holy experience. I have nothing to compare it to, this completeness I feel as I'm rooted deep inside her—but I know without a doubt there's nothing on earth that *can* compare to it. Every shift of her body pulls another gush from me, and I almost wish I could see the way I fill her up, the way I flood her insides to blend with her slickness.

I don't know exactly how long we'll be like this—locked together with no hope of escape—but I don't mind. I would stay like this forever if given the choice. I roll to my side, tucking her into my chest as she nestles closer. She fits so perfectly there, nuzzled against me.

"You should sleep," I tell her after a while. "You'll need your rest."

"Don't wanna," she mumbles.

I grin. "I'll be here when you wake up."

She looks at me, eyes wide and shining and so fucking *sweet*. "Promise?"

I tilt my head, pressing my lips to hers and letting them linger for several moments. When I pull away, a part of me worries that I'm helpless to stop the growing feelings I have for her, that she's taking everything I have left. Not that it matters, I think, since at this point . . . I seem to be giving it freely.

That same fear grips me—the one that comes from the uncertainty of what comes after this, of the idea of *losing* her after having just had her—and I hold her a little tighter to me, I pull her a little closer.

"I'm not going anywhere, Tess. I'm here. I promise."

And as she snuggles against me, content and sated and warm, I can only hope there's a chance that she might not go anywhere either, whatever that looks like. That even if her job takes her away from here . . . she might want something more.

That she might want it as much as I'm beginning to.

27

Tess

I CAN TELL my heat is waning on the second day. My head feels clearer, my need less demanding. I can't say why that disappoints me. The reality is I am a mess of sweat and slick and God knows what else, and I should be grateful for the reprieve, I really should. So why aren't I?

I snuggle into Hunter just a little closer as he sleeps, peering up at his relaxed expression as I revel in the warmth of his arm draped across my hip. It's been an intense forty-eight hours; I can honestly say that nothing about this experience has been something I would ever have expected—but as overwhelming as it's been, I've actually really... liked it. I've never felt as protected or as cared for as I have during this heat, and I know it's entirely because of Hunter.

It still makes me shiver when I remember some of the things he said to me, things like how he *owned* me, how I *belonged* to him. Rationally, I know it was nothing more than his instincts and a whole lot of hormones that most likely made him say those things, but I can't pretend I didn't like hearing it. What's more, I *loved* hearing it. And maybe that's just instincts and hormones too, but I still feel it.

I've spent most of my adult life making sure that everyone

around me was always taken care of—it's just in my nature. So being like this, having someone take care of *me* for a change, is . . . nice, to say the least. It's something I'm afraid to let myself get used to, because who knows how long I'll have it?

I close my eyes as I nuzzle into his throat, inhaling his calming scent and letting it wash over me, soothing my anxieties about what he might or might not have meant to say in the heat of the moment. For a little while longer, at least, I can simply enjoy the way he feels against me. He stirs when I press my hand to his chest, running my fingers through the dark hair there.

"What time is it?" he asks groggily.

I tilt my head back to meet his sleepy gaze. "Almost lunchtime," I tell him. "I checked my phone when I woke up."

"Have you heard from your brothers?"

He winces when he says it, and I know he's thinking about the moment when this little bubble of ours has to burst. When we're forced to return to the real world. Is he also agonizing over what that might mean for us?

"They texted me last night to say they're okay," I tell him. "They've got power where they are—they're staying in a hotel right now—and they said as soon as the roads are deemed clear enough to travel, they're going to head back this way." I run my fingers through his chest hair again, enjoying the soft sound of contentment it draws out of him. "Probably tomorrow."

"Tomorrow," he echoes, sounding not so thrilled. "Right."

I kiss the corner of his mouth, grinning against his scruff. "Plenty of time for you to take care of me again."

"Oh yeah?" He chuckles softly, turning his head so he can breathe in deep from my hair. "Your scent is waning," he tells me, sounding displeased. "Your heat might break before the day is out."

Disappointment floods me, and I know it's only because I'm not sure what comes after this. I want to ask him, to talk to him about what all this might mean, but I can't bring myself to. I'm too worried about what he would say, worried that it wouldn't be what I want to hear.

"I still need you," I tell him quietly, not feeling that demanding urge to have him but wanting him all the same.

He makes a low sound deep in his chest as he pulls me tighter against him. "I'm not going anywhere."

And as he rolls me onto my back, covering me with his larger-than-life body, I can't help but hope he means that.

AFTER MORE THAN three days without power, the afternoon brings more small projects and more makeshift sponge baths that have me starting to really miss the shower upstairs. I mean, yes, having Hunter's help has been a major point in the whole roughing-it scene, but still. A girl needs hot running water.

Not that he seems to mind in the slightest.

I've been lounging at the dining room table while he rehangs the curtains we took outside to beat the dust out of an hour ago, admittedly enjoying the way he tends to roll up his sleeves when he works regardless of the temperature. (I think that could be its own genre of porn, just saying.) My body is still sore and drained from everything we've done, and Hunter insisted on letting me rest for a while, as much as I protested.

"So Nate will be here tomorrow," I point out, making conversation. "Are you nervous?"

"Well, the future of the lodge is sort of hinging on this one guy and him not finding the place 'dingy' when he first sees it"—he looks back at me over his shoulder, but there's a teasing smile at his mouth—"so why would I be nervous?"

"It's going to be fine," I assure him. "This place looks like a whole new lodge even after a few weeks. Imagine what it will look like when we finish everything after the interview is over."

"What sort of things is he going to ask me, you think?"

"It's a short piece," I promise. "Just a little bit about you and the lodge and prime times to visit. Nothing major."

He nods his head as he breathes deep in relief. "I can handle that."

"Don't worry," I soothe. "He's going to love this place. You don't see rustic little places like this where I'm from. It's practically alien."

He leans back to fiddle with the curtains, opening them slightly until he's content with their placement on the rod. "Jeannie is going to be so smug about this."

"I *really* hope I'm around for that conversation."

Hunter makes an indignant sound. "I'll bet." He steps down from the stepladder to assess his work. "Does that look straight?"

"Well, considering you obsessed over that level for at least fifteen minutes..."

He shoots me a disgruntled look as he steps around the table to my side, still looking at the curtains. "I just want to make sure it looks right."

"You *are* nervous." I turn toward him on the bench, leaning on one elbow to prop my cheek against my fist. "That's so cute."

He cocks an eyebrow at me. "Cute?"

"Even big, scary lumberjacks can be cute," I tell him seriously.

"I can definitively say you're the only person on the planet who has ever called me 'cute,'" he snorts.

"Really? Not even during your streaking days? I bet someone thought you were *very* cute when you went out there butt na—"

It takes him no time at all to cross the minimal distance to tower over me, his hands coming to rest on either side of my body as they brace against the table behind me and effectively trap me below him where I sit. He leans down to press his lips firmly to mine, and my lashes flutter.

I'm a little short of breath when he pulls away, his mouth only inches from mine. "Did you just shut me up by kissing me?"

"It worked," he murmurs.

"That's not very nice of you, Mr. Barrett."

He makes some sound in his chest, one that makes me press my legs together. "I *really* don't think that should do what it does to me."

"Oh?" My hands come to rest on either side of his denim-clad hips, my fingers hooking in the loops as I pull him a little closer. "So does that mean you want me to stop, Mr. Barrett?"

"Tess," he groans.

I let my hand wander until I can palm him through the now-straining zipper, feeling *exactly* what my teasing is doing to him. I know my scent is still thicker than normal; I know that because he *told* me in a sort of a groan only an hour ago while we were eating lunch. "Because it kind of seems like you don't want me to stop."

His lips brush along my cheek, his mouth parted and slack—his breath catching when I pop open the button at his fly. His head lowers to watch as I drag his zipper down slowly, his cock already pressing insistently against the cotton of his boxer briefs as if he *really* doesn't want me to stop.

"Tess," he says again, his voice sort of choked this time. "You must be tired. You don't have to—"

I don't hear the rest of his protest, and honestly, I'd be willing to bet he forgets what he was going to say altogether when I tug down the elastic of his underwear to free him. Despite his imperviousness to the chill in the room that comes from lack of power, I can say definitively that I have no such resistance to it. Maybe it's something that will come the more I settle into my new omega designation. I know my hands have to be cold when they circle him. Maybe that's why he hisses through his teeth as my fingers curl around the hot, hard length of him—or maybe it's simply that I'm touching him. I like that thought better.

I'm not going to pretend I've ever particularly enjoyed oral. I mean, I was getting nothing from it in the past except a sore jaw well before I was acquainted with the enormity that is Hunter Barrett—but something about the way his breath seems to come unsteadily now, the way his fingers find their way to fist gently in my hair in an almost unconscious way . . . I find myself enjoying the effects of what I'm doing to him *very* much.

I know before I even start that actually fitting all of him in my mouth is going to be impossible, but I'm going for sexy here. Even in my limited experience with this, I doubt gagging will be a particularly attractive move. Last time was so rushed, so frantic—I didn't have time to properly enjoy everything I was doing to him. Now I let my fist slide down the velvety firmness of his cock, leaning in to press the flat of my tongue just under the head before I close my lips around it to suck.

"*Fuck*," he grunts.

If I turn up my eyes, I can see the way he's watching me; there's something wild in his expression that only spurs me on. I hold his gaze when I take as much as I'm able to, letting him push deeper into my mouth, keeping a tight pressure with my lips so that I can feel every inch of him as he moves over my tongue.

I doubt I can even get half *of him in my mouth*, I think distantly.

His hips jerk when I suck softly, making a wet sound that feels a little obscene. I tease the end with the tip of my tongue before swirling it all around the thick head, and the groan that tumbles out of his mouth when I dip it into the slit seems almost pained. His taste makes me dizzy, stirring up the ghost of that same need I felt when I was fully in my heat, making this just as enjoyable for me as it is for him, I think.

"Tess. *Tess.*"

I push my lips down the length of him slowly, looking up at him as innocently as I can manage while my mouth is so full. "Hmm?"

"I'm going to come," he warns me, sounding completely regretful. "I'm going to come in your mouth if you keep doing that."

I pull off him with another exaggerated sound, only because it seems to really rile him up. "You can," I tell him. "If you want to."

I'm lifted off the bench so fast I don't even know what's happening at first. Suddenly his hands are under my arms and he's tugging me upward to bring me right off my seat, plopping me down on the table as his mouth slants across mine roughly. His tongue slips inside to pet at mine as his hand tugs my hair a little less gently to angle me into the kiss, and all I can do is wind my arms around his neck to hold on.

"That's not where I want to come," he breathes against my mouth between kisses.

I'm surprised I can even make words, my voice sounding hardly like my own with the way it rasps out of me. "What's the alternative, Mr. Barrett?"

"Hmm." He gives me another slow kiss that has me leaning into it. "Aren't you cold?"

I don't tell him that my sweater and my fleece-lined leggings feel a little sweltering now, shaking my head instead. "Getting warmer by the second."

"Really?" For a moment, I'm actually put out by the way his fingers untangle themselves from my hair—until he reaches for the waistband of my leggings. "Then lift up."

I drop my hands to brace myself against the tabletop, lifting my hips to let him start peeling my leggings along my thighs and down my legs, with my underwear in tow. They slide over my wool socks to flutter to the floor and leave me in nothing else from the waist down, and I briefly wonder if I look ridiculous, half-naked in socks on a dining room table.

Not that Hunter seems to mind. He shoves the bench seat under the table with one swift movement of his foot, and then he's kissing me again, stepping between my legs and stealing my breath with both his tongue and the sudden sensation of his very warm, very *hard* length slotting at my core. He tilts his hips to let himself slide through my wet folds as if to coat himself in them, bumping my clit so that I shiver against him.

"You are"—he looks down to watch as he gives another slow, deliberate slide—"very hot here, at least."

I shift a little, struggling to hold on to coherent thought. "How sturdy is this table?"

"I don't know," Hunter tells me, his lips finding mine to curl lazily as he draws back to nudge at my entrance. "Guess we'll find out."

"*Oh.*"

I've lost track of how many times we've done this over the last few days, but even still, it takes me by surprise just how *much* of him there is. The way I'm sitting makes it easy for him to glide *deep* inside—my body welcoming him as he fills me up wholly. It's not as all-consuming as it was when I was fully in heat, but even still, the feel of him has my skin prickling with warmth and my insides twisting with want. Heat or no, I think that's just the effect he seems to have on me.

My nails dig into his shoulders when his hips meet mine, a rush of air escaping me, which he quickly swallows down as his mouth finds mine again.

"Fucking perfect," he mutters against my mouth. "How are you so perfect?"

"I'm not really that per—*Ah*."

His hips draw away to give me that slow, delicious friction as he pulls out, my eyes rolling back a bit as my belly tenses, flooding with warmth.

"Trust me," he sighs, easing inside again as I gasp with it. "You are."

He doesn't hesitate to do it all over again, forming a steady rhythm, in and out, that has me clinging to him tighter. He isn't looking at me—his gaze is fixed on the place where we're connected, watching himself push into me. My eyes drift closed as I lean in to press my lips to his throat, mouthing there softly as I push my fingers into his hair.

"*Hunter*," I breathe. "Right there."

He pulls out just to drive back inside, hitting the place that makes me lose my breath. "There?"

"*Yes*."

I feel one large hand at my shoulder, a finger hooking into my neckline to pull my sweater away, and then there's the hot wet of his tongue and his teeth as he sucks at a place near my collarbone, which damn near makes me forget my own name. I pull him tighter, which seems impossible given how little room there is between us as it is, and through it all Hunter never stops the way he rocks into me, moving a little faster with each thrust as his stuttered breath washes against my shoulder.

"Hunter," I huff at his neck. "Can you—? I just need—"

As if he can read my mind, I feel his other hand snaking between us, pressing against my clit, rolling the sensitive bundle under his fingertips as pleasure sparks between my legs and my thighs tremble.

"I love the sounds you make when you come," he rasps into my shoulder. He bites gently before he licks it, and I shudder as I remember what he said about my mating gland. "Can you come for me?"

"Keep—*Yes. Right there.* Don't—Please. Please don't—*Fuck, Hunter.*"

He grunts when I come apart, my entire body shaking against his as I moan through my orgasm. It seems to go on forever with the way he continues to drive into me, chasing after his own release and prolonging that humming current that seems to be coursing through every inch of my skin. He's loud and rough when he finishes, groaning nonsense that I can't fully catch. Words like *fuck* and *perfect* and *so good* are the only pieces my brain can pick up on.

I feel his knot swell, pressing against my inner walls, leaving behind that delicious feeling of fullness, and I think there's a good chance I might be a little addicted to the sensation. Will anything after this ever compare to him? Why does the thought of doing this with anyone else leave me irritated and a bit sad? I have to push the thoughts away, not wanting them to sour my mood.

His chest heaves against me as he holds me close afterward, his lips trailing along my jaw before they find mine. "I have no idea how we've gotten any work done this weekend."

"It's fine," I assure him. "I remember back in my high school health class they said you're supposed to share your body heat to avoid hypothermia in extreme temperatures."

Hunter smiles against my mouth. "I don't think this is what they meant."

"Whatever. Same difference."

I'm fully aware of how close he is—how *full* of him I still am—but none of this seems to faze Hunter. His face is hardly inches away from mine when his hands come up between us in that same adorable little would-be camera gesture as he makes a clicking sound with his mouth.

I bite softly at my lower lip. "Another moment you want to remember?"

He smiles as he kisses me again, and just when I think we might be here for a good while, there's a *click* above us, causing us both to turn up our faces as a sudden blast of slightly warm air begins to pour from the vent overhead. Hunter's surprised expression matches mine when his eyes find my face, and my lips tilt at the corners as I wind my arms around his neck once more.

"I guess they fixed the line," he comments.

"Oh my God, we can *shower*," I gush. I shift my hips, both of us wincing. "I definitely need one."

"I keep making a mess of you," he murmurs.

My smile widens as he closes the distance between us, brushing his lips against mine as he leans into the kiss. "I guess that means you should come clean me up then."

"Are you asking me to shower with you?"

"That's exactly what I'm asking."

"Hmm." He kisses me again, slower this time. "I can't promise you'll get clean."

I grin against his mouth. "Sort of the whole point."

28

Hunter

"EVENTUALLY I HAVE to take off this towel and get dressed."

My arms wind around her a little tighter, pulling her closer to me under her bedsheets. "I'm okay with one of those things."

"I'm just glad that we *can* lounge around in towels without freezing to death."

"You Californians and your working central heat and air."

"We aren't too keen on the cold where I'm from."

"Mm."

I'm only half listening now, my body lax and warm against her as my breath huffs into her hair. She curls her fingers around my forearms as she nuzzles closer, and I close my eyes and enjoy the quiet in what might be the last few hours of our little bubble. Since Jeannie has already called to make sure we're alive, I assume it won't be long before she comes to check for herself. Not to mention Tess's brothers will be back tomorrow, *and* I have the most important interview of my life to deal with.

"Oh my God," she says suddenly, jolting up so fast she jostles me as she lets out a surprised sound.

"What? What's wrong?"

"Ada probably thinks I'm dead," she groans.

"I think your phone is over there on the dresser," I tell her, sitting up.

She swings her legs over the side of the bed and runs for it, snatching it up in a hurry, then padding back across the room to wrestle with her charger, which has been plugged uselessly into the wall outlet by the bed all weekend.

"Do I need to worry about a visit from the FBI?"

She rolls her eyes. "Ada would probably trek this mountain by herself if she actually thought I was missing. I'm sure she's already badgered my brothers about why I've been MIA so long." She props her fist on her hip as she turns to eye my stretched-out form clad only in a towel, wiggling her eyebrows when I catch her looking. "Now, that's a shot for the website."

"I will toss you into the snow," I warn.

"Wow, rude."

I take a moment to just look at her as she powers on her phone, taking in her soft curves and her wild, towel-dried hair that falls carelessly against her shoulders. She looks so sweet like this, and her scent, which is still tinged with the last remnants of her heat, is so sultry that it makes me want to grab her by the waist and throw her on the bed to try to squeeze in one last round before it all ends—but I know she must be sore, so I refrain.

Still, if I stay in the same room with her for much longer when she's in nothing but a towel . . . there's no way I won't maul her again. Not with her smelling so sweet. With that in mind, I roll off the bed to root around for my discarded pajama pants.

"I'm going to go downstairs to check on the pipes," I tell her, needing an excuse to get out of this room. "Are you hungry?"

She shakes her head. "I'm okay right now."

I pull my pants up over my hips, then cross the space between us to give her a quick peck on the lips after shrugging into my shirt. "Okay."

"What was that for?"

My lips curl. "Just wanted to."

Her answering smile is brilliant, and I can't help but press another kiss to her lips, one that lingers this time.

"Pipes," she murmurs against my mouth.

I grin back. "I'm going."

She shoves me along with a nudge to my hip, and I begrudgingly leave her behind to go make myself busy. It's warmer now in the rest of the lodge, thankfully, so I don't have to worry about making sure Tess keeps herself bundled up while the old ducts try to catch up to the waning snowstorm outside.

The snow comes down in soft flakes now, the sky clearing up to let the sun shine through, which tells me the roads are likely being plowed as we speak. I'm not sure how I feel about the idea of giving up the little bubble Tess and I have made for ourselves, not quite ready to share her with others—even her family. I can honestly say I've never felt so possessive of another person, not even Chloe, and that thought should probably scare me. It should have me reevaluating things. But right now . . . it just brings me a sense of peace I've not had in a very long time, and I decide to enjoy it for however long I have it.

Because the idea of losing it is something I can't bring myself to think about right now.

I'M BUSYING MYSELF under the kitchen sink sometime later when I hear a commotion out in the foyer, the front door creaking open, and the sound of stomping feet following. The sounds instantly have me on high alert, the thought of Tess upstairs, still vulnerable at the tail end of her heat, putting me on edge. I pull myself out from beneath the sink and hurry my way through the kitchen and dining room to the foyer, where I'm taken aback by the sight of Tess's brothers piling in through the door with snow dusting their shoulders.

"Hey, man," Thomas says, stomping the snow off his boots. "Some fucking storm, huh?"

Chase shrugs out of his coat. "I hope our sister didn't freeze to death while we were gone."

"Where is she, anyway?" Kyle asks.

A few things happen at once. Their friendly faces and welcoming smiles do something to my insides that is a far cry from what they should; instead of putting me at ease, they have me grinding my teeth, the thought of Tess upstairs and smelling like heat making my body go taut with tension. My protective instincts go into overdrive, and before I can even catch the words coming out of my mouth, my voice projects with an edge that seems unlike me.

"You need to leave," I tell them, clenching my fists.

Thomas looks thrown. "Do what now?"

"Tess isn't ready to see you," I say, rising to my full height. The thought of someone seeing her like she is . . . it makes my alpha restless and agitated. "You can't see her."

Chase immediately goes on the defensive. "Excuse me? You can't fucking decide that." His head whips around. "Where is our sister? Tess? Tess!"

I don't know what has me acting this way; logically, I know that these are Tess's brothers and that they're no threat to her, or to me, for that matter, but the idea of a male—*any male*—seeing her even at the end of her heat has me feeling out of sorts. I can't make sense of it, but I also can't stop myself from acting on the feelings.

"I said"—I bump Chase with my chest, feeling a rage building inside that is entirely new to me—"you can't see her."

"The fuck, guy?" Thomas says, his voice rising. "What the hell is your problem?"

I hear an actual growl leaving my throat, and my skin ripples as if getting ready to shift. There's a humming voice inside me that screams *protect* and an even more alarming one that whispers *mate*—and there doesn't seem to be a shred of rationality to be found as I grab Thomas by the collar.

"If you so much as touch a foot to that staircase, I'm going to—"

"Hunter!"

My head whips around, and I spot a wide-eyed Tess at the top of the stairs, looking down at the scene before her in shock. I stare up at her with a parted mouth for a span of seconds, my chest heaving as I try to gather my bearings. With her this close, the hazy red that was clouding my vision seems to part—and all at once I recognize what the hell I've just done.

I let go of Thomas immediately, stepping away with bared palms as I struggle to catch my breath. "I—I'm sorry," I manage, still feeling a bit like I should be putting my body between theirs and hers. "I don't know what happened."

"You just tried to throw us out," Kyle huffs. "That's what happened." He looks up at his sister. "What the hell is going on here?"

Tess isn't paying attention to her brothers, rushing down the stairs to my side and pressing her hand to my chest, her eyes wide and looking as if she might be feeling as out of sorts as I am.

"Are you okay?"

Chase snorts. "Is *he* okay? Dude! He was six seconds away from hulking out on us!"

"Seriously, Tess," Thomas presses. "What the hell is going on?"

I keep my eyes trained on Tess, my brow wrinkling. "I'm sorry," I murmur. "I don't know what came over me. I thought about someone being near you right now, and I just . . ."

"I get it," she says with a nod. "It's okay."

"The hell it's okay," Chase says as Thomas roars, "Is someone going to tell us what's going on?"

Tess takes a deep breath, looking resigned. She gives my chest a gentle pat, turning her head to peer back at her brothers. I know this isn't how she wanted them to find out, and for that, I feel a pang of guilt in my chest. I'll need to apologize for that later too.

"Boys," Tess says with a sigh. Her hand glides down my forearm, her fingers finding mine and twining there, settling some of the restlessness still lingering inside me. "I can explain everything."

If the way her brothers are eyeing our intertwined hands is any indication . . . there's a good chance it will be *me* who gets my ass kicked here.

"SO . . ." CHASE STARTS. "You're a wolf person?"

"She said not to call them that," Kyle points out.

"I still don't understand how the fuck this happens," Thomas chimes in.

"I told you," Tess explains. "It's called a 'late presentation.' It's just something that happens sometimes."

"That doesn't explain why our *employer* tried to maul us," Kyle scoffs.

Tess shoots me a look, and I frown down at my lap, keeping my fingers firmly laced through hers. She seems to sense that doing so calms the more raging tendencies threatening to creep up with the close proximity of other males—brothers or no—and I'm grateful to her for indulging me, as ridiculous as it seems for me to be feeling these things in the first place.

"I'm sure you've heard what happens to shifter females," Tess says slowly. "Periodically."

"No." Chase cocks his head. "What happens to them?"

Thomas grimaces, leaning over to whisper in his brother's ear.

"Oh, *gross*," Chase says, making an *ack* sound. He shoots me a disgruntled look. "You've been *boning* our sister?"

I grit my teeth. "It's not so crass as that."

"I've read it's very painful for the female shifters," Kyle says, eyeing me. "If someone isn't there to . . . help."

I nod. "It can be, yes."

"Ugh," Thomas says. "Are you saying we should be *thanking* him for plowing our sister?"

My fist that isn't wrapped around Tess's hand clenches. "Don't talk about her that way, please."

"What's with you being so uptight anyway?" Chase asks. "You were ready to bite our heads off for wanting to see our own sister."

I take a deep breath, letting it out slowly. "Because of what we are, your sister and I are very . . . compatible. With her going into heat . . . it's hard for me to rein in my instincts. It makes me a lot more . . . possessive than I would usually be. Plus, it's been a long time since I've been near someone like her. It makes me even more . . . not myself." I take another deep breath. "I'm sorry. For the way I acted."

Tess squeezes my hand. "You didn't mean it."

"Why are you taking his side?" Chase grumbles.

Thomas leans forward in his chair. "So what does this mean? Are you guys, like, a couple now?"

"I—" My mouth falls open, thrown by the question, considering it's something Tess and I have yet to discuss. I turn my head to catch her equally distressed look, no doubt as lost for the answer as I am. I swallow thickly, keeping my eyes on hers so she can gather how sincere I am when I say, "I'm whatever she wants me to be."

Her breath catches and her eyes shine, her lips parting to answer as Chase says, "Oh, gag me. This is too weird."

"What will this mean for the job?" Kyle asks, more practical than his brothers.

I glance over at her, my brow cocked. "Nothing? Everything can go on as usual as soon as Tess is feeling better."

"Or now," she says forcefully. She looks up at me with a determined expression. "Nate will be here *tomorrow*, and we still need to finish staining the floors in the main room. I wasn't even sure we could get it done with just me and you, but with my brothers here . . ."

"Nate?" Thomas asks. "From the magazine?"

Tess actually looks sheepish. "Oh, yeah . . . I called him to see if he could sneak this place into the next issue. Give it a little boost."

"Oh God," Chase groans. "She's in love. They're going to have little wolf babies."

Tess's face flames pink, and I once again feel a small urge to pummel her brothers just for making her uncomfortable, but I wind an arm around her shoulders instead.

"Let's focus on the project for now," I tell them. "I'll pitch in as much as I can. Just tell me what to do."

A small smile touches her mouth. "You sure you're ready to be put to work?"

"Born ready," I tease.

"Good," she says. "Then we can start with—"

A sharp trilling sounds from Tess's pocket, and she frowns as she fishes out her cell phone, glancing at whoever is calling. When she notices the number there, her mouth parts, her eyes flicking up wildly to her brothers before she turns to catch my gaze.

"What?" I ask. "Who is it?"

She swallows, her face paling even as her scent tinges with anxiety.

"It's the producer from HGTV," she says.

Her brothers start to whoop excitedly, encouraging her to answer the phone, and when I hear her soft *Hello* after she puts the receiver to her ear, I know I should be excited for her, that I should be thrilled that she might be getting the opportunity she's been waiting for.

Instead . . . I feel a strange sense of dread.

29

Tess

MY HEART IS hammering wildly in my chest as I bring the phone to my ear; I haven't heard from the network in weeks now, and there was a small part of me that was beginning to think they'd forgotten about us altogether. I take a deep breath to calm myself, even as my brothers continue to bounce in their seats, and bring the phone to my ear.

"Hello?"

"Hello, Ms. Covington. This is Heidi Bosseler, with HGTV."

"Yes, of course," I hear myself saying over the thumping of my heart. "It's good to hear from you."

"And you too," she answers brightly. "I'm sorry it took so long for us to get back to you."

"Oh, that's not a problem at all," I assure her, rising from my chair, feeling a restless urge to pace. Doing so means I have to let go of Hunter's hand, and I miss the contact immediately. "We've been busy here in Colorado anyway."

"You certainly have," she chuckles. "We've been reviewing all the sample footage you've been sending over, and, well . . ."

I hold my breath, counting the seconds.

"We think it's fantastic," she finishes.

I feel a grin break out across my face, my entire body thrumming. "Really?"

"Really," she assures me. "We actually didn't have any doubts, with everything you've done so far, and seeing what you've been doing there in Colorado only solidifies our faith. We'd love to discuss moving forward with your own potential show here at the network."

I pump my fist, trying to tamp down the squee that threatens to escape me, and I catch sight of my brothers from the corner of my eye, shaking each other in premature celebration.

"We'd *love* to discuss it with you," I say emphatically. "We've only got a few more weeks here at the jobsite, and then I can—"

"Oh, no," Heidi says, a frown in her tone. "We'd like to get started right away, actually. We were hoping you could fly out on the red-eye tonight and get over here to Knoxville to discuss terms. We have a lot to do if we want to slot you into the spring lineup. No time to waste, I'm afraid."

I feel all my previous joy plummet down into my toes, leaving me feeling bereft. "Tonight? There was a big storm that just blew through here," I tell her. "I'm not sure if a flight out tonight will even be possible."

"I'll be happy to look into it," Heidi assures me. "But you'd be willing if we can get it booked?"

I glance at Hunter, who through all this has remained stoic, giving me nothing in terms of what he's thinking. He holds my gaze as Heidi prattles on, talking about flights and car services and everything I ever wanted—up until a few weeks ago. Now . . . I feel torn at the idea of leaving this place. Which is ridiculous, right?

"Sure," I answer when I sense she's done talking. "Let me just check with my brothers to make sure they can finish up here, and I'll call you right back, yeah?"

"Don't take too long," she says. "I'm going to go ahead and look into flight options and send you the details, if that's okay. We really don't have any time to waste."

"I totally understand," I tell her. "Talk soon."

I watch as Hunter rises from his chair, his expression still blank as he moves from the den into the other room. My brothers crowd me the minute I hang up the call, going on and on about landing the deal, about getting everything we wanted—but all I can think about is the man in the other room. The one I promised to be there for tomorrow.

And in all the times I imagined this—getting everything I ever wanted—I never imagined that there might be something I would want just as much.

I FIND HIM in the dining room, sitting at the massive wooden table with his fingers laced and his chin resting on his hands. He looks out at the snow through the big bay window, seeming lost in thought. I take the seat beside him tentatively.

"So I guess you caught the gist of that," I say quietly.

He nods. "Pretty much."

"Are you . . . mad?"

He heaves a sigh. "Of course not, Tess. This is what you've been working for."

"But your interview . . ."

He shakes his head. "I wouldn't even have the interview if it weren't for you. I couldn't possibly be angry with you over it."

"I told you I would be here," I point out.

He places his hand over mine on top of the table, glancing at me from the side. "Seriously, Tess. You've done enough. I promise."

"But what happens if they need me to start right away?"

His grip slackens, his mouth turning down at the corners so infinitesimally that I almost miss it.

"Then we'll figure something out," he says quietly. "Worse comes to worst... You're not the only contractor out there. I'm sure we can find someone to finish up for you."

His casual tone makes my gut clench; how can he be so cavalier about me leaving after everything? Doesn't he care?

"So, you're just... fine," I say. "With my leaving."

Hunter looks down at his hand resting over mine, his features still neutral, but his eyes... Sad, I think. They look sad. Or maybe that's simply me projecting.

"No," he admits. "I'm not fine. The thought of you leaving makes me feel like I'm being turned inside out, if I'm honest."

"Then maybe I can—"

"*But*," he cuts in, not letting me finish. "This is something you've wanted for a long time, from what I've gathered. You've worked so hard for this. You *deserve* this, Tess—and I won't be the one to stand in your way. Plus, think of your dad. He needs you too."

"But what about—" I swallow around the growing lump in my throat, feeling my eyes sting. "What about everything that's happened?"

He smiles at me gently, reaching to cup my cheek. "Sweetheart... We shared a heat together. It was intense. I'm sure that even now you're feeling the effects of it. But you won't *always* feel this way. In a few days... a week, maybe... you'll feel normal again. You won't feel like you need to be right here beside me at all times. And I can't let you even consider throwing away such an amazing opportunity for someone you barely know."

"But . . ."

"It's not the end of the world," he says, nodding his head as if to assure himself. "Maybe . . . maybe when you find the time you can call me."

I choke out a watery laugh. "On that ancient thing you carry around?"

"It gets the job done," he chuckles.

"So . . . that's it then," I say. "I just . . . call you when I can?"

It feels too paltry for what we've shared, not nearly meaningful enough to encapsulate the bliss of this last week. Or all the weeks since I've met him, really. Because if I'm being honest with myself, I think a part of me has been drawn to him from the start. And maybe that's biology or hormones or whatever else you want to call it—but I *feel* it, whatever it is. This connection between us.

Doesn't he feel it too?

"Tess . . ." He sighs. "You cannot let these past few days with me uproot everything you've worked for, do you understand?" His jaw tenses. "I won't let you. Not for this place. Certainly not for me."

There's a large part of me that wants to argue, that wants to scream at him for so easily tossing me aside, but deep down . . . I know he's right. I can't throw everything away just because of one amazing week. I can't do that to my brothers. Hell, I can't do that to myself.

It's only that something inside me is saying that if I leave here—if I leave him behind and chase after my dream—I'll never see him again. Why does that thought terrify me so much?

"Then . . . I guess I'll go pack my stuff," I say softly, the lump in my throat swelling to epic proportions.

Hunter nods. "Probably a good idea."

It takes all my willpower to pull my face from the cradle of his hands, then even more to drag myself from the table, leaving him sitting there looking so forlorn and lost that everything in me wants to run back and ask him to beg me to stay. But I know I can't do that, and I know he wouldn't even if I asked.

So I leave him there, alone, wondering if I'm walking toward my future or leaving it behind me.

BY THE TIME I've called back Heidi at HGTV to confirm I got her email about booking me a flight and packed up my stuff, I've gone way past downhearted. I'm miserable, desolate—I'm downright morose. Hunter hasn't so much as checked on me while I prepare to leave. Heidi sent over my flight details, which have me flying out in five hours, meaning Thomas and I have to be heading to Denver in less than one. So I have just over half an hour to figure out how to say goodbye to the guy who's wormed his way under my skin after spending the last few hours of my heat with him only this morning.

How do you just hug someone goodbye after everything we've done this week? How do I look him in the eye and tell him I'll call him after he held me for days on end? Is it even possible to get through something like that unscathed?

I zip up my suitcase, realizing I'm about to find out.

"Thomas said you're leaving soon."

I jolt at the sound of his voice, then turn to find the man in question leaning against my doorframe, filling the space like he owns it. His arms are crossed over his chest, one ankle resting against the other, and he looks so goddamn delectable right now that I want to unzip my suitcase, spill all my stuff onto the floor, and declare that I'm never leaving.

"Yeah," I manage. "Pretty quick."

Ask me not to go, I think desperately. *Ask me to stay.*

Would I? I wonder. I know deep down that I can't—that my dad needs me too much for me to even consider it—so why do I still want him to ask?

"Your brothers are confident they can get the rest of the floor stained before tomorrow, at least," he tells me.

I nod dumbly. "That's . . . good."

"I really appreciate you doing this for me," he says.

"It was nothing," I urge. "I wanted to help." That lump in my throat is a cantaloupe now; it's a fucking Fall Fest pumpkin. "He's going to ask about how this place started; you don't have to mention your parents, but if you're comfortable doing so, it would add a human element to your story—but *only* if you're comfortable. You should tell him about all the work you're doing on the lodge. I've got Kyle writing you up a list of the remaining projects as talking points. And if you get stuck, just—" I catch the way he's looking at me, a sort of wistful smile at his mouth. "What?"

"Nothing, it's nothing," he says, looking down at his feet. His lips curve upward, but his smile doesn't meet his eyes. "I just miss when you kept saying 'we.'"

The organ in my chest feels like it's in a vise. Like all the air in my lungs has whooshed out at once. "I could still stay," I start. "I could talk to Heidi, and I could—"

"No," he says gently. "You can't."

My eyes sting, traitorous tears collecting there. I can feel something like anger brewing in my belly, and I can't be sure if it's directed at his aloof demeanor or the situation as a whole.

"Just like that, huh? It's that easy?"

He frowns. "I told you it wasn't easy."

"Yeah, well." I plop down on the bed, shoving my socked foot into my boot. "Could have fooled me."

"That's not fair," he says.

I scoff. "Well, I don't think it's very fair that this morning you were touching me the way you were and now you're shoving me out the door."

"What do you want me to say, Tess?" His voice has taken on a slightly harder edge. "That I don't want you to go? What the hell would that accomplish? We both knew this had an end date. We both knew that you were going to leave once you wrapped this up, one way or another."

My mouth drops open. "Now who's being unfair?"

"I'm starting to figure out that *life* isn't fair," he says bitterly.

"Why does it feel like you're pushing me away?"

"Because deep down . . . you know there's nothing for you here. You have this whole big life to live, important things to do, and that doesn't involve some dingy little lodge in some nowhere town."

He doesn't say it with malice. No, his voice actually sounds fond. Like it's a joke between the two of us now.

"It's more than just some dingy little lodge," I tell him. "And *you* are too. But you have to realize that. I can't fight to make this work if you don't want it to."

"What is there to make work?" He averts his gaze. "I told you, Tess. We shared a heat together. That's the only reason you're feeling this way. In a week . . . you'll feel differently."

"Oh, fuck that, Hunter," I snort. "You don't get to hide behind that because you're scared."

"Scared," he echoes.

"Yes, scared," I assert. "You think it's inevitable that you're going to lose me, so you'd rather let me go without a fuss to save yourself the trouble later on, right?"

His mouth forms a tight line, and I know I've hit the nail on the head.

He clears his throat, looking down at his feet. "You have so much ahead of you. You and I both know that I would just hold you back. Deep down, you *know* that, Tess."

"Sounds like a crock of shit to me," I rasp, my voice sounding rough.

Hunter sighs, stepping deeper into the room and gathering me up in his arms. I go easily, nuzzling my face into his chest, inhaling his scent and trying to commit it to memory.

He kisses my hair, and I soak up the simple gesture like a flower in sunlight. I almost whine when he pulls away, his hands cupping the backs of my arms as he peers down at me, studying my face as if maybe he's doing a little memorizing of his own.

Ask me to stay, I scream silently. *Ask me.*

"It's just your hormones," he says soothingly. "That's why it feels like the end of the world. By tomorrow . . . you'll feel much better. You'll see."

I hear him, and I hear the sense in his words, but I don't *feel* it. Not even a little bit.

I'm opening my mouth to tell him so—to beg him to ask me to stay, to beg him to come with me, I have no idea what—but he robs me of all rational thought when he brings his fingers to his face, turning them into a square over his eyes and making a soft clicking sound as he takes a pretend picture.

"Really?" I say with a sniffle. "You want to remember *this*?"

His eyes are soft, his smile softer. "I told you, Tess. I want to remember everything."

"But not keep it," I say petulantly.

I can almost feel the way he wants to say something, and at this moment, I'm so close to begging for him to do so.

But he doesn't, and the hurt I feel at his silence keeps me from saying anything more.

If I'm honest with myself, I know why he's being like this. I know Hunter thinks he would just hold me back, that he would trap me here with no future, but I don't know how to tell him that isn't how I feel. I can't *make* him see that he's worth staying for, and . . . I know he's right about at least one thing.

I *can't* throw everything away for him.

But it would be nice to know that a part of him might want me to, as unreasonable as it sounds.

"I think"—he composes his features into something more manageable—"I'm going to go for a run."

"You're leaving? You won't see me off?"

The facade cracks, and I can see a sliver of pain—the same pain I'm feeling—bleed through in his eyes. "I can't watch you go, Tess," he says quietly. "Please don't ask me to."

"You're having an easy enough time watching me do it right now," I say quietly, feeling childish and hurt.

Hunter levels me with a look, his expression grim. "You were always going to leave, Tess," he tells me. "Maybe it's better this way. Easier, even. I'm sure you'll move on before you know it."

He gives me his back, leaving me there with my suitcase and a whole roomful of regret, and I feel his words cut at me like a knife, so final in their delivery. It's like he's counted on my leaving being inevitable. And I realize that he most likely has, if I really think about it.

I'm sure you'll move on before you know it.

It makes me wonder how much of a chance we ever stood in the face of that.

30

Hunter

THE LODGE FEELS emptier without Tess here, which makes no sense, given that she was only here for a few weeks. But in that time... her presence was so *large* that it almost seemed to brighten the place, to make it feel like more than what it is. I can still scent her in every room, so warm and sweet that it's like she's standing here with me.

And now she's just... gone. Because I practically pushed her out the door. I didn't fight, didn't beg her to stay like everything inside me screamed I should. Why didn't I do that?

You know why, something whispers.

Deep down, I know there's nothing here for her. Even if we were to try to make this work around her schedule... I'd do nothing but hold her back. I mean, really, what is there for her here? Nothing but a lodge that's barely making ends meet and a town that she could probably fit into a subdivision in her city. She can't thrive here. There's absolutely *nothing*.

Nothing except me. And it's no secret that I'm not exactly a prize.

I feel anger and regret swirling through me, a small part of me wishing I'd never touched her to begin with. I *knew* what would happen if I kept giving in to her, if I kept indulging in her sweet scent and her soft body and her softer heart—but I did it anyway. Like a fool.

I smile bitterly.

Appropriate, since I apparently never learned my lesson.

But then I think about her smile and her big brown eyes, which looked at me with such trust over and over again, and honestly . . . I never stood a chance, I think.

I do up the last button on the nicest shirt I own, feeling stiff in the rigid material and the slacks that were a surprise even to me when I found them in my closet. Tess's friend should be here anytime, and with every second that ticks by, bringing his arrival closer, my nerves skyrocket a little higher.

It feels silly now without Tess. What can I possibly say to this man to convince him that the lodge is as special as it feels to me? Sure, there have been a lot of good changes in the last few weeks, but there is still so much to do. And now there's a possibility that we'll be doing it *without* Tess.

Fuck.

As much as I try not to think about her, my thoughts always seem to find their way back to her. It's torture, really.

A knock sounds at my door, and my stupid heart jumps into overdrive, despite knowing there's no way that it could be *her*.

"Come in," I say.

Jeannie's head pokes around the doorframe, giving me an encouraging smile. "Your guy is pulling up the drive."

"Great," I say shakily, dropping down to the edge of my bed. "Now I just have to figure out how to not say anything stupid."

Jeannie frowns, moving deeper into my room and taking a seat next to me on the bed. "You're not going to say anything stupid."

"How do you know?"

"Because you love this place too much," she says. "Anything you say will just be a reflection of that."

I stare down at my hands in my lap, my lips pursed and my brow wrinkled as I consider that.

Jeannie pats my knee. "How about we talk about what's really bothering you?"

"What do you mean?"

"I think you know exactly what I mean, young man." She tsks. "Tess called me from the airport to tell me goodbye."

My jaw clenches despite the fact that I'm trying to look nonchalant. "Oh?"

"Yep. Sounded about as miserable as you look right now."

"I don't know what you mean," I say unconvincingly.

I peek over at Jeannie to catch her rolling her eyes. "Oh, come off it. The pair of you were trapped here for days, and I come back and the entire place smells like heat. I'm not stupid, you know."

"Yeah, well," I chuckle darkly. "Maybe I am."

"It's not stupid to admit you care about the girl," Jeannie points out. "And it's been clear to me for weeks that you do, even before all this heat business."

"I have no issues admitting I care about her," I say with a sigh. *The problem is, I think I care about her too much.*

"Then why are you sitting here moping? You could have told her how you felt."

"How do you know I didn't?"

"Because I know you, and you don't let yourself have good things easily. Too busy carrying guilt from an actual decade ago that isn't yours to carry."

"That's not—"

"Don't tell me it isn't true," she cuts in. "You've holed yourself up here on this mountain ever since your parents died, because you still feel responsible for what happened to them, and you think sequestering yourself in this place is somehow your penance." She cocks her head and gives me a pointed stare when I look back at her with an open mouth. "Am I wrong?"

"I don't know," I say too quickly. "I . . . You're not . . . *not* wrong."

"Baby boy," she sighs. "You're smart, and you've got a good head on your shoulders . . . but sometimes you can be a real dummy."

I rear back. "What?"

"Your parents loved you to pieces. They would hate the thought of you sitting around here blaming yourself for something that was a complete accident. They'd *hate* it if they knew you were still punishing yourself, and deep down, I think you know that." She shakes her head. "Maybe this is a conversation I should have had with you years ago, and I'm sorry I didn't, but something tells me you might be more open to hearing it now."

"Really? What makes you say that?"

"Because I've been watching you with that girl for weeks now, and you look at her just like I used to look at your uncle. Like she hung the moon."

"It doesn't matter," I say dejectedly. "There's nothing for her here."

"*You're* here, aren't you? I'd say you're plenty worth hanging around for."

"That isn't—"

"And for that matter," she says, cutting me off, "who says you have to stay married to this place? You've been holed up here so long, you forgot there's a whole world out there to explore."

"Are you saying I should give the place up?"

"I'm not saying that at all," she tells me. "But I'm saying you don't have to pour every waking moment into it. This place will always be here. We always find a way to keep it going. You don't have to give it your *entire* life to make sure that we do." She pats my shoulder. "You can let yourself have a life outside it, you know?"

I run my fingers through my hair. "We don't even know if Tess wants anything more from me, Jeannie."

"You're right," she says, startling me a bit. "We don't know that, because if I had to guess, you let the girl run off without telling her how you feel out of some silly, misguided sense of being all noble and deciding what's best for her without giving her an actual say, am I right?"

I open my mouth to answer, closing it just as fast when I realize that she is, in fact, one hundred percent correct.

"That's what I thought," she says smugly. "So now you have a decision to make."

My brow wrinkles. "I do?"

"That's right," she answers. "You can either keep going as you have been, giving your entire life to this place without taking anything for yourself out of guilt for something that wasn't your fault at all, or . . ."

"Or?"

"You can go get the damn girl."

I swallow thickly. "Are you suggesting I go after her?"

"I'm suggesting you take something for yourself for once in your life."

"What if . . ." I inhale a shaky breath. "What if she doesn't feel the same way?"

"Then you move on with your life," she says bluntly. "You keep pushing forward, but with a new attitude. One that lets you *enjoy* your life, not just suffer through it." She gives my knee a gentle squeeze. "But something tells me you aren't the only one."

"How can you be so sure?"

She taps her nose. "Because I am rarely wrong"—she leans in, giving me a knowing grin—"and you aren't the only one who's been throwing hung-the-moon looks."

I stare down at her hand on my knee, mulling over everything she's said and wondering if there could possibly be any truth to it. Could Tess really feel all the things I've been feeling? Is there actually a chance that she might want something more than what we've shared? And more importantly, am I brave enough to ask her?

Jeannie gives my knee a soft pat. "Tess isn't Chloe, Hunter. You know that, right? I know after someone breaks your heart, it feels like those cracks will never heal, but the funny thing about heartbreak is . . . the cracks leave plenty of space to let someone else in, and if you can let yourself do that, if you can take that leap . . . that person might just be the one who can seal those cracks right up and make you whole again." She grins. "And from what I can tell . . . Tess knows her way around some spackle."

I can't help the watery laugh that escapes me despite the fear that racks me as I consider what she's suggesting.

"Now go down there and do this interview—which you're going to knock out of the park, by the way—and then you think about what I've said, you hear?"

I nod slowly. "Okay. Sure, Jeannie. I can do that."

"Damn right you can," she says. "So go down there and get this shit done."

A chuckle escapes me, and I nod dutifully. "Yes, ma'am."

She stands, giving me one last stern look before she exits the way she came. I sit there for a moment, stewing over everything she's said, fear gripping me at the idea of putting myself out there, of taking that leap and risking plummeting to the ground all over again with no one to catch me.

Is it a risk I'm willing to take?

"WELL, I THINK that will just about do it," Nate says, smiling at me as he jots down a final note. His cameraman snaps another pic of the newly finished great room, and Nate stows his recorder in his pocket as he offers me his hand. "I appreciate you letting us come out, Mr. Barrett."

I shake my head, clasping his hand. "No, no, I should be thanking you," I tell him. "This is . . ." I chuff out a laugh. "This is great of you."

"It's nothing," he says, waving me off. "I owed Tess a favor." He flashes me a grin. "She must really like the place if she's cashing it in for you."

My chest squeezes, my lungs seeming to forget how to draw in oxygen for a moment. "Yeah, Tess is . . . amazing."

"Oh, the best," Nate agrees. He chuckles. "She called me this morning and basically demanded that I be gentle with you."

My breath catches. "She did?"

"Mm-hmm." Nate nods absently. "Seemed to be killing her that she couldn't be here." He winks at me. "She must really like *you* too, I'd wager, considering she spent twenty minutes telling me all about you and what I should expect."

"What . . . what did she say?"

Nate's eyes gleam with mischief. "Oh, just that you're kind of a grump, but it's all an act. That you're actually a big, soft marshmallow in lumberjack coating and would bend over backward for this place and everyone in it if you needed to."

"She said that?"

"Mm-hmm." He claps me on the shoulder. "It's nice to see her so into someone. She's always so wrapped up in her work . . ." He shakes his head. "Anyway, I'm really happy for you guys. You treat her good, you hear?"

I open my mouth to tell him that he's got it all wrong, that there's nothing *real* between Tess and me, but my lips close as quickly as I roll his words over in my head like unturned stones. I know for a fact that Tess's meeting was this morning, that she should have a million things to worry about concerning her literal dream, and yet she still took the time to make a call for me; she was still thinking of *me* despite all her own shit going on.

I feel frozen, unable to move as an emotion overtakes me that seems too big for my body, one that threatens to fill me up and overflow so that it's pouring out of me, taking over my entire being.

If you can let yourself do that, if you can take that leap . . . that person might just be the one who can seal those cracks right up and make you whole again.

And I realize all at once—because of something as simple as Tess taking time out of her day to make sure that I'm okay—that I want her to be that person. I want to let her into all the cracked pieces of my heart, to let her make me whole again, something that I'm starting to think only she can do.

"What the fuck am I doing?" I ask incredulously.

Nate looks confused. "I'm sorry?"

"Sorry," I offer. "I just . . . I need to do something. Are we all good here?"

He nods. "Oh yeah. We've got everything we need."

"I really appreciate this," I tell him. "Seriously. Thank you so much."

"It was my pleasure," he says with a smile. He gives me a wink. "Now go get her."

My mouth gapes. "How did you . . . ?"

"I have my ways," he says with a shrug. He leans in closer. "Between you and me, Tess's poker face is shit. And since she sounded as grim as you look right now . . . it's not hard to connect the pining dots."

"I . . ." I laugh incredulously. "Of course. Thanks again."

He waves me off. "Go, go. I can see myself out."

Before he's even finished speaking, I'm already running through the house, searching for the people I know I'll need to help me pull off what I have in mind. It's outside my comfort zone, what I'm planning, and it's well outside my wheelhouse, but I know deep down it's something I have to do. And if I don't . . . I'll regret it forever.

I find Thomas, Chase, and Kyle on the back deck, Chase smoking a cigarette as Thomas laughs at something Kyle has just said. Turning my way when I approach, they look at me with wild eyes when they notice how frazzled I must look.

"Hey, man," Thomas says. "You okay?"

"No," I say with a laugh. "Not at all." I can feel myself grinning maniacally despite my words, and I lean in to give them a pleading look. "I really need your help."

And I do. Need help. If I'm going to pull this off . . . I'm going to need a fucking lot of it.

31

Tess

"SO WE'RE WANTING to get you into our midseason slot," Heidi is saying. "We had a show that was just canceled for 2026, and we think *Rustic Renovations* will be the perfect replacement."

I blink back at her, processing. It's everything I want to hear, but my mind is miles away right now—specifically in Pleasant Hill, Colorado. I can't help wondering about Hunter's interview—how he's doing, if he's nervous, if he remembered to smile. It's making this meeting a hell of a lot harder to get excited about than it should be.

"That's . . . that's great," I manage with a smile. "I'm thrilled to hear it."

Heidi nods, her mauve-painted lips revealing perfect teeth as she snaps her fingers at her assistant, who scrambles over with a folder. "This is the proposal we've put together. It's mostly standard; it outlines your signing bonus and per-episode pay, as well as the locations and projects we already have lined up for you."

That makes me sit up. "I don't get a say in the projects?"

"Unfortunately," Heidi says with a slight frown, "there's a lot of legal stuff involved in this sort of thing—insurance waivers and such.

Things we have to take care of well in advance. It's just easier if we pick your projects." She gives me another reassuring grin. "Don't worry, we've all thoroughly scoured your channel, and we're more than sure that you'll approve."

I flip open the folder, skimming the contents briefly. I know I'll need my lawyer to look over everything, but currently I'm looking for the one thing that matters most. I release a shuddering breath when I see the signing bonus—thirty grand. More than enough to schedule dad's operation. Does it even matter that I don't get to pick my projects with that much on the line?

"This looks great," I tell her. "I'll need my lawyer to look over everything before I can sign a contract, of course—"

Heidi nods. "Of course."

"—but I'm pretty confident that we'll be agreeing to the terms."

It's not like I have any other choice, really.

"That's so good to hear," Heidi says, beaming. "We have your first project all lined up—we'll have you starting in two weeks."

Cold runs through my blood. "So soon?"

"Yes," Heidi says with a nod. "Like I said, we're fitting you into a canceled slot, so we need to move as fast as possible. Truthfully, we're already behind on filming." She gives me a pointed look. "So I hope that you won't need *too* long to look things over."

My mouth opens and closes as I think of the project I left behind, all the unfinished things still in Colorado, seeing it practically slip through my fingers. Seeing the man I left there slip with it. How could I possibly ask him to wait around for me while I undertake all this, knowing I'll have to abandon him in his hour of need?

"You can take the packet with you," Heidi tells me. "We'll need Legal to put together a formal deal agreement for you to sign if you say yes, but we can expedite that—don't worry. In fact, if you can get me an answer by Monday, I can guarantee we'll have you signed by the end of next week."

It's everything I've wanted, everything I've been dying to hear since this became even a remote possibility—so why the hell am I hesitating? I know deep down that I can't afford to, that no matter what my heart might be saying, I *will* be saying yes to this before Monday's end . . . I just didn't expect it to feel like this. I expected to feel accomplishment, to feel some sense of gratification at having reached the ending I've been working so hard for, and yet . . . all I feel is . . . empty, mostly.

But still I paste on a smile, tucking the packet under my arm as I rise from my chair and hold out my hand in offering for Heidi to shake. She takes it with a matching grin, no doubt knowing as well as I do that I won't be saying no to this. No matter how much it will hurt me to do it. Which is something I never could have anticipated.

And when I leave her office, when I step out into the bright waiting room, with its sleek tiles and cream-colored walls that feel like they're closing in . . . there's only one voice I want to hear.

". . . SO YOU just left?"

I sigh as I grip the steering wheel. "What choice did I have?"

"It sounds like you'd rather have made a different one," Ada says.

I've spilled my guts to Ada about everything that's happened the last few days—about the heat, about Hunter, HGTV . . . all of it. She listened patiently as I recounted everything we did and everything I felt, and she was thoughtfully quiet throughout all of it.

"He didn't really give me any other option," I tell her. "He barely acted like he wanted me to stay." Ada is silent as she seems to consider, and it makes me uneasy. "Well?"

"I'm thinking that I might understand where he's coming from," she says finally.

"What do you mean?"

"I just . . . I know what it's like to push everyone away because you think they couldn't want you."

My chest squeezes at her admission, and I know she's thinking of her own issues, of how she uses her humor and her jokes to hide the fact that she's most likely lonely.

"Anyone would want you, Ada," I tell her. "One idiot doesn't change that."

She sniffs. "I'm just saying, it sounds to me like Hunter was trying to protect himself from heartbreak."

"I would never hurt him," I argue.

"But it sounds like he might have a hard time believing that with everything he's been through, yeah?"

"Maybe," I admit. My breath comes a little shorter as I recall all that he'd said, and my voice is quiet when I ask, "Do you think he could be right? Do I feel this way because of hormones or biology or whatever?"

"I can't tell you that," she says. "There's no way I could be sure. But I know what it's like to be afraid of your own feelings, and I know what it's like to find out everything you thought was real never was."

"Ada, not every guy is going to be a bastard like Perry's dad," I tell her.

She blows out a breath. "Maybe you're right. But it's not about me right now. It's about you. Ask yourself, Tess. Do you think you really care about Hunter? Does it *feel* like it's just hormones?"

I let myself consider that, thinking about his quiet smile and his grumpy demeanor and his silly jokes at the most random of times, trying to imagine never experiencing any of it ever again. The thought fills me with immediate melancholy.

"It feels real," I half whisper. "Is that stupid?"

"Not if you feel it," Ada says. "You know your heart better than anyone else. And as scary as it is—and believe me, I know it is—sometimes you have to trust it. Even if it means you might get hurt. You'll never know otherwise."

"Maybe you're right," I say thickly.

"Of course I am," she chuffs. "I'm always right."

That gets a watery laugh out of me. "Of course you are."

"Are you going to be okay?"

"I think so. Maybe. I don't know."

"Just remember that you can follow your dreams without giving up everything you love," she tells me.

Love.

It feels strange to even think it, but it also feels odd how *not* strange it is. I've never felt longing like this, never felt this need to be with another person—to see them, to touch them, to simply be *near* them—and what else could that be if not love?

It's as terrifying as it is exhilarating.

"Thank you," I say. "I really needed this."

"I'm always here for you, babe," she assures me. "You know *I* love you."

"I love you too," I say with a broken sort of laugh.

"Now go rip off the Band-Aid and tell your parents everything you've told me."

"Maybe I'll leave out *some* parts."

She chuckles. "Probably a good idea."

"I'll talk to you soon?"

"I hope so. Sounds like you might miss my birthday though, superstar."

"I'm so sorry," I tell her.

"Don't be," she urges. "I'm happy for you."

"I'll call you later."

"You'd better."

I hang up the phone, feeling only slightly better than I did before.

THE DRIVE FROM the airport to Newport Beach takes barely half an hour—I'm bone-tired after two flights in a twenty-four-hour period—and I'm grateful for the proximity of my childhood home now more than ever. It's the same as always—red door, shingled roof that's seen better days, wide wraparound porch that holds memories of hide-and-seek and tag and hot cocoa while it rains—and I know that inside is an abundance of love and understanding that I can't get anywhere else.

Well, at least that's what I thought until very recently.

Mom's car is gone from the driveway, but Dad's old pickup is parked where it always is, and I realize after checking the time that Mom has most likely run off to her weekly book club meeting with her girlfriends. It's not ideal, since I wanted to tell them together, but I know if I don't get all this off my chest now, it's going to eat me alive. The excitement is too great, as is the strange forlornness that I can't seem to shake.

I knew from the minute I signed the contract that I needed to tell my dad in person, but now that I'm here . . . there's a wariness in me. Almost as if I'm worried he'll be upset that I've been keeping things from him.

I knock before testing the handle, then turn it and push the door open before calling, "Dad?"

"Back here," he says.

I find him in his old recliner, already lowering the raised leg rest and looking at me with pure confusion as he pulls himself from the chair. "Tess?"

"Hey, Dad," I say, moving to meet him for a hug. "Surprise."

"What on earth are you doing here? You're supposed to be in Colorado."

"I was," I tell him, moving to the couch, where he sinks down beside me. "But I came home because I have good news."

His forehead wrinkles, his brown eyes that are just like mine squinting under his thick brows. "News?"

I take a deep breath as I gather my thoughts . . . and then I tell him. About the first time HGTV tapped our shoulders, about the waiting game we've been playing while they deliberated, about the offer—all of it. He listens with rapt attention, letting me get it everything out before he releases a heavy breath.

"That's . . . Wow, Tess. That's fantastic." He chuckles softly. "Your mother is going to wanna whoop your ass when she finds out you kept all this a secret."

"I didn't want to tell you until I had good news," I explain. "I didn't want to get your hopes up."

"Get our hopes up?" He cocks his head. "This is *your* thing, kiddo. We would have just wanted to support you, is all."

"About that . . ." I chew on the inside of my lip, trying to find a way to come out and say what I need to say. "I haven't told you about the signing bonus," I say. "It's thirty grand, Dad. It's enough to schedule that operation."

His breath catches as he rears back, confusion painting his features. My dad is a proud man, and I've prepared myself for some pushback on this, so I'm already preparing my ten-point argument when he surprises me by throwing his arms around me, hugging me tight as he buries his face in my hair.

"Oh, hon," he says, his voice thick. "My sweet girl."

My fingers tangle in his shirt, my eyes prickling with tears. "I need you to be okay," I say, sniffling. "This will make sure that you are."

"Baby girl," he chokes out. "I'd have been okay regardless. You didn't need to do this for me."

"Of course I did," I argue. "Someone has to look out for you."

He chuckles as he pulls back, wiping at his eyes. "You've gotten real good at that over the years, haven't you?"

His hand touches my cheek, and I cover it with mine, feeling a tear slip out to collide with his fingers. He brushes it away, smiling.

"Tell me why you look so sad," he says.

I startle, my brow wrinkling. "What? Of course I'm not sad. I'm happy, Dad. Really happy. This is what I've been working toward for months. Why on earth would I be sad?"

"Kiddo," he laughs. "You've spent most of your life taking care of people, and I've always been so proud of you for that. It's just who you are. Ever since you learned how to walk, you've been offering up a helping hand to one person or another, but you can't fool me. You never could. I know when my baby is hurting."

My traitorous eyes begin to well with more tears, and I feel them spilling like I'm a little girl again, my heart aching. "They want me to start right away."

"And that's . . . bad?"

"I don't *know*," I cry. "I just . . . It's just . . ."

"Deep breath," Dad says. "In and out."

I do as he says, drawing in a steadying breath and releasing it slowly until the panic rising inside me starts to quell. I have so many feelings right now that I don't know what to do with.

"I met someone," I tell him. "In Colorado."

He looks surprised but masks it quickly. "You did?"

"I did," I say with a nod, and his hand falls from my cheek to hold mine in my lap. "And he's . . . Well. He's wonderful, really."

"And that makes you sad?"

I shake my head at his playful tone. "No. *No*. But he's—he's tied to that place. His entire life is there. He'd never leave it. And here I am in another state, about to be tied down to a contract for at least six months. Maybe more. I won't have time to *breathe*, much less visit. How can I ask him to wait for me? He barely knows me. I can't do that to him. But he's . . . he's lost so much already. I don't want to be another thing he loses. I just don't see how I can avoid it."

"That . . ." Dad nods solemnly. "That is a tough one."

He doesn't know the half of it. If I were to tell him everything—about my new designation, about the heats, the shifting, all of it—his head might explode. Probably a conversation for a time when I'm *not* already falling to pieces. Besides, I think that's definitely something I want to tell him and Mom at the same time.

"You know," Dad says. "You don't *have* to take this job. Not if you don't want to."

"Of course I do," I tell him chidingly. "Don't be silly. I *want* to. I just . . . I want him too. I want both, and I don't know if I can have that, and it's killing me."

"I'm sorry, kiddo," he says, sounding sincere. "I wish I had better answers for you."

I nod morosely, wishing the same thing.

"But I do know this," Dad says. "Love is rarely simple. It's not always like the storybooks or the movies. Love is damn hard. We don't always meet our person at the perfect moment, and we don't always get the ending we thought we would." He chuckles softly. "Trust me, I know. I've thought about endings a lot lately."

"Don't say that," I say, my voice tight. "You're going to be fine."

"Maybe I will," he says. "Maybe I'll get that pacemaker and last another fifty years, or maybe tomorrow I'll be a hit by a bus. No one can know for sure."

"If you're trying to cheer me up," I say, my voice breaking, "you're doing a terrible job."

"My point is," he goes on, "you gotta take what happiness you can *when* you can. There's only so much of it in this world, and when you find something good, you gotta hold on to it real tight and not let it go. Because tomorrow isn't guaranteed, hon, and happiness doesn't deal in what-ifs."

"What are you saying?"

"I'm saying if you care about this man of yours, you should tell him that."

"I don't want him to feel like he has to—"

"If you *don't* tell him," Dad stresses, "you'll regret it forever. Because, Tess? Take it from someone who's had to stare death in the face." He squeezes my hand. "There's no greater ache than the words we don't say. They're what haunts us forever, you hear?"

I press the heel of my hand to my eye, stanching the tears there. "I don't remember you being so poetic."

"Yeah, well. You live as much life as I've had to live these past few years . . . you start looking at things differently." He gives my hand another squeeze. "You gonna think about what I said?"

"I'll . . . think about it," I agree warily. Even if I'm not sure telling Hunter would do us any good.

"That's great." He pats my knee. "And, hon? I'm so proud of

you. It's one of those things I don't say nearly enough. You really have spent your whole life taking care of us in one way or another, and I want you to know I see that. I just wish someone could take care of you for a change."

Someone did, I don't say.

"Now," Dad goes on. "How about some coffee? We could slip a little whiskey in and celebrate."

"You know damn well you shouldn't be drinking," I scold.

He raises his hands placatingly. "Worth a shot, I guess. Besides, didn't you hear? Practically getting a new heart, it seems like." He winks at me. "Got my daughter to thank for that."

I give him a watery grin, shaking my head. "Go make the coffee."

"Can do, kiddo, can do."

I watch him shuffle off into the kitchen, mulling over everything he's said. I really didn't mean to spill my guts like I did, but my dad has a way of seeing right through me like no one ever has. I've never been very good at hiding things from him. It's a wonder I kept the HGTV thing a secret for so long without caving.

I lean back into the couch as I wipe my eyes, trying to focus on all the good that happened today. Trying not to think about everything I may have to give up because of it. I know I was right when I told my dad that Hunter is tied to that lodge, that there's nothing on earth that could make him leave it—and how could I ask him to? Not after everything he's suffered.

Maybe it's just one of those things that's not in the cards. Maybe we didn't meet each other at the right time. I can't even say if telling him how I feel would do anything but cause him heartbreak, and deep down, I don't know if I'll be able to bring myself to do that to him. I almost think it would be better to keep it all inside, if only to protect him.

You really have spent your whole life taking care of us in one way or another . . . I just wish someone could take care of you for a change.

I laugh scornfully under my breath.

Seems my dad was right.

A knock at the door makes me sit up, and I can still hear my dad moving around in the kitchen, so I holler at him that I'll get it as I rise from the couch, wondering if maybe Mom forgot her keys again and came home early. That thought makes me wince, because there really is a good chance she'll whoop my ass when I tell her the things I've been keeping from her.

God, I wonder if I can hide all the shifter stuff until I'm dead. That would be ideal.

I reach the door and wrap my fingers around the handle, preparing myself for one of her bear hugs that nearly crush me, already opening my mouth to explain my being here when I pull the door wide.

And then I freeze, shock trickling through me when I see who's on the other side—sticking out like a sore thumb in the California sunshine with his beanie and his flannel and his larger-than-life presence, because how on earth is he *here*?

I take a deep breath, barely managing to get a word out, and when I do, every feeling, every raging desire hits me with the full weight of a truck, coming back to me like I never left him, because—

"Hunter?"

32

Hunter

MY HEART IS trying to escape through my ribs when I knock on the door, but that could be residual terror from being on a plane for the first time in more than a decade. Part of me worries that she won't be here, that her brothers might have gotten things wrong, and then where the fuck will I be? Crying to her dad, whom I've never met? That will be a real riot, for sure.

I brace myself with my hands on either side of the door, trying to control the pounding of my heart as I consider how the hell I'm going to explain myself if Tess opens this door. What I'll say about why I'm here, what I'm feeling. How I'll convince a woman I've known for less than a month that I think she might be my forever.

But then the door opens, and I'm hit with her warm scent, which feels so right, here in the sunshine of her home; I'm met with her soft chestnut hair and her big brown eyes and her freckles and all the things that I've felt adrift without since she left. I see her, and suddenly I forget how to make words.

"Hunter?"

My mouth parts only to immediately close again, my throat bobbing with a swallow as I manage to eke out a "Hi."

"Hi?"

She looks confused when she says it, and why wouldn't she? I just flew about three hours nonstop in clothes that aren't meant for this place to see her, and now I'm standing here, and everything I thought I might say to her is out the window somewhere. Just . . . gone. Fluttering away where I can't catch it. Which is probably why the next thing I blurt out is:

"I love you."

She looks stunned, and why wouldn't she? I practically pushed her out my door yesterday, most likely making her think I was fine seeing her go, that I didn't need her. Which couldn't be further from the truth.

"I know it's too soon to tell you that," I go on, floundering. "But it's true. You blew into town and filled up my empty lodge in ways I didn't even know it needed. I've spent years, Tess—*years*—thinking I was fine, that I had all I needed. And then you showed up, and I realized I've been exactly like that dingy old lodge all this time. Nothing but a ghost of a shell parading around like I'm still living. I didn't even know what being content *looked* like anymore, until you."

I take a deep breath, feeling my panic rising at her shocked expression, but the words are barreling out of me now.

"I know I'm the worst choice for you. I'm moody and stubborn and live in the middle of nowhere, where there's nothing for you—but if you give me half a chance, I can change that. I'm realizing that the place I thought was my home is just like I was, just a shell. I didn't know what home looked like until I met you. And I want to *be* that for you. Whatever it looks like. Wherever that is. If you'll let me."

Her eyes are so wide they're almost covered by her bangs, and she does that adorable thing where she blows them out of her face, her mouth opening and closing like she has no idea what to say to all this. Not that I blame her. It makes me feel suddenly awkward and embarrassed, like maybe I've put her in a weird position. Which I have, probably. I definitely didn't think this through before I rushed to the airport, that's for sure. Hell, I didn't even pack the right clothes for this place. I don't even *own* clothes for California.

"I can go," I start, already backing away. "I can give you time to think about this, and if you don't feel the same way, I promise that's okay. I just needed to tell you. I couldn't leave things like they were when you left. I couldn't let you just be out there somewhere thinking it didn't kill me to watch you go. Because it did, Tess. It *killed* me. But what killed me more was knowing I didn't run after you. That I didn't tell you I would go *anywhere*, do *anything*—as long as I get to be with you."

"Don't you dare," she says, taking a step forward.

I pause. "Which part?"

"Leave," she says, her fingers reaching out to grab at my shirt. "Don't you dare leave."

"You don't . . . you don't want me to leave?"

"After that?" Her lips turn up in a grin. "You're not going anywhere."

"Then I'm going to need you to say something, Tess," I tell her pitifully, "because I'm kind of losing my mind here."

Her lips part as if she's going to speak, but then there's another wide grin, and she's pulling me to her, her lips crashing into mine as I feel myself melt into her.

"You got on a plane for me," she whispers against my mouth.

I nod. "I hated it. Hate flying. Felt like I was going to fall out of the sky at any moment."

"And they wouldn't even let you whittle on board."

Her voice is teasing, but I notice she still hasn't *said* anything.

"If this is your way of letting me down easy, could you just—"

"Hunter," she says.

I swallow. "Yeah?"

"I love you too."

I feel relief course through me, like all the adrenaline is leaving my system in one fell swoop. I breathe a little easier, stand a little taller, because the woman who holds my entire universe in her tiny little Fixit hands *loves* me.

"You do?"

"If you weren't here right now, I'd have been back in Denver by tomorrow."

"You're kidding."

"Not even a little."

"You mean I didn't have to fly?"

"It's so romantic that you did though. I still can't believe you're here. In California." She looks me up and down. "Wearing *that*."

"I don't exactly have beachwear." I grin down at her, feeling lighter than I have in years. "You really would have come back?"

"I was literally coming to the decision when you knocked on the door," she tells me. "You see, someone a lot smarter than me told me that it's the things we *don't* say that haunt us forever, and I realized . . . I didn't go to Colorado looking for anything. But I showed up, and suddenly my whole world was turned upside down. I had just lost my sense of self when I arrived at your . . . dingy little lodge," she says with a laugh. She reaches up to cup my cheeks. "But then there you were . . . This surly, stubborn, taciturn giant who frowned like it was his job. There was nothing at all that could have hinted you would turn out to be everything I didn't know I wanted.

You're kind and steadfast, and you think about everyone else around you even when you pretend that you don't."

Her thumb strokes at my beard, and I cover her hand with mine.

"I've spent my whole life taking care of other people, so I know exactly what it looks like to put everyone else's needs before yours. But with you . . . for the first time in a long time . . . I saw what it looked like to let someone take care of *me* for a change. And I didn't realize how badly I needed that. I had no idea how desperate I was for someone to take the reins so I could *breathe* until I met you." Her smile reaches her eyes, which look slightly wet now. "You see . . . I wasn't looking for anything when I came to you, but I *found* you just the same. And as it turns out . . . you're everything I never knew I needed."

"Tess . . ."

"So of *course* I was going to come back to you. I was going to march up to that lodge and make sure you *knew* that you were stuck with me now. That for as long as you'd let me, I was going to take care of you right back."

I feel a lump forming in my throat that is increasingly hard to swallow past, all of it feeling too good to be true, like at any moment I'll wake up and realize it's all been a dream. With that in mind, I lower my mouth to hers, kissing at her lips softly as I revel in her scent and taste, committing them to memory.

"I do want to take care of you," I murmur. "Whatever that looks like. Forever."

She giggles prettily, rising on her toes to let me sweep her up in my arms. I lift her from the ground and spin her as exhilaration fills me because I never could have anticipated this. Not in a thousand years. I never could have known upon meeting this tiny, fiery woman that she would be everything to me. That she would reach into me where all the cracks still reside, slipping past them and making herself at home to heal them from the inside out.

Because I can feel it. That this is what she's doing. Healing me.

And I can feel that it's only the beginning.

I'm kissing her furiously now, wrapped up in her soft scent and her warm mouth, so I don't hear it at first—the quiet *Ahem* from the doorway.

I jerk up to see a man only a few inches shorter than me, graying at the temples, with eyes that are big and brown and very familiar.

"Dad," Tess says sheepishly. "This is—"

"Hunter Barrett," I say stiltedly, thrusting out my hand even as I keep one arm wrapped around her.

I can't seem to let go of her now that I have her.

"Neil Covington," Tess's dad says, reaching to shake my hand. "I've heard a bit about you."

I cock an eyebrow down at Tess. "Have you?"

"Oh," Neil laughs. "Just a bit."

I clear my throat, putting a minimal bit of distance between Tess and me, feeling my neck heat as I realize what all her father must have just seen.

"I'm sorry to barge in like this," I say. "You see . . ."

Neil waves me off. "You had some things that needed to be said?"

"I . . ." My lips twitch. "Yes. A lot of things."

His eyes shift between the two of us, his grin widening. "Boy. Your mama really is going to have an ass whooping waiting for you, kiddo."

"You're probably right," she chuckles. She looks sheepish now too. "And I still have more to explain."

Neil whistles under his breath. "Whew. Well. You'd both better come inside. I got coffee made."

"That sounds great," I say tightly, still thinking about mauling his daughter.

I watch him turn back inside, then look down at Tess, who gives me an impish grin. "We have more to talk about too, I guess."

"You got the show."

Her brow furrows. "How did you know?"

"Didn't for sure," I say with a shrug. "But I knew you would."

"I know it will be . . . hard. For us. But—"

"It won't be," I tell her.

"But I have to—"

"You don't get it," I laugh, pulling her in closer. "You're kind of stuck with me now, Miss Fixit."

She beams back at me. "Is that right?"

"Afraid so. I told you. I'm with you. Whatever that looks like."

"They want me to start right away," she says forlornly.

I shake my head. "I'm due for a getaway."

"But what about the lodge?"

"It'll be there." I raise her hand to my mouth and kiss the back of it. "And like I said, you're not the only contractor out there. The place will get fixed one way or another. I promise, the work you've done won't go to waste."

Her eyes grow wider then, her lips parting as if an idea has struck her. It lingers for a moment, but then her face breaks out into a wide grin, and she throws her arms around my neck, kissing me soundly.

"You know, I get the idea it really won't."

My brow furrows. "What does that mean?"

"It means . . ." Her lips curve against mine, and my entire world is reflected in her smile. "I have some calls to make."

Epilogue

Tess

"NOBODY MOVE."

I hold my breath as my fingers brush against soft, dark fur, watching as Reginald *allows* me to scratch gently behind his ears.

"I can't believe I don't have a camera," Jeannie says in a hushed tone behind me.

I give the surly cat another scritch, a little more aggressively this time. "Months, Jeannie. I've known this asshole for *months*, and this is the first time he's *let* me pet him."

He blinks at me, looking bored, and I try for a smoothing motion of my hand down his back, which he also allows to happen.

"It's a miracle," Jeannie laughs.

"Hey, where do you want this stuff?"

I curse under my breath as Jarred's loud arrival from the other room scares off my would-be friend. Reginald pounces away only to look back like he's mocking me.

"Damn it," I huff. "You scared him."

Jarred rolls his eyes when I turn to glare at him. "That cat's just mean, Tess. You have to give it up."

"He likes *me*," human Cat pipes up, wandering into the giant den with a cookie tray. "You just have to give him food. He's a sucker for tuna."

"So where do you want this?" Jarred asks again.

I point bitterly toward the coffee table, and he sets the ice buckets there for me to arrange, placing the bottles of unopened champagne nearby.

It took weeks to finish the rest of the reno after I persuaded the execs at HGTV to let us make this project our pilot episode for the show; I thought it would take a lot more convincing, but once I pointed out how much footage we already had in relation to their short schedule, everyone seemed to agree that it was a no-brainer. Plus, the show has a reno budget going toward each property, so that allowed us to cover some of the bigger projects, like getting a new furnace, which Hunter hadn't been sure he could afford, thus a win-win.

"Place looks spiffy," Jarred notes.

I shrug. "We've been long overdue for a grand reopening, I think. We would have done it sooner if not for the show."

"God," Cat laughs. "Hiring Hunter onto your crew is the best thing that's ever happened to me. Those pictures of him in California added years to my life. I just love seeing everyone on the internet turning our Hunter into some mysterious sex symbol," she says with an actual cackle. "I feel like someone should tell them he still uses an address book and thinks a diverse wardrobe means different shades of plaid."

I smack her shoulder lightly. "Hey. Leave the plaid alone. I'm partial to it."

I smile as I think of how my followers constantly beg for more Hunter content; the first time I saw a post about Hunter's article online by someone thirsting over him was jarring, though in a pretty hilarious way. Mostly because I knew how ridiculous he would find the entire thing (and I was right). Still. It turned out to be nothing but free publicity for the lodge, so he doesn't complain *too* much. After Hunter's article was printed, it was less than three weeks before he started to get calls about availability at the lodge. And the sleuths on the internet piecing together that Hot Hunter of the Hills is *my* Hot Hunter of the Hills only makes business boom more. I guess he's more of an influencer than he first thought.

"We're here!"

I turn to catch sight of a smiling blond woman I never expected to see again. It was a surprise finding out that the same doctor who turned my world upside down was actually mated to Hunter's cousin, but after getting to know Mackenzie Carter, I'm actually kind of glad for it. It doesn't hurt to have a doctor in your corner to answer all your random questions.

Her towering mate trails behind her, looking so similar to Hunter and yet so . . . different. Noah is more refined, less rugged than his cousin, and it just makes me appreciate my grumpy lumberjack all the more.

Mackenzie sets down her tray of something baked and sweet that I don't recognize and reaches out to wrap her arms around me. "How are you? Settling in?"

Oh, right. That.

I don't think there will ever be a time when I don't smile about now permanently sharing a space with my sometimes-salty, sometimes-sweet lumberjack, especially since it means most of my nights involve snuggling or hot chocolate or toe-curling orgasms. I'd like to tell you a girl could get used to it . . . but this girl still hasn't, really. Leaving Newport to move here for good was a big change, one that Hunter insisted I didn't have to make. Although once the show was finished filming for the season . . . it just felt right. There's so much history here. Old memories and hopefully, in the future, a lot of new ones.

"Place looks nice," Noah comments, eyes moving around the space. "Very . . . new."

Mackenzie rolls her eyes. "He's still peeved you updated 'our' room."

"Well," I laugh. "*Your* room is basically the same. It just has a bigger shower now."

Noah's brow quirks, and he leans over to whisper something in Mackenzie's ear. Something that makes her blush and promptly smack his arm.

Mackenzie clears her throat, then asks, "Where should I put the cupcakes?"

I grin. "Kitchen is fine."

She drags Noah away by the hand, muttering something under her breath, and I have a feeling it won't be long before they're booking "their" old room soon.

"Is Ada coming?"

I shake my head at Cat, grateful that my Colorado best friend loves my California best friend as much as she does. "She had some stuff to take care of back in LA."

"I saw the announcement about the big exhibition. I can't believe she's mated now!"

"Yeah," I laugh, still having a hard time believing it myself. It was such a whirlwind, after all. "Me neither."

Not that I have any room to talk.

"Well." Jeannie claps her hands together, a quiet sort of smile on her face. "Let's stop dillydallying and finish setting up. Everyone's going to be arriving soon."

"Who would have thought?" Cat squeals. "A full house!"

"As far as grand reopenings go," I muse, "we really couldn't have asked for more."

Jarred makes a face. "Can you call it a 'reopening' if you never closed?"

"Shut up." I wave him away. "Go set some food out or something."

I hear him muttering something like *bossy* under his breath as his girlfriend pulls him away, laughing, and I cross my arms as I turn toward the big window to watch the snow falling softly outside. There was a time in my life when I thought I would never leave California. I'd been calling it home my whole life . . . but I don't think I really knew what home felt like. Not until I helped carry my stuff through the doors of the lodge, blending it with Hunter's.

Jeannie pats me on the shoulder before she goes. "You really did good, girl," she praises. "This place looks like it did the day I first saw it."

I reach up to give her hand a squeeze. "*We* all did this," I tell her. "*We* did good."

"Yeah," she says thickly. "Yeah, we did. I'll be in the kitchen if you need me."

I nod. "I'll be there in just a sec."

I hear her footsteps fading behind me as she leaves the room, and I continue to watch the snow with a bemused smile. I stay like that for longer than I mean to, and I scent him before I see him. The soft smell of sunshine and rain envelops me as thick arms wind around my waist, a chin tucking against my shoulder before lips press to my throat.

"You're slacking," he murmurs.

I roll my eyes. "I'm *living the moment*."

"Mm-hmm." I can feel his smile against my neck, his teeth nipping at the faded bite mark over my mating gland and making me shiver. "You do realize we are fully booked tonight, right?"

"It was probably that tasteful nude I posted of you on the new website," I say seriously. "The fig leaf was pretty small. I mean, they could practically see everything."

"If I didn't know how to use that damn thing—"

"By 'that damn thing,' do you mean a laptop from this decade?"

"—I might be worried you actually did that."

"Sorry, Grandpa. Your fig leaves are all mine."

"Your mom and dad send their love," he tells me.

I grin at that. "Can't believe they're missing this to go *camping* of all things."

"He's a new man now," Hunter chuckles. "Or so he says."

"I just hope they don't get eaten by bears."

"That doesn't happen as often as you seem to think."

"And I wonder who put the idea in my head?"

He laughs as he kisses my cheek, sighing when he rests his chin on my shoulder. "It's a pretty day," he says, squeezing me a little.

"I should take a picture."

"Live the moment, remember?"

I laugh, lifting my hands to my face to form a square as I click my tongue. "Yeah, yeah."

Hunter spins me then, his arms around my waist and his expression amused as he gives me that trademark Hunter sort-of-smile. The one I'm madly in love with—exactly like I am with everything else about this man who completely took me by surprise.

"Everything is nearly set up, anyway," I tell him. "They're setting out the charcuterie boards now."

He purses his lips. "It's just meat and cheese."

"But that doesn't sound *nearly* as fancy." I tap his nose. "Oh, what do you think of an ice sculpture, by the way?"

He turns his head. "What?"

"I was thinking it would be such a waste not to utilize your skills," I say with a straight face. "I mean, what is ice sculpting if not frozen whittling?"

He seems less amused now, his mouth turning down in a frown at my joke, and I laugh at his grumpy expression. I raise my hands again to take another mental picture of his narrowed eyes, knowing I'll be paying for that comment later, but, oddly enough, I don't mind in the slightest.

Hunter cocks an eyebrow at me. "Another memory you need, huh?"

"You just look so cute when you're annoyed," I coo.

He scoffs. "Cute."

"As a button," I tease.

He smiles at me then, not his usual tiny one but something full-blown and breathtaking—the smile that still catches me off guard no matter how many times I'm graced with it. His scent is a burst of joyful contentment, one that I pick up on him a lot more often now. It's insane to me that we crashed into each other's lives completely by chance, that an upheaval in my life could be the very thing that would deliver me more happiness than I ever thought possible.

"You know you did all this, right?" He gestures around the room. "We wouldn't be here without you."

"Don't sell yourself short," I tell him. "You helped." My mouth quirks. "I mean, sure, there would absolutely not be Wi-Fi at this place without me—I don't know how you'd even begin to set up the router—but still."

His eyes are narrowed again, but I can tell he wants to laugh. "I think you're kind of a brat."

"Well, I think"—I wind my arms around his neck, pulling him down to me—"you kind of want to kiss me."

His eyes roam over my face with a warmth like he's of a similar mind. "Only a stupid man wouldn't," he reminds me before he leans in to press his lips to mine.

There's still a whole slew of reasons why it's crazy that we're here. I still don't know much about classic rock, and I still have to show Hunter how to unlock his new smartphone half the time . . . but here, in this snowy little town of Nowheresville, with my surly but loveable mate, I learned what love is.

There's still a lifetime of *real* moments to experience . . . and I want to live every single one.

Acknowledgments

So as it turns out, sequels are hard. For all the love I have seen for *The Fake Mate* (and I am eternally grateful that everyone was so into the wolfy weirdness), it felt like there was so much pressure to deliver, to make Hunter and Tess's story just as dynamic. All I can hope for is that you loved them half as much as I do! (I did give you knot massaging, after all, which I am intensely proud of.)

As always, in the ever-ongoing parade of hand-holding, and in no particular order, I would like to thank:

Cindy Hwang, the best editor a girl could ever ask for, who possibly loves knots more than I do, and that's saying something.

My fabulous agency and my agent, Jessica Watterson, for being the best cheerleader and always answering her phone even when it's (usually) something silly I am bothering her about.

The amazing art team and Monika Roe, who came up with yet *another* banger of a cover, and the entire team at Berkley, for always making this process so fun and seem effortless (even when I know it absolutely isn't).

Keri, my sister by choice, for knowing every single detrimental thing there is to know about me and still loving me—there's no one I'd rather talk about knots with than you.

Kate Golden (wife), for always being up for a long phone call where I say mostly nothing except how much I think something isn't working and then making me believe everything will be okay anyway.

Elena Armas, for her continued love and support (and her amazing voice notes). I am *always* happy to see your name in my notifications.

Kristen (daddy), for always being the one to speak up and tell me when I'm being a stupid bitch (because I deserve that; you don't understand the number of ways I can be mean to myself)—this stupid bitch loves you very much.

Ruby Dixon, for still answering my emails after all this time, and also just for being an all-around genuinely lovely human—I probably would have had a breakdown long before this point if not for you.

Destinee, for being a knot-oisseur and wonderful friend. Getting to hug you this past year was a highlight, and I can't wait to do it again.

Vanessa, who is always down to tote around with me, to hold my hand *in person* when I need it—I am so grateful that this wide world of books brought me to you.

A wholehearted shout-out to the amazing bookstagrammers, bloggers, journalists, BookTokers, librarians, and reviewers who hype my books—your comments, posts, TikToks, and article mentions are sometimes the only things that keep me going, and I'm so grateful.

The readers... this is all for you, and I wouldn't be here without you.

And lastly my husband, who may not have a knot in the truest sense of the word, but definitely has a knot of the heart, so to speak, just a little something extra that makes me all aflutter—I love you, even if you can't turn into a wolf.

Keep reading for a preview of

The Final Score

The sequel to *The Game Changer*
by Lana Ferguson!

Abby

"ARE YOU SURE we're allowed to be down here?"

Lila rolls her eyes. "Kind of a perk of dating the owner's son."

I follow after her as she moves deeper into the inner workings of the stadium, the halls empty but a low murmur of voices coming from just down the way.

"Besides," Lila goes on. "You're his sister. You're practically in nepo-baby territory."

I snort. "Hardly."

Sure, my relationship with Ian has gotten a lot better in the last few months since our dear old dad ran off to California, but I heavily doubt that I could start using his name to throw my weight around. Definitely not to be practically sneaking down to the locker rooms.

"We're going to get in trouble," I hiss.

Lila shakes her head. "No, we aren't. Ian told me to bring him his phone. He forgot it back at the apartment." She throws an arm around my shoulder—something that is a bit difficult since I'm at least four inches taller than her five foot four—giving me a slight shake. "Live a little, Abby."

Live a little.

Seems like that's the motto most of the people in my life choose for me. In my last year of grad school for psychology and doing my very best to keep my nose clean so that I don't bring any more hardship to my brother than I already have, it's not a concept that comes to me naturally. I'm more of the *sit quietly in the corner* type. It's why I don't really have a lot of friends.

I watch as Lila raises her fist to the slightly cracked locker room door, giving three heavy knocks before shouting, "If your balls are out, cover them up!"

And then she just blazes in.

Ever since meeting Lila, I've admired her ability to run headfirst through anything standing in her way; this is also not a concept that comes naturally to me. Hence I remain outside the door, lingering against the wall.

"Brought your lucky jockstrap, Cupcake!" I hear her shout.

She's met with an answering groan. "Phone," Ian says. "She brought me my *phone*."

"Whatever you say," she hums.

I hear a series of whoops then, and assume she's kissing him. I assume this because it seems like the two of them can't be within four feet of each other without planting one on the other. And since I've been at their place every week for dinner for the last few months, I have been privy to a *lot* of kisses.

Animals, those two are. Animals.

I lean on the wall and let my head thunk back against it as I shut my eyes, letting the voices from the other room fade into the background as I mentally check off all the homework I need to get to tonight. Truthfully, I probably shouldn't have come to Ian's game, given how much work I need to get done, but I'd been so damned excited that he'd even thought to invite me, I couldn't bring myself to say no.

Before this year, my brother had been more of an idea rather than an actual person. I hadn't seen him in six years, and when we spoke on the phone—which was rare—it was stilted and awkward and not at all flowing with any sort of familial bond. It's not entirely his fault. I never knew what to say to him either. With the weight of all our father had done hanging over our heads—having me in secret out of wedlock, dumping me on Ian's doorstep after my mom died—and with the guilt of knowing that I'd practically ruined his life there for a while, it was easy to let myself sink into the background. Easier for everyone, honestly.

I still haven't really gotten used to being out in the light.

"Whatchya hiding out there for?" I hear a very familiar, very aggravating voice say from my right. "Afraid you'll see something in here you won't be able to forget?"

I crack open one eye, taking in the boyish grin flashing back at me, complete with an all-around perfect face that might make me swoon if I didn't know what a shit he was.

Jack Baker is the epitome of a playboy no-no. He's flirty, flighty, and the definition of a fuckboy—and there's nothing I like more than wiping that grin off his face. His big brown eyes and shaggy hair of a similar shade might inspire some to trip over themselves, but all I see is my dad in a slightly sweeter package. I'm sure he has a new woman every week, and I'll be damned if I ever put myself on the roster.

"Nah," I say back. "Don't worry. Forgot my microscope, so no danger here."

He just grins wider, undeterred. The dick. "I love when you talk dirty to me," he sighs. "But you'd need a telescope, not a microscope."

I cock my head, my nose wrinkling. "What?"

"Because," he says, leaning in a little closer, "it's as big as a planet."

He steps out into the hall, clad in nothing but his compression gear, which means that I can see every outline of his very cut body and if I were to look down—which I *won't*—I'm sure I would see ample evidence of his claims.

"God," I groan. "You really are the worst."

"I like to think of myself as adorably misunderstood."

"Whatever helps you sleep at night."

"So why are you hiding in the hall? Didn't want to come say hi?"

I shrug. "I'm not even sure I'm supposed to be down here. I get Lila, but I'm . . . Well. Just trying to keep out of trouble."

"No one cares," Jack laughs. "Come say hi."

"I'm fine here."

His brow lifts. "You're extra grumpy looking today."

"Yeah, well. I'm sleeping on a shitty twin bed every night, and I've got more coursework than I know what to do with. Excuse me if I don't look camera ready."

"Oh, don't worry, you're still hot." He cringes. "In an Ian way. I meant you look tired."

"I don't even know how to process what you just said."

"Well, you're like, really hot, but you also look a little like Ian. It's confusing. I mean, I consider myself to be sexually open to anything, but thinking about Ian naked is weird."

"Why would you think about Ian naked?"

"Because you look like Ian, and if I thought about you naked, eventually my brain would substitute Ian's face for yours, and that would be really weird for everyone." He frowns. "Damn it, now I'm thinking about Ian naked. I've seen it enough in the locker room, thank you very much."

"God, you're weird," I tell him. "And don't think about me naked."

"I'm not weird, I'm *medicated*," he says. "And sorry, too late."

"You know that little voice that tells you when you should keep your thoughts to yourself?"

He shakes his head. "Never had one. They don't make meds strong enough for that, apparently."

"Are you out here harassing my sister?"

Ian pokes his head through the doorway, frowning in Jack's direction.

Jack raises his hands in an innocent gesture. "Who, me? I would never. It's not like I have any sort of score to settle. It's not as if my best friend started boinking my sister and then just *continued on and made it a habit*."

"Did you take your meds today?"

Jack looks thoughtful. "I honestly can't remember."

Ian rolls his eyes. "Go get dressed and leave Abby alone."

"Fine, fine," he relents. "But Abby loves our banter. It's part of our meet-cute."

"There is no meet-cute," I argue. "I met you months ago."

"It's all about the endgame, baby," he teases.

Ian shoos him away, shoving him back into the locker room before stepping out into the hall with Lila in tow. "He's determined to punish Lila and me by being as insufferable as he can to you, isn't he?"

"That does seem to be the case," I agree.

Lila pats Ian's shoulder. "Abby and I are going to grab some food before the game starts, but we'll be back before the face-off, okay?"

"I'll be looking for you," Ian hums, leaning in to press his lips to Lila's.

I avert my eyes. Knowing them, there's always a fifty-fifty chance that they'll kiss longer than is appropriate for being in public. Thankfully, they cut this one short.

Doesn't stop Lila from slapping Ian on the ass.

"See you soon, Cupcake," she says sweetly, watching as Ian shoots me a wink before he walks back into the locker room, laughing as his teammates start jeering him.

Lila loops her arm through mine then. "Jack wasn't too much of a dummy today, was he?"

"It's fine," I assure her. "I can handle him."

"He means well, but . . ."

"He's a bit of a menace."

"Yeah," Lila laughs. "That. You learn to love it."

"I'll let you know when that happens," I say dryly.

She laughs harder, nudging me in the ribs. "Chinese or pizza?"

"Whatever's closest," I tell her, stomach rumbling.

She grins. "That's my kind of woman."

***

YOU KNOW, TO be the sister of such a popular player and the daughter of a legend, I sure don't know shit about hockey.

I watch Lila as she rises to her feet for the fourth time this period, shouting something about goaltender interference. Her face is turning slightly red, and I feel out of place just sitting here beside her, barely knowing what's going on.

She slumps back down in her seat with a huff, muttering, "Where the hell are your eyes, Ref!"

"Bad call?" I ask.

She rolls her eyes. "It's been the whole game."

"I guess one of these days I'm going to have to actually sit here and let you explain the rules to me," I laugh, my eyes following the Druids players as they move across the ice. I can spot Ian as he glides to the center of the rink, Jack close behind him.

"You'll get it eventually," she chuckles. "Basically, that player over there touched the goalie when he wasn't supposed to. That's why he didn't block the goal. No one but the goalie is supposed to be in the crease."

"The crease?"

She points to the shaded area in front of the goal. "There."

"Ah," I say. "Okay."

"You hate this, don't you?" she asks with a teasing grin.

I make a noncommittal gesture. "I don't *hate* it."

She eyes me with one brow arched.

"I'm just not much of a sports girl," I say with another laugh.

"Blasphemy," she tuts.

"Tell me what's happening now," I say.

"See Sanchez?" She points to one of the players. "He's got the puck. He's trying to get it into the other team's goal."

"Well, I knew *that* much."

"They're forcing him into the corner," she narrates. "Now they're battling."

I watch as Sanchez maneuvers his stick to try to win back the puck that the other team's player is attempting to swipe away from him.

"Now Jack is coming up, he's going to try to snag it," Lila tells me.

I can't help but let my gaze wander to him then—barely making out the shaggy ends of his hair that peek out of the edge of his helmet. Even from here I can see the look of fierce determination on his face. He looks so serious, so much more than he usually is.

As I watch, one of the opposing players swings around toward him, and Lila stands again, starting to yell, and all of a sudden that same player slams into Jack, pushing him into the boards roughly. Lila is shouting even louder as another player crashes into them, forming a full-on pileup as the corner of the rink becomes crowded with a mass of bodies.

"Penalty," Lila yells. "*Penalty!*"

She's still standing when the players start to move away from the corner, and it's only when they've skated away that it becomes clear that Jack is down, lying on his side as a flurry of activity ensues. I notice Ian skating over and kneeling next to him, the ref not far behind as Ian checks him over.

"What's happened?" I ask. "Is he okay?"

Lila doesn't answer, watching on with a concerned expression as she starts to move past me into the aisle to get closer to the edge of the rink. I follow her without thinking—but there are people already helping Jack from the ground, even though it's clear he isn't okay. There's a grimace of pain in his features, and Ian is helping support his weight by letting him brace himself against Ian's shoulder.

Jack is cradling his arm—the one he broke not so long ago—holding it closer to his chest as he and Ian maneuver off the ice. The ref has already called a time-out, and fans all around us are standing now, everyone watching to see if Jack is okay.

Lila takes off toward the Druids' bench where Jack and Ian have just exited. I push my way through the crowd to follow, both of Lila and I reaching them in time to hear the grunts of Jack's pain and Ian's soothing voice.

"You're okay, bud," Ian is saying. "You'll be okay."

"It fucking hurts," Jack groans, his voice taking on a panicked edge. "Is it broken again? It can't be broken again. I can't fucking miss out again."

Excerpt from THE FINAL SCORE

"We're gonna get you to the hospital, Jack," Ian tells him. "You're gonna be okay."

Ian spots Lila and me then, waving us over.

"He landed on his bad arm," Ian tells Lila. "They're gonna take him to the hospital to get an X-ray. Can you ride with him?"

"Obviously," Lila says breathlessly.

Ian nods. "I can meet you there."

"No," Jack says. "Finish the game. They need you."

"I'm not letting you—"

"Finish the fucking game," Jack says again. "You can come by after."

Ian hesitates for a moment, looking torn until he notices the determined expression on Jack's face. He nods once, frowning. "Okay. I'll meet you right after." He looks to Lila. "Can you text me what they say?"

"I will," she promises.

She seems to remember me then, turning to look at me pleadingly.

"Can you drive my car to the hospital? I'm going to ride in the ambulance with Jack."

"Of course," I tell her. "I'll be right behind you."

She gives me a grateful look, squeezing my arm once and dropping her car keys in my hand before turning back to her brother, where security is taking over for Ian, helping Jack through the crowd that is still standing and has just begun to cheer for him.

He raises his uninjured arm, giving them a tight smile, but there's something in his eyes that is so unlike him it actually stops me in my tracks.

Because Jack looks afraid.

He looks *very* afraid.

Illustration by Jessica Patrick

LANA FERGUSON is a *USA Today* bestselling author and sex-positive nerd whose works never shy from spice or sass. A faded Fabio cover found its way into her hands at fifteen, and she's never been the same since. When she isn't writing, you can find her randomly singing show tunes, arguing over which Batman is superior, and subjecting her friends to the extended editions of *The Lord of the Rings*. Lana lives mostly in her own head but can sometimes be found chasing her corgi through the coppice of the great American outdoors.

VISIT LANA FERGUSON ONLINE

LanaFerguson.com
 Lana-Ferguson-100078243151433
 LanaFergusonWrites

Ready to find
your next great read?

Let us help.

Visit prh.com/nextread

Penguin
Random
House